PRES
FOR ROMANCE

BY

MARIE FERRARELLA

AND

LOVE AND THE SINGLE DAD

BY

SUSAN CROSBY

Dear Reader,

I love babies. I always have, always will. Unlike a lot of my friends, I had absolutely no trouble getting pregnant. I also know, much to the embarrassment of my children, exactly when each of them was conceived.

Since holding my newborns in my arms and being a mom is something I cannot imagine not being part of my life, I can completely understand how the Armstrong Fertility Institute could be perceived as a beacon of hope to childless couples. This is the first book in a six-book series about the Institute and the people who are a part of helping to make the miracle of birth happen for couples desperate to have a baby. But, along with the miracles come secrets and intrigue… I hope that this book and the books that follow will entertain you.

Thank you for reading, and, as ever, I wish you someone to love who loves you back.

Wishing you all the best,

Marie Ferrarella

PRESCRIPTION FOR ROMANCE

BY

MARIE FERRARELLA

DID YOU PURCHASE THIS BOOK WITHOUT A COVER?
If you did, you should be aware it is **stolen property** as it was reported *unsold and destroyed* by a retailer. Neither the author nor the publisher has received any payment for this book.

All the characters in this book have no existence outside the imagination of the author, and have no relation whatsoever to anyone bearing the same name or names. They are not even distantly inspired by any individual known or unknown to the author, and all the incidents are pure invention.

All Rights Reserved including the right of reproduction in whole or in part in any form. This edition is published by arrangement with Harlequin Enterprises II B.V./S.à.r.l. The text of this publication or any part thereof may not be reproduced or transmitted in any form or by any means, electronic or mechanical, including photocopying, recording, storage in an information retrieval system, or otherwise, without the written permission of the publisher.

This book is sold subject to the condition that it shall not, by way of trade or otherwise, be lent, resold, hired out or otherwise circulated without the prior consent of the publisher in any form of binding or cover other than that in which it is published and without a similar condition including this condition being imposed on the subsequent purchaser.

® and ™ are trademarks owned and used by the trademark owner and/or its licensee. Trademarks marked with ® are registered with the United Kingdom Patent Office and/or the Office for Harmonisation in the Internal Market and in other countries.

First published in Great Britain 2011
Harlequin Mills & Boon Limited,
Eton House, 18-24 Paradise Road, Richmond, Surrey TW9 1SR

© Harlequin Books S.A. 2010

Special thanks and acknowledgment to Marie Ferrarella for her contribution to The Baby Chase miniseries.

ISBN: 978 0 263 88855 3

23-0111

Harlequin Mills & Boon policy is to use papers that are natural, renewable and recyclable products and made from wood grown in sustainable forests. The logging and manufacturing processes conform to the legal environmental regulations of the country of origin.

Printed and bound in Spain
by Litografia Rosés S.A., Barcelona

USA TODAY bestselling and RITA® Award-winning author **Marie Ferrarella** has written almost two hundred novels, some under the name Marie Nicole. Her romances are beloved by fans worldwide. Visit her website at www.marieferrarella.com.

To
Jessica and Nicholas
with all my love forever,
Mom

Chapter One

Dr. Paul Armstrong was deeply concerned.

His sister Olivia Armstrong Mallory could have never, by any stretch of the imagination, been described as robust or even glowingly healthy, but she sat in his office today, turning to him not just as her older brother, but as the chief of staff of the Armstrong Fertility Institute. He knew talking about this wasn't easy for his sister. She'd addressed half her story to the crumpled tissue she held in a death grip between her fingers in her lap.

How many times since he'd begun to work here had he heard this same story before? Too many times, and yet, not enough to become insensitive to it.

Olivia wanted to become pregnant and all her attempts, she had confided quietly, had thus far failed.

Even as he listened to her haltingly pour out her heart, Paul began to suspect that there was more to all this than she was telling him. Something beyond the hunger to have a child.

"Olivia," he pointed out gently, "you're being too hard on yourself. You're just twenty-nine—"

Eyes full of misery and unshed tears looked up at him. "And I've been trying to get pregnant for five years, Paul. Five very long, disappointing years."

This, too, he'd seen over and over again. The anguished faces of frustrated women, pleading for help, asking him to make the most natural of dreams come true for them. He'd never imagined he'd see this look on the face of one of his sisters.

"Olivia, there are other avenues. You could adopt a child," he tactfully suggested.

But he could see, even as he said it, that for Olivia, this wasn't the solution. She pressed a small, fisted hand beneath her breast, pushing against her incredibly flat belly. "I want to feel life growing inside me, Paul."

Though his heart went out to her, Paul felt bound to tell her what he told every woman or couple who came in to see him with this same dilemma. "It isn't all roses, Livy. There's a very real downside to being pregnant." Assuming, he added silently, that he could even get her there.

Olivia shook her head, her sleek black hair shadowing the adamant movement. "Don't you understand I don't care?" Reaching across the desk that separated them, his sister took his hands in hers in supplication. "I *really* want to be pregnant. Help me, Paul. Whatever it takes, help me."

The force of her words had him wondering again. He had to ask. "Olivia, is everything all right?"

Releasing his hands, his sister drew herself up in her chair as she squared her shoulders. "Everything's fine, Paul."

Her words only reinforced his concern. "You said that much too fast."

Olivia inclined her head. "All right, I'll say it slower. Every-thing's-fine." She deliberately drew out the sentence, saying it in slow motion and awarding it a host of syllables.

He would have laughed if he wasn't so concerned. "Livy, I'm your brother. You can talk to me."

"I *am* talking to you," she insisted. "I'm telling you that I want to have a baby. As the chief of staff you should be able to understand that." Blowing out a breath and clearly struggling not to cry, Olivia asked, "Now, can you help me?"

Though he had a tendency to be oblivious to the obvious at times, the irony of the situation did not escape Paul. The daughter of the famous fertility expert Dr. Gerald Armstrong was infertile. Somewhere, the gods were chuckling.

If he ever helped anyone at all, Paul thought, he should be able to help his sister.

"Yes," he answered gently, "I think there's a good chance that I can." Of late, there had been a number of allegations of wrongdoing, rumored to be made by a former disgruntled employee, of eggs and sperm being switched, research that was held suspect and too many multiple births, all of which had caused a cloud of suspicion to be cast over the institute and the work they'd done over the years. Paul had been going out of his way to try to right all of this. He began by luring the world-famous Bonner-Demetrios research team away from a prominent San Francisco teaching hospital and getting them to head up the institute's research operations here.

Just in time, he thought, looking at his sister.

"We've just scored a coup and managed to get two top-flight physicians to join our staff here. Both of them have been on the cutting edge of fertility research for some time now. I'm going to refer you to one of them."

Olivia nodded, desperately trying to draw hope from her brother's words. "What's his name?"

"Dr. Chance Demetrios. If there's any way possible for you to wind up getting morning sickness, he'll find it," Paul promised with a quick smile. Paul wrote a few words on a pad, then tore the page off and held it out to her. "I know he doesn't have patients today until later. Are you willing to go now?"

Olivia looked down at the slip of paper her brother had

given her, unable to read a single word. She sincerely hoped that another doctor would have no trouble deciphering the hieroglyphics. "Are you sure he can see me?"

Paul smiled the shy, boyish smile she remembered so well from their childhood, the smile she recalled gracing the lips of her protector. Derek, their other brother, was always the one in the foreground, gregarious, loud and charming. But it was Paul she always felt she could count on. Paul was the dependable one who spoke little, but meant every word he said.

"Yes," he assured her. "I'm his boss. Chance'll see you." Rising, he came around the desk and squeezed his sister's hand. "Sure there's nothing else you want to tell me?"

Olivia stood up and did her best to smile. "I'm sure."

That wasn't good enough for him. Paul tried again. "Maybe there's something you don't want to tell me, but should?"

"Only that I love you." Olivia rose on her toes and brushed a quick kiss to his cheek. Backing away, she held up the note he'd just given her. "Thank you."

Paul sincerely hoped that Chance was the magician the man claimed to be. "Anytime," he replied.

His sister left his office, closing the door behind her. Paul went back around to his chair.

He'd just managed to sit down when the door flew open again, this time without a perfunctory knock or even the pretense of formality. His other sister, Lisa—the head administrator at the institute—burst in with just a tiny bit less noise than a detonating cherry bomb. Ordinarily, she vacillated between looking harried and looking pleased because another happy couple had left the institute, pregnant and satisfied. Now she looked as if she was about to bite someone's head off.

"Do you know what he did?" she demanded angrily, slamming the door closed with a bang.

Paul had always found it was best to remain calm in the face of anyone's tirade. If he remained calm, he could assess the problem more accurately. "Who?" he asked mildly.

Lisa looked at him as if he'd suddenly turned simple on her. "Derek, of course."

"Of course," Paul echoed. Taking a breath, he patiently pointed something out—and not for the first time. "Lisa, contrary to legend and a handful of fair-to-bad movies, just because Derek and I are twins does *not* mean that I automatically know what he's thinking, so, no, I don't know what he did." And then he smiled indulgently at her. "But I'm sure you're going to enlighten me."

Lisa let out a loud huff and Paul would have been hard-pressed to say who she was angrier at right now, Derek or him. "He's gone off on his own, that's what he's done."

He was going to need more of a hint than that. "As in…he left?" He sincerely doubted that Derek would just run off at such a difficult time and leave his siblings to deal with the entire mess. But he had to admit that he and Derek often marched to completely different drummers and there were times when his brother's actions and motivation completely mystified him. Not only that, but of late, he seemed to be preoccupied.

"No, as in going off and hiring someone to— Now wait a sec—" Lisa held her hand up in case Paul was going to interrupt her "—I want to get this straight. 'Someone to help us *repair* our image.'" Then Lisa fisted her hands on her hips. "*I'm* head administrator here and Derek's gone and hired a PR manager without so much as saying boo to me."

Paul sighed. He lived and breathed his work to the exclusion of almost everything else, except for his family. Very seldom did he come up for air, much less to mingle in the everyday dealings of running the institute.

Paul asked his fuming sister, "What do you mean?"

"Public relations, Paul," she said, even more annoyed. "Derek went and hired a damn spin doctor."

"So what's the issue?" he asked, confused.

Lisa threw up her hands in desperation. "For such an intelligent man, you can be so dense sometimes. The point is, Derek is the chief financial officer—he isn't supposed to hire anyone without consulting us. Major positions are supposed to be filled by the three of us evaluating the candidate for the job, remember?" She didn't wait for him to respond before she went on. "If you ask me, I think Derek's beginning to envision himself as Caesar."

Lisa was the youngest and as such, she was given

to exaggeration. "Dial it down a notch, Lisa. I don't like Derek doing something like this without consulting us, either, but I think it's a stretch equating him with Julius Caesar."

"I'm not equating him with Caesar," she protested. "I think Derek *sees* himself as Caesar. The bottom line is," she said with a toss of her short black hair, "we don't need a PR manager."

Paul nodded. "At least we're in agreement about that."

It never occurred to her that Paul would see it any differently than she did. "Good, then fix it," she demanded. When he raised an inquisitive eyebrow, Lisa pressed, "Unhire her."

Even though terminating this unwanted new employee was his first inclination, Paul did want to be fair. That would mean talking to Derek and finding out just what his brother was thinking when he hired this person. "Where's Derek now?"

Lisa sighed. "I have no idea. You know how he is, social butterflying all over. But I *do* know where the new girl is," she said triumphantly. "She's in Connie Winston's old office," she said, referring to a recently retired officer of their board of directors. Lisa was clearly not finished with the topic. "You know, Derek's got no right to constantly usurp us like that."

Paul had always been ready to go the extra mile, giving everyone the benefit of the doubt. "Derek probably doesn't even realize that's what he's doing. You know he gets impatient when things don't go as fast as he thinks they should." Paul shrugged philosophically. "He doesn't have the patience of a scientist."

Lisa pounced on her brother's words. "Good thing you do. Now get rid of this woman and give Derek a piece of your mind when you find him."

He laughed, shaking his head. "If I gave all the people who I think deserve it a piece of my mind, I wouldn't have any mind left to use for myself."

Lisa's frown was back. "So then you're not going to tell Derek that he's got to stop making unilateral decisions?"

"I didn't say that, did I?" His eyes held hers until Lisa shook her head. "I'll talk to Derek," he told her, then added, "not that I think it'll do any good."

"You're probably right," she was forced to agree. "But you never know, maybe we'll get lucky. But first," she emphasized, "you have to give that woman her walking papers."

There were times when Lisa was like a hungry dog with a bone. She just wouldn't let go. Which meant he'd get no peace until he gave in. Paul rose again. "Connie Winston's old office, you said?"

Lisa nodded. "The three of us are supposed to be running this clinic. It's the Armstrong Fertility Institute, not Derek Armstrong's Fertility Institute. If anything, it should be Dad's name, not Derek's."

Paul put his hands on his sister's arms, trying to settle her before she got riled up again.

"Take a deep breath, Lisa—and calm down. There

are a hell of a lot worse things going on in the world. Derek playing king is really just small potatoes in comparison."

"Emperor," Lisa corrected doggedly.

He closed his eyes for a moment. He was *not* going to get sidelined with semantics. "Whatever."

Paul was fully aware that if he even attempted to put off this woman's termination, Lisa would continue bedeviling him until such time as he would make good on his promise. His sister meant well, he thought, but she tended to get far too worked up. Still, she was right. Derek shouldn't have just gone off and hired someone without even running the idea past them. This was a completely new post his brother had created.

Did they really need someone to try to restore the institute's good name? Or rather, their father's good name even though it wasn't imprinted on the front of the building?

Dr. Gerald Armstrong had always been a little larger than life when it came to the public eye. Paul was not ashamed to say that he revered his father and the groundbreaking work he had done. He'd gotten away from the boy he had once been. The boy who, when he was growing up, felt his father was accessible to everyone but his own family. He knew his mother felt that. Gerald Armstrong was always far too busy making a name for himself to enjoy the name he had already gotten, almost by accident: Dad.

Still, that was all water under the bridge now. A

man was what he was and Gerald Armstrong was an excellent physician, a visionary and the last hope for a great many women who had been told that they would never be able to hold a child of their own in their arms.

The rest of it—the feet of clay, the women, the preoccupation—well, that could all be forgiven, Paul thought, walking down the corridor to the office where, according to his sister, he would find his brother's latest mistake—and it really was a mistake, in Paul's opinion. Right now, they needed every last penny to be spent on research, not "spin." The research team he'd lured away from San Francisco did *not* come cheaply.

Approaching the until recently evacuated office, Paul knocked on the door, then knocked again when he received no answer. He was about to try again when a melodious voice told him to, "Come in." Apparently the focus of his sister's ire was indeed in.

He wasn't good at firing people. Actually, to his recollection, he never had. He'd always been satisfied with the people he'd selected. There was no need to fire any of them.

Twisting the knob, he opened the door and walked in, not knowing what to expect.

He wasn't prepared for what he saw.

She was sitting at her desk, a slender blonde whose every movement promised curves that would melt a man's knees. She looked up at him with the clearest, bluest eyes he'd ever seen. The word *beautiful* pushed its way through the sudden cobwebs that had taken his brain hostage. It took him a moment to realize that he wasn't breathing.

She did not look like someone who was hired to do battle with mudslingers. She looked more like a fairy-tale princess who had sprung up from someone's smitten fantasy.

The woman seemed to light up as she saw who was walking into her office. Her face became a wreath of smiles.

"Mr. Armstrong, hello." The young woman half rose in her seat, as if she was eagerly ready to hop to do his bidding at the slightest suggestion. "What can I do for you, sir?"

Bracing himself, Paul said in his kindest voice—because it wasn't in him to be cruel—"I'm afraid you're going to have to pack up your things and leave."

The smile on her perfect face faded, replaced by bewilderment. "Excuse me?"

He hated this, he thought. He tried again, sounding even more gentle than before. "I think there's been a mistake." Each word felt more awkward on his tongue than the last. This was *definitely* not his forte. "I mean, we really don't need a public relations person."

The woman was obviously not going to go quietly. "But you just hired me," she protested with feeling.

She didn't look angry, he thought, which surprised him. What she looked like was someone who was set to dig in. She still thought she was dealing with his brother, Paul realized. He needed to set her straight before he continued.

"No, I didn't," he began, but got no further in his explanation.

"Yes, you did," she insisted. "Yesterday. We were in your office and you distinctly said you were hiring me." Her blue eyes seemed intense as she peered at his face. "Is something wrong?" she wanted to know. "I haven't done anything yet, much less something that would make you want to fire me."

"I don't want to fire you," Paul said and it was true. "I wouldn't have hired you in the first place—"

"But you did," she reminded him with feeling.

"No, I didn't," Paul told her again. "That was my brother."

Her eyes narrowed and the frown on her face told him she wasn't buying it.

"Your evil twin?" she asked with more than a tiny trace of sarcasm in her voice.

Finally, Paul thought. "Actually, I don't generally think of him in that light, but now that you mention it, yes."

The young woman stared at him as if he'd lost his mind. "Excuse me?"

Any breakthrough he'd thought had been made faded like dancing dandelion seeds in the warm spring breeze. "Maybe I should explain—"

He could see that she was struggling to remain civil. Looking at it from her point of view, he couldn't blame her.

"Maybe you should," she agreed.

Chapter Two

Bravado was second nature to Ramona Tate. It always had been. Her chosen field of investigative reporting had only honed that ability. She could bluff her way through practically everything.

Because she had never gone through an ugly-duckling stage and had been a swan from the moment she came into the world, Ramona had to constantly keep proving herself. People naturally assumed that a) because she was beautiful, that meant she didn't have a brain in her head, and b) she'd gotten to her present stage in life because she'd slept her way there.

In both cases, nothing could have been further from the truth.

Blessed with a near-genius IQ, Ramona still had to work twice as hard as the next person to be taken seriously and to keep from being dismissed as "just another empty-headed pretty face." This while politely, but deftly and succinctly, putting men in their place if they decided to become too familiar with her. In the latter case, whenever "hands-on" experience was mentioned, her antennae instantly went up because most of the men she'd encountered took that to mean their "hands on" her body.

Ramona always made it perfectly clear that working and playing well with others did not refer to the kind of playing that could be done beneath the sheets. She fought her own battles and protected her private life—what there was of it—zealously.

Since wrongdoing on any level was something she abhorred, Ramona found that she took to investigative reporting like the proverbial duck to water. Even at her seemingly tender age of twenty-five, she had already broken a number of stories, revealing fraudulent practices at one of the country's larger life insurance companies, and exposing a doctor who had made a career out of bilking Medicare, submitting charges for the treatment of nonexistent conditions for nonexistent patients in order to collect Medicare's payments. Both stories had necessitated her going undercover to get the information she needed to substantiate her allegations.

Ramona had followed the same path here, at the Armstrong Fertility Institute. Once revered as a bastion of hope for the terminally infertile, the institute's outstanding success rate had bred a certain amount of envy, which begged for closer scrutiny. This scrutiny in turn gave birth to ugly rumors, some that were quite possibly well founded, others that almost certainly were not.

That was going to be her job—to separate fact from fiction, no matter how deeply the former appeared to be buried.

But Ramona had a far more personal reason to have gone undercover at the institute. She needed to gain access to the institution's older records in hopes of saving her mother's life. Her mother, who had raised Ramona by herself, had been diagnosed with leukemia less than six months ago. The prognosis was not good. If something wasn't done soon to stem its course, her mother had only a very short time to live.

Katherine Tate desperately needed a bone-marrow transplant. Ramona would have gladly given up hers. She would have given her mother any organ she could to save the woman's life, but, as happened all too frequently, her marrow wasn't a match. So the search was on for some miscellaneous stranger whose marrow might provide the cure.

There was, however, a glimmer of hope when Ramona remembered accidentally stumbling over a piece of vital information packed away in a long-forgotten box hidden in the back of her closet.

Katherine Tate was one of those people who never threw anything away, she just moved it around every so often from one pile to another, from one room to another. In one of her many, *many* boxes throughout the house was a bundle of receipts and bills dating back more than a couple of decades. Including a receipt from the Armstrong Fertility Institute for the purchase of donor eggs.

In between jobs and desperate for money, Katherine had sold a part of herself in order that "some poor childless couple know the kind of joy I do." At least, those had been her mother's words when Ramona had finally confronted Katherine with her find.

Now Ramona could only hope that the eggs had been used and that somewhere out there she had a sibling walking around. A sibling whose bone marrow would turn out to be a perfect match for her mother.

Finding this sibling was far more important to Ramona than breaking the story of any ethical wrongdoing on the institute's part.

But she wouldn't be able to do either if this bipolar man made good on his threat to terminate her before she even got started in her search. For that to happen, she needed to get entrenched here. She already knew that calling the institute's administration office with her plight was an exercise in futility. When she had, the woman on the other end of the line had briskly told her that accessing the old records would be a violation of those patients' right to privacy.

Yeah, right. As if the Armstrongs and their minions actually cared a fig about doing the right thing.

"You were hired," Paul began slowly, trying to carefully hit all the salient points, "by someone who didn't have the proper authority to hire anyone by himself."

Ramona felt her temper shortening.

"I don't understand," she said, hoping that the smile on her lips didn't look as fake as it felt to her.

Paul backtracked in his head, realizing that he'd failed to state the most obvious part, the part that would instantly untangle the rest. Or so he hoped.

"You see, I'm twins."

She stared at him, her blue eyes widening. "You are?"

That sounded stupid, he upbraided himself. "I mean, I'm one of twins. I have a brother," he told her. "He looks just like me. His name's Derek and *he's* the one who hired you."

Her expression never changed, but her tone was slightly incredulous as she asked, "You're not Derek Armstrong?"

Finally. The light at the end of the tunnel was beginning to materialize, he thought, relieved. "No, I'm Paul."

Twins. Damn, how had she missed that? She'd been so consumed with getting ammunition against the institute and being angry because they wouldn't just help her get at the information she needed to, hopefully, find a sibling, she'd completely skimmed over the Armstrongs' family dynamics.

She needed to be more thorough, Ramona told herself sternly.

Cocking her head, she scrutinized the man in front

of her, doing her best to give off an aura of sweetness. She knew that she could be all but irresistible if she wanted to be. She eased her conscience by reminding herself that this was definitely not for personal gain. This was for her mother.

"Now that you mention it, you do look a little more robust and athletic than you—I mean, your brother—did yesterday." She was five-seven, not exactly a petite flower. But the man before her was taller, way taller. He looked even more so since she was sitting and he was not.

Ramona raised her eyes to his in a studied look of innocent supplication. A look she'd practiced more than once. "So he—your brother—can't hire me?"

Now she was getting it, Paul thought. "Not by himself, no."

Again she cocked her head, employing a certain come-hither look as she asked him, "Can he hire me if you hire me?"

Why did he feel as if the ground beneath his feet was turning from shale to sand, leaving him nothing solid to stand on? "Not without Lisa's okay," he heard himself say hoarsely.

Another country heard from, Ramona thought impatiently, trying to remember exactly how many Armstrongs worked at the institute. Her smile never wavered as she repeated, "Lisa?"

Paul nodded, trying not to stare. Was it his imagination, or did she somehow suddenly look more beautiful? "My younger sister. She's the head administrator here at the institute."

That had to have been the cold voice on the phone, Ramona thought. "Does anyone else have a vote?"

He smiled and she thought he had a rather nice smile. It softened his features and made him appear less distant and forbidding.

"No, that's it," he assured her. "Just the three of us."

She nodded slowly, as if taking it all in and digesting the information. What she was really doing was casting about for a way to appeal to him and make him let her remain.

"Well," she said slowly with a drop of seduction woven in, "we know that I have your brother's vote. Do I have yours?"

For one unguarded moment, he could have sworn that he felt some sort of a sharp pull, an attraction to this young woman. But then he told himself it was just that he had always appreciated beauty no matter where he came across it. He certainly couldn't allow it to cloud his judgment, especially when it came to the institute.

Still, a public relations manager might prove useful, he supposed. Paul was honest in his answer. "I'd have to think about it."

She appeared undaunted. "Well, that's better than 'no,'" Ramona allowed.

Faced with her optimism, Paul wavered a little more in his stand, shifting in a direction he knew that Lisa would easily disapprove. "I tell you what. Let me talk to the others and we'll get back to you."

Ramona smiled. It made him think of a sunrise. Warm and full of promise. And then she looked just a tad shy as she asked, "In the meantime, would it be all right if I drafted a press release?"

"A press release?" Paul echoed, confused. "About what?"

"About doctors Demetrios and Bonner joining your staff. Mr. Armstrong—Mr. *Derek* Armstrong," she amended, "said that so far, no mention had been made of the transition. I think it would be a big plus for the institute, not to mention that it would be a huge draw, as well." Not that the institute actually needed it, she thought. The rich and famous flocked here, and the masses followed. "These two researchers are very famous in their field."

"I know," he said, amused that she believed she was telling him something he wasn't aware of.

"Of course you do." Holding her breath just so allowed the right amount of pink to creep into her cheeks. She instinctively knew that Paul was the kind of man who reacted to blushes, even though it was as out of date as a silver disco ball. "I just meant that it should be brought to people's attention. It's positive reinforcement." And then she flashed him another guileless smile. "I promise I won't do anything with the draft until I get your—all of your," she amended, "okays."

She sounded so eager and upbeat, Paul found that

he hadn't the heart to tell her to wait until after he'd won Lisa over. Lisa could be difficult at times, especially if she felt that her territory was being encroached upon and threatened. Her earlier tirade was likely only the tip of the iceberg on this matter.

"That'll be fine," he told her and then he quickly walked out of the room before he wound up agreeing to something else.

He needed to find Derek and have a few choice words with his brother for putting him in this situation. A few *very* choice words.

He found Derek just outside his brother's office, engaged in what appeared to be a very private conversation with one of the newer and younger administrative assistants. From the looks of it, it appeared that groundwork for far more than further conversation was being laid.

Suppressing a sigh, Paul inserted himself between the exceedingly perky young redhead in the platform heels and his brother. "Excuse us, please, um—" He had no idea what the young woman's name was.

"Danielle." Both the young woman and Derek said the name at the same time, which caused them to exchange more covert looks. Paul heard the assistant smother a giggle.

"Danielle," Paul repeated with a slight nod of his head, "I need to speak with my brother."

"Of course." Inclining her head, the administrative

assistant drew away. But not before she exchanged one more overtly steamy, sexy glance with the institute's CFO.

Paul walked into his brother's recently remodeled office and waited for Derek to follow. Which Derek did. Languidly.

The moment the door was closed, Paul immediately started talking. "What the hell were you thinking, hiring that young girl?" he demanded.

Derek looked at him, apparently confused. "Who?"

"The one sitting in Connie Winston's old office. Your so-called PR manager."

If he was aware of the sarcasm in his brother's voice, Derek didn't show it. "Oh, you mean Ramona Tate." Derek grinned broadly, obviously pleased with himself. "That was a real lucky break."

Derek was usually more intuitive than this. Ordinarily, he picked up on tension. Maybe his brother thought it would all just go away if he didn't acknowledge it. *Think again, Derek.* If nothing else, Paul wanted some of the ground rules reaffirmed.

"Some of us," he told Derek, "don't think so."

Derek laughed shortly. "By 'some' I take it you mean Lisa and you." Even as he said the words amicably, he knew the answer. Just as he knew that their baby sister was behind this confrontation. Even as a kid, Lisa was into power plays. As the youngest of the Armstrong children, she always wanted to come out on top, to be the one the others listened to.

Putting his hand on Paul's shoulder, Derek said patiently, "Paul, you're an excellent physician and a wonderful chief of staff here at the institute. If you ask me, you deserve a lot more credit than you're getting. But let's be honest, there's no denying that the institute needs help."

"I got us help," Paul pointed out tersely. "I got Demetrios and Bonner to leave their hospital and join the institute. In case you missed it, they're the cutting-edge research team who—"

"I didn't miss it," Derek answered crisply, cutting in. "But I just might have been the only one around who didn't."

Paul had absolutely no idea what that even meant. "What?"

"Exactly," Derek declared as if Paul had made his point for him. "What newspaper was that where the press release announcing their joining the institute was run? Oh, wait, it wasn't," he said with exaggerated enlightenment. "Because we had no one manning our PR desk to make that press release. But we do now," he concluded with a smug, triumphant smile.

Paul was easygoing up to a point, but he dug in now. If he didn't take a stand here, he might as well just lie down and have Derek walk all over him. "Not until Lisa and I agree to hire her."

"Then agree," Derek told him, trying to control his irritation. "Because she's already hired."

"Not exactly."

"What do you mean 'not exactly'?" Derek wanted to know. "I hired her yesterday."

"And I put her on temporary notice."

The smile evaporated instantly. Derek exploded. "For God's sake, why?"

Paul dug deep for patience. Derek, he knew, was accustomed to doing whatever he wanted to unopposed. But when it came to the institute, important decisions had to involve all three of them. They'd agreed on that when they took over the famous facility from their ailing father.

As if it was the first time, Paul doled his words out evenly. "Because you can't just go off and do this kind of thing whenever you feel like it without at least consulting Lisa *and* me."

"So you're going to let Ramona go because you're mad at me?" he asked in abject disbelief. Derek shook his head in amazement. "Boy, leave it to you to be such a cliché."

Paul's gaze became flinty. "Excuse me?"

Derek frowned, exasperated. "That old chestnut about cutting off your nose to spite your face. That's what you're doing."

Any moment now, his brother was going to throw a tantrum, Paul thought. "You're carrying on as if I just fired Woodward and Bernstein. That girl looks like she's barely out of high school, let alone college. We implant embryos here, Derek, we don't hire them."

Derek raised his voice to be heard over him. “Ramona Tate is twenty-five years old and she has impressive credentials—”

“Which I’m sure you checked thoroughly.” Paul couldn’t help the note of sarcasm that came into his voice. He sincerely doubted that Derek had done anything but glance at her résumé.

Derek squared his shoulders indignantly. “I was getting to that.”

Sure you were, Paul thought. “Want another old chestnut?”

Derek slanted a glance toward him, a suspicious look entering his eyes. “Like what?”

“Like you’re putting the cart before the horse.” In this case, he’d hired the woman and planned to rubber-stamp her references—if she even had any.

A deep chuckle escaped Derek’s lips. “Maybe you didn’t notice—and if you didn’t, you’d be the only one who wouldn’t—but this ‘horse’ has lines that could stop a charging rhino in his tracks.”

Paul sighed, shaking his head. “So this is about your libido.”

Derek rolled his eyes. “Unlike you, I have one, but in this case I was thinking of the institute.”

Paul leaned a hip against his brother’s desk. “This I have to hear.”

“There’s nothing wrong in having an extremely attractive—and able—woman to represent us. To be the ‘face’ of the Armstrong Fertility Institute.” Seeing that he was losing Paul, Derek hurried to add, "Which would you rather look at when it comes to getting your information, a gnarled, short, bald, fat man or an attractive young woman who makes your blood surge and makes you think of fertility just by *looking* at her?"

"I'd just as soon get it in a report on my desk."

Derek threw up his hands. "You're hopeless, you know that?"

Paul made no comment on that. He didn't feel he needed to defend himself. This wasn't about him, *or* Derek. This was about their father's legacy. "How much is she costing the institute?"

Derek rallied for a second defense. "Not as much as you would think—and Ramona is worth every penny of it."

Paul gave his twin a knowing look. "I'll bet."

"Get your mind out of the gutter, Paul. I was referring to the press release I asked her to prepare."

Was that why the woman had asked him if she could draft a statement? "About?" he asked cautiously, wanting to see if the stories agreed.

"Your dynamic duo, of course. Bonner and Demetrios bring their own sterling reputations to the table—just as you planned." Derek wasn't above trying to butter his brother up if he had to. "We get the public focusing on that, they'll forget the rumors."

He blew out a breath, then looked at Paul hopefully. "So how about it, Paul? Can we take her off notice and just watch her work?" He put his arm around his brother's shoulders in a gesture of solidarity. "I promise you won't be sorry."

There was no way that Derek could guarantee that. "And if I am?"

Derek laughed. "Not even you can be that much of a stodgy old man." Derek tapped his brother's chest with the back of his hand. "Loosen up, Paul. You'll not only live longer, but you'll get to enjoy yourself, too."

"I *do* enjoy my life," Paul insisted. And he did. He was dedicated to continuing his father's work and to granting childless couples their fondest wish. That was more than enough for him.

Derek merely shook his head. "Can't see how, but okay. Do you know where Lisa is?"

Paul laughed quietly. "Most likely sharpening her tongue so she can give you a good lashing."

"That's why I want to head her off," Derek confessed. "I was hoping to make a preemptive strike."

Paul thought of the expression on Lisa's face when she burst into his office earlier. "Too late," he speculated.

Derek was not easily defeated. And he had the ability to talk someone to death—or at least until he got what he wanted.

"Maybe not," he countered as he went off in search of their sister. Ramona Tate was staying and that was that. He was *not* about to tolerate being overridden. The institute needed to continue to make money and that was not going to happen if people—wealthy people—stopped coming to avail themselves of what they had to offer here. Their focus needed to be redirected to a positive image, and Ramona Tate seemed just the person to do it.

Both he and the institute would benefit from that.

Chapter Three

Ramona already knew that there was nothing in this small office that could help her with her investigation. If there was data that could openly incriminate one or more of the staff at the institute for engaging in the wrongful substitution of eggs or sperm, it wouldn't be readily accessible. She was also fairly certain that nothing tangible would turn up to back the claim that too many embryos were being implanted purely to up the success ratio.

There was no way she was going to learn how to access records that had been archived just by sitting here, staring at the walls. Ramona wasn't even certain that there *were* archived records. Since they might prove to be incriminating, they might have been destroyed years ago. She knew for a fact that they weren't on any database within the institute.

All she could do was hope that Gerald Armstrong, who ran this facility until ill health had forced him into retirement, had been vain enough to hang on to everything—good or bad—that even remotely testified to his accomplishments and his genius. From what she'd read and heard, the man had a more than healthy ego.

If the senior Armstrong had played God and implanted her mother's eggs into someone, she thought, adrenaline rushing excitedly through her veins, that *had* to have been noted in the recipient's file. She might be looking for a needle in a haystack, but at least she'd know that there *was* a needle.

Dr. Gerald Armstrong had been in charge of operations and treatments when her mother had sold her eggs to the institute, Ramona thought. Pacing about her small office, she wondered now if there was any plausible excuse she could come up with in order to gain access to the man. All she needed was about ten minutes. She knew that these days he led a fairly low-key, quiet life, hardly ever leaving his home. He was cared for and looked after by his very long-suffering wife.

It had to be hell for both of them, Ramona thought. Emily Stanton Armstrong came from a good family and had a high social standing in the community when she married the up-and-coming pioneering doctor. The woman spent her days planning charitable events and her evenings attending them.

From her research, Ramona knew that the good doctor had made sure that he got his share of mileage out of the successes the institute achieved. Handsome, dynamic and blessed with the gift of gab, rumor had it that Gerald Armstrong had more than one illicit relationship. Mrs. Armstrong cast a blind eye to his dealings and partied harder.

Now they were almost like two shut-ins—he, more often than not, relegated to his wheelchair, she to nursing a man she had quite possibly learned to loathe.

Not exactly the type of people she wanted to have anything to do with, Ramona thought. Still, she was not above using any means, fair or foul, to achieve her main goal: finding out if her mother's desperate action had ultimately resulted in a child who could save her life.

For now, though, Ramona had no choice but to stay in her office and wait for Armstrong—be it Paul or Derek, or perhaps even Lisa—to come and tell her whether or not she was to stay on as PR manager.

Because she wasn't the type to waste time by aimlessly surfing the Web, Ramona decided to do exactly what she'd told Paul she was going to do: draft a press release about the research team who had recently been enticed to add their names to the fertility institute's roster.

Even though she was only twenty-five, she already had established several strong connections within the media world. Pulling a few strings, she was certain that she could get sufficient coverage for Demetrios and Bonner's shift from working at a teaching hospital to bringing their research program to the Armstrong Fertility Institute.

And as for the public, she'd already learned that they were mercurial, as fast to revere as to condemn. All it took were the right words in the right place to achieve either reaction. For the time being, it served her purpose to give the Armstrongs a little something to put in the plus column.

Her mouth curved as she thought about it. If everything went according to plan, this would amount to the calm before the storm. Because, if her information turned out to be correct, she intended to bring the Armstrong Fertility Institute down so fast, the pompous family would wind up choking on the dust that was kicked up.

She crossed back to the desk and sat down to work. Pausing just for a moment to find the right first word, her fingers soon flew across the keyboard, trying to keep up with her racing brain and coming in a close second.

Engrossed in wording the release so that it would pop as a whole, Ramona didn't hear the knock on her door. She also wasn't aware of that same door being opened a beat later.

Paul slipped in unobtrusively, a considerable feat for a man who measured six foot one. But then, he had the kind of quiet, easygoing manner that allowed him to blend in with the scenery at will. Unlike his outgoing brother, who had never been known to fade into the background, even for a moment, in his entire life. The very act would have been against everything that Derek stood for.

She looked diligent, Paul observed, completely involved in her work. She was obviously intent on doing a good job.

Maybe Derek had been right in hiring this young woman after all, he mused. Maybe a public-relations spokesperson was exactly what they needed to give them that much-needed shot in the arm. Good works didn't count for very much if no one knew you did them, and the public, fickle at best in their loyalties, couldn't exactly be expected to embrace something if they didn't know about it.

Paul took a step forward and cleared his throat.

The sound caught her attention and Ramona raised her eyes. The next moment she was clamping her lips together, stifling a gasp. When had Armstrong come in? "How long have you been standing there?"

A slight smile curved his mouth. "Long enough to discover that you nibble on your lower lip when you're thinking—or was that fretting?"

Fretting. Now, *there* was a word she hadn't heard in—well, maybe forever. This man definitely had stepped out of the last century. Quite possibly the first half of the last century, she speculated.

"No, no 'fretting,'" she answered with a straight face. "You were right the first time. I was just thinking something through. Don't worry. There's nothing in what I'm writing that should stir up any kind of concern." She gestured toward the screen, which, given its position, only she could see right now. "It's just the institute doctors' backgrounds, plus I've added a little family history for each of them."

Personal histories had never really interested him all that much. They were just fillers, padding that was easily eliminated. It was what a person did, not who their parents were, that mattered. Though he had to admit that maybe his own background tainted his view of things.

Still, he asked, "Do you think that's really necessary?"

As far as she was concerned, a person's history was the most interesting part. She always wanted to know what made people tick, how they got to be the way they were. She sincerely doubted that she was alone in this.

"People like to know who they're dealing with. It makes the whole challenging process of fertility treatment a little more down-to-earth for them—and a little less like science fiction."

Leaning back in what she hoped would continue to be her chair for at least a modest amount of time, Ramona did her best to appear relaxed. The very act belied the knots in her stomach. She laced her fingers before her and tried to sound cheerful as she asked, "So, what's the verdict?"

Technically, there was no official verdict yet. He told her what was happening. "I managed to send Derek to Lisa to apologize."

Well, that didn't sound very heartening. "For hiring me?" she asked. This would be the part where she would have gotten up and told him what he could do with his apology. But she wasn't being herself, she was being a subservient employee. She assumed that was what Paul Armstrong wanted and she was willing to go along with it, as long as it eventually got her access to the archives.

"For hiring you without consulting with the rest of us," Paul corrected.

That still didn't give her the answer she was hoping for. "So you're letting me go?" she guessed. She had trouble envisioning the woman who belonged to that cold voice over the phone giving her a thumbs-up. Even so, there was absolutely no way she was going to go without a fight. "Because if you are, Dr. Armstrong, you're going to regret it."

"Are you threatening me, Miss Tate?" he asked quietly.

"No, I'm telling you that you need me," she responded with feeling. "I'm very good at my job." Ramona straightened and squared her shoulders.

She made him think of a warrior princess. He had no idea where that had come from, only that it seemed like a very appropriate description.

"I'd like you to read what I've been writing before you have security eject me."

Paul held up his hand to stop her before her mouth launched into double time. The woman was already talking faster than he could listen. He had a feeling that, like Derek, Ramona Tate could talk with the best of them, easily winning battles simply by wearing her opposition down.

"No one's ejecting you, Miss Tate," he assured her. "You have a temporary stay of execution."

The surprise came and went from her face in an instant. Had he blinked, Paul suspected he wouldn't have seen it at all.

"How temporary?" she wanted to know, banking down her eagerness.

"That remains to be seen," he told her. It depended on whether she actually got results that would do them any good. For now, he was willing to give her the benefit of the doubt. "Why don't we just take this one step at a time, shall we?"

"That's all I ever wanted, an opportunity to prove myself to you—whichever 'you' I happen to be talking to," she added with an amused smile. Rising, she cocked her head just a tad as she peered at him closely, her eyes swiftly taking inventory and reviewing everything she noted. And then she made her decision. "You're Dr. Paul," she declared with just a hint of triumph.

He hid his amusement. "What makes you so certain?" he asked.

Even though he felt that there was a world of difference between his brother and him, Paul knew that as far as looks went, he and Derek were close to interchangeable unless they were standing beside one another. It was only then that someone might notice that Derek was thinner, while he looked as if he availed himself of the gym's facilities whenever he could, which he did.

When they were younger, both of their parents managed to confuse one with the other, in part, Paul suspected, because neither parent ever really took the time to get to know either of them. Although, if he thought about it, Paul had a feeling that if his parents *had* taken the time, it would only have been Derek who would have garnered their focused attention.

It wasn't only the squeaky wheel that got greased, it was the noisy, silver-tongued brother who ultimately got all the attention.

Ramona smiled up at him. The smile penetrated clear down to his bones. "Your eyes."

He waited, but she didn't elaborate. "What about my eyes?" he pressed. He fully expected her to say something to the effect that they were dull, that Derek was the one whose eyes looked as if they held a host of secrets and the promise of excitement.

But she surprised him. "You're the one with the kind eyes," Ramona said. "Your brother's eyes are…unfathomable."

Maybe she didn't have such a happy way with words after all. Paul interpreted her meaning. "So Derek is the man of mystery while I'm the flat, two-dimensional one."

Her perfectly shaped eyebrows drew together into

a V. She looked surprised at his interpretation of her assessment.

"Not at all," she protested. "On an absolute level, you'd be the one who people would trust, Dr. Armstrong, not your brother. They'd go to him looking for a good time, not honesty."

Ramona firmly believed that it was never too early to begin laying groundwork in order to build a viable relationship. That was her goal at the moment to build a connection with Paul. She could accomplish more at a quicker pace if she had one of the Armstrongs in her corner, and Paul, although reserved, struck her as the one who was more real, more open. She had the feeling that Derek had his own, private agenda, one he meant to pursue no matter what. A man like that couldn't be manipulated.

Besides, Derek Armstrong was far too into himself to be of any use to her.

Paul shook his head ever so slightly. "I already said you had a temporary stay of execution, Miss Tate. There's no need to try to flatter me."

Annoyed with herself that she'd come across so transparent, nonetheless Ramona managed to rally quickly. "I wasn't flattering, I was telling it the way I saw it," she informed him simply.

She might have given him a simple answer, Paul mused, but he had the impression that this woman was anything but that. As a matter of fact, he would have been willing to say that, despite declarations of honesty and truth, there was something Ramona Tate was keeping back.

The fleeting thought intrigued him.

In case she believed he was fishing for more validation, he changed the subject. "By the way, about your references—"

Ramona was one jump ahead of him. She'd learned that a good defense was to have a good offense. "I have them right here." Reaching for her oversize purse, she pulled it toward her, then flipped the locks open. "Your brother said he'd be getting around to reviewing them eventually, but I think they should be a matter of record, don't you?" Taking out a light blue file that contained more than a few letters of praise, she offered the folder to him. "There's also a copy of my academic transcript and employment history," she told him.

Taking the folder, Paul opened it and scanned a few of the pages. There were letters from college professors and from news editors, some of whom had the logos of local TV stations stamped on them. One was from the *Washington Post*. He'd expected one letter, perhaps two. If asked, he would have said that she was too young for more than that.

"And you said that you were just twenty-five?" he asked incredulously.

Maybe Monty had laid it on a little thick, Ramona thought. Monty Durham was the computer geek/wizard she'd befriended in her first year in college. He'd been so grateful to have someone to talk to, he became

Sancho Panza to her female Don Quixote. There wasn't anything that Monty couldn't make a computer do, including spew out lies and make them look like gospel. There also wasn't anything that Monty wouldn't do for her.

"I graduated two years early," she told Paul by way of an explanation.

Which was true. Eager to start leaving her mark in the world, Ramona had opted for an accelerated course of study. It had allowed her to crunch four years of high school into three and then do the same with college. To make it work, she'd attended school year-round, picking up courses part-time in the summer. In her spare time, she had also worked any job in her field she could get her hands on. That in turn gave her a much-needed solid core for her résumé. Monty had done the rest, embellishing where he could. He was also responsible for half the letters of recommendation in the folder.

She was unusual, Paul decided, he'd give her that. "In my experience, most people like to extend their college experience if they can."

"Maybe so," she allowed. "But I wanted to get started with my life," she countered. "College was great," she added quickly, not wanting him to think she was bucking for some kind of sainthood, "but college isn't life. It's more like the TV version." Angling the monitor so that it turned in his direction, Ramona realized that she'd come full circle and made the offer again. "Would you like to read what I've written so far?"

That would probably be the best way to determine whether or not she could actually do them some good, he thought. Or if having her around was just Derek's way of having eye candy on hand.

"Actually, I would."

Smiling, she hit the key combination that caused the wireless printer in the corner to come to life. Within moments, it produced the four pages she'd composed. Ramona crossed to the machine and removed the sheets, then returned and handed them to Paul.

And that was when he realized that he'd gotten caught up in watching her move, and Paul found that for once he couldn't fault his brother for admiring Ramona's looks. He had to admit, the sway of her hips was something to behold. It was enough to even make a man believe in Santa Claus.

Chapter Four

Back in his office, Paul read through Ramona's pages.

Even if he wanted to, Paul could find no fault with the rough draft that she had given him to review. Obviously the new public relations manager definitely had a way with words.

Maybe, Paul thought, putting the four sheets of paper down on his desk, Derek was actually onto something.

There was a quick rap on his office door and before he could say, "Come in," the person on the other side of the knock did.

Speak of the devil.

Derek stuck his head in, holding on to the doorknob as if he was prepared to make a quick getaway. Paul couldn't help wondering if something was wrong. Derek seemed edgier to him these days. Was that just because of the tense climate at the institute, or was there more to it than that?

"You can stop holding your breath," Derek informed him cheerfully.

"I wasn't aware that I was." Paul waited for his brother to follow up with an explanation.

"Sure you were. About Little Miss PR's fate," Derek prompted when Paul continued to look at him quizzically. "I got Lisa to come on board with our decision."

"'Our' decision?" Paul asked, emphasizing the plural possessive. Was Derek trying to share the blame, or the glory?

"Sure." Derek looked surprised that he was even questioning that it was a joint effort. "You wanted to hire her, too, didn't you?"

"Well, yes, now," Paul admitted, because he had been won over, but he certainly hadn't started out that way. "However—"

Derek breezed right past his brother's "however" as he continued his narrative. "I convinced Lisa that we need a professional to help take the tarnish off the institute's reputation. Ramona stays."

Paul thought how angry Lisa had looked when she'd stormed into his office earlier. He shook his head in wonder. "Derek, you could probably sweet-talk the devil into giving you back your soul, couldn't you?"

Derek inclined his head. He saw no reason to argue. "If I had to." And then he grinned. The harried look he'd sported earlier faded as he asked, "By the way, you wouldn't be referring to our youngest sister as the devil, would you?"

Paul blanched. That was all he needed, to have Lisa think he was calling her names behind her back. "No, I would *never*—"

Derek laughed, waving away the rest of whatever his twin was about to protest. "Take it easy, Paul, I was only kidding. You're so nonconfrontational you wouldn't even call the devil a devil."

Paul read between the lines. "Are you telling me I'm spineless?"

Derek sobered for a second. His voice was devoid of any cynicism or sarcasm. For a fleeting moment, it almost seemed to be a tad wistful. "No, I'm telling you that everyone thinks of you as the 'good' brother. The nice guy."

There was something in his brother's voice, an unfathomable undercurrent that caught Paul's attention. This was the second time today that he felt as if a member of his family was hiding something, keeping something back. Prodding, he had a feeling, was going to be as futile with Derek as it had been with Olivia, but he wouldn't have been Paul if he didn't try.

"Is something on your mind, Derek?"

And just like that, the serious look in Derek's eyes

completely vanished. The cocky, confident air was back. In spades.

"Something's *always* on my mind, Paul." He winked broadly. "It's called responsibilities. Gotta fly. I'm heading out."

Paul tried to pin Derek down to something specific. "For the day?"

"For the rest of the week." That, Paul knew, was what he was afraid of. Of late, Derek behaved more like a hurricane, striking swiftly and then moving on just as quickly. "Maybe longer," Derek was saying. "Listen, I was going to help familiarize Ramona with the institute, give her a tour of the place, answer any questions she might have, that kind of thing. But now that I'm not going to be here, I'd really appreciate if you did the honors for me."

"Why aren't you going to be here?" Paul wanted to know. For his part, he was *always* here. Or at least it felt that way. He was not only chief of staff at the institute, but he saw his patients here, as well. Derek, on the other hand, hardly seemed to be present at all.

"Something came up" was all that Derek would say. "I need you to fill in for me. Will you do it?" To the untrained ear, it sounded as if Derek was giving him a choice.

But Paul knew better.

He frowned. He wasn't good with people in any prolonged capacity. And he was exceedingly bad when it came to making small talk. Despite their age difference—he was thirty-six to her twenty-five—he had a feeling that Ramona Tate was far more of a sophisticated creature than he was. This was out of his ballpark.

"Can't Lisa do it?"

Derek laughed shortly, dismissing the suggestion, or, in this case, request. "Lisa's got a lot on her plate right now, too. Besides, she'd be too busy sizing Ramona up to be of any help. You know how competitive our baby sister can get."

This was true, but she'd always been fiercely competitive with her three siblings—not, to his knowledge, with strangers.

"Why would she be competitive?"

Derek sighed, shaking his head. "She's female. In case you haven't noticed, brother dear, so is Ramona."

That was just the trouble. He *had* noticed. Really noticed. Ramona Tate was a stunning young woman. Just the type he could envision Derek—or their father, in his day—pursuing.

Without saying he would do it, he pressed Derek for some kind of specifics. "Where did you say you were going again?"

"I didn't."

And with that noncommunicative response, Derek closed the door and, for all intents and purposes, the institute's CFO vanished.

Paul sighed. That was so typical. There were times when Derek treated the institute as his own personal playground, someplace to pop in, stay just long enough to stir things up, then hop a plane and go back to New York, where he actually lived.

If that was even where he was going this time. Derek was a fine one to bandy the word *responsibilities* about. For the past few months, he'd certainly been shirking his while stepping on everyone else's toes, egging them on to pick up the slack he'd created.

Paul glanced down at the paper he'd just finished reading, his mind shifting to the problem Derek had left in his wake. He didn't have time for the so-called orientation tour that Derek had palmed off on him—at least not today. But he could tell the woman that she had her job and that, by the way, she'd done a rather nice one on the press release she'd just worked up.

Paul had never cared for empty flattery, but he did believe in telling someone if they'd done good work. It was something he'd learned not to take for granted. Praise was something that he'd never heard himself when he was growing up. His father hadn't been reticent when it came to acknowledgment, he just wasn't around all that much to begin with. It was hard to honestly comment on any accomplishments if you didn't know about them; if you hadn't been around to see or hear anything about them. Dr. Gerald Armstrong always seemed either to be *at* the institute he'd founded, or *on his way* to the institute.

Paul swore to himself that if he ever had any children of his own—something he was doubtful at this point would ever come about—he would never miss an opportunity to praise them if they did something well.

Hell, he'd even praise them for an *attempt* to do something well. People needed to be encouraged, especially children. That was why he'd initially become a doctor. To get the great Gerald Armstrong's approval. To get Gerald Armstrong's attention, at least for five minutes.

Neither really happened, but somewhere along the line, he grew to love his work. He supposed that made him one of the lucky ones after all.

Paul was just about to go see Ramona and discuss her release when there was another knock on his door. Had Derek changed his mind and decided to stay? He figured it was probably too much to hope for.

"Come in."

And he was right. It was too much to hope for. It wasn't Derek who walked into his office. It was Olivia.

"I saw your wunderkind doctor," she told him. There was no sarcasm in her voice. The title was bestowed in earnest.

Paul noticed that her face was flushed. Was that a good sign? Or a bad one?

"And?" Paul asked when she didn't continue. He gestured for her to take a chair.

She did, perching her weight on the edge of the cushion as if she anticipated the need to fly away at any moment.

"And he said there was a chance I could become

pregnant. Slim, but a chance," she added breathlessly, clinging to the word *chance* as if it were a lifeline.

Paul nodded. He more than anyone knew how iffy that statement was. But he was not about to rain on Olivia's parade.

"Well, he would be the one to know. There's none better," he assured her. For a moment, he sat there just looking at Olivia, debating whether or not to back away. He decided to try one more time to get her to open up. "Livy, is it Jamison?" he asked, referring to his brother-in-law, the up-and-coming junior senator from Massachusetts and media darling.

Olivia looked up sharply, a porcelain doll about to shatter. Her eyes were wary. "Is what Jamison?"

Paul had no idea how to phrase this, he just knew he had to get it out into the open somehow. He couldn't shake the feeling that there was more to his sister's unhappiness than just the failure to become pregnant.

"Is Jamison pressing you to become pregnant?" He knew how important lineage and legacy were to the Mallorys. They were practically their own dynasty, the young lions of the world, determined to leave their mark. Part of that involved offspring. "I mean, there are other ways to go, you know. You could adopt, or have a surrogate mother who—"

Olivia began shaking her head the moment he'd said that there were other ways to go. She didn't want to hear it.

"No. I want to *feel* this, to do this myself." Olivia

pressed her hand against her flat belly, splaying her fingers out beneath her chest.

Paul looked into her eyes for a long moment. "Having a baby doesn't solve anything, you know," he told her quietly. "It usually creates its own set of unique problems."

"I know that." There was tension wrapped around each word and he noticed that Olivia was clasping and unclasping her hands in her lap.

Paul pressed again, more succinctly now. "Are you sure everything is all right between you and Jamison?"

"Yes," she finally snapped. "Which is more than I can say about between you and me if you keep asking these ridiculous questions."

This wasn't getting him anywhere. Paul retreated. "Sorry. I'm just concerned about you, Olivia, that's all."

She pressed her lips together and took in a deep breath in an attempt to calm herself. "I appreciate that and I'm sorry, too. I really didn't mean to snap at you like that, it's just that it seems like everywhere I look these days, I see women either pushing a baby carriage or being pregnant and looking as if they're about to pop at any second. Everybody is pregnant but me." Her voice quavered and she looked down at her knotted fingers. "We've been trying for five years now. Five *long* years."

"Yes, I know. You told me," he replied gently.

Olivia abruptly rose to her feet, a deer about to flee. Paul rounded his desk, coming to her side. Though he wasn't a demonstrative person by nature, seeing his sister like this tugged on his heartstrings. He hugged her, albeit awkwardly.

"Everything's going to be all right, Livy," he promised.

"I hope so," she murmured against his shoulder. "I sincerely hope so."

There was yet another knock on his door. Undoubtedly that was his nurse, here to remind him that he had patients to see this afternoon. Anxious patients who felt exactly like his sister.

"Come in," he called out.

Ramona came in just as he gave his sister another bracing hug before releasing her.

Olivia stepped back.

Surprised, certain that she'd inadvertently walked in on something, Ramona instantly looked down at the rug as if it had suddenly become fascinating. "Oh, I'm sorry. I didn't mean to interrupt anything."

"You didn't," Paul told her crisply. "This is my sister Olivia Armstrong Mallory."

Ramona looked at the other woman, a wariness automatically entering her eyes. Another Armstrong. Another hurdle?

"Someone else who has to approve my being hired?" she asked politely.

Turning from the woman in the doorway, Olivia looked at him quizzically.

"Long story," Paul told her, forestalling any questions on her part. "And I have to be somewhere."

Olivia slipped the strap of her designer purse onto her shoulder. "So do I," she told him. "Thanks for getting me in to see Dr. Demetrios," she said, then nodded at Ramona before slipping out. "Nice meeting you."

But you didn't, Ramona thought. The fourth branch on the Armstrong family tree—this had to be Senator Mallory's wife, she realized—hadn't learned her name, making the introduction incomplete.

"She didn't," Ramona said out loud to Paul once the door was closed again.

That had come out of nowhere. Much like the woman herself, he observed now. "She didn't what?"

"Meet me," Ramona told him. Because Paul looked at her as if she'd just lapsed into a foreign dialect, she elaborated, "You gave me her name, but you didn't give her mine."

She was right. Paul lifted one shoulder in a careless shrug.

"She was in a hurry," he explained, then glanced at his watch. "And so am I."

"Then I won't keep you," Ramona promised, getting down to business. She subtly stepped into his path so that he couldn't leave his office without answering her. "I just wanted to know if you have any changes you want me to incorporate into the article."

His mind still on his sister's troubled demeanor, he looked at Ramona blankly. "Article?"

"The press release," she prompted. Seeing the pages on his desk, she pointed to them for emphasis. "That."

"Oh." What was it about this woman that seemed to drive any coherent thoughts out of his head? Paul glanced back at his desk, as if seeing the pages there would crystallize his thoughts. "No, no changes. It's very good just the way it is."

She knew she should let it go at that. But she couldn't. It wasn't vanity that prodded her, just a desire to make sure that everything was clear and aboveboard.

"Then you really did read it?" Her eyes held his. She liked to think that she could tell if a person was lying.

"Every last word," Paul assured her. And then he added, "You have a very fortuitous way with words, Ramona." There was genuine admiration in his voice. "I know learned colleagues who sweat bullets just to get out a paragraph. You whipped that whole thing out in what, twenty minutes?"

"Ten," Ramona corrected. "I spent the other ten praying."

Whatever he might have expected her to say, that didn't even come close. Maybe he'd misheard her. "Praying?"

Ramona nodded. He watched her hoop earrings swing in time to the rhythm she'd created. "That you'd come back and tell me that you've all agreed to let me stay on." She put on the most earnest face she could. "I really want this job."

It seemed odd to him that anyone would get so caught up or passionate about a public-relations position. "Why?"

Mentally, Ramona crossed her fingers. She really did hate lying, even though it did come with the territory. Right now, she needed to be convincing. Ultimately, in order to do what she had to, she wanted Paul Armstrong to think of her as an ally. The sooner she gained the man's trust, the easier it would be to gain access to other records.

"Because as far as I'm concerned, the work that's being done here at the institute is of paramount importance."

Even though he was still in a hurry, her words made him pause. Crossing his arms before him, he took a moment to study his newest staff member. "So this is a crusade for you?"

Ramona's already dazzling smile grew brighter. "In a manner of speaking, yes."

He wanted to believe her. Things would be a great deal simpler if he just could and let it go at that. Maybe the betrayal of their former employee had put him on his guard, making him more suspicious than he ordinarily was. Or maybe he was just being supersensitive, but for the third time today, he felt he was in the presence of someone who wasn't being completely up-front with him. Someone who, for whatever reason, was holding something back.

Although, he had to admit that when it came to Ramona Tate, he hadn't a clue what that "something" might be. He didn't know the woman well enough for that. It was just a hunch. A feeling.

He was being far too paranoid, he upbraided himself. There was no real reason not to believe that the young woman was being honest with him. After all, he was the one who'd posed the question, who'd prodded her. It was possible that Ramona was every bit as altruistic as she presented herself to be.

Possible, he reasoned, but was it actually probable? He really wasn't all that sure that the answer to that was yes. However, only time would tell.

Chapter Five

He should be on his way, Paul thought and yet, here he was, still lingering. Still sharing space with this woman with the expressive eyes.

"Derek asked me to take you on a tour of the institute and to give you a miniorientation," he told her.

Her natural curiosity kicked in. "Why doesn't he give me the tour himself?"

Paul took the question to mean that she would have preferred his brother's company to his. He understood that. People always gravitated to Derek. He was the outgoing one, the one with the ability to make people laugh. The one who could defuse any situation and had a story to fit every occasion.

Ordinarily, it didn't bother him to have someone prefer Derek over him. He was used to it. Why it bothered him this time was something he wasn't about to let himself explore.

"He had to leave," Paul told her.

She nodded, accepting the excuse at face value. "So, when do you want to get started? Now's fine with me," she volunteered.

She certainly did seem eager. "Unfortunately, I don't have time today. I have several patients scheduled for this afternoon."

Her eyes widened ever so slightly and he found himself being drawn in. "So you practice medicine as well as oversee the staff here."

"Yes, why does that surprise you?" he wanted to know.

She laughed, adding a touch of self-consciousness to the sound, as if she hadn't expected to be caught. She knew how to play her role well. "I didn't take you for a multitasker."

He knew he should have already been on his way to his other office. His sense of responsibility had him making a point of being early rather than just on time, but her reply caused more questions to pop up. He didn't think of himself as the kind of person that people formed any sort of impression about—unless they felt they had to or when being in contact with him directly affected their lives.

"All right, I'll bite. What *did* you take me for?" he asked.

There was no hesitation. Ramona had the answer all worked out. "Someone who is very focused. Who follows the rules. Someone who does one thing at a time and who does that one thing very, very well."

He realized he was watching her lips as she spoke and he looked away. "Sorry to disappoint you."

"You didn't," she assured him quickly. "Actually, I don't mind being wrong when it turns out to be a pleasant surprise." She said it with such feeling, he half expected her next words to be "gotcha."

But they weren't.

Realizing that she was waiting for him to say something further, he finally asked, "How's tomorrow for you?"

Ramona smiled before answering. As hackneyed as it might have sounded to someone had he voiced his sentiments out loud, her smile really *did* seem to fill the room with sunshine. Maybe he needed to get out more, Paul thought.

"Tomorrow's fine. What time?"

"Early," he told her. "I have a procedure scheduled for ten o'clock, so why don't we get together about eight—unless that's too early for you."

"No, it can even be earlier if you'd prefer. I'm a morning person," she volunteered cheerfully.

"Eight will be early enough," he assured her, all but riveted by her smile.

It took effort to look away and even more effort to

get himself to walk out of the office and put distance between them.

The problem was Ramona had started to walk out at the same moment that he did. They found themselves together in the doorway; their bodies wound up brushing up against one another. A host of shock waves seemed to travel right through Paul, and he pulled back instantly as if propelled by a live wire.

"I'm so sorry," he apologized quickly, hoping that she didn't think he'd done that on purpose. Had he been Derek, he realized, he probably would have—and then smoothed it over with his golden tongue.

Something else they didn't have in common.

Incredibly, her smile seemed to widen even more and there was a hint of laughter in her eyes as she absolved him of all blame.

"That's all right," she assured him as if she realized it had been an accident on his part. "And for the record, I don't bite."

Even though he opened his mouth to respond, Paul had no comeback for that. His mind had gone completely blank in the face of her smile. He was really going to have to work on that, he chided himself

Mumbling "Tomorrow," Paul hurried down the hall to his other office, grateful that he could retreat somewhere.

Ramona stood in his doorway for a moment longer, watching the quietest member of the Armstrong tribunal disappear down the corridor. She wasn't really sure what to make of Dr. Paul Armstrong. If she didn't know any better, she would have said that the man seemed almost sweet. But that wasn't possible, not given the overall circumstances.

One thing she did know was that Dr. Paul Armstrong was going to be the subject of some heavy Internet research tonight.

Time was that after she'd put in a full day's work, she'd head for her cozy little apartment, eager to enjoy a little well-deserved solitude. Dinner most likely would be something she'd have delivered. She'd wind up consuming it while sitting on her chocolate-colored sofa—purchased expressly to hide a multitude of sins, otherwise known as indelible stains—and channel surfing. It was her way of unwinding.

But these days, her own gratification, not to mention rest, was usually postponed, if not put on hold altogether. Instead, she would wind up swinging by the house where she had grown up. The house where her mother still lived.

The key phrase here, Ramona thought, changing lanes to pass a slow-moving SUV, being "still lived."

Ramona became aware that her grip on the steering wheel had tightened and she forced herself to loosen it—while still keeping a grip on her fragile emotions.

Once upon a time, not all that long ago, she'd been so eager to make her own way, find her own path in the world. But even as she did, she was very aware of the solid foundation she had in her life. Aware that if ever anything went wrong, or she needed a haven, she had her mother, someone who would always be there for her. *Always.* And if everything was falling apart around her, her mother could always make her feel that it was going to be all right.

Until now.

The threat of mortality, of death always hovering in the background, an invisible wraith that had the power to steal absolutely *everything* from her, was now ever present.

Ramona knew it was childish, but even so, on some level she felt that she could stave off the threat of her mother's demise for another day if she just swung by the house and saw her for a little while in the evening. Some nights, "a little while" stretched out into the wee hours of the morning. At other times, she didn't bother going home at all, crashing in her old room instead.

Turning onto her mother's street, Ramona was aware that she was once again holding her breath, the way she did now every time she came. She only released it after a swift scan of the surrounding area told her that there was no ambulance parked nearby, no paramedics rushing in or out of the New England–style house that, according to family legend, her mother had fallen in love with thirty-five years ago.

All clear, Ramona thought, pulling up onto the recently repaved driveway.

Taking a moment to collect her things—her purse and the state-of-the-art laptop that went just about everywhere with her—Ramona got out and locked her vehicle, then made her way to the front door.

She paused, juggling purse and briefcase, searching for the keys that habit always had her dropping into her purse the moment she took them out of the ignition. She knew she should just hold the keys in her hand, but that never seemed to happen. She always wound up playing a frustrating game of hide-and-seek in front of the door before locating her keys.

This time, Ramona didn't have to. The front door opened before she could pull her keys out of her purse again.

Katherine Tate, or what was left of her these days, stood in the doorway, one hand on the doorjamb to support herself. There was a slight smile on her lips as she looked at her daughter fondly.

"I thought I heard your car pull up." A tiny "yip" had her mother amending her words. "Actually, Roxy was the one who heard you pull up," she confessed, referring to the tiny, energized mix-breed puppy that was all but tap-dancing behind her, trying to get at Ramona. "How she can tell your car apart from all the others that pass by, I have absolutely no idea. But she's never wrong." Placing her very thin hand on her daughter's shoulder to anchor herself, the five-foot-two woman stood up on her toes in order to press a kiss on Ramona's cheek. "How's my famous undercover daughter doing?"

Shifting her briefcase to the same side as her purse,

Ramona linked her free arm through her mother's as if they were just two carefree girlfriends, walking and chatting, instead of a daughter who was attempting to unobtrusively guide her mother back inside the house.

"That's a contradiction in terms, Mom. If I was famous, I couldn't get away with being undercover. I'd be recognized immediately." With a wink she pointed out, "I'd rather be good than famous."

"To me you're both," Katherine declared with great feeling.

Ramona beamed at her mother, biting back a wave of fear. Life couldn't go on if anything happened to her mother, she thought.

Hear that, God? You can't have her. I need her too much.

"I can always count on you to pick up my spirits," Ramona said to her mother. Roxy eagerly scurried back and forth. It was the dog's way of showing she was happy to see her.

"Why?" Katherine asked, slipping her arm out and shutting the door behind them as they walked in. She flipped the lock into place then slowly turned around to face her again. "Do your spirits need picking up?"

They did, but only because seeing her mother like this, a shell of her former vibrant, youthful self, was always a shock to her system for the first few minutes. She didn't know why she expected her to look exactly the way she had a little over six months ago. Probably because she still liked to believe in miracles and secretly prayed that one would occur in the hours that she was away from the house and her mother.

But the miracle just didn't happen.

It will. As soon as I find who your eggs went to, Mom, it will, she silently promised.

"Just a tough day," she said, knowing Katherine expected some kind of response. Ramona attributed her own success as an investigative reporter as something that came naturally to her thanks to her mother, who would approach a subject from an endless multitude of angles until she got what she was after. Surrendering or giving up were never considered options.

Ramona was aware that her mother's breathing was becoming labored. It took very few steps to tire her out these days. Katherine sank down on the sofa in the living room. Roxy instantly hopped onto the seat beside her mistress. Smiling wearily at the dog, she stroked it as she looked at her and asked, "Where is it again that you're pretending to work?"

"I'm not pretending, Mom," Ramona corrected fondly. She thought of the article she'd written for the press release. It was damn good. Even Derek Armstrong's stone-faced evil twin had liked it. "I really *am* working."

"But you're also digging, aren't you?" The question was merely for form's sake. Katherine knew the kind of work her daughter actually did. She was exceedingly proud of the path that Ramona had chosen.

"Yes, I am," Ramona answered.

Except that no real "digging" had taken place yet. She needed to get to know people a little better before she could safely start asking questions without arousing suspicion. She had, she felt, a perfect cover in her role as public-relations manager, and the tour that Paul Armstrong had promised her was going to be an immense help in getting her started.

"So what is this place where you're working undercover?" And then, before her daughter could answer, Katherine's eyes narrowed. "It's not one of these so-called escort places, is it? Because I saw an exposé on one of those magazine programs the other night and I really don't want you associating with people like that."

Ramona suppressed a smile. Her mother still felt she could shelter her from the world's darker elements. In a way, she almost found it sweet. There was no way she could have ever reached her present position not having dealt, at least fleetingly, with the seamier side of life. But she'd never want her mother to worry and was rather relieved that she could set her mind at ease without having to lie.

"No, it's not a 'so-called escort place,'" Ramona assured her. "And honestly, Mom, the less you know about it right now, the better."

It wasn't exactly the truth. She just didn't want to raise her mother's hopes by telling her that she was trying to track down a possible sibling. If she told her that she was working at the Armstrong Fertility Institute, her mother would make the obvious connection: that she was there to get access to the archives and to locate the couple who had profited by her desperate donation. If there were no siblings to be found, her own disappointment would be difficult enough to deal with. Maintaining a positive attitude was exceedingly important right now.

Katherine drew her own conclusions from what her daughter *wasn't* saying. Her concern was palatable. "Then it *is* dangerous."

"No, it's not dangerous, Mom," Ramona was quick to tell her with feeling. "It's that if you don't know, you won't accidentally let something slip when you're talking to one of the checkers at the supermarket or the beauty salon. Or one of your friends. Undercover means just that—undercover. Secret," she added, though she knew it was overkill.

Katherine looked just the slightest bit hurt. "When have I ever betrayed a confidence?"

"I wasn't thinking of betrayal, Mom. I was thinking of being human and last time I checked—" Ramona patted the hand that wasn't stroking Roxy "—you were most definitely human."

Her mother sighed quietly. "At least for a little while longer. Then I'll be a guardian angel, watching over you."

Ramona completely dismissed the serious part of Katherine's statement, refusing to give it any credence by even insisting that her mom had more than a little time left. She defused the moment the way she always did, with humor. “I don’t think God lets you pick out your own assignments.”

“Why not?” Katherine wanted to know. “It’s heaven, isn’t it?”

Ramona didn’t bother suppressing her grin. “And your idea of heaven is watching over me?”

“Yes,” Katherine answered with feeling. It drained her meager supply of energy for a moment.

Ramona laughed and shook her head. “Oh, Mom, we’ve got to get you out more.”

“That would be lovely,” Katherine agreed wistfully. “The minute I’m better—if I get better,” she qualified, “you and I will do the town.”

“The minute you’re better—and you *will* be,” Ramona emphasized fiercely, “I’m going to get you a guy and the *two of you* are going to do the town. You can do the town with me anytime.”

Katherine rolled her eyes. Roxy, having lain down and been stroked into sleep, was snoring gently. “Oh, Ramona, why would I need a guy?”

Ramona grinned as she leaned over and patted her mother’s hand again. “It’ll come back to you, Mom. If not, I have a book I can lend you.”

Katherine laughed and Ramona paused to listen to the soft, melodic sound, thinking how very much she loved hearing her mother laugh.

She intended to move heaven and earth if she had to, in order to continue hearing that sound for the next half century or so.

* * *

It was late.

Very late.

Paul had already put in a full day and then some as far as he was concerned. He was actually on his way out of the institute when his pager had gone off.

A quick call to his answering service told him that the McGees were frantically on their way in. Allison McGee was spotting and they were terrified that she was going to lose the babies she was carrying. The woman at the answering service said that Marc McGee sounded as if he was the on verge of having a heart attack and was barely coherent. He was driving and shouting into his cell phone at the same time.

Paul knew that he could have easily turned their case over to one of the more than competent doctors on the staff, but he knew that seeing him would calm Allison down a little.

And besides, he felt a personal obligation to the couple, just as he felt a personal obligation to every couple he counseled and worked with.

So he called Marc and told the frantic father-to-be that he would meet them at the nearby hospital where he had surgical privileges. The McGees arrived in the parking lot, tires screeching, less than five minutes later. Knowing what part of town they were coming from, he judged that they'd have to have done eighty all the way. Paul and an attendant greeted them with a wheelchair and Paul personally helped Allison out of the vehicle and into the chair.

What he'd hoped was just an aberration had turned into a premature delivery. A rather difficult one at that, requiring the services of two other obstetricians besides himself. But at the end of the ordeal, Allison and Marc had two viable sons, both now sleeping peacefully in their incubators. They were alive and that was the only thing that mattered.

And he was beat beyond measure. If he tried to drive home now, he had a feeling that he would undoubtedly be the subject of headlines tomorrow: Head of Staff of Armstrong Fertility Institute Caught Driving Erratically and Arrested. Drug or Alcohol Abuse Suspected. Possibly Both.

Or at least something along those lines. The press loved building you up and then tearing you down and the institute, for the moment, was in the tear-down stage. Since he had absolutely no desire to fall asleep behind the wheel, he decided that he would be better off sacking out on the couch in his office for at least an hour until he got his energy back.

With a weary sigh, he lay down on the leather sofa. He was asleep within five seconds.

Chapter Six

Paul felt the beads of sweat forming along his forehead. His hair stuck to his forehead. His limbs felt too heavy to lift. He had no more control over any part of his body.

He was having that dream again.

The one where he was trying to find his way to his office and the more he walked toward it, the farther away the office became.

Frustration and anxiety filled him. His breathing grew more shallow. His lungs began to ache. He kept walking, going faster now.

The corridor shifted. Instead of going straight, it became a series of twists and turns that led him down unfamiliar hallways. And all the while his sense of urgency continued building. Building until it grew to almost unbearable proportions.

Just as he thought he finally saw his office at the end of the long, tunnel-like hallway, the ground beneath his feet disappeared and he found himself plummeting into a ravine.

The churning waters below threatened to drown him and then carelessly wash his body away, casting it wantonly where no one would ever find him.

Then suddenly, unlike all the other times he'd had this unnerving dream, there was someone touching his arm.

Someone grabbing it and shaking him.

Someone was saving him, keeping him from being swept out to sea. He was saved!

More frustration assaulted him because he couldn't make out the face of the person who had rescued him at the very last, possible moment.

And then he heard the voice—a woman who had hold of his arm, calling his name even as she shook him.

Somehow, he finally managed to open his eyes.

And then he saw her bending over him, her blond hair falling into her face, her hand on his arm. Holding him and keeping him from falling.

Startled, he bolted upright.

The ravine, the churning waters, they were gone. He was back in his office again. The same office where he'd lain down a few minutes ago to catch a short nap before driving himself home.

No, wait, it wasn't a few minutes ago. It was last night.

Except that, unlike last night, he wasn't alone. Ramona Tate was looking down at him, concern evident in her sky-blue eyes.

"Are you all right?" she asked, and he realized that this wasn't the first time he'd heard the question. She'd voiced it before, only then it had been part of his dream—or maybe he should start calling it his nightmare. *Nightmare* seemed like a far more fitting label for it.

Sitting up, he swung his legs off the sofa, trying to gather his dignity to him.

"What are you doing here?" he asked gruffly, dragging his hand through his hair.

"It's eight o'clock," she told him politely. When he continued staring at her, she added, "You told me to come in early for a tour. Introduce me to some of the other people, things like that. I knocked on your door first," she added. "You didn't answer, but I heard you moaning."

Scrubbing his hand over his face, Paul tried to focus. "I was having a nightmare."

Ramona nodded. "That's what it sounded like," she agreed. Her eyes washed over him, taking in every last detail, or so it felt to him. What was she thinking? he couldn't help wondering. "You never went home last night, did you?"

"One of my patients called in, or rather, her husband did. She was spotting and really afraid. I met them at the hospital. I seem to have a calming effect on her and her husband," he added with a shrug. A pain zigzagged up and down his spine. He'd forgotten how uncomfortable his sofa really was.

"And?" Ramona prodded.

The woman actually looked interested, Paul mused. "She delivered just before midnight."

Her eyes held his. "Everything went all right?" she wanted to know.

He laughed shortly. "Other than the fact that the babies arrived six weeks prematurely and that Marc McGee fainted at the first sign of blood, everything went just fine."

"Babies?" she echoed. One of the allegations making the rounds against the Armstrong Fertility Institute was that there were entirely too many embryos being implanted at one time, resulting in multiple births. "How many babies?"

Was that interest, or suspicion, he heard in her voice? He wasn't sure. "She had twins. Two boys. I think she was hoping for one of each, but the last few hours, she was just hoping they'd be alive and well—and out of her."

Her mouth curved warmly. "So you delivered them and then came in here to catnap?"

Paul shrugged dismissively. "Something like that."

He still looked tired, Ramona thought. She wasn't going to ingratiate herself to him if he felt that he had to drag her around when he was half-asleep.

"Look, if you'd like to postpone my orientation and go home to catch up on your sleep, I understand completely. We can do this tomorrow," she told him cheerfully.

Paul rotated his shoulders, trying to get the kink out. The sofa had definitely *not* been constructed with napping in mind. Still, though she'd given him an out, he didn't want to postpone the tour. He'd already postponed it once when he shifted it from yesterday to today.

"Tomorrow," he told her, "has a habit of never coming."

Tongue in cheek, she pretended to take this as a revelation. "You know something that the newscasters don't?"

He wasn't sure if she was kidding or not. "I just meant that life has a habit of interfering with things. If we postpone this now, who knows what might come up tomorrow? For all I know, there might be a bigger fire to deal with." He stretched, feeling several muscles line up in protest as he did so. "Just give me a couple of minutes to pull myself together."

She was more than willing to be cooperative. "No problem. I can wait in my office if you like. And, better still," she volunteered, "I can get you a cup of coffee."

The offer out of left field surprised him. "I thought that women didn't do that anymore, get coffee for their boss."

Were her eyes smiling or laughing when she looked at him? He couldn't tell. "Women don't like being *told* to get coffee. Volunteering to do it is a whole different story." She leaned in closer to him for a moment. Close enough for him to get a heady whiff of her perfume.

Something remote stirred for a second, then faded. "And in case you didn't notice, I was volunteering. You take it black, don't you?"

"Is that a guess," he wanted to know, "or are you clairvoyant, too?"

"Just a guess," she assured him cheerfully. "The percentages were in my favor," she confided. "You don't strike me as the latte type, or even the cream-and-sugar type."

"I strike you as the black-coffee type," he said and she couldn't tell if she'd affronted him, or if he was just trying to figure out what that actually meant. He seemed to be the kind of person who needed to have everything in black and white. He was, she silently promised him, in for a surprise. But for the time being, she'd play things his way.

Ramona nodded. "Basic. Good, rich, no frills."

He realized that for a second, his breath had backed up into his lungs. That did it, no more sleeping on the office sofa.

"Are you describing the coffee or me?" He didn't realize until he heard the words that he had said them out loud.

She smiled in response and for a second, he didn't think she was going to answer. But then she grinned impishly and said, "Both," just before she left the office.

Paul sat there for a long moment, staring at the closed door. He needed to get his day going, he reminded himself, not try to figure out the puzzles that hid behind Ramona's sparkling eyes and long, shapely legs.

Crossing to the door, he locked it and then went to change into the spare suit he kept on hand.

A shower would have been nice, as well, but that was a luxury he couldn't afford right now. He had a full schedule today, which was why he'd suggested doing the orientation so early. These days, he thought as he swiftly changed clothes, he always felt as if he was half a league behind in his life.

Someday, he promised himself, he was going to catch up.

Ramona was just looking at her watch for a second time, wondering if Paul Armstrong had decided to postpone her orientation tour after all when she heard the light rap on her door.

Rather than bidding him to come in, she opened the door, thinking that was the friendlier path to take. She was trying everything in her power to build a bond between them. If she was going to get anywhere, she knew she needed to erase that suspicious glint that came into his eyes whenever he looked at her.

Her immediate goal was to put him at ease and get him to trust her. If she could accomplish that, everything else would fall into place, both her primary reason for being here and the one she'd given her editor, Walter Jessup, so that she'd have his blessing and backing to be here.

"Hi," she greeted Armstrong brightly as she opened the door. "I thought maybe you'd changed your mind or forgotten about me."

"Not much chance of that," he said, commenting on the last phrase.

Paul sincerely doubted that *anyone* could forget about Ramona Tate once they met her. She wasn't the kind of woman who, left unseen, would just fade into some nether field. She had the kind of face that lingered on a man's mind long after she'd walked away. *Long* after.

Closing the door again, Ramona produced a tall container of coffee, strong and hot, and held it out to him.

"Coffee, as promised," she said.

It smelled rich and delicious. He was willing to bet any amount of money that this coffee had definitely not emerged out of any of the vending machines located on the first floor. Or *any* of the other institute floors for that matter.

Tempted, he took a sip and savored the outstanding brew for a moment. "Where did you get this?"

Ramona gestured toward the machine. "I brought my own coffeemaker to work." The machine, which first ground whole beans and then brewed the results, was sitting on a file cabinet that, when the last occupant worked out of this office, had housed countless piles of books and papers. "This way, I don't have to drop everything to go find Starbucks."

That sounded incredibly dedicated.

"I'm sure that when he hired you, my brother didn't intend for you to be chained to your desk for hours at a time."

Ramona didn't respond to his statement. Instead, she seemed to be watching him intently as he paused to take another sip.

"So," she asked, her voice a tad lower and more melodic, "is it the way you like it?"

Jarred, Paul blinked and stared at her. He must have heard wrong. "Excuse me?"

"The coffee." She nodded at the container he held in his hand. "Is it the way you like it?"

"Oh." For a minute, he thought she was asking him if he—

Unconsciously shaking his head, Paul banished the thought that had popped unwittingly into his head.

"You didn't like it?" Ramona asked, trying to make sense out of the way he was reacting.

She looked disappointed. Was she that sensitive? Or was this all an act for some reason he couldn't quite fathom yet?

"No. I mean yes, I did. And no, that wasn't why I was shaking my head." It felt as if his thoughts were all scrambled and it was only partially due to his waking up so abruptly. "I'm just trying to get the last of the cobwebs out of my brain."

She smiled and indicated the container with her eyes. "If you finish the coffee, I think the cobwebs will self-destruct on their own. Oh." She said the words as if she suddenly remembered something. Before he could ask if she had, she answered his question. "I brought pastries." She flashed a grin and a little ray of sunshine entered the room. It was becoming a given. "In case you wanted something sweet to go along with your coffee."

The sweet thing that he found himself wanting to go along with his coffee hadn't come from any oven, but because he was hungry, he forced his thoughts to zero in on the practical.

Ramona was taking the box she'd brought out of the double drawer where she'd put it. Placing it on her desk, she took off the lid and pushed the box closer toward Paul. He took one small muffin and sat down in the chair facing her desk.

She took a seat, as well. "I'm guessing this sort of thing happens to you on a regular basis. Spending the night here," she added when Armstrong looked at her quizzically.

She was right, but he had no idea where she'd gotten her conclusion from. He doubted that very many people here took note of the fact that sometimes his hours threaded themselves well into the night if the situation called for it.

"What makes you say that?" he wanted to know.

"Your clothes. You changed," she pointed out when he looked down at what he was wearing. "You keep a change of clothing in your office or locker or whatever. That means you've slept in your office."

He saw no harm in admitting to her that she'd deduced correctly. "It's happened a few times," he acknowledged.

Armstrong seemed almost modest. She prided herself on being able to spot a phony. Could he actually be the genuine article?

"You must be very dedicated," she observed with what she felt was just the right touch of awe.

He didn't know if he'd call it dedicated. He did feel a sense of responsibility toward the people who came to his father's institute.

"The people who come here looking for help are desperate," he told her without any fanfare. "We're their last hope. You tend to feel responsible for them as well as to them. If I'm only available to them on a strict schedule or when it's convenient for me, then I have no business working in medicine. Punching a time clock is for people who work on an assembly line. I'm in a different line of work," he concluded quietly.

She studied him for a moment. "You do extraordinary things here, Paul. You help people conceive babies. Some would say that's God's line of work." She smiled warmly, keeping her tone nonjudgmental. "I guess what I'm wondering is if you sometimes feel, well, godlike." Her eyes raised to his and pressed innocently. "Well, do you?"

The whole idea was completely absurd.

"Never once," he informed her firmly. Finishing the pastry, he wiped his fingers on the napkin she'd supplied and finished the last of his coffee, dusted off a crumb from his jacket and then looked at her. "Are you ready to take that tour of the institute now?"

She was on her feet immediately, closing the lid on the pastry box and abandoning her own coffee. She raised her face to his and told him, "I was born ready."

Paul had no idea why he felt she wasn't really referring to the tour, but was, instead, putting him on some kind of notice.

But he did.

A warmth, joining forces with anticipation, washed over him. He banked it down, but his pulse continued marking time at a heightened beat that only seemed to increase the closer he walked beside Ramona.

Chapter Seven

The tour through the institute lasted close to an hour. Because he was pressed for time, Paul moved quickly throughout the modern three-story building. Ramona kept pace with him and peppered him with questions every step of the way. Endless, probing questions.

If he didn't know any better, Paul would have said that it felt as if he was under interrogation. He'd never encountered anyone who was so incredibly and relentlessly curious about the place in which she found herself employed.

He took her to see the various meeting rooms and then on to the boardroom. When they arrived, Ramona walked in before he could move on.

"My God, this is huge," she breathed, looking around in awe. It felt as if her voice was echoing in the cavernous room.

It made him think of Alice when she first took stock of Wonderland. Ramona even had the long blond hair.

Where had that thought even come from? He shouldn't be evaluating her looks—just her skills.

Ramona took it all in, moving around slowly. The room was wood paneled and had floor-to-ceiling windows. It was a sunny day and there were prisms of light bouncing off the walls and the very large, elegant oak conference table.

Paul watched, mesmerized despite himself, as Ramona spun around full circle beside the windows before turning to look at him.

"I think my apartment is smaller than this. Why do you need such a large conference room?" Before he could answer her, she made her own guess. "Is it to dwarf the egos that might be here?"

Being caught off guard by this woman was beginning to be an unfortunate habit. "What?"

"A room this large makes a person feel small," she explained. "That might be handy in getting people to do what you want them to."

"I have nothing to do with the size of this room," he told her. "That was my father's design."

His father had been the one to choose this location to begin with and he'd been involved in every phase of its construction. Despite the fact that he had not been part of it for a while now, the institute bore Gerald's indelible stamp and would always be his building, even long after the man was gone.

"I see," Ramona said thoughtfully as they both exited the room.

He didn't like the way she said that. "What is it that you see?"

Keep it low-key, Ramona. You don't want to push the man away or put him on his guard. "Just that your father must be a very forceful man."

"At the moment, he's a retired man." Paul thought about his father, about how withdrawn and, on occasion, bitter the man had become. The senior Armstrong hardly ever left the house now.

She knew that Gerald Armstrong was retired, but she was curious if he still kept a finger on the pulse of "his" clinic. For some men, *retirement* was just a meaningless word. "Does he ever come in and see how things are going?"

Initially, his mother had tried to get his father involved in the institute again. It seemed rather an ironic turn, seeing as how Gerald's obsession with the institute had taken such a heavy toll on their marriage in the beginning.

Paul thought Ramona would abort her line of questioning when he told her, "My father's in a wheelchair." He realized that he should have known better. The woman just kept going and going.

"That doesn't stop some people," Ramona said tactfully.

"It does others," he countered. They were making their way back to the elevators. He couldn't keep his curiosity in check any longer. "Why are you asking so many questions?"

She looked at him with an innocent expression that seemed to say that the answer was self-evident. "How else am I going to find things out? By the way," she continued, stepping into the elevator car, "where are the archives housed?"

He stared at her for a moment, then pressed for the next floor down. "In the basement. Why?"

The answer was tendered in utter innocence. The doors closed. "I thought I'd take a look at them when I got the chance."

In less than a minute, the elevator doors were opening again on the floor below. "Again, why?"

"To get a sense of the institute's history," she told him as they got off.

He had no desire to have her rummaging through the files that were stored down there. For the most part, they were charts and records that belonged to some of the institute's first patients. "If you have any questions, you can come to me."

He was walking faster, she noted, and lengthened her own stride. Was he just trying to get this over with, or was he subconsciously running from something?

"You just wanted to know why I'm asking so many

questions," she reminded him. "I don't want to bother you any more than I have to."

It might have seemed like a good idea to Derek at the time, but he was back to being sorry that his brother had talked him into letting Ramona stay. That was going to have to change and soon. He didn't particularly want Ramona Tate digging around, disrupting the rhythm of things.

"As far as I'm concerned," he told her as they went down the corridor, "this position is a one-shot deal. And you've fired the shot, or you will sometime today I imagine."

It was her turn to be confused, Ramona thought. "Come again?"

"The press release about Bonner and Demetrios joining our staff," he reminded her. "You wrote it. You'll deliver it if you haven't already. That's why my brother initially hired you."

"Initially." She picked up on the word he used and emphasized it. "But that was just the beginning, Dr. Armstrong."

Paul stopped walking and looked down at her, a man whose overnight guest had just announced she was settling in for the next six months. "Oh?"

Ramona continued walking as if she was oblivious to the fact that he had stopped. "The way I see it, the institute is in a precarious state, like a forest in the middle of a really hot summer. There are bound to be fires. It's my job to put those fires out."

He resumed walking. "And what if there are no fires?" he challenged.

"Then I'll have a very stress-free job." She slanted a look at him, more than a hint of a smile on her lips. "But do you really think that will be the case?"

He didn't want to dwell on "fires" or public relations or baseless rumors that were running amok. He just wanted to do his job. "All I want to do is help couples have the families they've always wanted."

She wanted to believe him, to believe that even in this modern, fast-paced world there were still people who wanted to do decent things out of the goodness of their heart. But until she disproved those rumors that she'd come to investigate, she couldn't allow herself to be taken in by the innocent look in his eyes.

"I understand, Dr. Armstrong, but things are never as simple as we'd like them to be. It's my job to make sure that you can do yours without being hampered by innuendo or, more important, lawsuits," she told him, deliberately presenting him with a cheerful demeanor. "Public opinion can either be a wonderful tool, or a weapon."

He stopped right in front of the lab. "How old are you?"

"Old enough to be good at what I do." It sounded like an evasive answer, but she didn't want to give him a direct answer. She knew that Armstrong was thirty-six and to him, she undoubtedly looked as if she was just out of elementary school.

"I was only thinking that you seemed awfully young to sound so cynical."

She didn't think of herself as cynical, but she let it go. Instead, she said, "These days, cynicism is built into the DNA."

With a sigh, Paul shook his head and then pushed open the door to their state-of-the-art lab. He was proud of the equipment, proud of all the advances they'd made in the field because they were able to afford the kind of cutting-edge research to be done here.

Holding the door, he allowed her to walk in ahead of him.

Like the conference room, the lab was one large room. Unlike the conference room, it had two tables instead of one. The tables were waist high, equipped with sinks and a number of microscopes that were hooked up to projection screens and computers. There were several people in the lab at the moment, all dressed in white coats.

She'd heard as well as read a great deal about the newly transplanted research team of Bonner and Demetrios before she ever came to the institute. Consequently, she knew them on sight.

Only Ted Bonner was present at the moment. Chance Demetrios had an office in the building. Her guess was that he was probably there now.

Bonner did strictly research. He had the luxury of divorcing himself from the people who ultimately made use of the end product of his research via one of the doctors on the staff. This allowed him to throw himself wholeheartedly into his work. His failures had no faces on them, but then, neither did his successes.

She heard Paul take in a breath, as if he was bracing himself for some kind of ordeal. The next moment, she realized that *she* was the ordeal.

"Dr. Bonner," he addressed the exceedingly tall, exceedingly good-looking dark-haired man who was about to bend over to look into one of the microscopes, "I would like to introduce you to Ramona Tate. She's our new public-relations manager."

Shaking her hand, Ted quipped, "I didn't know you had an old public-relations manager."

"We didn't," Paul answered before he realized that Ted was joking. "This is my brother's idea. He thinks we need protecting." He flashed a semiapologetic smile toward Ramona.

Thinking to spare him, she made no comment. She was getting a great many mixed signals from this man and decided it was better to pretend to be oblivious to all of them.

She turned her attention to the man who was still holding her hand enveloped in his. "Nice to meet you, Dr. Bonner. Would you mind if I got back to you later sometime? I'd like to ask you a few questions if I may."

"I'll be looking forward to it," Ted assured her. "Anything I can answer now?"

She slanted a glance toward Paul. "No," she assured Ted. "Not now."

"Then I'll get back to work," he said, releasing her hand.

"What do you want to talk to him about?" Paul asked her the moment they walked out of the lab. He didn't bother to try to hide the suspicious look on his face. What was she up to? he wondered. Were all these questions normal? Was he so out of touch with the way things worked outside his small sphere?

She was ready for him. "Well, for one thing, I want to know what enticed Dr. Bonner and his partner to come here to do their research."

They walked down the corridor, each with a different destination in mind. He to his other office and she back to hers. But for now, they walked together.

"The lab they came from wasn't exactly third rate or shabby by any means," Ramona continued. "And there's a certain amount of inherent prestige being associated with a teaching hospital–slash–college the caliber of the one they came from." She stopped walking. He stopped a second after that and looked at her, waiting. "Did you offer them more money?"

He made no answer, trying to gauge what, if anything, he should say. Maybe, if he just waited long enough, she'd go away. Silence ricocheted between them.

Ramona pressed her lips together. "Dr. Armstrong, you need to talk to me if I'm to do my job and do you any good."

"It was a little more money," Paul finally admitted to her.

The inflection in his voice told her there was more. "And?"

Paul drew himself up. It was a purely defensive move. Knights running to man the castle parapets. "And I gave them carte blanche." He shrugged carelessly. "I thought that having them here would negate any bad publicity that might have cropped up."

"Aggressively heading that publicity off at the pass accomplishes that," Ramona pointed out. "For starters, I need to get that press release—released," she concluded, humor curving her generous mouth.

He glanced at his watch, blinking once to focus in on it better. "I have a procedure to get to," he reminded her—and himself.

"Then I should get out of your way," Ramona responded amiably. "Thanks for the tour," she added.

As far as it went, Ramona added silently. She noticed that the good doctor had conspicuously left out the basement with its archives. But she wasn't put off. She was confident that she'd find a way to get into that one way or another. Ramona had a very strong feeling that was where she'd find what she was really looking for.

At least, she sincerely hoped so.

Nodding at Armstrong, she turned on her heel and quickly headed back to her office. She had work to do: theirs, her editor's and, the first moment she could find an island of time when no one was around to catch her, her own.

Paul stood like a pillar, watching her leave. With

effort, he roused himself. He had no time to stand here like some pubescent adolescent, watching her hurry away, he silently chastised. He had a reputation to uphold. That reputation included never being late, especially not for a procedure.

How the hell had things gotten so damn out of control?

The question echoed over and over again in Derek's brain, haunting him.

Taunting him.

It had all started out so innocently. So harmlessly. A simple weekend trip to Atlantic City. He was going to be staying at one of the more luxurious casinos and, if time permitted, he figured that he'd indulge in a little gambling.

How was he to know that things would mushroom into *this*—an obsession that would threaten to completely ruin his life?

He'd never seen it coming.

In his defense, he'd never even *felt* the inclination to gamble before. But that had been *before* the first incredible rush had found him.

There was no other way to describe the feeling that exploded in his veins when turn after turn of the card rendered him the big winner at the table. It was an exhilarating, overwhelming rush. The closest he had ever come to a religious experience.

By the end of that first evening, he was staring at more money than he ever had before. And it was *his* money. Not his father's, not his family's or the institute's, but *his*. Exclusively.

He wasn't just one of Gerald Armstrong's sons, or the CFO of the Armstrong Fertility Institute, an empty title awarded him because of who his father was. At that specific moment in time, he was Derek Armstrong. *Winner*.

And then, when he returned to the table the next night, as mysteriously as it had found him, his winning streak abandoned him. Hand after hand, he lost. Desperate to recapture that magical feeling, to see that life-affirming envy in the other players' eyes, he kept betting.

And he kept losing.

At the end of the weekend, he'd not only lost all the money he'd won, but he lost twice as much as he'd brought to Atlantic City.

He began signing notes, barking that he was good for it. His luck remained bad. He only won enough to remind him that it was possible. Just not probable.

Eventually, the house stopped accepting his markers. That was when someone else did. And his life took a turn for the worse.

Addled by his desire to recoup his losses and to prove that his groundless certainty that he could win it all back if he just kept at it long enough was right, he went on to accept the loan for a large sum of money. The loan had come from a well-dressed, older man with the flattest eyes he'd ever seen.

And now, now he was in so far over his head that

he despaired he would ever break through the surface again. Lying on top of the rumpled bed in the shabby Atlantic City hotel room, he dragged both hands over his face in abject despair.

What was he going to do?

The demands for payments were relentless. And the threats, the threats frightened him most of all. Not just against his life, but against his parents and the institute, as well.

The threats hadn't been in so many words, but when he was late with his third payment, a payment that had become swollen out of proportion because the interest that had been slapped on it grew at a prodigious rate, his "benefactor"—as the man had referred to himself at first—quietly slipped him a news clipping. The clipping was from a West Coast newspaper from approximately six months ago. The photograph that was at the top of the article showed a once-famous hotel going up in flames.

"The owner of that piece of property didn't think he had to pay on time, either," was all the man said to him in that raspy voice that came across like a poor imitation of Marlon Brando in *The Godfather*.

Derek never asked who the benefactor was referring to. He didn't want to know. The lesson was crystal clear. If he didn't continue to pay off his loan on time, the institute would be burned to the ground.

He sold everything he owned and still, it wasn't enough. Having nothing left, immersed in maintaining a facade, Derek was left with only one source of money to tap. He handled the institute's finances. So he set aside his conscience and did what he had to do.

It was either that or watch the institute burn.

He refused to think of the consequences of his actions, but he knew they were coming.

And soon.

In the meantime, he would continue to burn the candle at both ends, trying to stay alive one more day. Hoping that, at the end of the day, there would be some kind of miracle that could save him. It was the only way he could go on. Searching for a miracle. And praying that his luck had changed.

Chapter Eight

Paul had to admit that the press release looked even better in newsprint than it had on the antiseptic white pages that Ramona had handed him to read several days ago.

He put down the first section of the *Cambridge Chronicle*. The periodical had been sitting on his desk when he'd walked in this morning, opened to the page with the pertinent article on it.

Aside from the Donner-Demetrios announcement, there was mention of the clinic's high success ratio, and the article brought attention to the fact that, not all that long ago, the institute was the first of its kind to offer hope to childless, infertile couples longing for a baby of their own.

The article ended by emphasizing that the institute was still on the cutting edge of the field, still leading the way. Hiring Bonner and Demetrios to conduct their research at the institute just ensured that they would continue on that path.

"So, has she earned her keep?"

Derek walked into his office grinning and looking extremely satisfied with himself. Paul wasn't aware that his brother had even bothered to knock.

"Did you leave this on my desk?" he wanted to know, indicating the newspaper.

That possibility hadn't occurred to him until Derek had asked the question. He'd just assumed that Ramona had left the paper to prove to him that she was doing her job.

"Had to," Derek responded. Rather than take a seat, he perched on the corner of the cluttered desk. It created the aura of looking down on his brother. Paul had a feeling Derek did it on purpose. "You walk around here the way you do through life, with blinders on. Not seeing anything until it's pointed out to you." Derek's grin grew wider. "I bet you didn't even notice that our new PR manager is one hell of a babe, did you?"

That's where you're wrong, Derek.

Whether or not his brother meant his question in a belittling way, he couldn't help resenting the way Derek said it.

"I noticed that she was a very attractive woman," Paul answered, "but I wouldn't have insulted her by describing her in those terms."

Derek shook his head. "Don't know how we can possibly share the same DNA and be so damn different."

"One of the mysteries of science, I guess," Paul replied coolly. Derek continued smirking at him. "And if you're here to gloat—"

"I am," Derek confirmed breezily.

Paul refused to rise to the bait. "One success doesn't make your case for you."

Derek stared at him, clearly surprised by this opposition. "Don't tell me you still want to get rid of her."

"What I'm telling you is that I'm still reserving judgment." Other places had a three-month period during which a newly hired employee could be let go if he or she didn't live up to expectations or performed poorly. Why not here at the institute, as well? "I see this place as being a tightly knit family. I'm not convinced that she belongs yet."

Derek laughed shortly, clearly not in agreement with his twin. "That's exactly your problem, Paul. The institute isn't a family, it's a business and as such, it needs to have people savvy about their particular sphere of business running it." Rising, he patted Paul on the shoulder. Paul pulled back from his brother's patronizing gesture. "But that's not your concern. You just go on doing you job and I'll make sure that you can *keep* on doing it."

Paul wasn't as dense as he assumed his brother thought him to be. He saw through the rhetoric. "I'm not handing over my right to challenge your decisions, if that's what you're after."

Derek pretended to snap his fingers like an old-fashioned villain and declared in a pseudoexasperated voice, "Curses, foiled again."

Paul relaxed just a little. "You're in a particularly chipper mood today."

Derek's grin broadened even more. "Why shouldn't I be? The sun is smiling down on our institute and all is right with the world." And then he added the crowning piece. "And I feel lucky."

Paul didn't understand what his brother might be referring to. "Lucky?"

"Lucky to be part of all this," Derek said, neatly smoothing out the unfortunate slip he'd just accidentally made.

Last night he'd left the table slightly better off than when he'd first walked into the casino. It was the beginning of a streak, he could feel it. He'd flown back to Cambridge early this morning, but he intended on going back again as soon as he was able to delegate his responsibilities for the upcoming weekend. He didn't want his streak to get cold.

"By the way," Derek interjected, stopping at the door just before leaving the office, "have you told her you liked the article?"

"I gave it my approval initially," he said evasively.

Derek continued staring at him. "I haven't had time to talk to anyone but you," Paul protested. "I haven't even left my office yet."

"Then leave it and go tell her," Derek prompted. "Everyone needs a little positive reinforcement once in a while. I'm guessing that you haven't given her any substantial feedback. I don't want to risk losing the woman to someone else—even if you do."

He hated it when Derek insisted on putting words into his mouth or second-guessing his thoughts. "That's not necessarily true," Paul contradicted.

"Such passion," Derek quipped, placing his hand over his heart. "Well, you've convinced me."

Paul held his tongue. Sarcasm wasn't something he indulged in with any sort of regularity, but his brother seemed to have cornered the market for both of them.

"I'll see you later," he told Derek, hoping that would help usher his brother out the door.

Derek paused again, his hand on the doorknob. "As a matter of fact, you won't. I have some unfinished business to tend to," he said evasively.

According to Derek, he had just been in New York. Unfinished business would indicate that he was returning there. "You're flying back to New York?"

"Yes."

His brother seemed antsy to leave now, but Paul still wanted to find out what was prompting all these trips. Was Derek involved with someone in the city? Or was there something else going on? "Mind if I ask why? You were just there."

Derek had his explanation ready. "I'm trying to hit up some corporate types for donations to the institute. That requires wining and dining and a lot of kid-glove attention, something you wouldn't know anything about," he pointed out, "because I take that burden off your shoulders."

That still didn't make any sense to Paul. "I thought that was why the institute holds several different annual fundraisers each year."

Derek sighed wearily. He'd never liked having to explain himself, especially when things were not quite what they seemed. "In case you haven't noticed, the price of everything is going up. If the institute was a play, I'd say we needed angels backing it," he explained, thinking that the metaphor was lost on his brother.

Paul let the hint of sarcasm pass. There was no point in taking offense. It wouldn't resolve anything. Another sigh, this time one that had nothing to do with impatience, escaped.

"Yes, we need angels," Paul murmured, more to himself than to Derek. Dealing in the creation of tiny beings was more in the domain of angels than anything else, he thought.

Derek had taken the opportunity to make good his exit.

Paul half rose in his seat. "Let me know how it goes," he called after his brother. Derek merely waved an acknowledgment without looking back.

* * *

"Good piece."

At the sound of Paul's voice, Ramona's heart jumped into her throat. She hadn't expected anyone to walk in and she was busy doing research on the institute and its founder, Gerald Armstrong. Caught off guard, doing her best to look surprised rather than guilty, it took her a second to compose herself.

"Excuse me, Doctor?"

"I saw the press-release article you wrote about Bonner and Demetrios in the *Chronicle,*" he explained as he came in. "Nice to see something in the newspaper about the institute without veiled accusations running through it."

Ramona's response was a knowing smile. Barely moving her hand so that she wouldn't call any attention to it or the monitor facing her, she deftly pressed down on a combination of keys that brought up a neutral screen. She had a feeling that the doctor wouldn't exactly be thrilled if he knew she'd been researching those very articles.

It looked as if she and Armstrong were finally getting on better footing. She needed to feed that. "By the time I get finished working on the institute's image, people are going to think of it as being on the same plane as the Grotto of Lourdes."

"Setting your sights a little high, aren't you?" he asked, amused.

She had never approached life any other way. "If

you set your sights too low, you never get to accomplish anything noteworthy. Life is a series of challenges. You're not going to meet them if you're sitting on the sidelines," she told him.

He turned her words over in his head and then laughed.

Was he laughing at her? She'd thought he was too polite and well mannered for that. "What's so funny, Doctor?"

"I just can't picture you on the sidelines of *anything,*" he told her honestly.

For a second, she was silent. And then she said, "Thank you," very quietly. "Do you realize that's the first time you've given me a compliment?"

He didn't want her to get carried away. "It's not meant as a compliment," he felt bound to tell her. "It's just an observation."

Another man would have taken advantage of that, she thought. Apparently *honorable* wasn't just a word in the dictionary to Dr. Armstrong. That definitely made him different from his father. So far, she'd compiled a rather formidable pile of dirt on the senior Armstrong, who'd been a womanizer—and there was enough to go around as far as Derek Armstrong was concerned. But she was after more than that. She wanted to find something that would substantiate the notion that Gerald had played fast and loose with patients' eggs and sperm, at times possibly even substituting an egg or sperm from donors rather than his patients. So far, she had nothing concrete.

And as for Paul, she hadn't uncovered *anything* on him yet. Not even a whisper of any sort of scandal much less wrongdoing. Either he was very, very good at hiding his tracks—or he was clean.

She was beginning to lean toward the latter.

"Well, I'm taking it as a compliment," she told him. An impulse hit her. Ramona glanced at her watch. It was only eleven. Early by most standards, but she'd been up since five. "You have any consultations or procedures set up?"

The question, coming out of the blue, caught him by surprise. "For when?"

"Now."

What was she driving at? he wondered. He'd come in early to catch up on some paperwork and to review several trials that had been conducted on a new kind of medication that just might be able to help with fertility. There were no appointments on his calendar today.

"No. Not until later."

"Good, then." Ramona rose to her feet. Ingrained manners had him rising, as well. "I'm taking you to lunch." She saw him look at his own watch. "An early lunch," she amended before he could protest that it wasn't officially lunchtime. "My treat." She took her purse out of the drawer where she kept it. "You can't turn me down. I'm celebrating."

Had he missed something? Or was the woman talking about the article making it into print? "Celebrating what?"

Her eyes crinkled when she smiled, he noticed. And she was smiling enough to light up two rooms. "My boss just gave me my first compliment," she told him cheerfully.

The woman was making entirely too big a deal out of this. "Ms. Tate—"

"Oh now, don't go spoiling it by going all formal on me," she chided him. "I've been here more than a week. Certainly that's long enough for you to remember my first name."

"I remember your first name," Paul protested. "It's just that—"

She wouldn't allow him to finish. "Good, then you can use it."

He found himself laughing and shaking his head. "Are you always this pushy?"

There wasn't even a moment's hesitation on her part. "Always," she confirmed. "I find I get more things done that way."

And with that, she led the way out of the office.

"So, how do you like working at the institute?" Ramona asked once they were seated at a table in Stella's, the quaint Italian restaurant a block or two from the clinic. The food was as old-fashioned as the decor and just as tasty as the aroma drifting in from the kitchen promised it would be.

The server took their orders and retreated, leaving them with bread sticks that were out of this world.

"Shouldn't I be the one asking you that?" Paul wanted to know, looking at her. Her hair looked somewhat darker in the dim light. It was medium gold instead of bright blond, Paul caught himself thinking. Either way, it was incredibly attractive.

"I already know how I feel about working at the institute," she answered. "But you must have had a hard time, trying to walk in your father's shoes." Her eyes were on his, looking for a reaction as she said, "If I had to guess, I'd say that Gerald Armstrong was a hard act to follow."

He shrugged. "I just try to do justice to his vision."

Paul loved his father, she realized, and couldn't help wondering if that affection was returned, or if the senior Armstrong had been too wrapped up in his work and in the women who'd fawned on him over the years to even realize the precious thing he was ignoring.

She bit off a piece of bread stick, then asked as nonchalantly as she could, "And, in your opinion, have you succeeded?"

His eyes narrowed as he picked up a bread stick of his own. "I thought you were asking me out to lunch, not an interview."

She needed to dial it back a little, Ramona told herself. She had a tendency to come on strong. That would be a mistake here.

"This isn't an interview," she told him innocently. "I'm just trying to get a few things more clear so that I can tell your story better when I get around to writing it."

He straightened, abandoning the last of the bread stick. "Tell my story to whom?"

"To the general public," she answered. "I was thinking of putting together a piece on the institute. You know, on how it came about, the changes that were implemented when you and your brother and sister took over, things like that. I want to send it to one of the papers that has a Sunday magazine. Part of the reason you have to put up with rumors and detractors is that not enough people understand what it is you do. I think that too many of them regard you as being on the same level as Dr. Frankenstein—trying to create life out of thin air and coming up with Boris Karloff."

He couldn't say that he liked the idea of being dissected in public, or even held up to scrutiny. Not because he had anything to hide, but because he was and always had been a private person. The spotlight was for people like his father and Derek. They enjoyed it. He just wanted to be left alone to do his work.

But for now, he made no protest. He could always do that later. "Who else have you interviewed?"

"No one." Which was true. She was relying on sources for that. "I thought I'd start at the top and work my way down."

Their food arrived, the aromas enticing them to start eating.

"If that's the case," Paul said, continuing where they had left off, "you probably should have started with Derek."

She waited until she'd taken a bite before contradicting him. "Derek's not at the top, you are." Then, in case he didn't understand her criteria, she told him, "Derek might be the chief financial officer, but you're the heart of the institute, Dr. Armstrong."

This was the first time anyone had ever accused him of having a heart, much less infusing its blood into the lifeline of the family business. It both pleased and embarrassed him.

"I'm hardly that," Paul told her, punctuating his words with a careless shrug.

"Oh, but you are," Ramona insisted. She smiled as she watched him shift in his seat. She was a student of body language. "I'm sorry, I didn't mean to embarrass you."

He wasn't about to confirm or deny that she had. "I'm just not accustomed to talking about myself."

"You weren't," she pointed out. "I was. So how *did* it feel, stepping into your father's shoes?" she pressed.

He thought of that first time, when he realized that he was flying solo. That his father was no longer there, making every decision, large or small, without consulting any of them. His father, in his eyes, had been a brilliant dictator.

"A little unnerving," Paul admitted quietly before he could think better of it and keep his own counsel.

Ramona nodded. "I would imagine. Did you ever want to override one of your father's accepted methods, but you hesitated because you felt he'd disapprove?"

Paul laughed quietly. He'd spent the entire first year constantly second-guessing himself. "Only every hour of every day."

"Well, the statistics I've seen so far seem to say that your success ratio is very, very high."

Ramona bit back the impulse to ask if that was due to implanting too many viable embryos. It was too soon to be that honest. She had to get him to trust her a bit more before she went after answers to questions like that.

But she couldn't help anticipating.

Chapter Nine

Looking back, in Paul's estimation lunch had gone by much too quickly.

Instead of being eager to make a hasty retreat, the way he'd anticipated when Ramona had first extended the invitation to him, he found himself wanting to linger even after the plates had been cleared away and the coffee was all but gone.

Which made no sense because he did have paperwork to catch up on. And besides, he'd never liked being subjected to questions, and lunch had been fairly littered with them, although she'd presented them amicably. Despite his natural tendency toward privacy and aversion to talking about himself, there was just something, some nebulous "thing" he couldn't put his finger on or explain, that had him enjoying this vibrant woman's company.

And wanting more.

"I guess we'd better go," she told him when the server finally cleared away their coffee cups. "You've probably got a full schedule this afternoon."

Ramona signaled for the check and when it arrived, he reached for it. She was faster and all but stole it right out from under his hand.

"I said it was my treat, remember?" Ramona reminded him.

His had always been a life of privilege. He wasn't accustomed to having someone else pay, especially not someone who was in his employ.

"Yes, but—"

Ramona guessed at what he was going to say. "You didn't think I meant it." She grinned as she continued, "Or is it that in the world you come from, men still pick up the tab no matter what?"

He didn't know if she was laughing at him, or just flashing another one of her incredibly sunny smiles. He would have liked to think it was the latter. "Perhaps a little of both," he allowed quietly.

"Well, I did mean it," she told him. "So you're going to have to adjust your thinking a little about the roles of men and women."

"You don't earn enough to toss money around like that," he pointed out.

That meant he'd reached for the check because he was being thoughtful. She wondered if Armstrong even realized that.

She offered a compromise. "Tell you what, I'll let you pay the next time."

Next time.

The words hung in the air like a red banner. As in going out to a restaurant again. Together. When had this been taken for granted? Paul felt as if he'd somehow grabbed hold of one of those horses on a merry-go-round and someone had upped the speed, making the carousel go faster and faster and preventing him from getting off.

Maybe he'd heard wrong.

"Next time?" he repeated.

"Next time," she affirmed. "As in some other time after this."

She'd unnerved him, Ramona realized. Paul Armstrong, in his own way, was rather sweet and sheltered, she decided. He was like a throwback to another century despite the fact that he was only eleven years older than she was.

The man was, she mused, utterly unlike his brother, and she was beginning to think that wasn't such a good thing—at least, not for her. Being in his company had a very strange way of blurring her parameters. She was going to have to watch that and keep sight of her priorities, Ramona silently chided as she surrendered her credit card to the waiter.

* * *

Going out to lunch with Ramona had thrown Paul off schedule, not to mention him, as well. Consequently, when he returned to the institute, he planned to stay and catch up on paperwork long after everyone else had left.

At least, that was his plan when he walked back into his office, but it slowly wound up changing over the course of the afternoon, as he caught himself thinking about his parents more than once. Especially his father.

That was Ramona's fault, he thought grudgingly. Her cheerful but endless questions had touched on his childhood and focused more than once on his father. That and the fond way she'd spoken of her own mother the rare time or two that the conversation had veered away from all things institute and shifted to her.

He caught himself envying her for the close relationship she shared with her mother. From what she'd told him, Ramona had grown up at a severe disadvantage, with a mother who frequently had to work two jobs in order to provide for things that he and his brother and sisters had taken for granted.

But no amount of privilege would outweigh the love Ramona had had while growing up, and from the sound of it, continued to have to this day. Paul and his siblings were closer to each other than to either parent. Their father seemed to always be away, busy at the institute or off to numerous conferences. Their mother never picked up the slack. Instead, she'd been distant, occupied with her society friends and obsessed with looking as if she had cornered the fountain of youth for her own private use.

If either parent took any notice of any of them, it was Gerald, who appeared to be marginally partial to Derek. Paul had a feeling that the founder of the fertility institute saw himself in Derek. Both were outgoing and outspoken—and very flirtatious, even silver-tongued. Paul knew he didn't possess any of these traits and that made him all but invisible to his father.

Listening to Ramona speak fondly of her mother, Paul found himself wishing that he had favorable memories of his parents to draw on in times of stress. Sure, he'd always loved them. But he had no illusions about the sentiment being returned. He knew that it was a one-way street.

He needed to do something to change that. Maybe he could begin with a little more close contact with both parents. It had been a while since he'd been back to the house where he and his siblings had grown up. It was more like a mausoleum than a home, but that didn't change the fact that he was long overdue for a visit.

The silent debate went back and forth for a while. Finally, just as the clock approached five, Paul powered down his computer and left.

Ramona, who was just getting off the elevator located on the far side of the corridor, saw him walk out the front entrance.

And made a mental note of it.

* * *

Maybe he should have called ahead, Paul thought as he approached the winding driveway. His parents might be entertaining and then he would be guilty of crashing their party.

But there were no valets racing back and forth, parking expensive automobiles. There wasn't even a single vehicle parked before the edifice that could only be described as a mansion. From the looks of it, his parents were alone.

That was in keeping with what was becoming, more and more, his father's reclusive nature.

For a moment, Paul thought of turning around and just going home.

But he was here now, he might as well stay, he told himself. Nothing was ever going to change if he didn't make an attempt to change it. Waiting for either of his parents to make the first move would only be an exercise in futility.

Leaving his vehicle parked in the driveway, he walked up to the three-story front doors and rang the bell. Several minutes later—long enough for him to think about leaving again—the door opened.

Anna, the Armstrongs' longtime housekeeper, looked surprised and then pleased to see him. "Well, hello," the older woman said warmly. Her eyes fairly sparkled as she smiled.

"I know," Paul responded as he walked in past her. "It's been a while."

"I was just thinking how nice it was to see you, Dr. Paul." The small, squat woman who had once been his nanny and had graduated to her present position when the old housekeeper retired, silently closed the door. "Your parents are in the front living room," she informed him. "Together for once," she added.

There was no judgment in her voice. It was just a simply stated fact. An unusual one since even when he was growing up, his parents were rarely in the same room at the same time, unless it was for a public function or there was a photographer involved.

"Thank you, Anna. You're looking well."

The woman smiled gratefully. "I'm looking older, but thank you for that. Will you be staying for dinner, Dr. Paul?"

He glanced toward the living room. The doors were opened, but at this distance, he couldn't see in. "Depends on how this plays out."

"I'll put up a plate," Anna told him confidently.

Lengthening his stride, Paul crossed to the living room. He stopped just short of the doorway, then quietly looked in.

Situated on opposite sides of the room, neither his mother nor his father seemed to notice him. Or each other, for that matter.

Theirs had been a marriage of inconvenient convenience. Gerald Armstrong had married Emily Stanton because he wanted a wife on his arm who had a pedigree and brought a considerable amount of money to the merger. Emily had married Gerald because even though the dynamic young doctor was socially beneath her, he was exciting and a future with him promised to be the same.

They'd both been disappointed in their expectations, but for the sake of appearances remained together. At least in theory.

As Paul stood there, silently studying these two people whose blood ran through his veins, his mother, beautifully groomed as always with every hair in place, was the first to notice him. If she was taken aback by his unannounced appearance, she covered it skillfully.

"Paul, what are you doing here?" Crossing to him, she brushed the air beside his cheek with a kiss. The same kiss she shared when greeting friends who weren't really friends. Stepping back, she appraised her son, searching for some kind of telltale sign of trouble. Artfully penciled eyebrows rose just the slightest fraction. "Is something wrong?"

He shook his head and forced a shadow of a smile to his lips. "Nothing's wrong, Mother. I just realized this afternoon that I hadn't been by for a while and thought I'd drop in on my way home."

His father, seated in the wheelchair he regarded as his prison, turned sharply away from the fireplace and looked at him.

"I'm not dead yet, if that's why you're here," Gerald snapped at his son.

"Didn't think you were, Dad," Paul said, keeping his voice mild as he came closer.

He went through a minor adjustment period every time he saw his father like this. Gerald Armstrong had been a giant of a man, both physically and in stature. But now, he seemed to have folded into himself, a whispered memory of the man he'd once been. All that was left was a booming voice that somehow seemed misplaced, as if it belonged to someone else and Gerald was just borrowing it for a little while.

Taking a breath, Paul tried to lighten the atmosphere a little. He smiled at his father and said, "Someone has a birthday coming up."

"Everyone has a birthday coming up," Gerald responded, scowling darkly. "Unless they have the good fortune to be dead."

Emily Armstrong waved away her husband's sour comment, then deliberately turned her back on Gerald and addressed her words to her son.

"Don't pay any attention to him. He's been in a mood all week. You have no idea what I've had to put up with." She sighed dramatically, her longing for the life she'd once led evident in every word she spoke. "I'm beginning to think I liked him better when he was busy with his work and his women."

Paul's eyes widened. He remembered the rumors, remembered, too, hearing Derek tell him that he'd made a play for their father's mistress after the senior

Armstrong had grown tired of her. Emily had been in the next room and Paul, horrified, had ordered Derek to shut up. He'd been foolish enough to think no one else knew about their father's wandering eyes and grasping hands, least of all their mother.

Even so, her comment caught him off guard. "Mother!"

To his surprise, his mother laughed. "You look stunned, Paul. What? You think I didn't know? That I believed all those stories of his about having to go off to conferences? *No one* goes to that many conferences," she jeered.

"You never said anything," Paul tried to explain.

Emily shrugged, turning her attention back to the liquor cabinet. Taking out a bottle of aged scotch, she poured the deep amber liquid into a glass. She took a long sip and savored the first taste for a moment before answering.

"I never said anything because there was no point in talking about it." And even if there was, she wouldn't have mentioned it to a child. Looking at her son's face, Emily anticipated what was going on in his orderly mind. He needed convincing. "There's a difference between not knowing and not caring." She slanted a glance at the man who was no longer handsome, no longer held any kind of attraction for her. "Sadly, I stopped caring a long time ago."

"What are you two whispering about over there?" Gerald demanded. Not waiting for an answer, he pressed one of the buttons on his right armrest. The automated chair instantly brought him right to them.

"Nothing that concerns you, Gerald," Emily answered evasively for the sake of peace. It was obvious she didn't want another scene.

"I don't believe you," Gerald snapped.

The evening degenerated from there.

Paul left right after dinner, feeling he'd done enough penance for one day. Possibly for a month.

It seemed to Paul that over the course of the next week and a half, Ramona Tate appeared to be everywhere. Their paths crossed at least half a dozen times a day. It got to a point that he was beginning to wonder if perhaps she had a global positioning satellite planted somewhere on his person that enabled her to find him wherever he went.

The thing of it was, he was beginning to look forward to seeing her.

Toward the end of the following week, Paul finally commented about it to Ramona. He tried not to make it seem as if he was calling her out on it, but he wanted an explanation. It almost seemed like too much of a coincidence.

When he walked into her as he was about to go into the lab and she was coming out, he said, "Our paths keep crossing."

The comment seemed to surprise her. "Now that you mention it, I noticed that, too."

"How do you explain it?" he asked, curious.

"Small building?" she offered with a beguiling smile. "There aren't that many places to go and since I can't really do my job sitting in my office for eight hours straight, per force I have to be mobile." Her mouth curved in that grin he had realized he looked forward to seeing far more than he should. "What's your excuse?" she wanted to know.

He stared at her, befuddled. Had she just turned the tables on him? "For what?"

"For turning up every place I am," she told him with a shrug.

The gesture was innocent and beguiling. The silky peasant blouse she wore slipped down her shoulder. She tugged it back in place under his watchful eye. He told himself he shouldn't be staring, but he couldn't look away.

"I don't know, you tell me." And then she pretended to hazard her own theory. "Maybe you decided you'd like to get to know me better and you don't know how to go about doing it."

He stared, stunned. "Ramona—Ms. Tate—" Words failed him.

She came to his rescue. "Relax, Dr. Armstrong. I'm only kidding," she teased. "I already told you, it's a small building. It's all coincidence. Now, if you'll excuse me, I have to take a trip up to the third floor." Stepping into the elevator he'd just vacated a few moments ago and that had been standing at the ready, she pressed the button for the third floor. "I have an appointment to talk to Dr. Bonner."

A score of red flags seemed to suddenly pop up in his head, as if warning him that something was off. Something was wrong.

"What are you planning on talking to him about?" he wanted to know.

"About his work, of course," she answered.

What kind of questions was she planning on asking the man? He thought that the threat of unrest was over. The article she'd written had appeared almost two weeks ago and since then, he'd heard no more rumors. Everything seemed to be fine.

So why was she talking to Bonner and who knew who else?

The last thing he saw before the silver doors closed was the expression on Ramona's face. She was smiling at him, but the look in her eyes was unfathomable. And that made him nervous.

Chapter Ten

It was hard to think of a mere thirty-eight-year-old as a science wunderkind, but that was exactly what the medical community had dubbed Ted Bonner. Even his detractors thought he was brilliant and his cheering section went on endlessly not just about his incredible mental acuity, but about his dark good looks, as well.

Ramona had always thought that intelligent, cerebral types came in dull shades of brown and gray. After being at the institute just a short while, she realized that she was definitely going to have to reassess the way she thought.

Though extremely busy, Bonner had agreed to pause for a few minutes and answer "just a few of your questions."

"A few is better than none," Ramona responded cheerfully. "Let's start with how the Armstrong Fertility Institute managed to entice you and Dr. Demetrios into leaving the university to join the staff here."

His mouth quirked in a smile. "Paul Armstrong said we could have carte blanche at the institute. That no one would interfere with our research and all he asked was to be given updates whenever we felt there was something noteworthy to share."

She noted that one of the lab technicians slowed her pace as she passed the good doctor. He was a heart stopper, all right, Ramona silently agreed.

"And how did this agreement with Mr. Armstrong differ from your previous employer?"

He laughed at the question. "The difference is like night and day. Previously, we were faced with a myriad of restrictions. It's a wonder we made any progress at all." Her puzzled look silently prompted him to elaborate. "Universities are *very* PC oriented. Or, more to the point, they're very fearful of being sued for one reason or another. They had all sorts of restrictions, rules and protocols for us to follow. And the massive amount of paperwork we had to do took away from actual lab time," he complained.

She watched his face for a telltale reaction as she stated her conclusion. "Then you and Dr. Demetrios must really be thrilled to be here."

He averted his eyes, glancing at something on the table before him when he answered, "Close to it."

Ramona read between the lines. "But?"

Again, he laughed. This time it was in self-deprecation. "Chance claims I wouldn't be satisfied in heaven," he said, referring to his research partner. "That I'd insist on rearranging the clouds if nothing else was off."

She could feel her pulse rate increasing. It took effort to keep the excitement out of her voice. "And what's off here?" she asked innocently.

He shifted his six-foot-four frame like a man who didn't want to be pinned down just yet. "I've got some reservations about the lab's protocols," he replied vaguely.

Again her eyes caught his. Was he guarding a secret, or was he just in the beginning stages of formulating his suspicions? And if so, what was he suspicious of? "For instance?"

Bonner let the bait pass him by. "I need to do a little more research into that before I feel comfortable enough to be more specific."

Damn it. So near and yet so far. She didn't want to give up, but she knew that she couldn't press too hard, either.

"It helps to talk things through," she encouraged. "You know, kind of like brainstorming. Maybe it's all just a misunderstanding…." Her voice trailed off as she mentally crossed her fingers.

But Bonner merely shrugged. "Maybe," he allowed. She could tell by his tone that he wasn't convinced—

but he wasn't about to say anything more, either. "But we each have our own way of doing things."

"No argument there." Although she'd dearly love to argue him out of this stance he'd taken. "Tell me, is it something that the institute has always done, or is it some new protocol?"

"Don't know the answer to that, either," Bonner admitted. "Most likely everything'll be cleared up once I go through the archives—if I ever get the chance to get down there." A timer went off, stealing his attention. Her time was up. "I've really got to get back to my work. If you'll excuse me?"

It wasn't a question, it was a statement, meant to politely usher her out.

Bonner obviously didn't want anyone looking over his shoulder as he worked, she thought. She could understand that.

"Of course." She closed the black leather-bound notebook she'd been taking notes in. "And thank you for your time."

But she was already talking to the back of his head as Bonner went to retrieve material from an incubator. Ramona quietly slipped out of the lab, passing several more techs scurrying about like mice.

The archives again, she thought as she got on the elevator. This just reinforced her desire to get into that basement room.

She was working on that, pressing for the first floor. She'd done her very best to be seen by as many people as she could so that everyone would come to regard her as a fixture here and wouldn't question her presence anywhere within the institute. Like the archives. It was time for her to find out just how she went about getting access to it.

Instead of going to her office when she got off on the first floor, Ramona took a detour and stopped by the medical clinic. Pushing open one of the glass doors, she walked into the waiting area. The large room was crowded to the limit with couples who were returning for procedures, there for counseling or coming in for the first time.

Looking at them, Ramona found that she couldn't tell one set from the other. Everyone had basically the same kind of expression, the kind of expression found on the faces of children on Christmas Eve, as they stared up at the skies and hoped that magic would briefly touch their lives and make their fondest wish come true.

"Lost?"

The softly voiced question came from behind her. She turned to see the clinic's receptionist sitting at her desk, watching her.

Wilma Goodheart had been at the institute practically from the very beginning and now, with the senior Dr. Armstrong gone, she regarded herself as its resident expert and historian. In her late fifties, she was the picture of the eternal, ever-efficient secretary.

"No, actually, I'm not," Ramona said, turning completely around to face her. "I came to ask you a question." Had Wilma not been loyal to a fault when it came to Gerald Armstrong and, by extension, his family, she would have actually had a ton of questions to ask the older woman. But since Wilma *was* loyal, she knew she would get nothing out of her that even hinted at the institute's secrets. "If I wanted to get some information from the archives, how would I go about it?" she asked, keeping her expression as innocent-looking as possible.

"You'd need a pass card to access the records room."

That sounded simple enough. But Ramona knew better than to be too confident. She took another tentative step across the semifrozen lake. At any moment, the older woman could grow suspicious and refuse to answer. "How do I get one of those?"

Wilma pursed her lips, something she always did when she was thinking. "What is it you want from there? Maybe I could—"

Ramona was quick to cut the woman off. "I don't want to impose on anyone. Besides, I'm not sure I know what I'm looking for yet."

Wilma scrutinized her, a hint of suspicion entering her brown eyes. "Then how will you know if you found it?"

"I'll know," Ramona told her with certainty. "It's just background information," she quickly added. "Maybe even the name of Dr. Gerald's first patient—"

"That's confidential," Wilma told her firmly. "I'm surprised that working in public relations, you don't know that."

"I'd use another name," she quickly assured the woman. "Maybe call her Patient One, something like that. But I'd want to see what she went through and how that was different from the procedures that are being used now." Ramona looked at the older woman who had willingly married herself to her work, clearly feeling that the institute was doing something extraordinarily good. Judging by the way Wilma's face relaxed, she'd found the right angle, Ramona thought.

"I just want to immerse myself in the institute's history. If I'm to do the Armstrong institute any good, I have to know everything about it first," she explained.

Wilma said nothing for a moment, then slowly nodded. "I suppose you have a point." She opened her middle drawer and took something out. She held out a plastic card. "I have an access card."

Though she wanted to snatch it, Ramona restrained her impulse. Her hand remained at her side. "That's good to know."

Wilma looked at her, confused. "You don't want the card?"

More than you could possibly know. Out loud, she continued with her charade. "Not at the moment. I need to get a list of questions together first so I don't wind up spending a weekend in there. But I'll gladly take you up on your kind offer when I'm ready."

Wilma put the card back in its place and shut the drawer. "Fair enough."

Ramona walked out of the clinic smiling to herself. This way, if the topic should come up, Paul's trusted receptionist could tell him that she'd been in no hurry to run off to the basement and go rifling through the archives.

Her plan was to wait until Friday, take Wilma's access card and then go down after everyone had left for the weekend. She wanted to go through the files at her leisure, without worrying that someone might walk in on her.

Ramona didn't bother to attempt to tamp down her excitement.

Hang on just a little bit longer, Mom. If there's someone out there with your DNA, I'll find them. I promise.

Paul glanced at his watch as he came to the end of the report he'd been working on. The same report he'd been struggling with for the past few days, that had kept him prisoner in his seat because he'd vowed he wasn't going to go home until he finished it, even if it *was* Friday night.

As if Friday nights were different from any other night, he mocked himself. He'd long ago sacrificed any kind of social life to make sure that the institute remained on the cutting edge of its field.

This meant at times having to wade through myriad rules and regulations. It was enough to make a man permanently cross-eyed.

He made a few notations, then sat back in his chair

and sighed. Well, the report was finally finished. It wasn't an outstanding piece of work, but it was finished.

Wanting to go, Paul forced himself to quickly reread the document.

Which was a good thing because on the third page, he came to a glaring empty space. That was when he remembered that he'd deliberately left the blank area to remind himself that he needed a particular set of statistics to hammer home his point. A set of statistics that weren't readily accessible because it had been bundled up with a large set of "precomputer" data and deposited in the room where they kept the rest of the files and folders that had not been input or scanned into the database.

Paul blew out a breath. He was tired and hungry. Monday was soon enough for him to go down there and retrieve the information.

No, he contradicted himself in the next moment. That would be putting things off, and he knew he'd spend the weekend being haunted by the omission until he finally came in on Monday morning and got the missing data he needed.

He might as well get it over with and do it tonight, Paul told himself. Otherwise, he was going to wind up sacrificing his weekend.

What weekend? he mocked himself. The only thing that made the following two days different from the five he'd just been through was that some of the time, he didn't come back into his office at the institute.

Well, if you did something about this attraction you're feeling for Ramona, maybe you'd finally have *a social life.*

Paul shook his head, pushing down his thoughts.

Opening his desk drawer, he took out the white plastic card he needed to gain access to the archives, picked up his briefcase and walked out of his office.

The lights in the building had been dimmed. It felt exceptionally lonely, he mused as he walked down the corridor to the elevator.

The sound of the car's arrival seemed amplified against the wall of silence. He got on and pressed the button for the basement.

Getting off the elevator, he turned right and made his way down the winding corridor. The lighting here was even dimmer than on the other floors. His destination had originally been used as a bank vault. When his father had bought the property for the institute, he'd had the existing building demolished, but he'd left the vault. Keeping it intact appealed to him for reasons the man never went into and no one—except his mother—even questioned that he'd seen fit to retain it.

When he reached the reinforced-steel door, he was about to slide his card through the slot when he saw that it wasn't necessary. The door was standing ajar.

The hairs on the back of his neck instantly rose. Who could be here at this hour? He debated calling 911, but decided to hold off in case it was one of the staff members who had access to the archives. He needed to check this out further.

Cautiously, Paul slipped in as silently as he could. Putting down his briefcase, he slowly crept toward the back of the vault where the files were actually kept. His father had taken an active part in designing the three-story building that was now the institute, and these plans had extended to renovating the vault, as well.

Gerald Armstrong had insisted that it not only have its own source of power, but a backup generator as well in case the city suffered another massive power failure like the one that had thrown the East Coast into darkness decades ago. In addition, he'd authorized that a very small powder room be added, as well. It was because of this last touch that the institute's "unique file room" had been the subject of more than one magazine article.

As he made his way in, Paul could have sworn he heard someone moving around in the center of the vault. Again he wondered who could be down here at this hour.

And then he had his answer.

There, directly in front of him, was Ramona Tate. She was taking pictures with what looked like the world's tiniest camera.

Paul was stunned. Was she spying on them? Collecting data for another fertility organization?

Even as the questions occurred to him, Paul felt anger bubbling up inside.

"What do you think you're doing, Ramona?" he demanded, coming forward.

Her nerves already pulled so taut that they were ready to break at any moment, Ramona's heart instantly flew into her throat. She screamed as she swung around. And then, when she saw that it was Paul, she breathed a sigh of relief.

Relief, however, was short-lived.

"I said, what do you think you're doing here?" he repeated. This time his voice was unnervingly cold and hard.

It took her a moment to collect herself. *Always go with the truth as your foundation.* Ramona sincerely believed that. It made for fewer mistakes in the long run.

She looked at him as if to silently say that was self-explanatory. "I'm just going through the files in the archives."

"You're photographing them," he pointed out angrily. "Why?"

She had an answer prepared for that, too. "So I don't have to come back again. This way, I can read through them upstairs instead of in this tiny, cramped space."

Because weakness of any kind embarrassed her, she didn't add that she was a claustrophobic. While closed-in places did not cause her to assume a fetal position, the sooner she was out of here, the better. That was one of the reasons she'd left the door open. She wanted to feel air coming in even though, logically, that was impossible, given her position.

"But *why* are you going through the files in the archives?" These were mostly patient folders and trials that belonged to his father. He didn't know what was in each file, but his protective instincts definitely kicked in. He might have never been close to the man, but he didn't want to see his father's name dragged through the mud, either.

"I'm preparing a piece on the institute—" She stopped and looked at him, slightly puzzled. "I must have told you that. Anyway, I just need a little history for background information. You know, how your father didn't give up despite X amount of false starts and near misses."

Paul picked up one of the folders she'd just been photographing and read the label across it. "You're in the patient files."

"It's a personal story," she replied, unfazed. "Don't worry, I'll change the names to protect the parties involved."

But Paul shook his head as he replaced the folder. "No, you won't."

Did he think she was that careless? "Yes, I will," she insisted.

"No, you won't, because you're not going to go through any more of the files," he told her firmly. "And you're not going to use the information from the ones you already photographed."

She still hadn't found her mother's file, but she knew it had to be here somewhere. She'd been down here for the past two hours and felt that she was getting close. All she needed was a few more minutes to find it. But he wasn't going to give her those minutes, she knew, looking at the set of Armstrong's jaw. She was going to have to come back later and it would undoubtedly be harder for her to get in. That really frustrated her.

"Why?" It was her turn to challenge him. "What are you afraid I'm going to find here?" The moment the words were out of her mouth, she realized that she'd pressed his buttons. Obviously he didn't like having his orders questioned.

"I think that's about enough. I want you to leave now. We'll discuss this on Monday." The tone he used promised that there would be no discussion, only a lecture. And he'd be the one giving it.

There was no point in arguing with him. He wasn't about to give in. She was just going to have to find an excuse to get back here and find her mother's file. She didn't care what it took.

For now, Ramona gave him a small salute. "You're the boss, Doctor," she told him.

He thought he detected a hint of mockery in her voice. "Yes, I am," he answered curtly.

She began to walk away. He was right behind her. Did he think she was going to make a mad dash back? "Are you planning on following me?" she wanted to know.

He was tired. He could definitely come back for the

statistics he needed on Monday. The report he'd worked on wasn't about to go anywhere over the weekend.

"Yes, I am."

She turned to look at him over her shoulder as she continued walking. "I'm not cattle that you have to herd."

"Never said you were." He pointed toward the door that was still standing ajar. "Now, just go." It was an order.

She didn't care for his tone. Still looking over her shoulder, she was about to tell him just that when she tripped over the briefcase he'd dropped. Thrown off balance, Ramona stumbled and pitched forward. Not wanting to smash her head against the concrete floor, Ramona grabbed the first thing she could to steady herself. The last thing in the world she wanted was to fall flat on her face in front of him.

Unfortunately, the first thing she managed to grab was the steel handle on the vault door. She yanked it toward her. The next moment, she heard an awful clicking sound. Her stomach seized up as she realized what she'd done. Praying she was wrong, she tried the door. And paled when she found it wouldn't budge.

"What are you waiting for? Go ahead," Paul ordered. He'd almost grabbed her himself when she was falling and was glad he was spared. He was fairly certain that it would have been the beginning of a huge mistake.

"I can't," she told him through gritted teeth.

He was in no mood for games. She was looking particularly gorgeous tonight, but she was becoming damn irritating. "Listen—"

"You said that when the building was constructed, this vault was left intact. Did anyone consider using it for a panic room?"

What an odd question. And one that could be asked far better outside this enclosed area than in. "Not that I know of, why?"

She sucked in air before answering. Was it her imagination, or was she choking? There was distress in her eyes as she turned around to look at him. "The door's locked."

His eyes narrowed. She had to be pulling his leg. He hadn't thought that her sense of humor would be on this low a level. "What do you mean 'locked'?"

"As in 'won't open.' As in 'trapped.'" Did he really need any more synonyms? "I—accidentally pulled it shut when I tripped."

She was putting him on to see his reaction, Paul thought. "No, you didn't."

"Fine." She stepped to the side and gestured toward the steel door. "Have it your way. *You* open it. I really hope you can," she added.

But he couldn't.

Chapter Eleven

Paul had hoped against hope that Ramona was mistaken—that she hadn't pulled the door shut all the way when she'd grabbed it. But one fruitless tug told him she had.

He turned away from the immobile steel and looked at her. "It's locked."

"That's what I said," Ramona retorted, her voice quavering. With effort she desperately tried to keep her voice from cracking. Panic was waiting just beyond the perimeter to grip her in its bony fingers.

Damn it, he'd been meaning to put in safeguards against this very thing happening, but it was one of those nonpressing things he felt comfortable about putting off. He was far from comfortable now.

Searching for a way out, he found none. "I don't think you understand what I'm saying," he told Ramona.

"It's locked. I got it," she said sharply. "I told you."

Ramona took in a shaky breath. She needed to calm down. But confined places made her think of graves. It was only because she was so desperate to get the information she needed for her mother—and to secure the information that would give credence to the rumors that her editor had her investigating—that she'd even stepped into the tomblike room.

She looked at Paul hopefully. "But you can override it, right?"

"Override it?" Paul repeated. What did she think he was, a magician?

"Yes, as in making it open up again. You know, with a code or a master card or something like that." She was beginning to sound like a babbling loon, she chided. With effort, she got hold of herself. "You're the chief of staff," she argued when he continued looking at her as if he was still waiting for her to make sense. "You're supposed to have some kind of extra power over the rest of us."

"I must have missed that in the manual," he quipped. "No 'extra powers' to speak of."

Oh, please let him be kidding. "Then you can't open it?"

"It's a converted bank vault," he needlessly pointed out.

"I know what it is." She banked down the hysteria that was beginning to enter her voice. "But I still thought—"

"That means," he continued as if she hadn't spoken, "it's on a timer."

A timer. A timer meant that it was set to a specific hour. Like every hour on the hour or something like that. She could handle an hour. Maybe. "So when does it open again?"

He glanced at his watch. There were times when he forgot not only the time, but the day. His watch had both. "It's Friday."

"Yes. So?" she prodded, waiting for him to tell her something she could cling to.

Paul realized that he was going to be stuck with this woman for an entire two days and three nights. He met the prospect with conflicted feelings. Some he understood and others he didn't want to understand. They were far too personal, far too stirring. They had no place here.

"The vault opens again at 8:00 a.m. on Monday morning."

"Monday morning?" It was all Ramona could do to keep from screaming out the words. "You're kidding, right?"

"Unless someone comes and overrides the timer from the outside, no, I'm not kidding," Paul told her. "The door won't open until Monday."

"But we can't stay here that long."

Although he liked the idea of being alone with this woman, having her trapped in order to do it was definitely not what he would have had in mind. "I don't think there's much choice."

For a moment, desperation reduced her thought process to nothing, freezing it in place as panic encroached upon her. Focusing every fiber within her, she willed herself to calm down. Once she did, she remembered. She had her cell phone with her.

"There's always a choice, Doctor," she retorted happily. Flipping her phone open, she tapped out 911, only to get nothing. She tried again before she looked at the tiny illuminated screen. "There're no signal bars," she noted numbly. "There're always supposed to be bars." She looked up from her phone to Armstrong's face. "They promised bars," she lamented, referring to the commercials about her service provider. "Why aren't there bars?"

"That's probably because they never tried to use their phones in an underground vault."

She wasn't going to accept defeat. She couldn't. "Do you have your cell phone on you?"

He always kept it in his pocket. "Yes, but the result will be the same," he warned her.

Maybe he was wrong. Maybe there was something wrong with her phone. She didn't care what the reason was, she just wanted a signal.

"Try it," she ordered. She was no longer an employee trying to curry his favor—she was just a woman on the verge of a breakdown for a completely embarrassing reason and she knew it—which made it all the worse to bear.

Rather than argue, Paul took out his phone and tapped out the three numbers. "Nothing," he declared in response to the quizzical look in her eyes.

She could feel the panic in her chest. "You seem awfully calm for someone locked in a vault until Monday morning," she accused.

Maybe he was doing this to teach her a lesson for snooping where he didn't want her to, she thought. Ramona grasped on to the slim sliver of hope, praying she was right.

"Panicking isn't going to help us any," he pointed out.

She still didn't want to give up. "Isn't there some way to signal someone?" she wanted to know. "What about the security guards?"

Paul reviewed the men's responsibilities in his mind. "There're video cameras throughout the building. They monitor them in the security room." The room was off to the side of the building.

Oh, thank God. "Well, there you go," Ramona said, relief coating every syllable. "They'll come down when they see us."

"*If* they see us," Paul corrected. "There's no camera in here. Hardly anyone ever comes down to look through the archives," he pointed out.

Ramona could almost feel her heart sinking in her chest. She looked around the room as if the walls literally *were* starting to close in on her. Thoughts of suffocation began to crowd her head. "How much air do we have?"

"That's no problem," Paul was quick to assure her. "The original designer made sure there'd be plenty of air circulating through here so that whatever people had in their safe-deposit boxes wouldn't eventually dry out. My father maintained the system for the files he had stored here."

For a second, she closed her eyes and murmured, "Thank God." And then her eyes flew open as other, possibly insurmountable problems occurred to her. "What about other things?"

"Other things?" he repeated, not following her line of thinking.

"Food, water…" She didn't feel like getting personal right now, but there was no way around it. "Bathroom facilities," she concluded uncomfortably.

"There's a watercooler behind the last cabinet." He pointed to the right. "And for reasons I never understood, there's also a powder room located on the far side." He indicated the opposite wall. "As for food—" Well, there they struck out. "Nobody was ever supposed to be down here long enough to get hungry."

Two whole days without food. People didn't starve after two days, right? She tried to make the best of the situation. "Oh well, I've been meaning to go on a diet," she murmured. Her biggest problem wasn't food, it was keeping her thoughts under control and not panicking.

Paul's eyebrows drew together as he looked at her. "Why would you want to do that?"

"Because I'm overweight." According to her scale, she was three pounds over her ideal weight. She'd been meaning to cut back a little. She just hadn't thought about doing it while locked in a safe.

When she looked at Armstrong, he made no secret of the fact that he was still scrutinizing her. "No, you're not."

In the midst of her mounting panic, Ramona paused to look at the chief of staff in surprise. She wouldn't have thought that he'd even notice something like that. She realized that in his own unassuming way, he'd just given her a compliment—while sealed inside a vault.

"Thank you," she murmured.

There was air, there was air—he'd told her so and he wasn't the kind of man to lie, she tried to console herself. So why did she feel as if she was suffocating? Was it just her mind playing tricks on her?

"Won't someone wonder where you are?" she asked hopefully.

It was Friday evening. Everyone he knew had plans. Plans that didn't include him. His time was usually spent working or making plans for the coming week's work. This weekend, like most, he was going to spend by himself.

"No," he told her quietly. And then he looked at her as the same thought occurred to him. Just because he wasn't panicking didn't mean he wanted to be here until Monday morning. "How about you? Someone's going to miss you if you don't show up tonight or tomorrow morning, am I correct?"

Since she had such a sporadic work schedule, she knew her mother would just assume she was working. Katherine Tate wouldn't dream of interrupting her when she was working, so there wouldn't even be an attempt to call her.

Not that that would lead to anything anyway, she thought, looking at the nonreceptive cell phone in her hand.

She shoved the phone angrily into her pocket. "No," she answered, "I don't."

"I find that impossible to believe."

Ramona looked at him. Armstrong wasn't being sarcastic, he was serious. She repressed her fraying temper.

"You have no idea how much I wish you were right. But you're not." Her voice sounded ragged to her own ears as she asked him, "What are we going to do?"

Paul studied her for a moment. It wasn't his imagination. There were now beads of perspiration forming along her hairline. It still wasn't hot enough in here for that sort of reaction.

"Are you all right?" he asked. "You look a little—" Paul searched for the right word. "Spooked," he finally said. "Definitely agitated."

"I'm fine," she retorted. This was not the time to

reveal a weakness. She didn't want to have the fact that she had claustrophobia getting around.

But it seemed to be too late. "No, you're not," he countered. And then he realized what he was seeing. "You're claustrophobic, aren't you?"

"No," she snapped. And then she drew in a lungful of air. What was the point of denying it? He was going to find out soon anyway. She didn't know how much longer she could maintain this facade. "Yes. Yes, I'm claustrophobic," she retorted.

It didn't make sense. "But I've seen you in elevators."

Yoga and a few other crutches had taught her how to cope within a situation for a limited amount of time. "I can usually keep it under wraps as long as the confinement is for a short period of time." She glanced around the room again like a caged animal. "Not eternity."

"Unless you're a fruit fly, Monday morning is hardly an eternity away," he told her, hoping that putting things into perspective would help her cope.

Ramona made no answer. Instead, she looked down at her palms, which were growing progressively sweatier. She rubbed one hand against the other in an attempt to dry them off. The sweatiness continued.

He was a doctor, Paul reminded himself. His first obligation was to his patient and while Ramona was not his patient, in the typical sense of the word, it took no stretch of the imagination to see that Ramona Tate was sorely in need of a physician to help her cope with the predicament they found themselves in.

"The first thing we need to do," he told her, taking her hand and leading her away from the steel door, "is get your mind off the situation."

Was he delusional? "We're *in* the situation," she reminded him sharply. "In a small, steel-walled, 'situation' that could at any minute suffocate us. Snuff us out just like that."

"Not unless the air stops being pumped in," he pointed out.

She looked up to the air vents. "There's a thought." Her throat tightened in fear.

"There's a backup generator in case this one fails," he told her.

She searched his face. His eyes were kind. She shook her head. "You're just saying that to make me feel better."

"Yes," Paul admitted. "I would. But luckily, I don't have to. My father left nothing to chance," he assured her. "The basement is hooked up to the system that runs through the rest of the institute. There are backup generators in case of a major power failure. Don't forget, we have donor eggs and sperm stored here. We can't afford to have the refrigeration system break down, even for a small amount of time. If we actually lost power, any stored embryos we have would be destroyed in a matter of hours. Even a short amount of time would likely have an adverse effect."

All right, so there was air. That still didn't keep the

walls from feeling as if they were closing in on her, but at least she'd die breathing.

She slowly took in a breath and then released it just as slowly in an attempt to calm her erratic pulse.

"Better?" Paul asked her gently. He was still holding her hand.

He was trying to be nice, she thought, feeling somewhat guilty for what she'd been up to. She knew she couldn't blame him for this situation since it was really her fault they were locked in. The fact that he wasn't blaming her said a great deal about his character. Paul Armstrong was a really decent man, she decided.

"Better," she acknowledged in a quiet voice.

She was lying, Paul judged. The beads of sweat were still there, dampening her bangs. But at least she wasn't breaking down yet. Maybe he could still divert her attention, get her mind on something else.

There was an old sofa, a castoff from one of the consultation rooms, pushed up against one of the walls. It had been placed here rather than thrown out so that when someone did come down to the archives, they could go through the files and read whatever they needed in comfort. He led her over to it now.

"Why don't you sit down here and talk to me," he encouraged.

She stared at him blankly. Was he going to interrogate her? Did he suspect what she was actually doing down here? "About?"

As he sat down, he lightly tugged on her hand, silently urging her to take a seat, as well. "Anything you want."

Ramona sat down. She licked her lips, thinking about the fact that she'd skipped lunch today and her stomach was reminding her that it felt damn empty.

"How do we get out of here?"

"Monday morning, the time lock will be released," he told her patiently. She looked away. He saw the building panic in her face. "Look at me, Ramona. Look at me," he repeated more firmly but still kind. When she did, he continued, his voice reassuring, patient. "It's going to be all right. Fear is just a trick our minds play on us. This is a big room, just a big room, nothing more. Not a tomb," he said, looking into her eyes. "A room."

"Are you sure there's no way to get someone down here?"

"I'm sure. Everyone but the security guards is gone. We had an emergency earlier, but we managed to stabilize the woman enough to transport her and her husband to the hospital. She's resting comfortably now and, more important to her, she's still pregnant," he added.

He had a nice smile, she thought. Why hadn't she noticed that before? "You really are into this, aren't you?"

She had a way of hopping around from topic to topic. He wasn't sure what she was referring to. "Into what?"

"Making couples into parents."

"Yes."

She tried desperately to concentrate on the conversation. "Why?"

"Because I know that the people who come here to the institute, ready to give us their last penny, to borrow more if need be, just for the privilege of having a baby, will make wonderful parents. Because that's what being a good parent is all about. Sacrifice. Putting the child in front of your own needs. If it's in my power to help them, it would be unconscionable for me not to."

She nodded. "It must make you feel a little like God, doing that. Creating life."

"I'm not the one 'creating it,'" he protested. "And I certainly don't feel like God. If you want to follow the creation route, I'm just an instrument in all this. If God doesn't want it to happen, then nothing I do will make it so."

Ramona was quiet for a moment, reading between the lines. "So you've had failures."

He thought of the looks on the women's faces when he had to tell them that the procedure hadn't resulted in a pregnancy. Thought of the way his sister Olivia looked when she came into his office a couple of weeks ago, desperate. Each time he lost a battle, it took a piece out of him. "Sadly, yes."

She prodded a little further. "Then not every embryo takes?"

"No." He really wished it would. Each failure, to him, represented a child who would never be born. "That's a matter of record," he told her. His eyes held hers for a long moment. "Was that what you were looking for? The failures?"

The question had come out of nowhere and in her present state, she wasn't as prepared to answer as she should have been. She almost stuttered as she made the denial. "No, I told you, I'm doing a piece on the institute's history and—"

He cut her short. "I know what you told me." Paul moved in closer to her. "Now, I'm interested in the truth."

"I *am* telling you the truth," she protested, doing her best to sound indignant. She couldn't quite carry it off.

"All right," he allowed patiently, "then tell me the *whole* truth."

Maybe it was the claustrophobia kicking up another notch and stealing oxygen from her brain. For whatever reason, she felt she had to give him something more than she had. He was surprisingly too intuitive to be satisfied with her pat alibi.

He understood the bond between mothers and their children, she mused. Suddenly, she knew what piece of the truth to give him.

Taking a breath, and then another because the first didn't feel sufficient, Ramona began. "As it turns out, putting this in the 'truth is stranger than fiction' column, a couple of decades ago my mother donated her eggs to the institute."

He kept looking at her, wondering if she was fabricating this story on the spur of the moment. But a moment later, he decided that she looked too distressed to be making it up. Either that, or she was one hell of an actress. "And you're trying to find out if you have siblings?"

"Not exactly," she corrected. "I'm trying to save my mother's life."

Chapter Twelve

Paul's eyes met hers. On the scale of one to ten for dramatic statements, the one she'd just uttered was a ten. If she meant to capture his attention, she'd succeeded.

"I'm listening."

Ramona suppressed any last-minute doubts. What did she have to lose? He couldn't take her to task for being concerned about her mother, he wasn't the type. And if she gave him this, it might make him stop looking for other reasons why she'd ventured down here, quite apparently far out of her comfort zone.

Maybe he'd even help her find the file.

"My mother has leukemia. And it's progressing." She paused a beat to keep her voice from quavering.

"The doctor said she's going to die without a bone-marrow transplant." Ramona bit her lower lip. The pain in her voice was something she didn't have to fake. She experienced it with every word. "Mine's not a match. She has no brothers or sisters. Neither do I. At least, none that I knew about—" She took a breath. "And then I remembered."

"Remembered what?"

She told him just the way it happened. "That when I was a teenager, I stumbled across an old box of receipts and what looked like bills in the back of my mother's closet—I was looking for a pair of her shoes I wanted to borrow," she explained in case he was going to ask why she was rummaging through her mother's things. "Mixed in was a medical statement for a donation she'd made years ago. She donated her eggs to the institute." Her eyes were on his now. "I need to know if they were even used and if so, by whom and whether the implantation resulted in a viable birth."

There was silence for a moment, and then he shook his head. Ramona wondered if she'd set herself up for a fall. Had she been wrong about him after all? Was he strictly by the numbers with no heart?

"Why didn't you just tell me what you were looking for?"

"Because I had no idea what your reaction would be," she said honestly.

"Under the circumstances, did you really think I'd say no?"

"I didn't know you. If I asked and you said no, you might have decided to put safeguards in to prevent my looking. This was too important to take a chance on that. My mother's life depends on it."

She wasn't aware that she was crying until she saw Paul reach into his pocket and take out a handkerchief. Very gently, he took her chin in his hand and wiped away the tears that were sliding down her cheeks.

The movement was so delicate, so kind, Ramona could feel her heart swelling in her chest. None of her safeguards were in place.

Her eyes met his and their gazes held for what felt like eternity.

Again, she stopped breathing, but this time her fear of small, enclosed places had nothing to do with her response. Or with the sudden increased beating of her heart.

Without realizing she was doing it, Ramona silently willed him to kiss her. If she kissed him first, it would throw everything off. She didn't want seduction—because it would be seen as that—to be perceived as part of her arsenal in going after the evidence to substantiate her story and, in hindsight, that would be what Paul would think.

But if he kissed her, well, these things happened sometimes, especially under the unusual circumstances that they found themselves in.

The fact that she was willing him to kiss her had nothing to do with her ultimate goals was something she wasn't going to think about now.

* * *

Paul knew he shouldn't.

He was a grown man with better-than-average self-control. He always had been.

And maybe that was the problem. He'd used it so often, held himself in check in so many different ways—be it denial of his own desires, or simply holding his temper in check when it came to dealing with Derek—that something felt as if it was cracking inside him now. He wanted—*needed*—to break free. To act on these feelings and unexplored emotions that were rushing over him now.

Maybe it was the look in her eyes that finally pushed him over the edge. He really wasn't sure.

The pure, basic fact of the matter was that he slipped his fingers into her hair, framed her face with his hands and brought his mouth down on hers slowly enough for her to pull away if she so chose.

But she didn't pull away.

Instead, she offered herself up to what was happening, making the kiss between them flower into something far more powerful than what it was intended to be. It wasn't a kiss to console, or comfort, or support. Rather, it was something so powerful that it overwhelmed both of them.

Paul felt his control shatter and Ramona's lips met his own. Suddenly, passion and desire were all around him, urging him on, making him realize that he wanted her. Not just to hold, not just to kiss, but to have. He wanted to make love with her.

The last time he'd made love with a woman seemed light-years away; he couldn't even summon up a face, a name. Hell, right now, he realized, as fire raced through his veins, he'd have trouble summoning up his *own* name.

There was nothing and no one, only this woman whose very presence was sending him into an emotional tailspin. And that unnerved him.

Badly.

This was better, better than she'd even imagined. The taste of his lips excited her to the point that it took supreme effort not to begin tearing at his clothes. She couldn't return his passionate kisses, couldn't get caught up in the fever pitch that seemed to be sizzling between them. Because he would think she'd planned it all. And he'd hate her even more than he would once he found out who she really was.

The thought chilled her for a moment, but then her need to be with this man, to feel his hands on her, to have him come to the ultimate union with her, overwhelmed everything else. All she had was the moment and she meant to savor it for the thrill that it was. Later would have to take care of itself. She wanted Now.

A moment ago—or maybe a lifetime ago—they'd been sitting sedately next to each other on the sofa. Now their bodies were pressed against one another. The instant she felt his hands, pulling her blouse from her waistband, her fingers began to tug at his shirt, all but ripping away buttons as she yanked them through the buttonholes.

She could feel her breath growing shorter, but this time it wasn't because of any sort of panic. This time it was because of anticipation. Anticipation that blazed through her body like a wildfire as they discarded their clothes in a growing frenzy.

Paul couldn't believe this was happening, that he was really *so* immersed in this woman whose soulful eyes had gotten through his carefully constructed reserve.

But he had to regain at least a modest amount of control over himself, he thought fiercely. Though he felt the heat of her response, he had to be sure that he wasn't just forcing himself on her because her claustrophobia had rendered her defenseless. He wanted their joining to be mutual.

She was beneath him on the sofa, the movement of her body setting him ablaze. But he had to give her a chance to back out. So, with extreme effort, Paul pulled himself back just far enough to give her room to slip out from under him, and looked down into her face.

She was breathless, but it didn't bother her. She was that wrapped up in what was happening, that wrapped up in these extreme, delicious sensations that were holding her in their grip. And suddenly, the building crescendo halted like a video on pause.

She felt air along her skin as he created a space. Was he getting up? Now?

"Is something wrong?" she asked in a voice that was hardly above a whisper.

As she spoke, her breath trailed along his skin, tightening his groin. He wanted her with such an intensity that he almost broke.

"Wrong?" he echoed. "It's never felt this right," he confessed, even as he counseled himself to dole out his words sparingly.

She didn't understand. Her body was all but screaming for his. "Then why did you stop?"

He watched her lips move. It took everything he had not to press his against them. "Because I want to make sure you don't want to change your mind."

"We're taking a vote?" she asked incredulously.

The next moment, she heard him laugh, the sound rumbling along her abdomen and breasts, teasing her almost to the breaking point. Her core was moistening, aching to accept him. She didn't bother with words. Instead, she framed his face with her hands and brought his mouth down to hers.

Bathed in kisses that Paul pressed along her neck and shoulders, Ramona felt she was more than ready for him when Paul finally locked his fingers with hers and slowly entered her body.

Ramona gasped as the first forceful wave of a climax exploded through her. She began to move her hips frantically in order to reach the next plateau.

And then the next one.

By the time they reached the ultimate limit, they were both drenched, breathless and almost beyond exhaustion, but content.

She felt herself falling back to earth after what amounted to a surreal experience. Paul Armstrong was easily the very best lover that she had ever had. He had surprised her with his technique, his gentleness and his prowess. Ramona kept her arms wrapped around him. She was holding on so tightly that she didn't think she was ever going to release him.

And part of her didn't want to.

She didn't want this moment to pass. She didn't want the world, with its myriad complications, to descend on her, robbing her of this wondrous sensation.

But all too soon he was rolling off her, sitting against the arm of the sofa, leaving open space next to her. Ramona doubted very much that this was just a random choice on his part. He knew, she thought, knew that the other way would make her feel hemmed in and stir up her claustrophobia all over again now that the temperature of her blood was returning to normal.

As he looked at Ramona, Paul searched his brain, trying to find something reassuring to say. Something that would let her know that this wasn't the way he ordinarily behaved, even under these extraordinary conditions.

He wanted to apologize—but he was only sorry if she felt compromised in any way. Because, looking at it from his own point of view, he was as far from sorry as a man could possibly be.

But how could he express any of that without

sounding as if this had all somehow been carefully plotted out and rehearsed?

Paul began haltingly, clearing his throat. He got no further than whispering her name. "Ramona…"

Ramona pressed her index finger to his lips, silencing him. For some reason, she had a feeling she knew what he was about to say and she didn't want him to agonize over what had just transpired.

"I know," she murmured.

And she did. She'd found out everything she needed to know about what had just happened between them just by looking at him. It was there in his eyes. And it was enough for her.

He looked at her quizzically. "You do?"

Touching his cheek, she smiled at him. He could almost feel that smile radiating warmth within his chest. "Yes."

Was the woman a witch, or just good at second-guessing? He had to ask. "And what is it you think you know?"

Funny, she never thought of herself as being particularly insightful when it came to men, at least not on a personal level. When it came to breaking news, she could read them like a book. This was different. It was as if, having made love with him, they were connected on a deeper level.

"That you didn't plan this. That you don't generally do this kind of thing and that you want me to know that you weren't trying to take advantage of me."

Paul stared at her for a long moment. It stretched out so far that she thought she'd really overstepped the line this time. Maybe she'd gotten it wrong after all. Maybe he had just fooled her.

No, she silently insisted. He wasn't that kind of person. She had to be right about him.

And then he said, "When you filled out your résumé, under special skills, why didn't you put down mind reading?"

Yes, she was right after all. Pleased, Ramona grinned. Grinned from ear to ear before answering his question. "I didn't want to brag."

"I see."

Propping himself up on his elbow, he lightly swept her hair from her face. There was a feeling going through him. He couldn't really begin to describe it. The closest he could come to it was admitting to himself that he felt happy. Lighter than air and really, really happy. He'd never felt that way before.

"It would have been nice to be forewarned, though. I wouldn't have bothered talking as much as I did. You could have just read my thoughts."

She laughed then, shaking her head. "You consider what you did a lot of talking?"

"For me."

"I see."

Just looking at him, all she wanted to do was kiss him again. And again. And then follow that to its natural conclusion one more time. Maybe two.

Giving in to her impulse, Ramona bent her head and pressed a kiss just above his collarbone. The small, guarded sigh that escaped his lips as she did so thrilled her and fueled her inclination to repeat at least part of what had just gone before.

Pressing him back against the sofa, she shifted so that this time she had the upper position. It wasn't about first moves anymore. It was about enjoying each other while the rest of the world was still at bay.

Ramona wreathed his face and neck with a string of fleeting, light kisses that she dispensed with growing fervor.

As spent as he thought he was, Paul had no choice but to rise up and offer her a return on her investment.

They made love again and then again after a sufficient amount of time had passed, turning the small confined former vault into a miniparadise where each had found his soul mate, as temporary as that might turn out to be.

And during all this time, the one constant that remained was that Ramona forgot about her fears.

All she felt was wondrously alive.

Because of him.

Ramona hung on to that for as long as she could. And, without being aware of when and how it actually happened, she dozed off in his arms.

Chapter Thirteen

"Breakfast," Paul announced the next morning, his voice cutting through the last layer of sleep swirling in her brain.

Ramona blinked several times to focus. Somehow, Paul had managed to get up without waking her. He'd had to be part contortionist to have managed that feat.

He'd gotten dressed as well, putting on everything except his white lab coat. That, she now realized, he'd draped over her to give her some semblance of privacy.

Again, she was caught off guard by his thoughtfulness. There was so much more to the man than she'd originally thought.

Sitting up, holding his lab coat pressed against her,

Ramona looked at the energy bars that were in the palm of his hand. She couldn't remember anything ever looking so good to her. Controlling the impulse to grab them as her stomach all but moaned in its emptiness, she looked up at his face instead.

"Where did you get those?"

He nodded toward the worn, black leather object that had tripped her and set off this chain of events last night. "I forgot I had them in my briefcase."

"Anything else in your briefcase, like coffee? Or a shower?" she asked longingly. She could use both—and a toothbrush, she thought, running her tongue over her teeth.

Paul smiled and shook his head. "Sorry, just these two energy bars."

"Don't be sorry," she told him. And then a thought hit her. "Unless you're not planning on sharing them with me."

"Actually, you can have them both." Paul deposited the energy bars next to her on the sofa. "I'm really not hungry."

The hell he wasn't, she thought. He was just making that up so that she wouldn't feel guilty eating both bars. She might be incredibly hungry, but she still had a conscience.

"Oh, don't get all heroic on me. How can you not be hungry?" she wanted to know. "If you don't have something, you're going to start nibbling on the first thing you find—like me."

His smile widened. "Not completely without merit."

The bars were identical. Raspberry flavored with chocolate drizzled over them. She picked up the one closest to her. "I bet you say that to all the girls you fool around with in the vault."

The very memory made him smile more broadly. It took effort not to pick up where they had left off last night. "That would be a minuscule number—as in one."

Ramona smiled at that, and, as he'd already noted more than once, her smile seemed to light up the entire area.

She looked down at the lab coat. "I think I'd better get dressed before I start in on this little feast," she quipped, nodding at the energy bar.

"Right."

Before she could ask, Paul turned his back to her, allowing her a little privacy, even though what he *really* wanted to do was tell her that she didn't need to get dressed again. Just looking at her stirred up other hungers. He tried to think of other things.

And remembered. "You said something last night about looking to see if you had any siblings."

"Yes," she answered guardedly.

"You realize that means invading the privacy of former patients."

For a second, she stopped tugging on her blouse. She knew all about those ramifications, but her cause was too precious, too important to let those concerns make her back off.

Was Paul going to stand in her way after all? "Yes," she replied haltingly, watching his back.

"You're going to have to proceed very cautiously," Paul warned her. "Otherwise, you're going to be leaving yourself—and the institute—open to a lot of legal red tape, not to mention the possibility of being sued by former patients if you wind up approaching them."

She released the breath she was holding. He wasn't telling her not to do it, he was telling her to be careful.

"I understand." Gratitude mingled with relief all through her. "You can turn around now," she told him. "I'm dressed."

More's the pity. Paul's expression never gave him away as he faced her again. "All right then, let's get to it," he said.

She was left to wonder what "it" was for only the briefest of seconds. Paul crossed back to the files and she realized that he was going to help her look. Energy bar in her hand, she scrambled to her feet.

Guilt almost got the better of her. Guilt because she hadn't been completely honest with him about her intentions.

The photographs she'd been taking weren't meant to be used as background material for a feature highlighting the positive side of the Armstrong Fertility Institute's history the way she'd told him. They were to cast light on its dark side. On the practice of substituting viable eggs and sperm for the ones that would never successfully produce a healthy child.

"I need to know the name your mother used when she made her donation," Paul was saying to her as she joined him. "Plus the year the procedure was done and, if possible, the name of any doctor she might have had contact with at the institute." He looked at the boxes of files before him. "The information we're looking for could be filed under any number of names," he told her.

Despite her inner turmoil, at the moment Ramona was busy savoring the taste of the energy bar she'd just unwrapped. It took a great deal of control not to wolf it down in three bites, but she managed to hold herself in check.

"There was no doctor's name on the statement," she told him. "And I don't recall the date, but I do remember the year." She gave it to him. "And I remember that my mother had used her maiden name, which struck me as odd at the time. It was Katherine Donnelly." She pressed her lips together. "Not much to go on, but—"

Ramona stopped midsentence. Was that a noise behind her? Her heart leaped. If she didn't know any better, she would have said it sounded as if someone was opening the vault door. But that was probably just wishful thinking on her part.

Even so, she crumpled up the empty wrapper and ran toward the steel door, bracing herself for disappointment. Paul, she realized, was right behind her.

"You heard it, too," she cried.

He had no time to answer.

The door *was* opening.

In less than a heartbeat, Ramona and he found themselves looking at Derek. It was hard, Paul thought, to say who looked more surprised, him or his twin. While beside him Ramona cried a relieved "Thank God," both he and his brother echoed the same question.

"What are you doing here?"

Derek, though, followed up his question with another one. His brother looked from him to Ramona and made no effort to hide a knowing grin. "Did I just interrupt something?"

It was Ramona who immediately answered. "Yes, suffocation."

On the heels of that, Paul explained, "We got locked in." But he saw that it wasn't enough. There was suspicion on his twin's face, that and an expression that bordered on a smirk. He knew the way Derek's mind worked. His twin was a womanizer and saw the world in those terms. "I came down to find some old files I wanted to check out for a report I was writing. Ramona is a great researcher, so I brought her with me to assist."

Maybe it was a good thing that there was no breeze down here, Ramona thought, because if there had been, it could have knocked her over just now. She only barely managed to keep her surprise from showing as she stopped short of contesting Paul's words.

The man was protecting her reputation. Somehow,

without knowing it, she'd managed to stumble across an old-fashioned knight in shining armor.

"And you?" Paul was asking his brother. "Why did you come down here?"

Instantly, another smile popped up. Derek's smile was all encompassing—and fake. Paul knew his twin far too well to be taken in by it. Still, he didn't bother to challenge his brother when Derek told him, "I just wanted to see how far back the files in the archives went. I was curious," he ended a bit lamely. "Keeping up with files wasn't exactly Dad's forte."

Paul let that slide, as well. He'd ask Derek more questions when they were alone. He owed his brother the courtesy of that rather than cornering him in front of someone outside the family.

Derek deftly turned the conversation back on them. "How did you get locked in?"

He was looking at Ramona when he asked the question, Paul noted.

"Long story," Paul answered. "Right now, all I want is a shower and a change of clothes. And something to eat that doesn't belong in the granola family."

"Ditto," Ramona chimed in with feeling. She was already turning on her heel to leave. Paul was quick to fall into step beside her.

Derek hung back as they walked out. He deliberately waited until his brother and Ramona had boarded the elevator and the doors had closed, separating him from them.

Satisfied that they were gone, Derek got down to business.

There were secrets down here in the old files, he thought, secrets that had to be worth something to someone. If he had a choice, he wouldn't do this, wouldn't go this far. But he had no choice. He was desperate enough to use anything at his disposal, whether it was ethical or not. Because, in the long run, it meant his life.

"We didn't get the information you were looking for," Paul said to her once the elevator doors opened on the first floor.

Getting off, Ramona was acutely aware of that fact. "I know." She couldn't have exactly gone rummaging around with his brother standing there. "I'll go back as soon as I can if you don't mind, but right now, I just want to assure myself that the sun is still in the sky and I can take in as much air as I want."

He smiled and reminded her, "You could in the vault, too."

Considering that the circumstances could have contributed to a complete breakdown on her part, she had a lot to be grateful to him for. "Logically, yes. But being claustrophobic doesn't have anything to do with logic. I really want to thank you for helping me get through that ordeal in one piece."

She saw him smile again and marveled at how the expression completely transformed him. Gone was the somber chief of staff. In his place was the young, sensually attractive man he somehow managed to keep hidden during the normal span of the day. The man who had made love with her last night, who had made her forget her fears.

"It was a dirty job," Paul responded, tongue in cheek, "but someone had to do it." And then he sobered slightly, as if the topic he was about to bring up deserved a display of decorum. "When do you want to come back to look for your mother's records?"

She glanced at her watch. It was a little after nine in the morning. "Would one o'clock be all right?"

It was Saturday. He had no firm plans for today. Spending time with her would definitely brighten it. "Fine. I can pick you up at your apartment if you like—"

She hadn't expected that. "You're coming, too?" Ramona didn't even try to hide her surprise. Why did he want to come with her? Was it because he still didn't trust her?

Paul nodded in answer to her question. "Two sets of eyes searching through the boxes will cut your time in half."

Relief briefly passed over her before guilt set in. He was being noble again. God, he was going to hate her once the other shoe dropped.

The thought weighed heavily on her. Far more heavily than when she thought she was trapped inside the vault and her claustrophobia had bordered on becoming unmanageable. She didn't want to seem ungrateful, but she really did want to be in the archives alone. She hadn't finished researching the topics she was being paid to flush out.

"Are you sure I'm not taking you away from something?"

"Very sure."

Paul resisted the impulse to slip his arm around her shoulders and pull her to him just for a moment. He didn't want to crowd her, but he had to admit to himself that there was something special about her. Something he wanted to explore. He'd never felt like this before about a woman. He wanted to see if it was the beginning of something wondrous, or if, like those old songs that littered musicals more than half a century ago, it was "just one of those things" that would eventually just fade away.

He wasn't a man anyone could ever accuse of being impulsive, but he allowed impulse to take over now. "Want to stop somewhere for a proper breakfast?" he asked her.

It was on the tip of Ramona's tongue to say no. The more she got involved with this man, the worse her lie of omission was going to seem to him. He was going to be furious with her and she was certain that there was nothing she could say that would convince him that she wasn't trying to use him.

Because, initially, she had.

He's going to think that no matter what, she silently

argued. She might as well enjoy what little time she had with him before the earthquake hit.

Nodding, she said, "Sounds good to me."

"Then let's go." He ushered her toward the front entrance. "I know this really great place that's open 24/7. Food just like mother used to make. At least," he amended as they stepped outside the doors, "your mother."

She looked at him. Bits and pieces were falling into place and he was becoming progressively more and more human to her. A good man who didn't deserve to be betrayed. "Didn't your mother cook?"

He laughed shortly. "I'm not sure my mother could find the kitchen with a compass. She's a Stanton," he told her. "Stantons, according to my mother, were born above menial things like cooking and other family-involved enterprises. They had a social standing to maintain, charity balls to throw and attend."

Ramona could feel her heart going out to him. What a lonely child he must have been. More than ever she was grateful for her mother—and more determined than ever to find the information that might save her life. "I am so sorry, Paul."

He believed her. He hadn't said it to make her pity him. Paul shrugged her sympathy away. "When you do without, you don't know what you're missing."

The same, he added silently, could be said about lovemaking. His previous experiences had convinced him that lovemaking and everything that went with it was way too overrated. Without emotion, sex for its own sake wasn't satisfying for him.

But he didn't feel that way anymore, not since Ramona had all but knocked his socks off last night.

He stopped by his parking space. Since it was Saturday, the lot was nearly empty. Ramona's vehicle was parked several yards away. "Do you want me to drive, or do you want to follow?"

She wouldn't have thought that Paul was sensitive to this extent. He was giving her a choice. Ordinarily, she would have said that a man like Paul was accustomed to making decisions and giving orders without regard for other people's feelings.

God, was she ever wrong about this man.

And maybe, just maybe, all these rumors that were flying around about the Armstrong Fertility Institute, his "baby," were just that. Rumors. Baseless rumors.

At least she could hope.

"I can appreciate the fact that you haven't written up your notes yet into any kind of final draft, but what, exactly, *do* you have?" Walter Jessup's voice crackled over her landline.

Ramona felt her heart sink in her chest. This wasn't a conversation she wanted to have now, but she knew she couldn't put her editor off. That was why she'd picked up the phone despite having caller ID and seeing his name on the LCD screen.

Big mistake.

After sharing a prolonged breakfast with Paul and discovering that the man she'd made soul-satisfying love with was a fascinating man in so many different ways, she'd all but floated home, humming off-key and grinning like some silly, love-struck schoolgirl.

Love-struck. Good word, she thought with amusement. Softer than being struck by lightning, but just as powerful.

What a difference a few hours had made in her world, she'd mused with a sigh as she'd unlocked the door to her apartment.

The plan had been to take a quick shower, change and meet Paul back at the institute, where he was going to help search for her mother's file.

Which meant that she couldn't do any other research, but that was okay with her. Her mother took precedence over that.

But she couldn't come out and say that to the man who was presently losing his temper on the other end of the line. The man whose call she shouldn't have taken.

Ramona tried to placate Jessup as best she could. For better or for worse, he was, after all, her boss. "I went through their old files—"

Jessup's mood instantly shifted. "Fantastic! Knew you'd come through. And what did you find out?"

She stifled a sigh and did her best to sound as positive as she could without giving him anything. "I'm not sure yet. I just took pictures of a number of the files. I haven't had a chance to go through any of them yet." She crossed her fingers that that would be the end of it for now.

It wasn't. "E-mail the files to me," Jessup instructed.

"But I just said I haven't read them yet." That wasn't entirely true, but she didn't want to hand the man anything he could actually use until she sorted it—and her own feelings—out. "It could all be nothing. I've just got a few rough notes to go with my research."

"I understand all that," Jessup barked impatiently. "I also understand that I sign your paychecks and I'd at least like to see some kind of return for the money that's been invested in this project. Now, e-mail those damn photographs to me. Do I make myself clear, Tate?"

"Yes, sir."

He had a perfect right to ask. He did, as he said, sign her paychecks. But that didn't stop her from putting conditions on her cooperation. She owed it to Paul, not because she'd slept with him, but because it was the decent thing to do. In her rush to find her mother's file and to earn as much money as she could to help defray her mother's medical expenses, she'd almost forgotten the meaning of that word. *Decent.* Her mother would have been heartbroken if she'd known.

"All right, Walter. But you have to promise to let me do the story my way. Don't give any of this information to some third-rate hack out to do a hatchet job on the institute just because he can."

She heard the editor pause for a long moment. The

silence worked its way into her nerves. And then she heard him grind out the words "All right."

Ramona wasn't convinced. "Your word, Walter. I want your word."

There was no indication of any emotion, good or bad, in Jessup's voice. He said, "You have my word," as if he was reading the words off a cue card.

"I'm holding you to that, Walter."

"Fine. And I'll be on the lookout for those photographs. Be sure you send them, Tate." The threat in his voice was barely veiled. The next moment, Jessup broke the connection.

Ramona hung up the phone and went to her desk.

She couldn't shake the feeling that she was making a mistake as she sat, holding the small, plug-in camera in her hand, waiting for her computer to power up. But there was little else she could do. She was going to have to send Jessup the files.

Chapter Fourteen

It was a little over a week later when Lisa burst into Paul's office like a petite hurricane. He looked up, silently wondering if a refresher course on doors, doorknobs and their function in the scheme of things might not be out of order.

Any mention of that topic instantly died as his sister, looking angrier than he could recall seeing her of late, demanded, "Have you seen it?"

A quick search of his memory banks came up empty. "I might be able to answer that question better if I knew what you're referring to, Lisa," he said, deliberately using a calm voice and hoping it might rub off on her.

He'd just been contemplating asking Ramona to spend the weekend at a bed-and-breakfast he'd come across this morning while doing a little research. Paul sincerely hoped that his sister's tirade wasn't going to take too long or interfere with his plans.

Lisa contemptuously tossed a magazine on his desk. Paul looked at it and read its name. He was not unfamiliar with the periodical. "The latest issue of *Keeping Up with Medicine.* I must have my copy here somewhere." Picking it up, he offered her back her copy.

Lisa made no effort to take the magazine. Her expression was stony. "Obviously, you haven't read the table of contents."

"I haven't had the chance." An uneasiness began to weave through him although he couldn't quite pinpoint the source. "Why? What's in it?"

"Look at page thirty." Lisa was seething as she bit off the words.

Paul dutifully turned to the page in question. He wasn't prepared for what he saw. His heart all but stopped as the title of the article jumped out at him: Armstrong Fertility Institute: Answer to a Prayer, or Beginning of a Nightmare?

He quickly skimmed the first paragraph in silence. The tone of the piece told him that the article was strictly focused on character assassination. In short order, he scanned the title page and the last paragraph. There was no byline. Credit for the article went to Anonymous.

He could understand Lisa's anger, but his was compounded. He didn't want to think what he was thinking—but he couldn't help it.

Paul felt a fire burning a hole in his belly. Reining in his outrage, he looked up at his sister. His voice was low, dark. "Who wrote this?"

Lisa shrugged in frustration. "It doesn't say. I've already called the magazine, but they gave me the standard runaround. They 'can't reveal their sources,'" she told him. "Whoever this writer talked to knew a lot. They've got material in there that goes way back to when Dad was running this place." Lisa clenched her hands at her sides. "How did they *get* that kind of information?" she demanded angrily.

And then her eyes widened.

Paul was oblivious to the light that had suddenly come into his sister's eyes. Neither did he notice the shift in demeanor as she mumbled, "I've got an idea. I'll get back to you on this."

Lisa left far more quietly than the way she'd entered. Paul was lost in his own thoughts, entertaining his own set of suspicions. Suspicions that caused him to be, in turn, angry, furious and incredibly disappointed. He tried to tell himself to reserve judgment, not to jump to any harsh conclusions until he talked to Ramona.

But everything pointed to Ramona being the culprit.

He had walked in on her in the vault taking photographs of the files. Taking photographs, for God's sake.

All sorts of bells should have gone off when he saw

that. Industrial spies behaved that way, not company PR managers.

How obtuse could he have been?

Almost against his will, Paul followed his thinking to its logical conclusion—and he didn't like it.

Had everything been a lie? Had Ramona seen a way to use him, to placate him with her body so that he didn't ask her any more questions?

And that story about her mother, was it even real? Or was that just a product of her fertile imagination, created on the spur of the moment and fashioned out of something she'd noticed while going through the files?

He didn't want to believe it. But how could he *not* believe it? Sick at heart, he skimmed another two paragraphs in the article Lisa had brought to his attention.

This had Ramona's stamp all over it, he thought. Phrases jumped out at him. Phrases he'd heard her use.

Paul didn't want to dignify any of what he read in the article with a public denial, but he, Lisa and Derek were going to have to put their heads together and do some heavy-duty damage control here. The institute would suffer otherwise. For all he knew, it might already be too late. Coming on the heels of the formless rumors, this just might be a death blow.

He couldn't allow that.

Damage control. The thought struck him as ironic. Supposedly, that was what they had Ramona for, to implement damage control. But what they had actually done was to naively invite the fox into the henhouse.

He shook his head. Despite *everything,* he still wanted to believe Ramona wasn't responsible, that someone else was behind this. Someone with a vendetta against the institute or against his father or perhaps one of the three of them.

He was going to have no peace until he confronted Ramona with this article. No matter what the outcome, the sooner he got that over with, the better.

But first, he needed to check something out. Paul turned his chair to face his computer keyboard and began to type. Each strike of a letter cost him.

Ramona caught her lower lip between her teeth.

She reread the figures twice, then lifted the sheet on her desk to look at another spreadsheet that was just beneath it.

She wasn't wrong.

Wow. She hadn't even been looking for this when she started going through the files. The figures had caught her eye quite by accident.

There was a discrepancy.

A very large discrepancy.

No matter what she did, the tallies just didn't add up. Somehow, unaccounted for money was disappearing between spreadsheets. It wasn't obvious, but it was there, buried beneath invoices and laughable charitable write-offs. Laughable because a place like the Armstrong Fertility Institute didn't have charitable write-offs, it had A-list clients, some who came in through the front door, others who slipped in quietly via the "special" entrance, unwilling to let the public in on their private pain of infertility.

Here and there were Mr. and Mrs. Average American who had scraped together everything they had in order to obtain the one precious thing they *didn't* have: a baby. But none of the records, some of which went back over two decades, showed that any of the procedures were done pro bono. Everyone paid, some more handsomely than others, but everyone paid.

And yet, there were write-offs. How could that possibly be?

The word *embezzlement* popped up in her head in big, bold neon letters. It was a horrible thought, but it was the only explanation.

She had to tell Paul.

Derek might have been the one who hired her, but there was something about him that held her at bay, that didn't allow her to completely trust him. And as for Lisa, well, so far she hadn't gotten close to the woman, so the issue of trust hadn't been allowed to take root one way or the other.

But Paul was another matter. He'd gotten to her. Beneath his somber exterior was a kind, sensitive man who was also one hell of a lover. The corners of her mouth curved, remembering.

The doctor, bless him, was still trying to track down whoever had gotten her mother's eggs for her. The whole file was encoded to safeguard the recipient's identity, but Paul told her he was doing his best to get it deciphered. God knew he didn't have to go this extra mile for her, and yet he was. He understood what she was going through.

Which in turn made things very difficult for her.

Ramona sighed. She wanted to tell Paul what else she was up to, but she knew that the minute she made a clean breast of it, everything that had happened between them—that *was* happening between them—would be held suspect. And she would lose him.

And she couldn't even blame him.

Ramona drew in a ragged breath, wishing she'd never gotten involved in this investigation. But, in an odd way, if she hadn't, she would have never met the man who'd set her whole world on its ear and sent it spinning.

You can't miss what you never had.

Paul had told her that the evening when they'd gotten locked in the vault. And she knew that the converse was right, because if she ever lost him, she would be acutely aware of what she no longer had. Of what she'd lost. With all her heart she hoped she would never find out what that felt like.

And yet, how could she not? She just couldn't envision a happy ending to this.

Ramona heard the sharp rap on her door and hoped that whoever was standing on the other side would be quick about whatever they wanted. She wanted to talk to Paul as soon as possible.

She managed to successfully cover her impatience as she said, "Come in."

When she looked up and saw Paul walking in, her heart did a little dance in her chest. She wondered if she was ever going to be able to look at the man and not think of that night in the vault. It was almost as if she'd been born all over again that earthshaking night.

Paul was frowning.

It never occurred to Ramona that the frown was directed at her. She just thought that something had come up at work that displeased him.

Or maybe he had an inkling about what she'd just discovered. After all, he was an extremely intelligent man. Far more intelligent than she thought anyone gave him credit for because of his quiet demeanor.

Flashing a smile, she said, "I'm glad you're here, Paul. I was just about to come looking for you."

Yes, he just bet that she was. Undoubtedly to tell him another lie, or pump him for more information.

"Oh?"

There was something in his voice, something that didn't sound quite right, but she had no clue what it could be, so she plowed on.

"Yes, I found something you might be interested in." Ramona turned the spreadsheet around so that he could see it more clearly. "This was in the database," she explained, "but I printed it out. It makes it easier to follow. I work better with paper and pen," she added.

He wasn't looking at the spreadsheet in question.

He was looking at her. And still frowning. "Yes," he said darkly, "I know."

It wasn't her imagination. There *was* something wrong. She wanted to ask him what it was, but first, she needed to bring this matter to his attention. He needed to be made aware of it.

"I think someone is embezzling from the institute." He looked at her sharply. "Here," Ramona coaxed, "look at this." Pointing to one column on the first page, she then indicated another column on the second sheet. "Somewhere between these two points, this amount of money disappears. And this isn't the only place. It happens several times with different entries. I double-checked the figures, but the totals I come up with don't change." She leaned back in the chair, knowing this had to be hard for him to take in. "I think you're going to need to call in a forensic accountant."

For a moment, Paul wavered, not knowing whether to believe her. If she was right about someone embezzling funds, then this could be disastrous. It was tantamount to one more nail in the institute's coffin.

On the other hand, he reminded himself, this could just be another example of Ramona's artful camouflage, designed to draw all attention away from herself.

He knew what he *wanted* to believe, but that didn't make it true.

Ramona narrowed her eyes. Something was really off. "You don't seem very upset about this," she noted. "Am I wrong?"

That was when she noticed that he was holding a magazine in his hand, rolled up the way someone would when they wanted to kill an annoying insect that crossed their path.

"Have you seen this?"

Paul tossed the magazine on her desk, watching Ramona's face for her reaction. The initial surprise gave way to another expression. Guilt?

His heart froze.

Struggling to keep the extent of his anger under wraps, he pointed at the magazine. "I think you'll be particularly interested in the article beginning on page thirty."

Even before she opened the magazine, Ramona could feel her heart sinking in her chest like a clay pigeon that had been shot down. Her fingers felt almost numb as she turned to the page he told her.

Oh God, he did it. Jessup went ahead and wrote the article after I'd begged him not to.

She didn't have to read the article to know that it was slanted. She could see the truth in Paul's eyes.

How did she make this right?

She took a breath and began to plead her case. "Paul, I can explain—"

Pain shot through him. The last shred of hope that she was actually innocent of this died the second Ramona uttered those words. She *was* responsible.

And everything else that came before, and after, had been a lie.

"I don't want to hear it," he told her coldly, cutting

her off before she could start to weave another web to ensnare him. "I don't want to hear another lie. Just pack up your things and go." He saw her jaw slacken and fall open, but no words emerged. No further lies. "And I wouldn't put the institute on your résumé if I were you," he advised sarcastically. "Because I won't be giving you a letter of recommendation."

Oh God, he was hurt. And it killed her that she was the cause of his pain.

He had to hear her out. She had to make him understand, she thought frantically. "Paul, please, you have to let me explain—"

He couldn't allow it. Because he still cared. Still wanted to believe that this was all a mistake. That she hadn't betrayed him. And if he let her talk, he'd wind up being swayed.

Being made an even bigger fool of than he already was.

"No," he cut her off gruffly. "There's no point. I can't tell the difference between your lies and your half-truths."

"I *wasn't* lying," she cried, desperate to have him understand the situation that had developed. "I mean, I was, but that was only a small part of it. The rest of it, it was all true."

There was pain along with the contempt in his eyes. She was responsible for that. She had to make this right, to turn it around. But now, caught by surprise and shell-shocked, she couldn't even think straight.

"And why would you expect me to believe that?"

he wanted to know. "Just because you say so? I have your word for it, is that it?"

He was mocking her and he had a perfect right to, she thought. All she could do was answer his question as honestly as she could and pray that somehow it would work itself out. That he would believe her. She'd just been trying to do her job and earn some money. She had never planned on falling for him.

"Yes," she cried breathlessly.

"So I have the word of an artful liar," he reviewed coldly. "Is that what you're telling me?"

Every word that he said, every cold look in his eyes slashed at her heart. She reached for him, to make contact, to touch his arm, but he pulled it away. He wanted no part of her, she realized.

"Paul, I didn't—"

"Save your breath, Ramona." And then, to her surprise, he laughed shortly. "At least you gave me your right name, and if I'd had half a brain in my head—because my brother clearly didn't—I would have stopped to look you up on the Internet before ever agreeing to have you stay on."

His mouth curved in a humorless smile. Ramona braced herself. She knew what was coming.

"There were a number of reprinted articles on the Web with your name on them." Scanning them, he'd felt like an idiot. "You're quite the investigative journalist, aren't you?" His eyes narrowed as his mouth hardened. "You must have had a hell of a laugh at my expense."

Oh God, this was getting worse by the second. She would have given anything to undo it, to find just the right thing to say to make him believe her. But she had nothing. Nothing but the truth, which he didn't believe. "I didn't laugh at you, Paul. I never laughed. You opened my eyes—"

"Oh, please," he said dismissively. "Begging doesn't fit your image. By the way, that bit about your mother, that was a really nice touch. You *really* had me going there for a while." When he thought of the time he'd devoted on what amounted to a wild-goose chase… There was a reason he devoted himself to his work instead of socializing. He could depend on medicine. Trusting his instincts when it came to a woman only made him act like a fool. "I even tracked down that so-called sibling."

"Then there *is* one?" Her eyes widened. There was hope, real hope for her mother. At least this was going to turn out right. "Who?" Ramona cried.

"Oh, no." Paul shook his head. He wasn't about to get sucked back into her lies. "I'm not going to have you bothering some stranger just to continue with this charade of yours. Better luck next time," he retorted.

Turning on his heel, Paul walked out. He slammed the door in his wake.

Numb, Ramona stood there, frozen, the slammed door reverberating in her chest.

Chapter Fifteen

He began missing Ramona the moment he told her to leave.

It had been a week now. A week since the article in the medical journal had changed the steady, progressive path he'd been on. Not having Ramona in his life had created a melancholy within him that was becoming a greater and greater burning pain in his gut.

Waking, sleeping—what little he got of it these days—the pain was always there. Haunting him. Reminding him that she was gone.

He'd never gone through this kind of thing before, never cared enough about anyone to hurt the way he did now.

He would have thought, with all the turmoil that Ramona's article had created, that he wouldn't have time to feel anything except outrage. He, Derek and Lisa had all scrambled to release statements to the press that amounted to some very fancy damage control. It seemed to have taken hold and, for now, the furor was beginning to die down again.

Between that, doing a little investigative work of his own and seeing to his patients, two of whom had just discovered that they were finally, *finally* pregnant, he was busy enough this last week for three people.

It didn't matter.

He still missed her. The feeling was a part of everything he did, everything he thought. And a piece of him hoped, however irrationally, that there was some kind of explanation for what had happened. Hoping that the betrayal *wasn't* a betrayal but something else.

Yeah, like what? Face it, buddy, you were played. Now get over it and move on.

Paul knew that *that* would be the right thing to do, the smart thing, to move on with his life. But he just couldn't do it. What was he supposed to move on to? And how?

Sitting at his desk now, he glanced at his calendar. It had been years since he'd had a vacation. Maybe it was time for him to take one. But go where? Do what?

Wherever he went, he would be taking his malaise with him. That wasn't a solution.

It occurred to Paul that he didn't even have a close

friend to turn to, no one to vent to or share these jumbled-up feelings with. Despite the very short time they'd spent together, Ramona had been the one he'd talked to more than anyone, even more than the members of his family. They all expected things of him. She just wanted him to be *him*.

Yeah, right, so she could pull the wool over your eyes.

Enough with this pity party, he upbraided himself. He had work to do. There was no time to behave like a mooning adolescent. He was way too old for that.

Feeling lost and caged at the same time, it took Paul several minutes to realize that he was staring at a folder on his desk that he didn't recognize. Where had it come from? He was fairly certain that he hadn't placed it there, even though the space on his desk was far from orderly this week.

How long had that folder been there?

He was really losing it, Paul thought, dragging a hand through his dark, wayward hair. This *had* to stop. He had to get a grip.

Pulling the folder over, he opened it. Inside were two spreadsheets. He recognized them instantly. They were the ones that Ramona had tried to get him to look at last week. The day he fired her.

His first impulse was to sweep them into the wastebasket. Instead, after a moment of mental wrestling, he began going over the figures.

Ramona had been right, he thought darkly as he continued to review the spreadsheets. The figures *didn't* tally. If she hadn't pointed it out to him, he might have never even noticed the shortfall. He didn't focus on the money end of it beyond making sure that the department was properly funded to provide him with the things he needed to continue his work.

If he had noticed that they were short, he would have just chalked it up to a mistake and corrected it, maybe even funding it out of his own pocket. But the "mistake" occurred in several other places, affecting a number of totals.

Too many to be a coincidence. Someone was playing with the numbers, stealing the money. Why?

Briefly he considered the theory that Ramona was behind this. It could be just another smoke screen she'd set up to divert attention from what she was actually doing. But then he went back to the database where she'd gotten her original figures. Hitting File Stats showed him that no changes had been made to alter the figures during the time that Ramona had been working at the institute.

The data he was looking at had been input by someone else, someone who worked here before Ramona started. Someone who was robbing the institute and had been for what looked like several months now.

Paul stopped and rocked back in his chair, thinking. He was going to have to get someone more knowledgeable than he was to untangle all this and then hopefully track it down to the person who was responsible for the embezzlement.

There was no other word for it. *Embezzlement.*

He wouldn't even have known about this if not for Ramona.

He also wouldn't have been gutted and vivisected if it hadn't been for her, he reminded himself. And he, Derek and Lisa wouldn't have had to scramble to reverse the media's harsh opinion of the institute—and his father—if she hadn't written that damn article.

Oh hell, how stupid could one man be? he berated himself. He'd actually told himself, when he first saw the article, that she couldn't have written it. That she wasn't the type of person who could do something like this. She wouldn't have betrayed and used him this way

Well, obviously, she could and she did and wishing seven ways from sundown that she hadn't would not change a damn thing. *Now* it was time to move on.

He picked up the landline, about to tell his assistant to put a call through to Harvey Nordinger, a discreet accountant who could conduct an audit without arousing anyone's suspicions, when someone knocked on his door.

Paul replaced the receiver. The accounts weren't going anywhere, he'd make the call later. Maybe this was Derek to tell him if there'd been any further progress defusing the volatile situation the accusations in the medical journal had brought about.

Ever the optimist, he thought wearily. "Come in."

* * *

On the other side of the door, Ramona took a deep breath.

Here goes nothing.

Pasting a broad smile on her face, she swung open Paul's door and walked in.

Had she not had an iron backbone, the look on Paul's face would have destroyed her.

"Hello, Paul." She'd thought of addressing him by his formal title, but somehow, calling him "Dr. Armstrong" seemed artificial, especially after the moments—hours—they'd shared.

She did her best not to focus on the last part.

For a split second, when he saw Ramona in the doorway, his heart had skipped a beat. But then the memory of how she'd lied to him, how she'd used him, kicked in with the force of an angry mule.

It didn't help. He still cared about her.

Damn it, why was she here? He was too vulnerable to see her now—because he knew he wanted her badly enough to forgive her anything.

He couldn't have her talking her way back into his life. Not until he could think clearly.

"Get out," he told her.

Rather than comply, Ramona calmly looked at him and said, "No, I won't." Just before she turned around and locked the door. "Not until you hear me out." Taking the key out of the lock, she underscored her statement by slipping the key down the front of her blouse.

Did she think he wouldn't go after the key there? Or was she hoping he would? "That's a little melodramatic, don't you think?"

"Maybe." She patted the region between her breasts, pushing the key against her skin. "But I also know you're gentleman enough not to try to retrieve it."

His eyes narrowed as he envisioned the key's hiding place. "Don't count on it," he warned.

Actually, there was very little she wanted as much as having his hands on her right now. The only thing that trumped that was the desire to make him listen to her—that and getting him to forgive her.

She shook her head. "I know you better than you know yourself." She took an envelope from her purse and placed it on his desk.

He eyed it, but made no attempt to reach for the envelope. It remained where she'd placed it. "What's this?"

"A signed and dated statement from my mother's doctor that he diagnosed her with leukemia six months ago." Why wasn't he picking up the envelope? Did he think it was a trick? "Dr. Richard Sanger is one of the best oncologists in the state." She raised her eyes to his. "If you don't believe him, I also brought along a copy of my mother's lab work. It's all there."

This time, the envelope she took out of her oversize purse was a thick manila one that made a small *thud* when she dropped it on his desk.

"I wasn't lying to you. My mother *is* seriously ill

and she *does* need a bone-marrow transplant. I took this assignment because I needed the money and because I needed to find out if she had any other children I could reach out to." She took a breath, trying to subdue the building panic she felt. "I don't have much time."

She was handing him the proof on a silver platter. The last of his unfounded hope splintered. "So you did write the article in that journal."

"No," she insisted. "My editor wrote it. When he called to see how far along I was and I told him I'd only taken photographs of the files, he made me send him the photographs and my notes. I told him I'd only do that if he didn't have someone else write the article. I also told him I needed time to separate fact from rumor. He gave me his word he wouldn't have anyone else write it." Anger entered her voice as she continued. "Technically, he pointed out when I called him on this, he'd kept his word. He wrote the article himself."

Paul's frown deepened. "Potato, po-tah-to," he concluded sarcastically.

Ramona laughed shortly. "That's what I said to him when I gave him back his advance—and quit."

That surprised him. "You quit?"

She knew he wouldn't believe her. That was why she'd brought proof. "You want to see the letter of resignation?" As she asked, she began digging through her purse. "I can't work for someone I can't trust."

Getting up, Paul rounded his desk and put his hand

on hers, bringing her search to an end. "That won't be necessary. I believe you."

Suspicion, created out of fear, warred with relief. She raised her eyes to his again, searching to see if he was telling her the truth. "Why now?"

"Because you were right about there being monetary discrepancies. Because I've already called around, making inquiries, and found out that your mother's on the transplant list." It had taken calling in a string of favors, something he'd never done before. It had also taken bending a few rules, something else he'd never done before. But this was for a woman who, God help him, he loved.

She would have rather that he'd believed her on his own, without searching for proof, but she couldn't exactly blame him, seeing as how she had come to work here with a hidden agenda, determined to substantiate the rumors about unethical practices conducted at the institute.

Renewed hope suddenly flourished through her. "Does that mean that you'll give me the name of my mother's child?"

"I don't know the name," he told her, and her heart sank. "But I do know the name of the family."

Paul was being literal, she realized. He'd thought that she was asking him for a first name. That was only of secondary importance. Where she could find this sibling was what came first.

"Oh, thank God. What is it?"

First things first, he schooled himself. "Before I tell you that, I have to tell you that you might have been right."

Thoughts were swirling in and out of her head, making it hard for her to concentrate. Making it even harder to follow what he was saying without some kind of cue card. "About what?"

"About misconduct going on. Not now," he quickly amended because he didn't want her to think that he was in any way responsible for it, "but during the years when my father ran things."

This wasn't easy for him. There was no love lost between Paul and his father, but he'd always had the utmost respect for the man as a physician and as a pioneer in his field. What Gerald Armstrong had done to up his success rate, to forge a reputation as being *the* person to come to in order to solve infertility problems, cast a dark shadow across all his true accomplishments.

"From what I could ascertain, the recipient of your mother's 'donation,'" Paul said delicately, "had no knowledge that her own eggs weren't being used. According to the records, the recipient couldn't produce healthy, viable eggs. But she had been adamant about having my father use her eggs along with her husband's sperm to create an embryo. From what I saw in my father's notes, he knew if he did, the procedure was doomed to failure. So he made a substitution without telling either her or her husband. The result," he told her, "produced a little girl—and a great many generous monetary donations to the institute over the years."

She only wanted to know one thing. "And their name is?"

He hesitated for only a moment, his dedication to the patient's right to privacy warring with his desire to possibly save the life of her mother. Life won out over privacy.

"Welsh. Hayden and Estelle Welsh."

Her eyes widened as the information sank in. "The New York Welshes?" she cried, stunned. "As in richer-than-Rockefeller Hayden and Estelle Welsh?"

Paul nodded. "The very same."

She closed her eyes for a moment, both overjoyed to finally discover that she had a sibling, someone who might be able to save her mother, and at the same time significantly daunted—because approaching this young woman who had grown up believing that Estelle Welsh was her biological mother was not going to be easy. The young woman had absolutely no idea about her real origins. Most likely, she would think she was being lied to for financial gain.

But to save her mother's life, Ramona was more than willing to walk through the very gates of hell if she had to. Cornering an heiress should be a cakewalk in comparison.

"Thank you," Ramona said with sincerity. She knew that telling her had to cost him. He had gone against his principles. "Thank you for tracking all this down for me—for my mother," she amended, since she had a feeling he was still angry at her for her initial deception. For not trusting him enough to be honest from the start.

She couldn't read the expression on his face. Was he still angry, or had he gone on to indifference? She wasn't sure which was worse.

Taking a breath, she knew she couldn't leave until she told him everything. "I just want you to know, I never meant to hurt you. And I never meant to fall in love with you," she added in a much lower voice, saying it almost to herself. "It just happened."

A flicker of surprise came and went from his eyes, but he gave no other indication that he had even heard her. "There's more," he told her.

Ramona's face lit up with hope. "More siblings?" she asked eagerly.

She'd misunderstood, he thought. "No. But I managed to pull a few strings." He wasn't about to go into any detail as to what favors he'd called in. That was for him to know, not her. "Your mother's at the top of the recipients list now."

Tears instantly filled her eyes as Ramona steepled her fingers before her lips to keep the sobs back. Pulling herself together, she murmured a heartfelt, if perforce, very quiet "Thank you." Blinking back tears, she reached down her blouse into her bra and drew out the key she'd hidden. She held it out to him. "I guess you'll be wanting this now."

He took the key from her. Contact with her skin had

made the metal warm. Paul closed his fingers around it, savoring the heat.

"There's no hurry," he told her. "The door can stay locked a little while longer."

A ray of sunshine stirred inside her. She told herself not to entertain any false hopes. But, being the optimist she was, she couldn't help it. "Oh?"

He answered her question with a question of his own. "Were you serious just then?"

"I was completely serious about everything I said," Ramona told him solemnly. "What part are you referring to?"

There was a hint of a smile on his lips. "The part where you said you fell in love with me."

Had she made a mistake, letting that slip out? Paul probably felt as if she was putting him on the spot, cornering him. "I'm sorry. I didn't mean to make you feel uncomfortable—"

His eyes held hers as he cut her off. "Did I say I was uncomfortable?"

"No, but—" This time she was the one who stopped herself abruptly. "Paul, where is this going?" She knew where she wanted it to go, but she couldn't read her own feelings into his words. It would be too disappointing when she turned out to be wrong.

"I don't know yet," he admitted, measuring his words out slowly. "I've never been in this kind of situation before." Sitting on the edge of his desk, he put his hands on her hips and drew her to him. "Although, when two people feel like this about each other, it usually ends with some kind of ceremony," he theorized, and then added, "generally a wedding."

Ramona's mouth fell open.

She'd come here to try to convince him to forgive her. This was something she hadn't even contemplated because she felt it was too far out of her reach. "A wedding?" she echoed.

He was going too fast, Paul thought. But that was because he had no experience with this. The proper way to conduct a relationship, the proper way to do *anything* with a woman was really out of his realm of expertise.

"I'm not rushing you," he assured her quickly. "We'll take it one step at a time. But I want to warn you that I mean to do everything in my power to convince you to say yes." The more he talked about it, the more right it felt to him. "Being with you made me see that the world comes in colors, not just black and white. I want you with me forever, Ramona, so that I never take myself so seriously that I forget why I'm doing all this again."

She couldn't begin to find a word for the way she felt, but *stunned* would have to do until she came up with something better.

Her head was spinning. "Are you asking me to marry you?"

"Yes. No," he said almost immediately after he'd said yes. "Eventually," he finally amended. "When you get used to the idea."

Ramona grinned and her eyes began to shine. "I'm used to it," she declared.

He'd expected that convincing her to marry him was going to take a few months, not a few seconds. "Really?"

"Really," she murmured just before she offered up her mouth to his.

He took the hint instantly.

* * * * *

Don't miss the next story in the new Cherish™ continuity, THE BABY CHASE.
Olivia Armstrong made the perfect match when she married junior senator Jamison Mallory. The only thing missing from their picture-perfect life is the baby they both desire. Will the Armstrong Fertility Institute be the answer?
Don't miss
The Family They Chose
by
Nancy Robards Thompson.
On sale February 2011

LOVE AND THE SINGLE DAD

BY

SUSAN CROSBY

DID YOU PURCHASE THIS BOOK WITHOUT A COVER?
If you did, you should be aware it is **stolen property** as it was reported *unsold and destroyed* by a retailer. Neither the author nor the publisher has received any payment for this book.

All the characters in this book have no existence outside the imagination of the author, and have no relation whatsoever to anyone bearing the same name or names. They are not even distantly inspired by any individual known or unknown to the author, and all the incidents are pure invention.

All Rights Reserved including the right of reproduction in whole or in part in any form. This edition is published by arrangement with Harlequin Enterprises II B.V./S.à.r.l. The text of this publication or any part thereof may not be reproduced or transmitted in any form or by any means, electronic or mechanical, including photocopying, recording, storage in an information retrieval system, or otherwise, without the written permission of the publisher.

This book is sold subject to the condition that it shall not, by way of trade or otherwise, be lent, resold, hired out or otherwise circulated without the prior consent of the publisher in any form of binding or cover other than that in which it is published and without a similar condition including this condition being imposed on the subsequent purchaser.

® and ™ are trademarks owned and used by the trademark owner and/or its licensee. Trademarks marked with ® are registered with the United Kingdom Patent Office and/or the Office for Harmonisation in the Internal Market and in other countries.

First published in Great Britain 2011
Harlequin Mills & Boon Limited,
Eton House, 18-24 Paradise Road, Richmond, Surrey TW9 1SR

© Susan Bova Crosby 2010

ISBN: 978 0 263 88855 3

23-0111

Harlequin Mills & Boon policy is to use papers that are natural, renewable and recyclable products and made from wood grown in sustainable forests. The logging and manufacturing processes conform to the legal environmental regulations of the country of origin.

Printed and bound in Spain
by Litografia Rosés S.A., Barcelona

Dear Reader,

It's probably obvious to say that I've never created a hero I didn't totally, absolutely adore. Why would I write any other kind of man? They've all shared certain characteristics: honesty, loyalty, kindness, intelligence, wit. Who doesn't want all that in a hero—or a human being, for that matter?

But a fictional hero needs to be more than what's expected. He's generally a man who accepts huge challenges and takes the necessary risks to meet them. He needs drive and guts above and beyond the average.

Donovan McCoy is such a hero. He's worked hard and achieved success professionally, but where has that gotten him personally? Then, at the peak of his career, Donovan discovers he's a father. Now what? What constitutes success now? How does he balance work and home? It's an issue that many parents battle, whether married or single.

I hope you enjoy Donovan's journey to discovering what's really important in life, and how he goes about achieving it.

Susan

Susan Crosby believes in the value of setting goals, but also in the magic of making wishes, which often do come true—as long as she works hard enough. Along life's journey she's done a lot of the usual things—married, had children, attended college a little later than the average coed, and earned a B.A. in English, then she dove off the deep end into a full-time writing career, a wish come true.

Susan enjoys writing about people who take a chance on love, sometimes against all odds. She loves warm, strong heroes; good-hearted, self-reliant heroines; and will always believe in happily ever after.

More can be learned about her at www.susancrosby.com

To Patti Rueb with gratitude for your ego-boosting notes, and your friendship.
And Robin Burcell, yet again. You know why.

Chapter One

Donovan McCoy tossed his duffel bag into his rented SUV, then ran a mental checklist of his briefcase contents—e-ticket, passport, voice recorder, laptop, cell phone. Chargers? He needed to double-check that he'd gathered all of them. An hour ago he'd added a stack of Internet research to pore over during the flights. Last night he'd said goodbye to his family at a farewell barbecue, thirty-two goodbyes, to be precise, from his eighty-nine-year-old grandmother to his two-month-old niece.

The McCoy clan knew how to throw a party.

Donovan shut the car door with more force than necessary. He was on edge this morning. Not wanting to analyze why, he strode back up the walkway to his brother's house. A car pulled up, a shiny red Miata, the convertible top down to take advantage of the warm July day.

"I hear you're leaving," the driver called out.

Laura Bannister. He'd managed to stay in town for two months without any one-on-one conversations with her. Intentionally. Their long-ago-but-brief history amounted to a single event when she was a freshman in high school and he was a senior. She'd made him an offer he'd been smart enough to refuse, but had regretted his decision ever since. Even though fifteen years had gone by, the memory hadn't faded.

Donovan ambled over to her car, studying her as he went. Her hair was down, rare for her, and wind-tossed, even rarer. He'd never seen her looking anything but perfect—sedate, elegant and neat. Her wild look wasn't the image he wanted stuck in his head from now on, not this accessible, sexily messy woman with the ash-blond flyaway hair, her trendy sunglasses hiding eyes he recalled were hazel and always direct.

He rested an arm on the top of her windshield, checked out her white shorts and pink tank top. Her nickname around town was "The Body."

"It's Tuesday and you're not working, Laura?"

"I'm playing hooky."

"Hell froze over? Pigs flew?"

She gave him that look, her lawyer look, the one that set a person in his place. He'd always found it sexy.

"So, where are you headed this time?" she asked.

"I'm going to mosey down Mexico way. Do a follow-up on the article I did last month for *NewsView.*"

"Is it risky?"

"Guess I'll find out."

She shoved her sunglasses up into her hair and squinted against the sun. "Your family loved having you home for so long."

"I'm sure Joe'll be glad to have his house to himself again." His brother hadn't said anything, but Donovan figured he'd overstayed. Which might be a clue that he shouldn't wait another twelve years to take a vacation and be in such need for time off.

"You're probably right," Laura said. "I've lived alone for so long, I'm not sure I could ever adapt to sharing space with someone."

"You and me both." He was glad they hadn't had this conversation anytime in the past two months. He didn't want to discover anything in common with her. She was five foot eight, shapely, stunning and smart—a deadly combination, the kind of woman he went for. And a complication he didn't want….

Because she was from here, Chance City, his hometown, the place he'd left behind without regrets the day after high-school graduation fifteen years ago.

"I should let you get on the road." Laura settled her sunglasses back in place and grabbed the gearshift knob.

He tapped the windshield to get her attention.

"What does Laura Bannister, ex-beauty queen and attorney-at-law, do when she plays hooky?"

"Just that—I play. It's a day of self-indulgence. I had a massage, and now I'm going to go home, take a swim, then stretch out on a lounge chair and read something other than case files."

An image flashed in his mind, based on an old e-mail from his brother Jake. "I heard about the bikini you wore at a Labor Day party last year."

"Did you?" Her mouth curved into the sexiest smile he'd ever seen, her lips glossy and pale pink. "Well, I don't bother with a swimsuit at home. Too confining. Bye, Donovan. Be safe."

He decided not to stare after her like a randy teenager as she drove off, although he felt like one, so he went inside to make a final check of the house. From the dining-room table he picked up a copy of a photo his nephew had taken of the whole family at the barbecue last night. The teenager had rushed home and printed copies for everyone, had even put Donovan's in a travel frame, now tucked away in his duffel. People always had a hard time believing he had five sisters, two brothers and seventeen nieces and nephews. Now he had proof to show.

It'd been a good couple of months, especially spending time with his brothers. Jake, older by four years, had gone fishing with him, like the old days. Joe, younger by three years and the baby of the family, had become a man—probably long ago, but Donovan had finally spent enough time with Joe to recognize his maturity.

And his loneliness. But that was for Joe to figure out.

With nothing left to do, Donovan poured himself a to-go cup of coffee, checked his briefcase for the chargers, then headed out. The phone rang. He debated whether to let it go to Joe's answering machine. Most people called his cell phone, so it was probably a telemarketer.

But because Donovan was in stall mode, he picked up the phone.

"Oh, good, I caught you in time. This is Honey." The forthright woman owned the Take a Lode Off Diner, the local gathering place where truth and gossip mingled freely, but he couldn't hear the usual diner noise in the background.

"I'm headed to the airport right now, Honey. What's up?"

"There's a woman here at the Lode looking for you."

"Who?"

"Didn't catch her first name. Blond. British. Last name sounded like Bogart, maybe?"

"Bogard," he corrected automatically. Anne Bogard. What the hell was she doing here, especially after all these years without contact?

"Donovan? Are you there?"

"Yeah." Now what? "What did you tell her?"

"That I would see if you'd left town yet."

He should trust his instincts and ask Honey to say

she hadn't caught him. But curiosity—and something even stronger—changed his mind. "Send her here to Joe's, please, Honey."

"Will do."

Donovan shoved his hands in his pockets, memories assaulting him. He and Anne had ended their relationship over five years ago. They'd both been covering the war in Afghanistan, both freelance photojournalists working as close to the front lines as possible. It was where he'd made his name, garnering credibility and a few awards, opening up his world, personally and professionally.

The breakup with Anne had been bitter, neither of them willing to compromise their blossoming careers for a personal relationship. He'd seen her name on a byline now and then, but her career hadn't gone the same way as his. He took every chance in the book. She played it safe, for several years writing character pieces, and articles about members of royalty from all over Europe, but nothing at all lately, not that he'd seen. A far cry from their time dodging missiles.

He was over her. Had been over her for a long time. Yet his heart pounded when he saw a dark blue sedan park in front of the house. Should he wait for her to knock? She knew he was home and waiting for her, so it hardly made sense to stay inside.

He opened the front door, stepped out.

Her car door swung open—

Not Anne. It was Millie, Anne's mother. She raised her hand, gave a tentative wave.

Dread curled inside Donovan, burning hot. If Millie had come all the way from Great Britain to see him, the news couldn't be good.

On autopilot, he kept moving down the walkway as she came around the front of the car.

"Hello, Millie," he said, questions rushing through his mind.

"Donovan. You're looking well."

She hugged him, sending all that red-hot dread skittering through him. She wasn't a hugger. It had taken him a while to get used to, because his mother hugged everyone, long and hard.

He waited, mind whirling, pulse racing, heart thundering.

"I'll tell you straight out, then," she said. "Anne died last month."

His world tilted. "What happened?"

"Lymphoma. She fought it for a long time."

Shock hit him, followed immediately by grief. She'd been so beautiful, so vital. "I'm very sorry, Millie. She was an incredible woman."

"Yes, she was." She paused. "I suppose you're wondering why I've come."

He nodded, especially since he was rarely here, had never given out this address as his.

She looked ready to speak, then clamped her mouth shut. "I'll just show you, then."

She opened the back door of the car and held out

her hand. A child emerged. A boy. With black hair and blue eyes.

Like me, Donovan thought, as Millie confirmed it out loud.

"This is your son, Ethan."

Chapter Two

Donovan brought Millie a mug of tea and Ethan a glass of milk, then set a plate of his mother's home-made chocolate chip cookies on the coffee table.

Ethan. His son. A son he'd been denied for almost five years.

Why? What possible reason could Anne have had to keep his own son from him?

"Had enough time to get used to it?" Millie asked Donovan as he joined her on the couch. Ethan played quietly with race cars from Joe's toy cupboard, but looked up now and then at Donovan, his gaze serious. So far, the boy hadn't said a word.

No, Donovan hadn't had enough time yet, but he

needed answers. He leaned toward Millie. “Does he talk?”

“Oh, yes. He’s a regular chatterbox, that one. He’s had a long day, that’s all. Give him a little time, and he’ll be right as rain.” She sipped her tea. “Lovely, thanks.”

“Don’t you think we should discuss this privately, Millie?”

“Perhaps you should read the paperwork first.” She passed him a portfolio a couple of inches thick, filled with folders and envelopes. “I’d start at the top. It’ll make more sense that way.”

Because he needed to know the big picture before the details, he sifted through the folders and envelopes to determine the contents. He found legal documents—Anne’s trust, Ethan’s birth certificate with Donovan’s name listed as father, Anne’s birth certificate. One envelope held a journal, the first entry being the day she learned she was pregnant. The final entry on Mother’s Day, two months ago. Another envelope contained pieces of Ethan’s artwork and crafts, from first scribbles to more complex collages.

“There’s more,” Millie said. “In my suitcase.”

Ethan had put away the race cars and was now building a tower with interlocking plastic squares. His mouth was set in concentration, a dab of chocolate at one corner.

Finally Donovan went back to the beginning and opened the first envelope in the stack, a handwritten letter from Anne. He closed his eyes for a moment, then began to read.

Dear Donovan,
I know you will never forgive me for not telling you I was pregnant, and then keeping Ethan from you. I didn't want a part-time father for my son, especially a father who accepted all dares and took all risks, one who journeyed far and wide to tell the truth to the world.

I'd wanted the same kind of career for myself, as you know, but I gave that up to become a full-time parent, something you wouldn't have done. I wanted Ethan to have stability, so I chose to raise him myself. Consistency is critical for a child.

As he got older I changed my mind, mostly because my mother begged me over and over. So, I was going to involve you, I promise you that, but then I was diagnosed with lymphoma. It changed everything. I needed to make memories with my son so that he would remember me. I couldn't do that and share him with you at the same time. My mother has photo albums for you, and we shot lots of videos.

Please keep my memory alive for him. And please stay in touch with my mother so that Ethan will continue to know her. You have a large family, which will be a boon for him, particularly while you're on assignment, but Mum needs to be part of that family, too.

Finally, I hope you prove me wrong, that I've worried for no reason. I almost asked my mother to keep Ethan, maintaining the consistency he needs, because I'm afraid you'll let someone else in your family raise him. I know how much your career matters. Your search for truth and justice has driven you to places most nonmilitary people never go. I've seen your scars, both physical and emotional. It's a young man's game, and you're still young. I don't see you giving it up like I did. But Ethan has already lost me. I hope you keep that in mind while deciding what to do next.

Thank you for the gift of my son. He made my life worthwhile.

We were both too selfish, Donovan.

Anne

Donovan folded up the paper and slipped it back into the envelope. Selfish? About what, his career? That was true. He wouldn't have been selfish about his son, however. She hadn't given him a chance to show that. She'd been the selfish one. And she was right—he would never forgive her for that.

"Questions?" Millie asked.

He nodded. "But I want to read everything thoroughly first. You're not going to rush off, are you? I need to talk to a lawyer. You might be needed."

"I wouldn't drop him off and leave. He needs transition time. He's become quite attached to me, as you can imagine."

An anchor in a swirling sea. Yes, he could imagine any child needing that. "How would you feel about staying with my mother? I can get you a motel room, if you'd rather, but—"

"In for a penny, in for a pound," she said cheerfully.

He smiled for the first time since she'd driven up. "Exactly."

"I'd like to know the people my lad will be spending his life with, so a couple of days would be grand. If you're quite sure your mum won't mind."

"If I took you to a motel, she'd just drive up and get you, so, yes, I'm sure she won't mind. I'll stay at Mom's, too. This is my brother Joe's home. I don't have a house here in town." He gestured toward the stack of paperwork. "His birth certificate says he was born in Maine."

"Anne didn't plan it that way. She was there on a job interview to teach at the university since her writing wasn't going to pay the bills entirely, but she went into labor. He was a month premature."

"I thought women couldn't fly in their last trimester."

Millie cocked her head.

"I've got five sisters. I hear things," he said, trying to make light of it. But it was typical of Anne that she'd taken such a risk. She'd probably convinced some doctor to give his approval.

"Well, you know Anne," Millie said, echoing his thoughts. "She ended up getting the job and staying on."

"Why would she choose Maine, of all places?"

"She said it was because you wouldn't think to look for her there."

That confused him. "With very little digging, I could've found her. I saw her byline occasionally. I could've contacted her publisher."

"But you never did, did you? Maybe she wanted you to find her, I don't know. Why didn't you come looking for her?"

"Because it was over."

"It didn't occur to you to find out if she was pregnant after you split up? You'd been together quite a while."

Six months. Long enough to have fallen hard for her, but not long enough for her to feel the same. "It never would've occurred to me that she wouldn't contact me to say she was pregnant." *Selfish.* He had a feeling that word was going to come up a lot.

He focused on Millie then. "My mom and grandmother drove to Sacramento this morning, but they'll be back in a few hours. Would you mind staying here while I go talk to my lawyer? I'll let my brother know, so he doesn't come home to find you without warning."

"That would be all right."

He walked over to where Ethan was playing, his tower a couple of feet tall and wobbly. His child, and he hadn't even touched him.

Donovan laid a hand on Ethan's shoulder. The boy jerked back a little, and Donovan quickly released him.

"I'm your father."

Ethan nodded.

Love rushed through Donovan, a powerful need to protect this sad, worried child of his. "I'd like to give you a hug," he said, trying to keep his voice steady.

Ethan looked at Millie, who smiled and nodded. "Go on, then, love. It's okay."

Still Ethan hesitated.

"Maybe later," Donovan said, disappointed but understanding. "I have to go somewhere for a little while, but I'll be back. I promise I'll be back. If you want to rest, there are two bedrooms. You can use either one. Or you can just keep playing."

"I'll play, thanks. These toys are wicked fun."

Donovan laughed at the New England term, although said with a slight British inflection. "Yes, your uncle Joe has a wicked-good toy cupboard."

He wrote down his cell phone number and gave it to Millie; then he escaped.

Escaped. There was no other word for it, he thought, as he got into the car he was supposed to return today. He needed to cancel his flight, too. He did that as he drove, then called Joe but only got his voice mail.

"Hey, it's me. Listen, I haven't left town. Something came up. Give me a call as soon as you get this. Thanks."

He pulled up in front of Laura Bannister's house. Knowing she was probably in her backyard sunbathing—without a confining bikini—gave him a little bit of mental distraction from thinking about how his life had just been turned upside down and then spun on its axis.

Because everything had changed. Everything.

Donovan sat in his car, trying to right himself. The spinning slowed, as did his heart rate. He'd been trapped by enemy fire more than once, and this felt just as terrifying.

He wished he had Laura's home number. He could get her office number, but that wouldn't help. So he walked to the blue-painted front door and rang the bell. After a few seconds, he tried again. One more time.

The door opened. She must have looked through the peephole because she didn't show surprise. Her face was pink from the sun. Her skin gleamed with sunscreen and sweat. She wore a pink-flowered shift with skimpy straps over bare shoulders, which meant she really had been sunbathing in the nude. Too bad he didn't have the time or inclination to let his imagination take that picture and run with it.

"Donovan?"

He said the words out loud for the first time. "I have a son."

Chapter Three

Laura gauged the tension in Donovan's body, the restrained emotion in his eyes, and invited him in.

"Grab something cold from the refrigerator," she said, gesturing toward the kitchen. "I need to change."

He headed that way. She rushed into her bedroom, pulled on a pair of cropped pants and a blouse, twisted her hair up with a big clip and then grabbed a legal pad and pen.

From the living room, she spotted him outdoors, a bottle of water hanging loosely in one hand, the portfolio he'd brought in the other. He moved closer to her pool, staring into it. Although not large, it was pretty, and set within a small forest for privacy. Peace and quiet reigned, a paradise of her own creation.

Laura didn't join him right away but studied the tall, ruggedly handsome man. She'd tried to avoid him the whole time he was home, but he kept popping up everywhere she went—parties, picnics, even at the diner when she dropped in for lunch or coffee. They were polite to each other, but never engaged in conversation, not just the two of them alone, anyway. It'd been especially hard this trip, because he usually came home for only a few days, and then was gone again.

And she'd never known a man who intrigued her more or whom she needed to steer clear of more.

She couldn't think about that now, or that time in high school, either. She opened the glass doors and joined him. "Do you want to stay out here or go inside?" she asked.

"You choose."

"Inside, then. It's cooler."

"I'm sorry I interrupted your day of self-indulgence," he said, coming back to life a little.

"Oh, well. It was self-indulgent of me, anyway."

He barely smiled. "I think I have need of a lawyer."

They both sat. He took an overstuffed chair. She perched on the sofa so that the coffee table would be handy for paperwork. "And since I'm the only family-law attorney in town, you settled for me?"

"If I didn't think you were the best, here or anywhere, I wouldn't have come to you."

Right answer. He seemed a little more relaxed finally,

so she opened up the discussion to business. "Okay. So…you have a son?"

"Ethan. He'll be five in a month."

Laura listened to his story and sifted through the documents.

"What happens?" he asked. "Do I adopt him?"

"No need. You're listed as his father. But, Donovan, are you sure he's yours? We should verify."

"There's a picture on Mom's photo wall—my first day in kindergarten. It could be Ethan. And the timing is right. I don't question his paternity."

His cell phone rang. "I'm sorry, Laura. I need to warn Joe that they're at his house."

While Donovan explained the situation to his brother, Laura reread Anne's trust documents, but what she really wanted to read was her journal. Too bad there wasn't a legal reason for that. She thumbed an envelope that he said contained a personal letter from Anne.

Donovan noticed. He put his hand over the phone. "Go ahead."

He'd loved her, that much Laura had figured out from the way he talked about her. He was angry and hurt, too, but he'd loved her. He was also a family man, and the fact that he hadn't known about his son all this time had to be devastating. It didn't matter that he'd left his home and family so many years ago. They were still the most important people in his life.

And a son? She didn't know how much of a change

he would've made in his career decisions, but he certainly would've done *something.*

Anne implied in her letter that he would let his family raise the boy, only visiting now and then. Laura wasn't so sure about that. She also didn't know how many options he had. He was at the top of his game. How could he make a huge change at this point in his career without risking it entirely?

"Sorry," Donovan said, slipping his phone into his pocket.

"How did Joe react?"

His mouth tightened. "I can't repeat his words to a lady—which is not the word he used to describe Anne."

Brother protective of brother. Family ties. Laura's experience with them were minimal. Her parents had divorced when she was a baby, and her mother hadn't remarried. As a family-law attorney, however, she saw all kinds of familial relationships and had come to appreciate what she had with her mother.

"You probably heard me tell him to get it out of his system right now," Donovan continued. "I won't tolerate any bad-mouthing. She's my son's mother. That's all that matters."

"That's commendable of you."

"I'm not as uncivilized as some people think."

She raised her brows. "You've changed overnight?"

After a moment he laughed. "Thanks. I needed that."

"Anytime you need to be insulted, just come to me,"

she said, sitting back, letting herself be aware of him as a man again, not a client.

She saw him check her out, something he always did, always seeming…interested. No, it went beyond that. *Attracted.* She'd been wondering for a long time how it would feel to make love with him—since before she knew what making love really meant.

"What's next, Laura?"

"Give me the rest of the day to study her estate issues. Do you have a will?"

"Yes. It's in Joe's safe."

"Bring it to my office tomorrow, and any other documents you have. Life-insurance policy, brokerage account information, whatever else you can think of. Do you own a home?"

"I don't own anything. I have investments, of course."

"You'll want a trust drawn up. And you need to decide on a guardian, should something happen to you."

He didn't say anything for a few seconds, then pushed himself out of the chair. "I should get back to Ethan and Millie."

Laura handed him the portfolio, minus the documents she needed, and followed him to the door. "Give my office a call in the morning. I'll fit you in." She gave his shoulder a friendly pat, then let her hand linger long enough to feel his muscles tense. "What are you going to do?" she asked.

"Get to know my son."

"And after that?"

He turned around, breaking contact. "I don't know. This particular scenario hasn't been on my what-if list. Thanks again for letting me interrupt on your day off."

"No problem. Donovan? How do you feel, finding out you're a father?"

"Bonded. Possessive. Worried. I don't want to mess up, you know? He's already been through more than any little boy should."

"Don't expect perfection of yourself."

"Why should I expect less than usual?" He half smiled. "I know I have a lot to learn, Laura, and I'm probably going to mess up along the way. I'll count on you to point out when I'm falling down on the job."

The last thing she wanted was to get close enough to him to do that. She would do her job as his attorney, but that was it. "I'm sure your big, boisterous family will let you know," she said.

"Family sees a different truth from friends."

She considered that, understanding what he meant but deciding not to keep the conversation going, because she had an urge to hug him, to get body to body with him—and not just to comfort.

Laura watched him drive off then returned to her house. She still had plenty of time to relax by the pool before she started on Donovan's case, but she was more anxious to dig into Anne Bogard's life—and to get the job done. She couldn't afford to spend a lot of time with him.

She'd already surprised herself when she'd stopped by this morning to tell him goodbye. Her relationships were casual for a reason. A very good reason. She wasn't marriage material. Period. She said as much to every man she dated, believing in full disclosure. Some men were grateful and continued a casual relationship, others backed away.

The end result was always the same, anyway—they left. Which hadn't caused her any heartache. *Yet,* she thought, as she picked up Donovan's paperwork and headed for her office.

By the time Donovan returned to Joe's house, not only was Joe there, but their older brother, Jake, too. They both were sitting in Joe's truck in the driveway.

As Donovan approached the truck, the brothers climbed out—Joe, ponytailed and athletic, and Jake, newly married and a father to two-month-old Isabella. He looked like the adventurer he was, long and lean, with dark brown hair and probing blue eyes.

"Joe filled me in," Jake said.

"I don't suppose you helped me out by telling Mom and Nana Mae, too?" Donovan gave Joe a steady look.

He laughed. "I left the easy stuff to you, Donny."

"Right." He glanced toward the house. He wasn't as reluctant to tell his mother as his grandmother. There had never been a McCoy born out of wedlock. She would have something to say about that.

"How do you feel?" Jake asked.

"Probably about the same as you when you came home and found Keri nine months pregnant."

"Turned out okay for me."

"I expect it's going to turn out okay for me, as well." He was grateful to have Laura helping, too. "Do you want to meet him?"

"I thought you'd never ask."

The three brothers were headed to the house when a car honked. Donovan recognized that horn. His mother and grandmother were back from Sacramento.

Aggie McCoy, a sixty-seven-year-old widow of ten years and the dictionary definition of "mom," leaned out the driver's window. "Why're you still here, Donny?"

His brothers gave him I'm-sure-glad-it's-you-and-not-me looks. He walked over to the car and crouched, greeting his mother and his paternal grandmother. "I have some news."

Before he could tell them, the front door of the house opened and Ethan stepped onto the front porch, stopping there.

"Ethan." Millie came up beside him. "I told you to stay inside."

"I waited and waited. He didn't come in."

The image of Ethan standing hopefully at the window jarred Donovan. He had a lot to learn about fatherhood. "It's all right, Millie. I'm sorry I kept him—and you—waiting. Please join me."

Millie took his hand, nudging him forward.

Donovan set a hand lightly on Ethan's shoulder. This

time he didn't flinch. "Mom. Nana Mae. This is Ethan. My son."

"Well, of course he is," Aggie said, opening her car door and getting out as Jake went around the car to help their grandmother out.

"And this is his grandmother, Millie Bogard."

Aggie ignored Millie's outstretched hand and hugged her instead, one of her classic all-engulfing hugs. Donovan knew his mother must have a ton of questions.

Nana Mae came around the car on Jake's arm, using her bright purple cane to help steady herself on the other side. "I'm Maebelle McCoy," she said, her voice strong. Then to Ethan, "I'm your great-grandmother. Everyone calls me Nana Mae."

Ethan stared wide-eyed, keeping his hand firmly in Millie's as the introductions continued with his uncles.

"Ethan, would you go inside with your uncles and Grammy for a minute, please," Donovan said. "I need to speak to Grandma Aggie and Nana Mae. I promise I'll be there in a minute."

"Okay," he said, looking relieved, then racing ahead of the adults.

When the door shut, Donovan took a steadying moment. "I'm sorry I didn't get to warn you. I didn't have any warning myself. They just appeared. I'm hoping you won't mind if they stay with you for a few days, Mom. Me, too, for that matter, while we all make the adjustment."

"Of course I don't mind. Where's his mother, Donny?"

"She died a month ago. Anne Bogard."

"Without telling you about Ethan?"

He nodded. "I'll explain later. For now I don't want to keep him waiting. He's still unsure."

"Well, of course. There's plenty of time."

He turned to his grandmother then. "I'm sorry, Nana Mae. I know he's the first McCoy born out of wedlock. I hope you won't hold it against me, since I didn't know myself."

"You should have."

Her tone wasn't accusatory or angry, but matter-of-fact. And it silenced him. He should have taken the time to find out before he wiped Anne out of his life, as she had him. It was irresponsible of him.

"You're right," he said to his grandmother. "No excuses."

She patted his cheek. "You'll be a good father. I always knew it."

She headed toward the house, taking careful steps, refusing his arm, giving him a moment with his mother.

"How can I help you the most?" Aggie asked.

"I don't know yet. Opening your house to us is the first step. I have a lot of decisions ahead."

"Including about your job."

"Especially that. I can only imagine what Nana Mae would think of me if I left anytime soon."

Her blue eyes, the exact same color as Donovan's,

twinkled. “I’ve been Maebelle McCoy’s daughter-in-law for forty-nine years. One thing I know about her—she’ll love you no matter what.”

The front door opened. Ethan stood there, waiting, silently reminding Donovan of his promise to meet him in the house in a minute.

“And so it begins,” his mother said.

She was right. It was a new chapter, probably the longest one in his book of life, but at this point, mostly blank pages waiting to be written on.

Chapter Four

Millie and Ethan went to bed at eight o'clock, exhausted from their long journey and the emotional roller coaster of the day. Restless, Donovan took off for a walk. He considered his options. He could go to Joe's house three blocks away and have a couple of beers while they watched a Giants game, giving his overloaded mind a break from the relentless thoughts bombarding him. But he was tired of noise. He needed some quiet, which was rare for him.

It wouldn't be dark for another half hour or so. He walked the streets of his hometown, seeing it anew. He'd always appreciated the beauty of the place. Nestled in the foothills of the Sierras, the land was green, the air clear. The miners who'd come to the Mother Lode of this part of California in the 1850s had not just mined for gold, but settled the town. Many of the houses built over the years since still survived. Those who built new generally chose designs to fit in with the surroundings, whether Victorian or contemporary log cabin.

Donovan passed a house with a for-sale sign in the front yard, a smaller "offer pending" tacked across it. Jake and his new wife, Keri, had made an offer, having decided to move into town from Jake's cabin outside the city limits. The old Braeburn house had been vacant for months, ever since the Widow Braeburn had been moved into a nursing facility, so the transition into the four-bedroom Victorian should be quick.

Donovan turned right at the corner and realized he was a block from Laura's street. He wished he had a reason to stop by, but he hadn't even gathered all of the paperwork she wanted, was still waiting for some information to be faxed or e-mailed before he went to her office tomorrow.

He could've kept going past her block and on to the park nearby, but instead he intentionally walked toward her house. She was out front, watering the garden herself, using a hose instead of her in-ground sprinkling system. Donovan couldn't name many flowers beyond roses and daisies, much to his landscaper-brother Joe's disgust, but it didn't take knowledge of the names to appreciate Laura's yard. It bloomed with mostly pink and purple flowers, punctuated here and there with a few white blossoms. Her cottage-style house was small, white and homey. He would've expected something more sleek and contemporary for her, not this cozy place. Even the neighborhood was mature, with few families, mostly just singles or older couples.

You're making yourself old before your time, Laura Bannister.

Her back to him, she couldn't see him coming up the sidewalk. She also wore earbuds connected to a music device in her pocket. She'd changed back into the cool shorts and tank top she'd been wearing early that morning when she'd stopped by in her car.

Donovan couldn't take his eyes off her. There was a reason she was called The Body. A man could put his hands anywhere on her and enjoy either full curves or smooth planes. Her skin looked touchably soft, as did her hair.

He came up behind her, tapped her on the shoulder to get her attention.

She spun around, using her hose as a weapon, and soaked his shirt.

He shouted a laugh, grabbed the nozzle but ended up turning it on her. She shrieked, yelled his name and danced away, as he angled the nozzle toward the ground. She reached over to turn off the faucet, then plunked her fists on her hips and scowled.

She looked magnificent.

It was the first time he could remember seeing her ruffled. Well, the first time in fifteen years, anyway.

"Sorry," he said.

"I'll bet."

He smiled. She could win any wet T-shirt contest, anywhere, hands down, especially with that nice lace bra revealed.

A couple of teenage boys rode by on bicycles, staring. Donovan eased in front of her, blocking their view. One wolf-whistled. The other crashed into a parked car. Donovan looked at Laura, whose eyes sparkled. He laughed.

She crossed her arms, but he could see she'd relaxed.

"I *am* sorry," he said. "I hadn't intended to get you wet. I was just reacting."

"I believe you. It's funny you came along when you did. I'd just been thinking about you, wondering how you were doing, hoping you were okay. You already needed time away?"

"He's asleep. He and Millie were wiped out. And, yes, I needed some time alone." He moved past Laura and wound the hose on its reel. "I suppose you're used to that kind of reaction. Those boys," he said.

"It's no different from yours." She walked up the steps to her front porch. "You're just quieter about it. You always have been."

He followed, even though she hadn't actually invited him. "You check me out, too."

She made a noncommittal sound, then opened her

door and went inside, leaving it open, which he took as an invitation. He followed, shutting the door behind him.

"I'll toss your shirt in the dryer, if you want," she said before disappearing down the hallway.

His shirt wasn't soaking wet, just a wide stripe down the middle that would probably be almost dry by the time he walked home. But since it suited him to hang around awhile, he peeled his shirt over his head and waited for her to come back.

When she returned, she'd changed tops. As she walked by him, she swiped his T-shirt out of his hands. He followed as she went into the kitchen and then the laundry room at the other side. She gave his bare chest as much of a look as he'd given her wet T-shirt out front.

It made him smile. He liked a woman who was sure of herself, sure of her sexuality, someone who could match him in bed, sometimes taking over. She would be a match.

He also knew they were treading in dangerous waters. The interest had been there for years. It wouldn't take much for it to get much more personal.

Or maybe she was just getting even for what had happened—had *not* happened—years ago, and had decided to tease him with the intent to reject him. Well, it didn't really matter. He needed a distraction, needed not to think about Ethan for a little while. Or Anne. Laura was as fine a distraction as he could ever wish for.

The dryer started tumbling and she returned to the kitchen, where he stood looking out her window. It was almost dark.

"How about a glass of wine?" she asked.

He would've preferred beer. "Sounds good."

She poured from a bottle already opened. "Shall we sit outside by the pool?"

"And let the mosquitoes use us for appetizers?"

"They should be gone by now." She passed him a wineglass, then led the way to the backyard. They settled in two lounges, didn't say anything for a few minutes. He wondered what her thoughts were, since his own were deeply involved in a graphic fantasy.

"How was the rest of your day?" she asked finally.

He tried to focus again. "Um, it was good. He's a great little kid, and not surprisingly overwhelmed by all the new people in his life. We kept it to a minimum, but we'll add more tomorrow. He's got cousins a few years older, so that's going to be helpful. And he's gone to preschool since he was three, so I figure he's pretty well socialized."

"He's accepted you already?"

"No. I didn't mean to imply that. But one good thing Anne did was to tell him about me. She'd even shown him pictures. And Millie did some research, found out I was here and had talked to him about me during their trip, and about the fact she would be going back to England. She laid good groundwork."

"I'm surprised she didn't contact you first, rather

than just showing up. Or let you come to them, instead, and be in his own environment."

"So was I, but I figure Anne must have assured her I wouldn't shirk my responsibility. Or Millie decided a surprise attack would be best." Anger swooped in and pecked at him, as it had many times during the day. He'd missed five years with Ethan. Five long years.

"It looks like you'll be sticking around Chance City," Laura said. "Any decisions on your job?"

"I won't go anywhere for a while, that much I know. We need time together, for the two of us and for him to get to know his family. I want him to feel comfortable and settled first."

"There's nothing you could do here or from here?"

"There are probably jobs to be found, but something I'm interested in? Passionate about? I sure haven't come up with any ideas."

"I've heard that most journalists are frustrated novelists. Any interest in writing a book?"

"I've thought about it." He had contacts. Maybe now was the time to put out feelers. "I've got enough based-on-a-true-story material to write ten thrillers, but I'm not sure how well I'd do being cooped up in front of a computer all day. I love being in the field, interviewing people, getting into the action."

"Getting injured. Fearing for your life. Mmm-hmm. I can see the appeal."

He laughed. "It's rarely that touch-and-go."

"So you exaggerate in your articles?"

"You read my work?"

Her mouth tightened, as if she'd revealed something she hadn't wanted to. "I subscribe to *NewsView,* and you write frequently for them."

"They pay the best."

"What will happen with the Mexico job you were headed to today?"

"It gets put on hold. No one else will write the story, if that's what you mean. It's not as time-sensitive as some. I've been in touch with my editor at *NewsView.* He understands what's going on." He gestured toward the surroundings. "You've created quite an Eden for yourself."

"My decompression tank." She sipped her wine. "Have you read Anne's journal yet?"

"Started to. It's pretty painful at the beginning, so I put it aside for now."

"I can't imagine being in your shoes, finding out you have a child after all this time. It must be very helpful having your family."

He stared into space, considering her words. "I think it's harder in some ways." He turned toward her, set his wineglass on a nearby end table. "It's like there's a spotlight on me, following my every move. Everyone will want to have input, you know? All five of my sisters have children and are not shy about offering advice—ever. All but one are older than me, have always mother-henned Jake and Joe and me. My oldest sister, Cher, is fifteen years older than I am, got married at eighteen, has children in their twenties. It's a helluva formidable group, this family of mine."

"I would have no idea what that's like."

He knew her father had left when she was young, so it had been only her and her mother. Laura had always been a loner, even in high school. Donovan graduated three years ahead of her, so he'd only gotten news about her secondhand, from Joe. She'd never tried out to be a cheerleader or run for class office. The boys teased her, as teenage boys always did, not knowing how to deal with a smart, beautiful girl like her. And the other girls didn't welcome her into their groups, probably because they felt threatened by her.

When it came down to it, though, it'd been her responsibility to find friends for herself, and she hadn't done it. On the other hand, she'd ended up as valedictorian, gone on to college and entered beauty pageants, winning the Miss California title, then Miss U.S.A., then was first runner-up for Miss Universe, shocking everyone. Not just because she'd done so well, but because she'd put herself out there like that when she'd stayed behind the scenes in high school.

Then she'd gone to law school and had been practicing law ever since, here and in Sacramento. But even now, she stayed on the fringes, showing up at events, yet not doing anything to call attention to herself.

"I didn't mean to bring the conversation to a halt," she said, setting her empty glass next to his. "When I said I wouldn't know what having a big family was like, I wasn't whining. I was stating a fact."

"I didn't take it that way. I got lost in thought, that's all. And I'm not saying I'd trade my family for anything, just that in some ways I'd like to take off with Ethan and not come back until we've gotten to know each other first, without others interfering."

"Why can't you do that? He won't start kindergarten for a over month. Take some time."

"I'll think about it. Thanks for inviting me in, Laura. I didn't know how much I needed to blow off a little steam." He grinned. "Although I do know of better ways to do it."

She gave him that sexy lawyer look. "I'm your attorney."

"Okay, so, once everything is handled and you're not my lawyer anymore?" He tried to look as if he were teasing her, making a game of it, when he was absolutely serious.

"Unless you take your business to someone else, I'll still be your attorney. It's unethical."

"Meaning, if I fire you, you'd be interested?"

The dryer buzzed, loud and long. The ensuing silence slowly refilled with the sounds of crickets and frogs, seeming to chastise Donovan personally for his foolishness.

He sat up and swung his legs over the side of the lounge. "Are you seeing anyone right now?" he asked.

"My answer doesn't matter. Ethics do."

"Humor me. It's not like you're representing me in a murder trial, you know."

"No," she answered lightly, then stood and headed into the house.

No, she wasn't seeing anyone? Or *no,* she wasn't going to humor him by answering?

After a minute he smiled, gathered the empty wineglasses and followed. He rinsed the glasses and set them on her kitchen counter just as she came into the room with his shirt and handed it to him.

"Thank you," he said, moving closer to her. "We've got unfinished business."

"Water over a very old dam, Donovan."

He watched a vein throbbing visibly in her neck, a noticeable reaction to their conversation.

She took a step back. "What part of 'I'm your lawyer' don't you understand?" she asked, even as goose bumps rose on her skin.

He backed away, drawing his shirt over his head and down, then apologizing.

"Accepted," she said.

"You'll still be my lawyer?"

"Of course."

"Damn."

She laughed, which was what he'd intended.

"Bring Ethan and Millie with you tomorrow, please," she said.

"Sure. Good night, Laura."

"Night."

She shut the door right away behind him, so there was no awkward moment of whether to turn back and wave. She'd already dealt with it.

He made the walk to his mother's house, his thoughts in more turmoil than when he'd left. He never pushed women, had always accepted no as a final answer. Yet he'd pushed Laura to the point that she'd had to remind him about ethics. Him, of all people.

His mother was seated in a rocking chair when he climbed her porch steps. "Everything okay?" he asked.

"Quiet as clouds. Poor little tyke. What a big day he had."

Donovan eased onto the porch swing, crossed his feet and set it in motion, his arms stretched along the back. The stars had come out. Not the brilliant blanket it sometimes was when there was no moon, but a scattering.

"Big day for you, too, son," Aggie said.

"Yeah. Big day." Whatever event might have taken first place in his life before had been drop-kicked into second now.

"You'll need to register him for kindergarten right away, so there's a space for him. Carly said she'd go with you, if you want."

"I'll manage on my own, thanks." And so it began. Sisters already taking charge.

"Ethan'll need a physical. Doc Saxon can do it."

I know, I know. "Millie brought his medical records,

including immunizations. Should make the transition easy. I need to get him on my health insurance."

His cell phone rang, his brother Jake.

"Good news," Jake said. "We got the house. We'll officially have a fifteen-day escrow, but they said we can move in tomorrow, if we want, and just assume that all the paperwork will go through fine."

"That's terrific."

"It is, but what I'm really calling about is to ask if you want to live at the cabin. We decided to keep it as rental property."

Jake's one-bedroom-with-an-office log cabin would be perfect. It was off the beaten path a little, so he and Ethan would be separate from the rest of the family but still close enough to keep the connection tight.

"That'd be great, thanks, Jake. Perfect. How soon can that happen?"

"The more help you give, the sooner you can move in."

He laughed. "I knew there'd be a catch."

"You would've helped, anyway."

Yeah, he would have. "Do I have to paint?"

"Probably. And Keri's been making noise about some new fixtures in the bathrooms. That job you had with Bud Hollenbeck could come in handy."

Bud was the best, although slowest working, plumber in town. Donovan has spent one summer working with the man. It had settled Donovan's mind about getting out of town, since the jobs available to people here in the tiny bedroom community were mostly in the trades or tourist related. He'd had different dreams.

Jake had left home because he felt he didn't fit. Donovan had a calling.

"You never forget how to seat a toilet, do you?" Jake asked, laughter in his voice.

"Unfortunately not."

"We'll give you the first month rent free for your help."

Money wasn't an issue, which Jake knew. Donovan didn't own anything, had invested and saved, because his job wasn't exactly the most secure. "It's a deal. I walked by there a while ago. House looks in pretty good shape, but the yard needs work."

"Keri's dying to get her hands into the earth. *Her* earth, she's calling it. She wants to be planted, then let her roots go deep."

After a few more minutes Donovan hung up. Aggie smiled. "They got the house?"

"Yep. And he's offered to rent me the cabin."

He saw the disappointment in her eyes. She liked having them all staying with her. With so many children and grandchildren, people were in and out of the house constantly, but it wasn't the same as having someone living there, someone she could pamper—and mother.

The screen door creaked. Ethan pushed it open an inch and peeked out.

Donovan hurried over. "You okay, buddy?"

"I just wanted to make sure you were here."

Progress. "I'm here. Do you want to sit with me for a while?"

"On the swing?"

"Yes."

"Okay. But not in your lap."

Donovan was hungry to hold him, to comfort him and keep him safe, but he did what Ethan asked, just picked him up and set him on the swing. He brought his knees up and wrapped his arms around them.

"Hi, Grandma," Ethan said quietly.

"Hello, little man."

Ethan giggled at that, then nestled his chin on his knees.

"Did something wake you up?" Donovan asked.

"Mum did."

Donovan glanced at his mother, who lifted her brows. "Did you have a dream about her?" he asked.

"No. She was here. She sat on my bed and talked to me."

"What did she say?"

"That she loves me." He said the words matter-of-factly.

"That's nice." What could he say to that? "Um, do you see her a lot?"

"Just sometimes. She doesn't look sick anymore, so why can't she come back?"

Donovan closed his eyes for a moment. His first big test. "It's good that she doesn't look sick anymore, isn't it?"

He nodded his head against his knees.

"But you know that when someone dies they don't get to come back, right?"

"I know."

"We usually only have pictures and videos of them. You're pretty lucky that you see her now and then. But she can't come back, not like before, anyway." He put a hand on Ethan's back, glad that he accepted the touch easily. "But she'll stay with you the rest of your life, Ethan, in your dreams and in your heart. She'll never stop loving you. Okay?"

"Okay." He yawned, then after a minute, leaned against Donovan. Pretty soon he was asleep.

Donovan scooped him up and carried him to bed, tucking him in, kissing his head. He stood over his son for a few minutes, watching him sleep, his heart pounding, love flowing.

"Well done," Aggie said when he returned to the porch.

"Thanks."

"You know it's just the beginning of the questions, right?"

"I guessed as much. I figure I need to be as honest as possible, as I would with anyone else."

"Just trust your instincts. You'll do fine."

"I feel like I have to have better instincts than the average person, Mom. I'm coming into this late. I wasn't given a chance to start at the beginning and grow with it."

"You'll see. It'll be okay."

It had to be, he thought. Because failure wasn't an option.

Chapter Five

From her desk, Laura watched Donovan pass by her office window. She couldn't see the boy or his grandmother, but assumed they were beside him. He was taller, and probably blocked the view.

Laura heard the front door open. She smoothed her hair as Donovan greeted her mother, Dolly, who ran the Chance City office. Usually Laura would walk into the reception area to greet her clients, but his voice was enough to freeze her in place.

She'd done little else but think about him last night and this morning, especially the way he'd looked stretched out on her lounge, shirtless.

It was like being in high school again, a time when

she'd trailed him in the hallways, trying not to let him see her, her heart thumping. Then when she'd finally worked up the nerve to talk to him—

A boy bounded into view and stopped, framed by her doorway. Donovan was right. There was no doubt about paternity.

Ethan smiled. Laura smiled back and went to say hello to him. She rarely interacted with children, the exception being children of clients, and Donovan's baby niece, but then Laura didn't have to figure out what to say to an infant.

"My name is Laura," she said. "What's yours?"

He stuck out his hand. "Ethan."

"Very nice to meet you," she said, shaking his hand.

"Very nice to meet you, too."

He had a sweet smile and wonderful manners, which spoke highly of his mother.

"Good morning, Laura."

She looked up, tried to put on an expression as businesslike as her blue suit. "Hello, Donovan. Ethan and I have introduced ourselves." She extended a hand to the woman at his side. She was probably in her early fifties, slender and blond, with rosy cheeks and soft blue eyes. "I'm Laura Bannister."

"Millicent Bogard. Call me Millie."

"Please come in."

Ethan climbed onto the chair in the middle, then spotted a display case in the corner and hopped off to go look at the contents. "Wow! You must be the Queen of America."

The case contained some of her sashes, crowns and even a scepter. She knew it was too much like bragging, but her clients got a kick out of having a beauty pageant winner as their attorney. And this was her hometown, after all. Her most prestigious prizes were in her home office.

To Laura they represented so much more than winning a pageant. They'd meant financial survival through college and law school.

She joined Ethan at the case. "They're all kind of flashy, aren't they?"

"Sparkly! That one's brilliant," he said, pointing to a scepter and sounding very British. "I could fight with that. Take that! And that!" He mimed dueling with a phantom partner, his expression intense.

"Ethan," Donovan said, caution in his voice.

He stopped, then trudged back to his chair. "I *know.* Behave." His tone was long-suffering.

Laura made eye contact with Donovan and smiled, as did he. She took her seat behind her desk and thumbed through the papers he'd stacked there.

"I hope I brought everything," he said.

"I'll check it all out later." She turned to Millie. "I'm so sorry for your loss."

"Thank you. Anne was lovely. A little headstrong, you know, but a lovely girl, and a good daughter."

Ethan climbed from his chair and onto Millie's lap,

his sneakered feet bouncing so much that Millie had to lay a hand across his shins. Laura saw yearning in Donovan's eyes.

"Ethan," Laura said, then waited for him to focus on her. "What do you think of your new town?"

"It's good."

"You have a great big family now." Laura tried to imagine it. Her mom meant the world to her, but the idea of so many siblings and cousins was daunting. Especially since the McCoys were always in each other's business, and she liked her privacy.

Ethan looked serious. "Grammy says they're like friends but better. I only met my uncles and Grandma Aggie and Nana Mae. But we're having a party tonight and everyone will be there. You can come."

"Please," Donovan prompted, looking just as hopeful as Ethan.

"Pleeease." Ethan dragged out the word, grinning ear to ear.

Laura felt backed into a corner. The McCoys were famous for their big family parties. Even spur-of-the-moment, as this one would be, there would be tons of food, plenty of noise, and spontaneous dancing. "Maybe I can drop in for a little while," she said, hedging.

"Will you bring that?" He pointed to her scepter.

"Ethan, that's like a trophy for Laura," Donovan said. "You know what a trophy is?"

He nodded hugely. "I got trophies for soccer and T-ball."

"You wouldn't want anyone to play with them, would you? What if they got broken?"

"I wouldn't like that."

"Okay, then."

Laura was satisfied that Ethan was making the transition into his new life just fine. Not that she could've done anything about it, but she'd had enough experience dealing with broken families that she could recommend counselors. At the moment, she didn't think it necessary.

"Did you meet my mother out in the reception area?" she asked him.

"That's your mum? She's pretty, too."

"Thank you," Dolly said from the doorway, fluffing her red hair dramatically. "How about you come play with me for a while, handsome?"

He looked at Millie, who said, "We won't be long, love. And I saw a basket of toys out there."

He left the room with Dolly, who shut the door behind her.

Laura turned to Millie. "Is there anyone who might try to claim that Ethan should be with them instead?"

"Donovan's his father. No one disputes that."

"That fact doesn't necessarily stop people from trying to make a claim. Not that Ethan could be taken away, but legal battles can happen. It's…inconvenient. And expensive. Did Anne have a significant other who might challenge Donovan?"

"No. No one. Oh, she dated some, but Ethan was her whole life, even before she got sick."

"And are you asking for anything from Donovan?"

Millie's eyes widened. "Like what? Money? Anne left me some. I don't need more."

"I noticed that in the trust. I was thinking more along the lines of visitation requests."

"Let me step in here," Donovan said. "Millie can come visit as often and for as long as she wants. If she wants to move here, I'll help her get settled. And if coming here isn't feasible for her, I'll make sure that Ethan goes to England to visit."

"That's very generous, Donovan," Millie said, her eyes taking on a sheen.

"You're his grandmother. You're his direct connection with Anne. That's important."

"Thank you."

"Do you have any questions?" Laura asked Millie.

"Anne's lawyer answered all that I had before. Is there anything I'll need to sign? Because I expect to be leaving day after tomorrow."

"Already?" Donovan asked, his surprise evident.

Millie patted his arm. "You've seen how he turns to me instead of you. It'll help if I'm out of the picture." She looked expectantly at Laura then.

"If I come across something in the paperwork, I'll let you know in time, Millie. Now, if you don't mind waiting in the reception area with Ethan, I need to speak to Donovan for a minute."

"Of course."

"Alone at last," Donovan said, a few seconds later, setting the tone. He smiled, slow and sexy.

She resisted his flirting. "I thought we settled this last night. Are you going to continue to tease me, knowing nothing can happen between us?"

"My time will come. I'm just keeping you primed for that moment."

She laughed. She wished she didn't feel flattered by his attention, and wasn't totally drawn to him in every other way, especially watching him in the role of father. Her father had left when she was two, with promises to visit often, according to her mother, anyway. He'd never come back.

"So, Millie's leaving," she said, changing the subject.

"That was the first I'd heard of it. I'm sure she's right about it forcing Ethan and me to become a unit, but I think she's also anxious to go home. She's been caregiver for a long time. I imagine she needs some time for herself."

"While you no longer have time for yourself." She couldn't imagine what that would be like, having someone totally dependent on her. She didn't even own a pet.

"True."

An interesting response. A statement of fact only. He was good at that.

She opened a folder. "Who are you naming as Ethan's guardian?"

"Jake and Keri."

"They've agreed? I know that seems like a dumb question. It's a technicality."

"They've agreed."

"Actually, you need to designate two guardians—one for Ethan, and one for the estate. It can be the same person, or you can choose someone else for the estate. Sometimes it's better that way. No emotional involvement."

"You mean, like you?"

"Yes. Or anyone else."

"Let me think about it. I'll let you know."

"When you've decided, I'll give Jake a call. We'll need to adjust for this change in his own estate documents, in case something happens to him."

"We sure plan for a lot of contingencies."

"Planning pays off."

Donovan nodded. "Have you heard that Jake and Keri are buying a house around the block from you?"

"Which one? There are a couple in different directions." She almost held her breath, waiting for his answer.

"The Braeburn house on Poplar Street."

Relief eased into her refilling her lungs. Not the Denton house.

"Ethan and I will be renting Jake's cabin for now."

Which meant he wouldn't be in town anymore, but a ten-minute drive away. No more going out for a walk and stopping by. Which was probably a good thing, given their attraction.

"Good for them. I know Keri wants to be closer to

the action—and the family," Laura said. "I reviewed everything you gave me yesterday. Anne's trust is straightforward. I'll get the transfer of funds started."

"I want all of Anne's money to go into a trust for Ethan."

"Including the insurance payout?"

"Yes."

"Okay. Payable to him at what age?"

"Twenty-five. I can lower that later, if I want, right?"

"Of course. Or raise it, for that matter. But don't you want it available to him for college?"

"I'll take care of part of that, and he can earn part of it."

Laura knew he'd made his own way in the world, without help from anyone, so it didn't come as a surprise that he would want Ethan to do the same. "All right. I think that's it for now. I'll call you if I have questions."

"And you'll come to the party tonight? It's at Mom's."

"I'll try."

"Laura, you told Ethan you'd come. You can't disappoint him."

"I told him *maybe.*" A tiny bit of panic struck her. She didn't want to get too involved.

"You'd better believe he didn't hear the maybe." Donovan stood.

Laura came around her desk to walk him to the door. "I feel a need to caution you. I've observed a lot of situations where children come into a new household, whether it's foster kids or newly adopted—which is similar to what you're experiencing. There's generally a honeymoon period where kids are extremely well behaved or extremely badly behaved. Ethan is going to feel abandoned. You can't avoid that. So, just know that how he acts now, especially after Millie leaves, isn't necessarily how it will be when he settles in. Be patient and, above all, be consistent. You'll find your own path together."

"Thanks. I've already noticed he's much more comfortable with women, which says a lot about how he's been living." They had reached the door. "This is the Laura I know," he said, touching her hair briefly. "Hair up, business suit, makeup, heels. I've seen another you, a more relaxed you. Which one rules?"

"Different looks for different occasions, but still all me."

"Layers."

"I certainly hope so." She spoke quietly so her words wouldn't breach the door.

"Say you'll be there tonight, Laura."

"I'll be there." She didn't have to stay long, after all.

"And you'll stay more than ten minutes." He grinned. "Yes, I've figured you out a little."

She didn't want to fall for him, but he was making it difficult. She liked his boldness. He was a brilliant reporter, honored and respected. He hadn't gotten that way by sitting back and waiting for something to happen.

"I'll stay at least fifteen," she said. "What can I bring?"

"I heard you don't cook."

"No, but I shop very well."

He smiled. "Why don't you just bring yourself? We'll have tons of food. Six o'clock."

She wouldn't go empty-handed. "That's a sweet boy you've got."

He nodded, then opened the door. Ethan looked up, his expression hopeful. "There's an ice cream shop next door. Did you know?"

"I had no idea."

"My favorite is chocolate. Grammy likes vanilla."

"Good to know."

"I have money, you know," Ethan said. "Grammy gave me some."

Donovan knelt down to him. "I was having fun with you, son. I'd be happy to treat you to an ice cream. Want to come along?" he asked Dolly.

"I never pass up an ice-cream cone."

"Laura?"

"I have a client due any minute."

"We're only going next door."

She was being a stick-in-the-mud because she didn't want to get close to him, and to Ethan. There were good reasons not to. Excellent reasons. Sanity-saving reasons.

"Next time, maybe," he said, ending the silence. Then they were gone, and the office seemed enormous and quiet.

She returned to her inner office and desk. After a few

minutes she heard the front door open. She went to greet the expected client, but it was Donovan, carrying an ice-cream cone, mocha almond fudge, her favorite.

He didn't say a word, just handed her the cone and left. As he opened the door, her client approached.

"Hey, George. Laura's running about ten minutes late," Donovan said, throwing his arm around the man's shoulders. "Come have an ice cream with me first."

"If you're sure."

"Positive. Laura won't mind."

The door shut behind them. Donovan winked at her as they walked by her window.

And Laura sat in her chair and savored the ice cream for the full ten minutes, trying to remember the last time she'd just had fun with a man. It'd been a long, long time.

Chapter Six

The McCoys were spread out for Ethan's welcome party from Aggie's front yard, to inside the house and on into the back. Donovan watched over Ethan as he played out front with a few of his cousins, a little shy but warming. He was the youngest by several years. Most of the women were in the kitchen putting the final touches on their potluck items, laughing and teasing each other, their voices drifting through the screen door.

The sound was familiar and relaxing.

Even though they'd just given him a send-off barbecue two days ago, everyone seemed happy enough to be back for more. And if Ethan was a little overwhelmed by the number of relatives, he didn't show it beyond a little extra clinging to Donovan's hand. Ethan probably would've been clinging to Millie, instead, but she'd busied herself with the food preparation, purposely making herself unavailable to him.

Only two non-McCoys were there—Millie and Dixie Callahan, Joe's ex-fiancée, who'd recently moved in with Nana Mae to help care for her, without Nana Mae knowing she was being taken care of.

Donovan was on the lookout for the other non-McCoy invited guest, Laura, and to watch Ethan ride a bicycle with training wheels that one of the cousins was passing down.

Everyone came with gifts, all of them in grocery bags, for which Donovan was grateful. He didn't want to sit and unwrap gifts for an hour. But he admitted to being curious about what kinds of things they'd brought.

He spotted Laura from a block away. It was an especially warm evening. Maybe her skin would be pink and dewy from the long walk....

She was wearing another formfitting summer dress, the neckline not too low, the hem midthigh. She'd left her hair up. He'd bet if he commented on it, she would say she was cooler with it off her skin. He didn't really mind, because it exposed her long, tempting neck, but he did like the messy look he'd seen yesterday after she'd been sunbathing at home.

He moved to the sidewalk to greet her, noting that she also came with a Nordstrom shopping bag, but he could see colorful wrapping paper inside, with kid-appealing robots printed all over it. Ethan pedaled up, coming to a stop between them.

"Hi, Laura!"

"Hello, Ethan. Looks like you're having fun." She smiled at Donovan but quickly returned her attention to the boy.

"Guess what? I'm related to all these people. I have aunts and uncles and cousins." He leaned close to her and whispered, "I can't remember everyone's name yet."

"Maybe they should wear name tags until you do."

He scrunched up his face. "That's silly."

"Why?"

"Because I can't read."

After a moment, Laura started to laugh. Ethan chimed in, giggling in delight, not really getting what made it funny, but going along with it.

She reached into her bag and pulled out a package. "This is for you."

"It's not my birthday for a whole month."

"We talked about this, son," Donovan said. "It's a welcome party. I'm getting presents, too. But you have to wait until later to open the packages."

The boy sighed. "Thank you, Laura, but I have to wait until later."

"No problem." She slipped it back into the bag.

"We're about to eat," Donovan explained. "Presents after dinner. Mom's rules. It drags out the anticipation." Which worked in his favor, because it would force her to stay through dinner and beyond. It would seem rude if she left before Ethan opened his gift from her. Sometimes life just worked out perfectly.

"Dinner's on!" someone yelled through the screen door.

"Hey, bud, ride your bike through the gate into the backyard," Donovan said, "so it's not sitting on the sidewalk."

"Okay." He took off, leaving Donovan and Laura to follow.

"Thanks for coming," he said.

"My pleasure. He looks happy."

"It's an ongoing process."

"And you? Are you happy?"

He hesitated long enough that she stopped, putting her hand on his arm to halt him, too.

"What?" she asked. "You aren't happy?"

"It's not that. I can't say this to anyone else." He shoved his hands in his pockets. "I'm in over my head, you know? I have all these nieces and nephews, but I've never spent much time with them, and certainly never been responsible for them. Joe's got all the kid experience, since he's never left Chance City. I know he babysat when he was a teenager. Even now he takes the kids places. Fishing, ball games, lots of different activities. I don't know how to relate."

"From what I've seen, you're relating just fine. In fact, I'd say you're a natural."

"I haven't been tested yet. It's all fun and games so far." He put his hand at the small of her back, urging her forward so they could join the family in the backyard, then didn't let his hand drop until they were almost in sight of everyone. Her dress was damp where he touched her. Something about that aroused him. Maybe just the vision of them working up a sweat while they made love—hot summer nights made even steamier in bed sharing body heat.

He wondered if part of her allure was that he couldn't have her—

No. He'd avoided her during the two months he'd been home because he knew it couldn't go anywhere, and he wanted his visits home to be uncomplicated. It'd been a conscious choice. He'd rather ignore her so that he wouldn't sleep with her than have to ignore her because he *had* slept with her.

Donovan watched his mother sweep Laura into a hug, saw Laura stiffen and pull back as soon as she could. She fished a bottle of wine from the paper sack she carried and gave it to Aggie, which made Donovan smile. His mother would put it aside for a special occasion, and probably never serve it because it was way too special.

Donovan let Laura fill her plate, waiting for her to come back to where he'd saved a seat for her. She surprised him by not even looking his way, but heading to where Dixie and his new sister-in-law, Keri, sat, the two women a study in opposites. The curly-haired blonde, Dixie, was about five-five and blessed with the perfect hourglass figure. Dark-haired Keri stood a couple of inches taller and was reed slender, having lost the pregnancy weight in a hurry.

Putting Laura between them defined the contrasts even more. She was taller than Keri, blonder than Dixie and a perfect balance between Keri's slenderness and Dixie's voluptuousness.

Donovan filled his plate, then sat at a picnic table, glancing at the women occasionally as he ate, wondering how they'd all become friends, then deciding that while they were different from each other in visible ways, there were similarities. All three women were comfortable in their own skin, and were confident and strong—matter-of-fact, no-punches-pulled women. He'd always recognized what Joe had seen in Dixie all these years, and couldn't believe he'd let her get away. As for Keri, Donovan had come to recognize what Jake saw in her, how she made his life better, richer. It had taken Donovan a long time to trust her, but it was part of his nature to be skeptical.

Yet he already trusted Laura.

"You look like you've got dessert all scoped out."

Donovan jolted at the sound of Joe's voice as he sat beside him, his own plate heaped with fried chicken and potato salad. Donovan gave his brother a quelling look. "You know I never turn down cherry pie."

Joe laughed. "Is that what you call Laura? Cherry

pie?" He picked up a drumstick and eyed it casually, too casually.

"You can't say I don't have good taste," Donovan replied, knowing it was useless to argue the point.

"Nope. Sure can't. I can still picture her in that bikini she wore to David Falcon's party."

"Me, too," Jake said, joining his brothers. "I almost asked her out a few times over the years, but I had a feeling she'd chew me up and spit me out. You're a braver man than I, Donny."

"Don't you have a baby to take care of?"

"Isabella is sleeping. Where's *your* child?"

Donovan stood in a hurry. He'd been so wrapped up in sneaking glances at Laura, he'd forgotten Ethan.

"He's fine," Jake said, exchanging a grin with Joe. "He's sitting on the grass over there with part of our village." He pointed to where Ethan sat with five of his cousins, smiling tentatively.

Donovan lowered himself to the bench again, feeling like an idiot, but knowing his brothers wouldn't embarrass him in front of the others. Parenting was a brand-new role.

"What time are we getting started tomorrow on your house?" Donovan asked Jake.

"Smooth change of subject." Jake grinned. "Early. So far, I've lined up about fifteen people. We'll paint tomorrow, and pull up carpet. There are hardwood floors under the carpets. We're hoping they won't need too much work. We figure we can be set up and moved in within ten days. But we've got a ton of stuff to buy. We plan to leave most of the furniture that's at the cabin. Is that okay with you?"

"Are you kidding? That'd be great."

"You'll need a bed for Ethan." Jake turned his head at the sound of a baby crying. He stood, then went to meet their sister Darcy, who held and bounced Isabella as she came out of the house. Darcy turned sideways, not letting Jake take her. She kept moving toward Keri. Jake followed.

Donovan watched in amazement as Laura reached for the baby instead of Keri. Almost instantly, Isabella quieted.

"The baby whisperer," Joe said.

"What?"

"That's what they all call Laura."

It was news to Donovan. He hadn't figured her for a kid person at all, but especially babies. She generally left kids alone, although she certainly seemed at ease with Ethan. "I didn't know she was that close to Keri. I've seen them talking at some of the parties, but that's all. She was at Jake and Keri's wedding."

Joe picked up his empty plate and Donovan's to toss. "Laura turned thirty this year, like Dix and me. Maybe she's looking for a change. Trying to get involved more."

Donovan zeroed in on Joe. "Does that mean you're looking for a change?"

Joe shrugged. "I've been doing the same thing for a whole lotta years, you know?"

"To great success."

"Yeah. That's the problem." He started to walk away, then turned back, a hint of a smile on his lips. "Can I get you some cherry pie?" He gave Laura a quick glance.

Donovan wished it was that easy—just order her up and she would appear. She would be sweet and tart, too, just like his mom's pie.

Joe didn't wait for an answer. He didn't have to.

Ethan came running up. "Is it time to open Laura's present now?"

"Five more minutes, bud. Let everyone finish eating."

"But—"

"Patience, Ethan. There are a lot of gifts to open, not just Laura's."

Ethan walked back to where his cousins sat, kicking the ground as he went. Donovan smiled at the universal body language of being denied something. He shifted his gaze to Laura, who still held the baby but was watching Ethan. She made eye contact with Donovan and smiled, too; then Keri said something and Laura passed her the baby.

Donovan waited to see if Laura would join him, since he was alone now and she no longer held the baby, but she continued to sit where she was, looking back at him, the smile on her face leaving by degrees.

He wanted her. He wanted to see her naked, to kiss her for hours, to seek the warmth inside her and find satisfaction. Then he wanted to do it again.

A plate of cherry pie dropped with a thud on the table, then Joe landed beside him. "You've got it bad," he said. "You know she's untouchable."

"That should stop me?"

Joe raised his brows. He scooped up a forkful of lemon meringue pie, his favorite. "I forget how much of a pit bull you can be."

"Did Dixie make the lemon pie?" Donovan asked innocently.

Joe ducked his head. "Tastes like hers."

"Are you ever going to fix things with her?"

His younger brother continued to eat without comment.

"Okay, if you're not going to fix it, are you going to start dating?"

"Maybe."

"You're in a tough spot."

"Yeah," Joe said. "The hazards of living in a small town."

"Dixie's in the same position, I imagine. Are you sure there's no hope? You've got sixteen years invested in this relationship."

"Like I don't know that?"

Donovan saw Ethan make his way to Laura and lean against her armrest. They talked easily. Ethan kept trying to see around her to the baby, but Isabella was nursing, and covered by a blanket. Keri looked peaceful in the midst of all the noise and chaos of the McCoy clan.

A loud whistle pierced the air—Nana Mae. It always made Donovan laugh to hear her, now eighty-nine, whistling like a stevedore, a skill she'd passed down to most of her grandchildren and great-grandchildren.

"Thank you, Nana Mae," Aggie said from where she stood under the patio roof. "I think it's time to open presents, so if Donny and Ethan would join us, please?"

With a small, embarrassed-looking smile, Ethan came across the lawn to hop into one of the chairs on the patio, next to a table stacked with bags.

Donovan joined him, but the whole time they unwrapped gifts, he kept an eye on Laura. He couldn't let her slip out. Not when he intended to walk her home.

Ethics be damned.

Chapter Seven

Father and son approached the whole present-unwrapping event with similar reluctance, Laura noticed. Ethan peeked into bags first then drew out the contents, whether it was a new toy, a used toy, pajamas or a bathing suit, with the same shy look.

"It really isn't my birthday yet," he said once, drawing laughter.

Donovan seemed almost embarrassed for a while, too, then got into the spirit of the moment. He'd been gifted with a box of "It's a Boy" cigars, a first-aid kit, coupons from several people for babysitting, a booster seat for the car and lots of products to start his own household—kid shampoo and pump soap, but also the other basics like dish soap and laundry detergent, and other kinds of cleaning products and utensils.

Laura had given them a pass to a family fun center in Sacramento, where they could play miniature golf, ride bumper boats and drive race cars.

Her gift to Ethan was the last one unwrapped. He ripped open the colorful paper to find two plastic swords upon which she'd glued a whole lot of fake gems. She'd had so much fun tracking down the toy swords in just a few hours and then decorating them like her scepter.

"Wow! Donovan, look! Brilliant, isn't it? Thanks, Laura."

Everyone went silent. Ethan noticed. He looked around. Donovan slipped an arm around his shoulders. "Maybe you could call me Dad."

Ethan looked unsure. "Oh. Okay. Dad."

Donovan ruffled Ethan's hair as people began talking and moving around, clearing off serving dishes. Laura decided to slip out, but she couldn't leave without telling Aggie goodbye and thank you.

"You're not leaving yet, are you?" Donovan asked, coming up beside her.

"Isn't it over?"

"Nope. We're just going to make room to dance."

"I don't dance." She just wanted to get away from the noise, to have her quiet house envelop her. Calm her. Having spent the evening watching Donovan—

"You don't dance?" He said it as if she were un-American or something.

"I have two left feet."

He looked down, then shook his head. Music filtered from outdoor speakers. People partnered up—husbands and wives, adults with kids, kids with kids. The song was neither fast nor slow, but that awkward tempo in between. He took her into his arms.

"Donovan, please. I really don't want to do this." But he'd already pulled her close, drawing her body-to-body with him, and suddenly she wanted to be there, even if she stepped on his toes.

"Not so bad, hmm?" he asked.

She didn't answer. Couldn't answer. Her heart was lodged in her throat. Every nerve ending did pirouettes throughout her body. But she was also aware that a lot of people were watching them. So while she wanted to lean against him and use the excuse of dancing to snuggle close, she pulled back a little, putting some space between them, and stumbling over his feet at the same time.

He laughed, low and sexy. "You're so obvious."

She met his teasing gaze. "About what?"

"About wanting me. You'll even trip just to get closer."

"In your dreams."

"Oh, yeah. Dreams, for sure." He whispered into her ear, "Hot ones. Detailed ones."

Laura had dated a lot, but no one like Donovan. However, she had always been direct at the beginning of the relationship, never really allowing any man to court her, or tease her, or tantalize, as Donovan was doing, but keeping things simple instead. She didn't know how to respond to his…wooing.

"Are you going to fire me?" she asked.

"I can't. Yet."

Ah. There it was. The anticipation. He was an expert at creating it. He was putting her on notice that once his legal needs were met, the professional relationship would be terminated and a more personal one would begin. She was safe as long as she continued to do work for him.

"I wonder how often you're speechless," he commented idly.

"I wonder how often you're humble."

He laughed then, full-throated and appreciative—and everyone looked, and smiled.

"I need to go home," she said, moving out of his arms, keeping a composed smile on her face for appearance's sake. He didn't try to talk her out of it, so she was able to say goodbye to people, including interrupting Ethan's swordplay with a cousin to give him a hug.

Laura walked through the side gate and out to the street. It wasn't dark yet, but the air had cooled to a more comfortable temperature than on her walk over. She hadn't gone twenty feet before Donovan jogged up beside her. She stared straight ahead, not acknowledging him. He kept silent, too, just matched her step for step.

She tried not to laugh. Tried hard. She'd almost succeeded when he started whistling "Ain't She Sweet."

She laughed then, and shoved him. His eyes twinkled.

"Why aren't you home, putting your son to bed?" she asked, choosing a safe topic.

"The party isn't over. He's still playing. Your gift was perfect, Laura. It opened him up. Did you notice that?"

She'd noticed he'd gotten more comfortable as the evening went along, but didn't consider her gift the catalyst. "I probably should've asked you first if you objected to toy swords."

"I don't know what I do or don't object to yet. I'm taking it day by day. But as a former boy myself, I think it's fine." He was quiet for a while, then, "He called me Dad."

She heard the emotion in his voice. "I gathered that was the first time. It was kind of cute how he called you Donovan."

"It sounded really strange, coming from him. I have to keep reminding myself that he just lost his mother, and I need to be careful not to push him about anything. It was spontaneous. We hadn't talked about what he should call me."

She squeezed his arm. They walked along in silence for a block or so.

"You don't like crowds much, do you?" he asked.

"No."

"Are you claustrophobic?"

She could say yes, use it as an excuse, but it wasn't the truth. "No."

"I've seen you at a lot of events, large and small. You're never in the middle of the action."

"Is that worthy of a headline?"

"I'm curious. You're personable, you don't seem shy, yet you hang back."

A lot of people jumped to incorrect conclusions about her, mostly based on her pageant wins, as if that would turn her into an extrovert. She'd entered pageants to earn prize money and scholarships, and had come out at the end of law school debt-free. Not many people could say that.

"I apologize, Laura," he said. "That probably sounded like criticism. I really am just curious. I mean, you go to these events, but don't participate, so, naturally, I wonder why."

"Sometimes someone railroads me into going," she said, eyeing him. "Even uses a child to do it."

"I'm always looking toward the goal. That's my fatal flaw."

"You mean winning."

"Is there a difference?"

They kept walking, past homes where children played in front yards and parents sat on porch swings, watching. Most people waved. Small Town, U.S.A. It did still exist. Not that everything was perfect. There was crime, of course, but people really did look out for each other.

"Want to stop by Jake and Keri's new house? Peek in the windows?" Donovan asked.

"Sure."

Suddenly the quiet between them seemed peaceful. Natural. She relaxed.

"This is nice," he said after a while.

"Yes."

Silence again. And it was okay again. When they reached the house, they walked up the steps to the porch. The curtains were pulled aside.

"Looks like we'll be having a garage sale," Donovan said, peering in. "Jake said the house comes as is. That's a lot of furniture in there."

"*Old* furniture."

"Antique?" he asked.

"Maybe, but doubtful. If it'd been valuable, someone in the family would've taken it out. You've all got a lot of work ahead of you."

"You wanna come help?" He bumped shoulders with her. "I could line you up with a pressure washer. You could wear your world-famous bikini and spray down the siding."

She shook her head. "You never give up."

"There'll be time for that when I die."

She admired his attitude, frankly, but she wasn't about to give him ammunition when he created enough on his own. "I'll be helping Keri, I'm sure, but it'll be after work hours. I'm in Sacramento two or three days a week, remember." Maybe she would invite everyone for a swim when they were done. She could pick up food from a deli near work and bring it home with her.

"I've noticed that you and Keri, and Dixie, too, for that matter, have been hanging out," he said.

"Yes." She'd been making an effort to have girlfriends, something she'd been missing, always afraid to reveal herself to anyone. Almost every relationship she had was superficial, and she'd come to recognize that—and be appalled by it, even though she knew the reasons why.

"That's it?" Donovan asked. "'Yes'?"

"Yes, I have been hanging out with them more," she said, teasing him.

"You are tough. I'd like to see you in action in a courtroom."

"I don't end up there often. Only if a divorce case gets really nasty and we have to take it to court to resolve it. I pride myself on being able to get people to come to a determination without it going that far, though. Most of the time I can follow through."

He sat on the top step, inviting her with a gesture to join him.

"Is that part of your reputation, then? Negotiating amicable divorces?" he asked, waving at a couple out walking.

"Those are also extremely rare. A couple may start out thinking they can keep things cool between them, but it doesn't always work. Where emotions are involved, there's always reaction. Plus, friends and family interfere, as well, a big cause of difficult divorces. But I do my best to keep things on task, especially where kids are involved. So many of them get so hurt."

"Did you become a divorce lawyer because of your own parents' divorce?"

She tucked her hands in her lap. "I do family law, which isn't exclusively divorces, but pretty much you're right. It was ugly."

"So that's what drives you?"

"Partly. Been there, done that. It helps."

"You never saw your father again?"

She pulled her body closer, clasping her hands tighter, leaning forward more. "No. Never."

"Do you know if he's alive? If you have half siblings somewhere?"

"I have no idea."

"Never wanted to find out?"

She eyed him directly. "Hey, newsman, just because you have a huge, loving family doesn't mean those of us who don't are searching for that. I've never felt denied."

He hesitated a few beats. "You're right. I apologize. And, believe me, sometimes I think you're the lucky one."

She would like to see him at work. He adjusted quickly to changes in conversation and situations, probably a critical skill for a top-notch journalist who needed to experience something in order to write about it to his personal standards, especially in war-torn countries.

Laura admired that about him. A lot. The list of pros about him kept growing.

She stood. "You should probably head back so you can tuck your son into bed. I'm fine walking home from here."

"It's on my way back to Mom's." He stood, as well, then placed his hand on the small of her back as they headed up the walkway.

As it had earlier, the touch of his fingers sent her pulse racing. Need filled her, almost painfully.

Maybe she would be the one to fire *him* as a client….

She stopped that thought cold. "How do you think Ethan is going to react to Millie leaving? Has he talked about it with you?"

"He alternates between being okay with it, probably because he's been so busy, and being sad. He understands that she's going. I don't think he really understands how far away she'll be, and that she can't just drop in. Fortunately, we'll have Jake's new house to work on, and then getting settled in the cabin, and then kindergarten. It should keep him busy."

"So, you're not going to take him away for a while?"

"I decided not to. We'll have privacy at the cabin. And he'll need people around him, too. He tends to seek out women. That's his comfort level. I don't want to interfere with that transition. I don't know, Laura, I'm just trying my best to figure out what works. I'm used to knowing what I'm doing. I'm not sleeping well, I can tell you that."

They reached her house and stopped at the head of the brick walkway. "Thanks for the company," she said. If she'd had pockets, she would've stuffed her hands in them. She clenched them into fists instead. "I'll give you a call when your paperwork is ready."

He did jam his hands in his pockets. His gaze dropped to her mouth. He took a step closer, still staring, slowly moving up to her eyes.

She waited, logic having taken a vacation from her brain, desire filling the space instead. She'd always loved his mouth.…

"Good night," he said. He eased around her and headed down the street.

Laura let out a long, slow breath. She'd wanted him to kiss her. Wanted it bad. She would've let him, too, right there on the street in front of her house. In public.

Shocked at herself, she moved toward her house. Her phone was ringing when she opened her front door. When she picked it up, all she heard was someone whistling "Ain't She Sweet." She listened until he let the last note fade out into one long, drawn-out sound. She hung up the phone gently.

It should've made her smile. Instead, her throat burned and a lump formed. She went into her office and pulled her high school yearbooks off the shelf, sat cross-legged on the floor and thumbed through them, something she hadn't done in years—probably since she'd graduated.

Her hair was perfect in every photograph she came across of herself, her smile exactly the same. Her pageant smile, she realized. Teeth showing, eyes vacant. She found Donovan's senior portrait. He looked confident. Cocky. She found other pictures of him—student-body president, newspaper editor, debate team, homecoming king. Big man on campus.

She closed her eyes, remembering the day she'd finally worked up the nerve to approach him. Lots of boys had pursued her, but she knew it wasn't for her mind. Donovan hadn't given her a second glance, which was probably why she wanted him. She figured he would appreciate that she had a brain and could use it, not be intimidated by her. And she thought he was the hottest guy on campus, wanted him without knowing exactly what it was she was wanting. She knew the basics of the birds and bees, but she'd had no idea she could lose all common sense over a guy.

He certainly had no idea how much it had cost her to go up to him in the school parking lot and introduce herself. Determined not to wait a day longer, she'd been waiting for an hour before he finally showed. His was the last car there.

"I know who you are," he'd said.

"I really like you," she'd blurted.

"Uh. Okay." He jingled his keys in his pocket and looked around. *Now* she could recognize that he'd been looking for someone to rescue him from an awkward situation. But that was then.

Maybe a smart girl would've noticed and not forced the issue. She was smart, but not about boys. "I'd like to kiss you."

His eyes widened. He took a step back. But she lunged, planting her mouth on his. He grabbed her arms and moved her away from him. "What the hell are you doing?" he asked. "Are you crazy?"

She was. Crazy in love with a boy she knew nothing about, just that she wanted to be with him. “You don’t have a girlfriend. I asked.”

“So?”

“So, how about me?”

He frowned. “What are you offering, exactly?”

“What would you like?”

Laura could almost laugh about it now. She’d been so naïve. Her knowledge of sex was minimal, just a concept she’d seen in books and movies. She didn’t understand the emotional commitment it entailed, good or bad.

“Look,” he’d said calmly, being much more mature than she. “I’m flattered, okay? But you’re too young, you know?”

He’d softened the blow by telling her that. She recognized now he’d just been being kind to her, letting her down easy.

“And in two months,” he’d added, “I’ll be out of here. I’m not coming back.”

“Why?”

“Because there’s nothing here for me except my family. I want to travel the world. I want to do something important. Don’t you?”

She hadn’t known yet. She was only a freshman in high school. How could she know what she wanted three years down the road? Still, she would have two months to change his mind. If she worked at it, she could do that.

"I want to be with you," she said.

"I don't know how else to tell you I'm not interested," he said, clenching his jaw, his frustration with her finally letting loose. Then he'd gotten into his car and driven away, leaving her standing in the empty parking lot, her face red, her heart broken. She'd never approached a boy again. Never went on a date in high school. Lots of boys looked, but none of them asked her out. She had an invisible *Go Away* sign on her forehead.

Then a month after she graduated, she learned she had uterine cancer, a secret only she and her mother knew. Her world had turned upside down, and hadn't fully righted itself since.

And now family man Donovan McCoy was the last man she should get involved with.

The problem was—she wanted him as much now as she had at fifteen. She should be discouraging him, but she couldn't seem to do that as she could with any other man.

She closed the yearbooks and set them aside. She couldn't have him then because he had bigger plans for himself. She shouldn't have him now because he would want more than she could offer.

That left her stuck in limbo, attracted but unable to act on it. And dangerously close to falling in love with a man she shouldn't love, one who shouldn't love her back.

Because she could never give him what he wanted most, even if he didn't realize it yet—a family.

Chapter Eight

The night was mid-July hot. No breeze stirred the air. The sun would set in an hour, bringing a welcome drop in temperature. Until then, Laura's swimming pool was the best place to be.

Donovan sat on the edge with Joe, their feet in the water, which couldn't really be called cool. Wearing a life vest, Ethan clung to Donovan's ankles and bobbed in the water. A few teenage nieces and nephews played Marco Polo at the other end.

Most of the family had spent the past two days sanding, painting, cleaning and decluttering. They would hold a garage sale the next day, Saturday. Aggie would run the show. She loved wheeling and dealing.

Joe elbowed him. "Are you as disappointed as I am?"

"About what?"

"That Laura's wearing a one-piece bathing suit."

Donovan studied her as she refilled a potato-chip bowl and talked to Keri, who had Isabella in her arms. No, he wasn't disappointed—well, he was disappointed for himself, but he was content that no one else was seeing her that way. She wore not only a one-piece but a loose, hot-pink blouse over the plain black suit.

"I hadn't thought about it," he finally said to Joe, who laughed. He'd obviously been goading Donovan.

"Much," Donovan amended. It'd been a nice surprise when she'd stopped by Jake and Keri's house to invite them all for dinner and a swim when they were done. About half of the family accepted the offer. The pool was full.

Nana Mae came through the back door then, Dixie with her. Dixie hadn't been able to help much with the house because she attended cosmetology school in Sacramento during the day, but she would undoubtedly help over the weekend. Despite the awkwardness between her and Joe since she'd broken off their engagement, she was still one of the family. Longevity counted.

Guilt dropped over Donovan's shoulders as he watched Nana Mae settle in a chair. He hadn't spent any time alone with her since Ethan had arrived. Donovan needed to change that before she started giving him The Look, the one she'd directed at any of them when they'd misbehaved as kids. The Look was much more effective than anything she might shout.

Too late, he realized. She was giving him The Look right then. Even from across the pool he could see her crystal-blue eyes firing displeasure at him. Donovan had been on the receiving end of that particular expression much more than the rest of his siblings.

"Come in the water with me and play," Ethan said. He'd stayed close to Donovan ever since they'd taken Millie to the airport that morning, but hadn't called him Dad again yet.

"Please," Donovan reminded his son.

"Pretty please, with a cherry on top."

Donovan slipped into the pool. Ethan climbed on his back and clung to his neck, his chin resting on Donovan's shoulder.

"I miss Grammy," he said.

"Of course you do."

"When can I see her again?"

"Probably at Christmas. But you can call her, you know."

"Now?"

"She isn't home yet. It takes a long time to get to England from here. She'll call us when she's home."

Ethan moved his hands from Donovan's neck to his shoulders, relaxing a little. "Let's go pull Laura into the water and play with her."

The idea appealed to Donovan, too, although differently. "An excellent plan, my boy." He swam quietly toward where she'd taken a seat on the edge, watching Jake dipping Isabella in the water, her arms and legs moving wildly, splashing water everywhere.

"*Laur*-a!" Ethan shouted in a singsong voice. "We're coming to *get* you."

Donovan grabbed her ankle before she could get away. She yelped. Ethan giggled, a joyful sound to Donovan's ears. Then she fell into the water with a splat, sputtering as she surfaced.

"We *got* you," Ethan said happily.

"His idea," Donovan added.

"And a four-year-old boy holds all the power? You couldn't say no?" She shoved her hair out of her eyes, and kept that now-familiar forced smile on her face.

"I'm almost five."

"Yeah. He's almost five." Donovan loved when she got on her high horse about something.

She tried to pull off her wet blouse. Donovan helped her, then tossed it onto the deck. By the time she turned around, any signs of annoyance were gone. She stole Ethan away from him, and they went off and played. Appreciating how she'd turned the tables on him—and knowing when to admit defeat—he got out of the pool and went to visit his grandmother. Dixie had just hopped into the pool, too.

Donovan wiped the water from his face, kissed Nana Mae's cheek, then sat in the empty chair next to her. She wore a new hairstyle, a frequent occurrence now that Dixie was there to fix her hair every morning.

No more mass of permed curls, but stylish, chic looks that took ten years off her.

"You've been avoiding me," she stated.

"Guilty."

"Am I so formidable?"

He sort of laughed. "You even have to ask?"

"I don't mean to be." She looked puzzled by the very idea of it.

"You don't know the reach of your power, Nana Mae."

"Power? Me?" She thought it over for a minute. "Okay. I'll accept that, since I think you're really talking about respect. Anyway, that's no excuse for ignoring me."

"I have no legitimate excuse, except I've been busy." He leaned back, keeping an eye on Laura and Ethan as they held hands and jumped up and down. Maybe she'd had the notion that by wearing a one-piece black suit, she wouldn't draw anyone's attention, but seeing her jump like that? If he was alone, he would salute.

"Yes, dear, I know you've been busy, which is why I'm not going to pester you about it. But as soon as Jake and Keri have moved into the house, and you've moved into the cabin, I expect to see you."

"I'll take you to the Lode for lunch."

"That would be lovely."

"I'm sorry I disappointed you," he said then, getting the worst of it out of the way now, not wanting to have it festering between them.

She settled her purple cane in front of her, resting

both hands on the crook, looking thoughtful. "I know the McCoy legacy carries with it a lot of pressure, Donny—no children out of wedlock and no divorces. But I think the very fact that legacy exists has made us all more careful, more responsible. Even the ones who marry into this crazy clan feel a different expectation for themselves. It doesn't hurt."

"And I didn't live up to that expectation. No one regrets that more than I do, since I missed five years of my son's life. I didn't get to see his birth, or celebrate all those firsts."

"Do you think marriage to Anne would have worked?"

"I would've made it work."

"She seems very selfish."

"Self-protective, I think. And angry. But also selfish," he decided. "So was I."

"You still would've done your duty."

Yes, he would have. But would he have been happy? Content? Enjoyed forever-after love? They were questions without answers. He was into fact, not speculation. "I'd prefer not to discuss Anne anymore. What's done is done, and she's not here to defend herself."

His grandmother stared into his eyes for a few long seconds, then patted his cheek. "You're a good boy."

"Thank you."

"And you've got eyes for Laura Bannister, I see."

"I'm male."

She laughed, then looked toward Laura. "That girl could use a good, strong partner at her side."

"That *girl* is stronger than most men."

"Maybe. But don't equate strength with need. She needs the same things that everyone else does."

He didn't want to get into it with his grandmother. He didn't even know how he felt about Laura, except he wanted to strip her naked and not let her out of touching range for, oh, say a year or so. "How about letting me figure out one life crisis at a time?"

Her eyes twinkled. "I believe I can do that."

"Your hair looks very nice," he said, turning to another subject. "Must be nice having a live-in hairdresser."

"I'd rather she and Joe got back together. I've tried to talk to her about it, but she threatens to leave whenever I bring it up. And it's not that I need someone living with me, you know, but I do enjoy her company. Plus, the reason she came to stay with me in the first place was to be able to go to school full-time. She's so close to finishing."

"Here's your prune," Laura called out, sending Ethan toward Donovan, who grabbed a towel and wrapped him up. As warm as the evening and the pool were, Ethan was shivering, his body having had enough of the water.

Taking a chance, Donovan lifted Ethan into his lap and held him close. For once, he didn't even squirm, making Donovan very happy. How could he love someone so fast, so completely? It hadn't taken more than a minute and would last a lifetime.

As they waited for Ethan to stop shivering, Nana Mae tried to talk to him, but she was the only person who turned him shy. He would nod or shake his head to answer a question. He spoke if he had to, but with as few words as possible.

Laura climbed out of the pool then, emerging like some kind of water goddess. She tilted her head to one side and wrung out her hair. Her bathing suit gaped just enough to tease.

"You should get Laura a towel, Dad, and let her sit on your lap for a minute. I'm all warmed up."

Nana Mae laughed quietly. Donovan didn't dare look at her.

"She'll be fine, bud. She wasn't in the water as long as you."

"Oh. Can I get a cookie?"

"Just one. We need to leave pretty soon."

"Aw, man."

Donovan didn't know how he felt that Ethan had learned that particular phrase from his teenage cousins. He didn't want Ethan growing up too fast.

Ethan slid off Donovan's lap and scurried over to the food table, choosing a cookie about the size of his face, it seemed, and probably the equivalent of four cookies.

The pool emptied out, the long, hard workday catching up with everyone. No one asked if they could help clean up, they just did, even as Laura kept trying to tell everyone to leave it. Hadn't she been around his family enough to know that wasn't how they did things?

He saw her finally give up and accept their help. She'd tied a brightly colored skirt around her waist that undulated as she moved. He caught her looking at him several times as he and Joe moved patio furniture back in place, while at the same time keeping an eye on Ethan, who had curled up on a chaise.

Laura grabbed a dry towel from a stack she'd put out and tucked it around him, bending to whisper something in his ear. He smiled, but his eyes remained closed.

"Looks like they've bonded," Joe said.

"I think she's a safe haven in a sea of rowdy McCoys. He's still working at sorting us all out."

"Either that or he's as infatuated as you are."

Infatuated? Was that it? Donovan was on fire for her, certainly. And he got a kick out of riling her to see her reaction. She smelled good, too, which always drew him closer. He liked when she stood her ground as much as he liked that she sometimes got nervous enough to back away. Infatuated? It was a good enough description, he supposed.

Joe dropped a hand on his shoulder, bringing Donovan out of his stupor. "I'll give you a ride home. Looks like Ethan will be deadweight to carry."

"Thanks. I need to tell Laura goodbye first."

He tracked her down in the kitchen, alone, everyone else gone except for Joe. She was bent over the dishwasher, adding silverware, her very nice rear in his direct line of vision. She sure made it hard to resist her. He must have made a noise, because she spun around.

"I figured you'd already gone," she said.

"Without saying goodbye? My mother raised me better than that."

"According to your mother, you were the most stubborn, independent, doesn't-play-well-with-others child she bore."

"That's probably true. But I still learned manners." He moved closer. "To say please. To hold doors open. To tell the hostess goodbye."

She didn't say anything, just watched him suspiciously.

"And to say thank you." He bent close and kissed her cheek.

She went absolutely still. He felt a moment, just the tiniest moment, where she leaned into him, her hand brushing his arm as if to steady herself.

He moved back. Their eyes met. Hard to resist, for sure.

"You're welcome," she said in slightly more than a whisper. "I had fun, too."

"See you tomorrow?"

She found her voice. "I imagine so. I told Keri I'd put new shelf paper in the kitchen cabinets."

"I'm in charge of installing the new toilets."

"Sounds fun." Her eyes twinkled.

"I'm flushed with anticipation."

She laughed then, and he decided to leave on that note.

He was aware of her following him into the backyard

and saying goodbye to Joe. Donovan lifted the sleeping Ethan into his arms, then headed for the front door. Joe preceded them, so the door was already open. Donovan stopped to give Laura one last look. She ran a hand over Ethan's hair. Donovan felt her other hand slide down his spine, stopping at the small of his back, as he had done to her a few times.

Get the damn paperwork finished up, he ordered her silently. He wanted to see where this relationship could go.

She smiled as if aware of his thoughts and her own power, maybe even happy to be causing him discomfort? "Good night, Donovan."

Like hell it was going to be.

Chapter Nine

A week passed, during which Donovan ran into Laura now and then, usually at Jake and Keri's house. Every time, he would ask how the paperwork was coming along. Every time, she would say, "Patience."

The anticipation was killing him, was even interfering with the decisions he needed to make about his future. Consequently, for the first time in his memory, he was procrastinating. He and his brothers generally took after their father, a man who'd worked hard, never missing a day on the job until he keeled over and died of a heart attack at the age of sixty-one. Donovan was twenty-three when it happened, and every year the loss grew bigger.

"Daydreaming?" Jake asked, coming up behind Donovan as he finished installing a new medicine chest in the master bathroom, the last job on his to-do list. Tomorrow the new furniture would be delivered, and they could begin to settle in and make it theirs.

"Thinking about Dad."

Jake leaned a shoulder against the bathroom doorjamb. "He's been on my mind a lot, too."

"How does it happen that I miss him more now than ever?"

"You've been too busy until now? You're a father yourself?" Jake looked around. "He would've loved working on the house with us."

A carpenter turned general contractor, John McCoy had lived for moments like this—family helping family. Pitching in. Getting the job done quickly, but doing it right.

"Do you think he was happy?" Donovan asked.

"Who?" Joe asked, coming up beside Jake and peering into the now-completed bathroom.

"Dad," Jake and Donovan said at the same time.

"Of course he was happy." Joe stepped around Jake and into the room. "What a change. Does Keri like it?"

"Keri is thrilled," the woman in question said, joining them, sliding her arm around Jake's waist. He pulled her close. "It's sparkling clean, too. Did you do that?" she asked Donovan.

"Your husband did the honors."

She angled closer to Jake, setting her hands on his chest. "I find that incredibly sexy."

Jake laughed, then kissed her.

Donovan hadn't had that kind of relationship in a long time, if ever. That playfully sexy banter and teasing-foreplay kind of rapport. His longest relationship had been with Anne, and it'd been intense and serious.

"Hey!" Donovan said. "I put up the cabinet. Don't I get a kiss for that?"

"Get your own girl," Jake said, tucking his wife against him.

"I can think of one," Joe said.

Keri smiled. "Me, too."

Donovan felt like a teenager, but he asked anyway. "Does she talk about me?"

"Not one word."

He tried to swallow his disappointment.

"She's very good at keeping confidences, you know. Comes in handy in her profession."

"I agree, but how does not saying anything mean she's interested?"

"It's something she *could* talk about. She chooses not to, which gives it more importance, at least in my book."

"Plus there's that whole X-rated-look-in-her-eyes thing," Joe added.

"That, too," Keri agreed lightly.

Donovan's cell phone rang, displaying Laura's office

number. "Are you ready to toss ethics to the wind?" he said instead of hello.

A beat passed. "Well, not today, but I'm free tomorrow."

Crap. Not Laura, but her mother. "Hi, Dolly."

"Hey, sugar." She was laughing like crazy. So were his brothers and sister-in-law.

"What's up?" he asked.

"Laura wanted me to notify you that your papers are done and ready to be signed. If you want to stop by and pick them up, you can have the weekend to read through them. Then we'll arrange for some witnesses when you sign on Monday or Tuesday, or whenever you want."

"Okay, thanks. Sweet 'ums," he added.

She laughed as she hung up.

He looked at his watch. "I finished my official to-do list," he said to Jake. "Anything else you can think of?"

"I'm sensing there's somewhere else you'd like to be."

Donovan shrugged. "Only if you really don't need me for a few hours."

"Take the whole day, if you want. You've already done more than I would've thought humanly possible."

Donovan *had* pushed himself all week—as a distraction, as a way to vent frustration, and, of course, to help Jake and Keri get moved in as soon as possible. As much as he loved his mother, he was ready for his own space, and to build his relationship with his son.

On his way home, he stopped by Laura's office, making a detour next door first.

"Hey, there, sugar," Dolly said, grinning.

"Hey yourself, sweet 'ums. I brought you a bribe." He handed her a strawberry ice-cream cone.

She reached for it. "I'm taking a lick first, just in case I can't go along with whatever favor you're going to ask and I have to give it back."

He smiled. He didn't know Dolly well, but he had, on occasion, wondered how such a gregarious woman could be Laura's mother. Or maybe the point was that he didn't know *Laura* well enough.

Donovan started to speak, but Dolly held up a finger. "One more."

He sat in the chair across from her desk. "Go ahead and finish. I'll wait." He whistled tunelessly, looking around the room.

With one bite left, she hesitated, the bottom inch of the cone in hand. "What do you need?"

"Laura's in her Sacramento office today, right?"

"Right."

"I need for you to get me an appointment with her late this afternoon."

"That's all?" She popped the final bite into her mouth. "You didn't need a bribe for that."

He leaned back and crossed an ankle over his knee. "Well, there's a little more to it."

Her brows arched high.

"I don't want her to know I'm coming."

"Afraid she won't see you otherwise?"

"*Sure* of it."

She drummed her fingers on her desktop, studying him, then stopped abruptly. "Okay. Under what name?"

"Cory Spondent."

It took her a second, but then she laughed, a big shout of appreciation. "You don't think she'll figure out it's you?"

He grinned back. "Not until it's too late, I hope."

"She's pretty smart."

"It's something I admire about her."

"I figured you would. Okay. So, what reason can I give her assistant for your appointment?"

"Trust."

"That you want to have her put a trust together for you?"

"No. Just trust."

Her smile turned soft. "Okay." She picked up the phone and made the arrangements, then passed him a large packet that had been sitting on her desk. "Four o'clock. Her assistant's name is Moses. He likes butterscotch sundaes. No walnuts. He's allergic."

"Good to know." He stood. "Thanks, Dolly."

"Donovan? She's put up some pretty solid walls."

"I've noticed. Patience isn't usually a virtue of mine."

A thoughtful look came over her face, as if debating what to say. He waited. Sometimes he could be as patient as Job.

"I'm going to paint you a picture," Dolly said finally. "Do you know that house on Denton, the big old white Victorian?"

"Sure. Wraparound porch. West windows face the park. In complete disrepair."

"Exactly. When Laura was a little girl, we used to walk by there on our way to the park, and she would always stop and stare at it. She called it the *It's a Wonderful Life* house. Not because it looked exactly like the movie one, but because she thought having a house like that would give her a wonderful life."

He got it. She might appear to be sensible and logical, but inside there was a dreamer, too. He needed to remember that.

"So," Dolly said. "Even though patience isn't one of your virtues, try."

Or leave her alone. He heard the unspoken request as clearly as if she'd said it.

What she didn't know was he'd never wanted like this. And he wasn't about to deny himself unless Laura said no.

He didn't think she would say no.

"Your last appointment is here." Moses stood just inside Laura's door.

She glanced at her computer, pulled up her daily calendar. "Did you already give me a file on…" She read the name, Cory Spondent. "Cory. It's a *him,* I assume?"

Moses, twenty-six, tall and as skinny as a birch tree,

looked flustered, a first for the usually cool, easygoing man. "I forgot."

Speechless, she stared at him. He never forgot anything. Ever. "Are you okay?"

He nodded.

"Can you put a file together while I'm talking to him, please? It's a trust he's interested in, right? He's—" She stopped, her gaze zipping back to the computer screen. Cory Spondent? She laughed.

"Send Mr. McCoy in, please. And I'm sure he'll want coffee."

Moses stood aside, and Donovan came in, a manila envelope in hand, obviously having been waiting just outside the door instead of in the reception area.

"Cory Spondent?" she said, gesturing to him to take a chair opposite her desk. She knew why he'd come. So did her body. Blood raced through her, scorching hot. Almost two weeks—plus fifteen years—of anticipation swirled and stormed.

"You laughed," he said. "I heard you."

"Well, of course. I do give you points for creativity, but I don't know why you bothered." *Yes, you do.*

"Just wanted to surprise you."

"Were you going to be in Sacramento anyway?" *No, he'd planned this, just this.*

"I came here specifically to see you." He laid the packet on her desk. "Nice office. A little on the stodgy side."

She didn't take offense since she agreed with his assessment. The firm was old and respected, and the furnishings reflected it in the dark woods and deep-tone colors. The walls were thick, not allowing voices to drift down hallways or room to room. "So, Donovan, what's going on that couldn't wait until I got home?"

I'm glad you couldn't wait.

"The paperwork is done, Laura."

Bells seemed to toll at the statement.

"It's time," he added.

"I'm your lawyer," she said, knowing that was about to change.

He leaned forward and plucked one of her business cards out of its brass holder, then set it on her desk right in front of her. "Which one of these attorneys do you respect the most?"

Her finger shook just a little as she pointed to a name. "But he's a partner. All these men are. I think you'd be happier with Monique Davis. She's an associate, like me."

"See if she's available. Please."

Moses came in with a mug of coffee while she made the call. Donovan set it on a coaster on her desk without tasting it. He leaned back casually, his body seeming relaxed, but his eyes were focused directly on her, his jaw as tight as hers felt.

Over the next interminable minutes, papers were signed and witnessed. Then when the room was empty except for the two of them again, Donovan got up and headed to the door.

She held her breath, stunned. He was leaving? Why? To drag it out further? To wear her down even more with anticipation? To—

He shut the door and walked back toward her, coming around the desk, and setting his hands on her armrests.

"You're fired, Ms. Bannister."

"Good." Everything was simple now. She would know, finally, what it was like with him.

She grabbed his shirt and pulled him closer, but he took the final action. He kissed her, and it was every long-held fantasy come true. His lips were soft and demanding, his tongue gentle and seeking, his breath hot and tempting. She'd been waiting half her life for this moment.

He slipped his arms around her and pulled her out of her chair so that they were body to body, deepening the kiss and contact, groaning, gentleness turning flatteringly fierce. He slid his hands down her back, curved them over her rear, pulled her snugly against him. Sounds came from inside her that she didn't recognize and couldn't control.

"This isn't the place," she said, tipping her head back as he ran his lips and tongue down her throat into the deep V of her blouse.

He touched his forehead to hers, his breath wavering. "Do you need all your girly stuff?"

"Girly…stuff?"

"Yeah. Makeup. Lacy nightgown. You know. Frills."

"As opposed to what?"

"Coming with me right now to a hotel. As is."

Laura was torn. She wanted it to be good. Not perfect—she was realistic, after all, and firsts weren't ever perfect—but good. Memorable. Waiting until they got back to Chance City wouldn't make a difference. Nor would a sexy nightgown. They were both too anxious to deal with the trappings.

"Let's go, newsman. Correspondent."

He chose a large, pricey hotel walking distance from her office, a place big enough to offer some anonymity. Then instead of going to the front desk he guided her to the elevator banks. From his pocket he pulled out a card key.

"You planned," she said as soon as the elevator doors shut. She leaned into him when he put his arm around her and kissed her.

"I hoped." He cupped her face. "I figured the odds were in my favor, but I had to allow room for your feelings about the matter, which I didn't want to presume."

The bell pinged, and the doors opened. They ran down the hall, stumbling, laughing, anticipating. He surprised her by sweeping her into his arms and carrying her inside, her briefcase banging against the doorjamb. She didn't know what he meant by the grand gesture. Maybe nothing. She didn't want to read anything into it.

"You *really* planned," she said, looking around. He'd folded down the bedding, leaving just the bottom sheet, the huge, beckoning expanse of a king bed.

Champagne on ice on the nightstand. Chocolate-covered strawberries. Drapes drawn.

"I'm not a barbarian." He set her down. "Champagne?"

"Later. Much later."

"Laura." He grabbed her hands and held them against his chest. "I have to be home tonight. As much as I'd like to spend the night with you, I can't. Ethan—"

She put her fingers against his mouth. "I understand." She didn't want their relationship to be public, anyway, needing to see where it was going first—if anywhere. For now she just wanted him.

Laura let her suit jacket drift down her arms, then tossed it onto a chair. She stepped out of her high heels, kicking them aside. The rest was up to him.

And he knew exactly what to do and how to do it. How to let the backs of his fingers brush against her skin as he unbuttoned her blouse. How to ease down the zipper of her skirt and slip his hands underneath the fabric to push it to the floor in a bare whisper of sound, her blouse quickly joining the skirt. She didn't wear pantyhose in the summer, so she was left wearing only high-cut white panties and a matching lace bra.

"You have tan lines," he said, surprise in his voice. "So, your story about your bikini being confining was just that? A story? You don't sunbathe in the nude. You just meant to stir me up."

She looped her arms around his neck. "It worked, too, didn't it?"

"Yeah." He kissed her, lingering until she couldn't get enough of him. "The idea of you naked by your pool turned me on, big time. As I'm sure you know. But the tan lines? Very sexy, too."

He took his time then, looking and touching, teasing and promising, her skin on fire from his caresses, from the need. He ran his fingers through her hair, freeing it, finger-combing the tangles out. "You know what people call you?" he asked.

"The Ice Queen?" she guessed.

He looked startled. "Not that I've heard. They call you The Body."

"You mean men. Men call me that."

"Some women probably, too," he said with a grin, reaching for her bra clasp.

She stopped him. "Let's catch you up first." She went to work on him, undressing him as slowly as he'd undressed her, revealing his body to her appreciative eyes and hands. Scars marred his skin here and there, some looking much more serious than others, a visual reminder of the risks he took—*liked* to take. He kept himself in shape, but wasn't overdone. She didn't like the overly brawny look. He was perfect—strong arms, broad shoulders, a wide chest with a dusting of black hair that arrowed straight down his body.

Kneeling, she ran her hands down that tempting line and under his briefs, not rushing the unwrapping, the unmatched pleasure of discovery. She heard him suck air between his teeth as her fingertips grazed his velvety hardness. His thighs went taut; then he hooked his hands under her arms and pulled her up. Her bra was off in an instant, her breasts filling his hands, her nipples sucked into his mouth, teeth scraping, tongue circling. He moved her back until her knees hit the bed and she landed with a bounce. He wasn't slow or gentle removing her panties—nor did she want him to be. She wanted him over her, around her, inside her.

"You are incredible," he said, harsh and low, as he ran a hand down her body, barely touching her, just enough to drive her wild. "Perfect."

She could hardly catch her breath. "So are you." She wrapped her hand around him, guiding him, needing him.

He squeezed his eyes shut for a few moments. "You're on the pill?" he asked, impatient.

I can't get pregnant. "It's taken care of," she said, closing her eyes as he pressed into her, stretching and filling. Then he went motionless, letting their connection just be. She didn't know whether it was her pulse or his she felt—maybe both—but it pounded where they were joined. The absence of movement stretched out the climax she felt building, second by second. He lifted his head and kissed her, hot, wet, openmouthed, mimicking the act itself but not moving his hips, just staying there. She clenched around him.

"Yes," he whispered against her mouth. "Keep going."

He was giving her control, yet he was completely in control, too. Equals. Partners. Light-headed, she tensed and released him rhythmically until his body shook and hers arched. Then at exactly the same moment, they moved in need, melded in desire, soared in satisfaction.

She'd never felt closer to any human being in her life.

And it was perfect.

Too perfect. Scary perfect.

She wrapped her arms around him as he collapsed against her, feeling the sting of tears, and a huge, hot lump in her throat.

How had she ever thought it would be simple?

Chapter Ten

Donovan jammed a pillow against the headboard and tucked his hands behind his head as he waited for Laura to emerge from the bathroom. After all the wondering, the anticipation, and then the incredible pleasure, he should feel relaxed….

He was more tense than ever.

Every reason he'd created for steering clear of her had been valid. She was a banquet, a feast for the eyes and mouth. He should be satisfied, but hunger for her growled, demanding to be fed again. A taste of her wasn't enough.

The door clicked open. He enjoyed watching her walk toward him, but kept his gaze on her face, needing to read what was there. She'd taken a long time in the bathroom, much longer than he would've expected.

Second thoughts, maybe?

No. She would've come out wearing the robe hanging on the back of the door. Instead she was gloriously naked, sexy tan lines and all. Her smile was small and tight. Why? She didn't look as though she'd been crying.

Donovan scooted over, holding out a hand to her, pulling her close, wrapping her in his arms. She let out a long, slow breath and slipped one foot between his.

"Are you okay?" he asked, his breath stirring her hair.

"I'm fine."

She wasn't fine, that much he knew. He needed to see her eyes. "Want some champagne?"

"Sure."

They sat up. He opened the bottle without ceremony and poured two flutes, passing her one, touching the lip of his glass to hers but not saying anything, not sure where he stood. He took comfort in the fact she hadn't gotten dressed.

After they'd each taken a sip, he offered her the plate of chocolate-covered strawberries. He'd had fantasies about feeding them to her, but that didn't seem like something she would enjoy at the moment.

He waited for her to finish eating the first one, then said, "You're quiet."

"I know. I'm sorry."

He was afraid to ask why. "Can we talk about it?"

After a few seconds, she laughed, low and soft.

"That cost you a lot, didn't it? You don't want to talk about it, whatever *it* might be."

"Not really. But I do want to know why you're so quiet." Usually he didn't second-guess anything he did. Maybe other things hadn't mattered as much as this. It was taking every bit of his control not to pull her under him and take her again.

"I'm just feeling a little overwhelmed," she said.

"In what way?"

She brushed his hair, then rubbed his earlobe between her fingers. "You have to understand that this is something I've wanted since I was fourteen—and I didn't even know what I was wanting. Every time you came to town since then, every time I saw you at a wedding or a barbecue or whatever, it was brought home to me again. You've been kind of an obsession."

"And now it's been fulfilled and you're disappointed?"

"On the contrary." She flattened her hand on his chest. "I want more. Lots more."

"I'm willing to accommodate that."

She smiled, then let her hand drift down his chest, his stomach, his abdomen and beyond. "I can see that you are," she said. "It's also complicated now."

He clenched his teeth as her fingertips danced over him. "In what way?"

"The relationship has to be private. Stolen moments. Can you do that?"

It wasn't what he wanted, but he understood what she was saying, and why. There would be too much speculation from his family, putting pressure on them. And then there was Ethan. Donovan didn't want to confuse his son by being gone overnight, and he couldn't invite Laura to stay over at the cabin after they moved in.

But he wasn't giving her up. "I can do that, Laura. Can you?"

She took his champagne flute and set it on the night-stand with hers, then straddled him, settling herself exactly where he wanted her.

"I don't want to give this up, newsman."

"Neither do I."

"Would you be saying the same thing if I were dressed?"

He was glad she'd recovered her sense of humor. "What do you think?"

She took the lead then, and he let himself enjoy the view and the ride. He thought he'd last longer, be able to take more time, use more finesse, but need stopped him from keeping any kind of control—not to mention she kept bringing him to the brink, and then stopping at the pivotal moment. Finally he pulled her down, rolled over and started a rhythm designed to bring them both to climax quickly and mutually again, their bodies and needs attuned.

The moment she hit the peak, he let himself, as well. He thought he'd been satisfied before, but this time went so far beyond it. Sated, maybe. Replete.

Happy.

Now, *there* was a word that hadn't defined him lately.

"Wow," Laura said, her breath hot and shaky against his shoulder.

Which, he decided, summed up how he felt, too.

"Do you want to leave separately?" Laura asked Donovan when they were both dressed and ready to go, their idyll over. Her body ached pleasantly. She wished she could curl up with him and sleep for a while.

"I don't think there's a need for evasive maneuvers," he said, his back to her as he put some tip money on the nightstand.

She heard laughter in his voice. "We're both recognizable around Sacramento, both have had our photos in the newspaper a number of times, our own claims to fame. Local kids make good."

"Tell you what. I won't feel you up in the lobby. How's that?"

She realized how ridiculous she was being. So what if they were seen together? "Dumb, huh?"

"A little." He put his arms around her, but kept her at a distance where they could look at each other. "I imagine it's important to maintain a certain image for your firm."

She toyed with the buttons on his shirt. "My stodgy old firm?"

He smiled. "I said your *office* was stodgy."

"The office reflects the firm." She'd accepted the offer to work for them because she could build a practice quickly there, which had been important to her.

"How long until you make partner?"

"Never. I split my time, so I'm never going to work the eighty hours a week to bring in the necessary revenue to be offered a partnership. They brought me aboard and allowed me to work part-time because of my pageant background, frankly. They didn't say so, but I knew it. They like being able to tell clients that. It gives them a certain cachet."

"Are you okay with not making partner?"

"It's not that I couldn't, because they keep asking me to come aboard full-time. But having my own firm, where no one tells me what to do, satisfies me more than a partnership would. I could work in Chance City full-time if the McCoys would start getting divorces...." She grinned, then kissed him.

He deepened it, then turned it tender, lingering. "I'll walk you to your car," he said finally.

Her automatic refusal of his chivalry didn't come, as she would have expected. After all, it wasn't even dark yet. But some woman she didn't recognize said in her own voice, "Thank you."

They held hands as they walked down the hall and then waited for the elevator, but once inside they let go, standing about a foot apart, each watching the panel of lights as the elevator descended.

They reached the lobby level. The doors opened, revealing a man and woman facing away but turning toward them.

Joe and Dixie, Laura realized. What were they—No. Not Joe. Another man with a ponytail.

The color drained from Dixie's face, as it probably had from her own, Laura thought. Donovan recovered first.

"Hey, Dix," he said as he and Laura stepped out of the elevator.

Dixie's face not only regained its color but turned deep pink. "Um, hi." She looked as if she wanted to ask them what they were doing, then thought better of it. Because she would have to explain herself?

"This is Rick Santana," she said without further explanation of who he was. "Rick, these are my friends Laura Bannister and Donovan McCoy."

There was hand-shaking all around, then a moment of awkwardness.

"Rick and I are going upstairs to the restaurant."

"We just came from upstairs ourselves," Donovan said.

"Early dinner?" Dixie asked.

"We met to discuss legal issues."

Laura lifted her briefcase.

"Oh." Dixie leaned over and pressed the up button again. "I'll see you later, I guess."

"Nice to meet you," Laura said to the man. They got on the elevator. As the doors were shutting, Laura made eye contact with Dixie, who mouthed, "I'll call you."

Donovan shoved his hands in his pockets. "Looks like Dixie's finally over Joe."

"Or trying to be."

Their mood turned somber as they left the hotel, not touching, not speaking, the thrill of the past few hours tempered by seeing Dixie out with another man after sixteen years of only seeing her with Joe.

"Are you going to tell your brother?" Laura asked.

"To what purpose? He's already gone from fun-loving Joe to serious Joe, a stranger we hardly recognize. I don't want to see him nose-dive further."

"Maybe it would help him move on."

"Possibly. And now that we've seen her out with someone else, maybe she'll tell Joe, so that he can do the same," Donovan said.

"I'm surprised he hasn't. They broke up, what, about nine months ago?"

"Joe's more complicated than he seems."

It was Friday evening in downtown Sacramento. The streets and sidewalks were bustling. Soon the clubs would be jammed, music reverberating, the dance floors full. She hadn't indulged in the club scene for a long time. Suddenly she wanted to break free of her quiet routine, to have fun, flirting with Donovan the whole time, teasing him, testing her own limits.

But he was a family man now, with responsibilities.

They reached her car in the huge, dark garage under her building.

"Where are you parked?" she asked.

He pointed to a brand-new silver SUV two cars away.

"You bought a car."

"I picked it up this afternoon."

So many questions came to her mind. She asked none of them. He would tell her when he'd made his decisions about his future if he thought she should know. But buying a car seemed to signal…something.

Laura opened her door and tossed her briefcase on the passenger seat. She slid the key in the ignition and then lowered the top. She loved her little red Miata, and since it was a warm evening and her hair was already down and messy, she decided to enjoy the night air.

Then it struck her. "Um, Donovan?"

He slid his hands around her waist. "What?"

"My hair's a mess."

His gaze drifted over her. "A sexy mess."

"Dixie would notice something like that, and not just because she's a hairdresser."

"Meaning, she didn't buy that we were upstairs hashing out some legal business?"

"Exactly."

"What will you tell her?"

"I don't know. But I'll let you know, so you're aware."

"Okay." He pulled her close. "No more wondering," he said into her hair.

"No more wondering. And worth the wait." She felt him relax into her, was surprised it even entered his mind that she wouldn't have felt that way. He always came across as confident.

He kissed her, still tasting of strawberries and chocolate, neither of them having drunk much champagne because they would be driving home. She kissed him back, wishing it didn't have to end.

"Always leave 'em wanting more, hmm?" he said finally, as if reading her mind, something they seemed to do with each other frequently.

She flattened her hands on his chest, could feel his heart thumping, steady and strong. "When will you move into Jake's cabin?"

"Monday or Tuesday. It's going to complicate things for us, isn't it?"

She nodded. He couldn't just walk from his mother's house after Ethan fell asleep. "It's going to take some planning."

"Spontaneity is overrated."

"Says the king of spontaneity," she said with a smile.

"I've learned to adjust quickly."

"Which is the definition of spontaneous, isn't it? I'm a little more routine oriented."

"I've noticed that," he said, pulling her close for a final hug. "Will you consider it too chauvinistic if I follow you home?"

She slid into the car and started the engine. "See if you can keep up, newsman."

He cupped his ears. "What'd you say? Keep it up? I think I've already proven that."

"Show-off."

"Lucky you," he said, backing away. "I'll call you."

She zipped out of her parking space. Because she had a monthly pass instead of needing to stop and pay at the exit gate, she was on her way quickly, but he caught up with her before she got on the freeway. They played cat and mouse the whole trip home, each taking a turn getting ahead, then being behind, neither of them exceeding the speed limit by much. He let her exit first, then followed her home and waited as she parked in her garage. She waved before she shut the door.

Then she was alone. And already lonely.

Chapter Eleven

"Can I honk the horn, Dad?"

"That's not how a gentleman calls on a lady." Donovan put the car in Park and turned off the engine. He hadn't called ahead to ask Laura if it was okay to stop by, but he and Ethan were taking their first drive together in the new car, and Ethan wanted to show it off to Laura. "In fact we *should* call first," he said, pulling out his cell phone.

"She sees us! Hi, Laura!" Ethan unhooked his seat belt as Laura stepped outside. It was ten o'clock, but she was still wearing a robe, soft pink and midthigh length. Her hair was up in a big clip.

She stopped just outside her door. Her newspaper

was a foot away. After a moment she picked it up, then waved in their direction.

"We got a new car!" Ethan shouted. "We came to take you for a ride."

Even from a distance, Donovan saw her tense. He got out of the car and headed toward her, telling Ethan to stay put.

"Sorry," he said quietly, when he reached her. "He's excited. I was just going to call you, and then you opened the door."

She looked incredible, her face makeup free, her hair less than perfect, her nipples pressing at the light fabric. He'd had dreams about her last night. Hot, erotic dreams based on reality now rather than fantasy. He knew what she looked like naked. Knew the sounds she made when she climaxed. Knew how her skin tasted, her own unique fragrance.

"As you can see, I'm not ready to go anywhere."

"You slept in."

She hesitated a beat. "I had a hard time getting to sleep."

"Me, too. You should've called. We could've talked each other to sleep."

"I hope I'm not *that* boring."

"You're—"

"Hey! What about me? I wanna talk, too," Ethan called, leaning out the window.

"He sounds pitiful," Laura said, smiling slightly. "Why don't you let him out of his jail, Dad?"

Donovan whistled, then waved for him to join them. Ethan started to climb out the window. "Stop! Use the door, son." He jogged over, reaching the car as Ethan slid to the running board, and then the sidewalk.

"It's stuck."

Because Donovan had the childproof lock on. He'd forgotten. "You need to wait until I open the door for you."

"Why?" They headed back to see Laura. "I'm a good climber."

"We'll talk about it later," he said as Ethan took off running and threw himself against Laura. Donovan wished he could do the same.

"Please," Ethan was saying, dragging out the word.

"I haven't gotten dressed or even had breakfast yet."

"We can wait for you. I could go for a swim."

"No swim," Donovan said, but otherwise stayed out of it. If Ethan could convince Laura to join them, Donovan would be happy.

"If you're sure you don't mind waiting," Laura said as they all went inside. "Help yourself to anything you find in the kitchen. There's fresh coffee, Donovan."

He poured himself a mug, then a glass of orange juice for Ethan. They went into the backyard, Donovan taking the newspaper with him. He settled Ethan with the only toy in sight, a plastic car that must have been left after the party. Donovan glanced through the paper, something he hadn't done much because the local edition left a lot to be desired. He generally got his news online, needing the broader scope. He'd written a few articles recently, stories he'd been able to gather by phone and Internet; plus, he'd been working on something else that could pay off, in time.

He set the paper aside and sipped his coffee, leaving Ethan to play on his own, something his son rarely did, always wanting company, usually not content to create any games for himself. Donovan had been the opposite as a kid, going off on his own a lot, eavesdropping on conversations in public places, creating stories in his head from what he heard. He loved his family, but he'd craved time alone, although obviously he couldn't remember what he'd been like at age five.

Ethan never wanted to be alone, not even to play in Aggie's family room, which was stuffed to the gills with toys and games. Donovan didn't think his reluctance was only from the upheaval in his life, but a pattern. Anne had probably spent every nonsleeping minute with him. Who could blame her for that?

After a while, Laura emerged, looking cool and fresh in white shorts and a blue T-shirt. She was taking bites of a bagel smeared with cream cheese.

"Are we headed anywhere in particular?" she asked.

He stood, happy to see Ethan putting away the car without being asked. "We have boxes of our things to deliver to Jake's cabin, and some of theirs to bring to the new house. Then we thought we'd head up the mountain a bit. That okay?"

"That's fine." They all piled in the car, Ethan chattering, Donovan totally aware of Laura. He could hear his pulse in his ears, his muscles tightening as memories assaulted him.

"Rides smooth," she said a couple of minutes later, patting the console.

"Yeah," he said, looking her over suggestively. "Best ride I've ever had."

She raised her brows. "Best ever? That must be saying something."

"Laura," Ethan said. "I have my own DVD player. Wanna see?"

"What did we decide about the DVD, Ethan?" Donovan asked, glancing in the mirror long enough to see disappointment settle in his son's eyes.

"Only if the trip is at least an hour long."

"Tough dad," Laura said under her breath.

"Building character."

She laughed then. "Yeah, we'll see who wins this battle."

They pulled into Jake and Keri's driveway and spotted another car parked near the little cabin nestled among oaks and pines.

"Dixie's here," Laura said, sitting up a little straighter.

"Son, you can go on ahead to the house, if you want. Laura and I will catch up in a minute."

"Okay."

Ethan raced across the open space. Dixie came onto the porch and waved at him.

"Are you going to talk to her?" Donovan asked Laura.

"Not here. I expect she'll drop by."

He put a hand over hers. "It was hard not kissing you this morning. And getting harder by the minute."

"You're still referring to kissing?" She wore that sexy smile he loved.

He remembered a moment last night when they'd been lying side by side, facing each other, not talking, and she'd looked like that—content, self-confident and showing a hint of power. Or maybe *knowledge* was a better word; the knowledge that she knew how much she affected him.

He ran a finger down her arm. "Remind me why we're keeping this relationship secret."

Her smile disappeared. "You know every reason, and if you're thinking about ignoring them, this isn't the time or place to discuss it." She grabbed the door handle and climbed out.

He didn't get it. What was wrong with him asking that? They had to be careful around Ethan, of course, but around others? Did it matter?

He watched her for a minute, noting her usually easy stride was stiff and rushed. She stopped as Dixie came down the stairs. They talked briefly before Laura continued up the stairs to the cabin and Dixie headed to her car, without a glance toward Donovan.

"Dix!" he called out, hurrying to join her.

She barely looked at him. "I need to pick up Nana Mae in ten minutes," she said, hooking her purse straps over her shoulder, jangling her keys.

Like Joe, she'd gone from outgoing to restrained since they'd broken up this last time. The two of them used to be the life of whatever party they'd attended, but not anymore.

Was it grief? Were they mourning what they'd lost? Would they heal?

Donovan came up beside her. "I just want you to know that I understand your need to move on. You've been like a sister to me. I want you to be happy."

She tossed her hair, looking like the Dixie of old. "You don't know anything, Donny."

Startled not just by the words but by the harsh tone in which they were delivered, Donovan clamped his jaw. "Feel free to explain."

She shook her head. "I can't. And I'm late." She opened her car door.

"You need to tell Joe," he said. "It'll set him free, too."

She closed her eyes for a few seconds. When she spoke again, her tone held more resignation than harshness. "Joe's always been free. He made sure of it." She got into the car, then looked up at him. "He's just like you and Jake, you know. Except he never left home."

What the hell was that supposed to mean?

He gave up, and headed back to his car. His gaze swept the area, the trees surrounding the property, the cabin set back into a grove. He'd been here uncounted times, yet he'd never noticed how dark it was, and right now it was almost noon in the middle of summer, as good as the light gets.

Jake came across the yard toward him, carrying a large box. "You look…confounded," he said, using one of Nana Mae's favorite words.

"The story of my life these days." Donovan pulled his boxes from the back end of his SUV, opening up space for Jake's to be added.

"I was surprised to see Laura with you and Ethan."

"Ethan's invitation."

"Uh-huh. And you, as the adult, had no say in the matter." Jake hefted a box, waiting for Donovan to do the same.

They walked side by side.

"Nothing to say?" Jake asked.

"Wait until Isabella can sweet-talk you. You'll find it hard to deny her."

"You know, I might've bought that if you hadn't taken so much time to think about it." Jake climbed the stairs.

Donovan followed him into the house, then kept going to the bedroom to stow his box of clothes. The house was so dark that lamps were turned on in every room. He remembered liking Jake's cabin before—it'd felt like a man's place. Which was probably the problem Keri was having with it, and why she wanted to move. It'd been a place for Jake to decompress after a tough security assignment, a job Jake no longer did. And it wasn't a place for a family.

Ethan and I are a family.

He returned to the living room. Ethan was engrossed

in a television program about fishing. Laura held a cooing Isabella.

"I'm thinking it's a really good thing that Laura lives around the corner from us," Keri said to Donovan. "Isabella had been crying for a half hour. Laura walks in? Instant calm. You're free evenings and weekends, I hope, Laura?"

"Send up a smoke signal. I'll be there."

Donovan moved next to Laura and his tiny niece, whose forehead he kissed, her baby scent mingling with Laura's perfume. He straightened slowly, made eye contact with a very serious-looking Laura. She took a few steps back and turned away, making baby noises to Isabella.

Donovan picked up the last packed box from the porch and took it to his car. Jake had already taken care of the rest.

"Do you need these delivered right away?" Donovan asked his brother.

"I don't think so. Why?"

"We're going to take a drive, but I could go back to town and drop the boxes off first, if you want."

"We've got plenty to do in the meantime."

Donovan wished he could talk to Jake about what Dixie had said—that Joe was like them—but he couldn't, not yet, anyway. He wanted to give her time to tell Joe she was dating.

"Everything going okay with Ethan?" Jake asked.

"He's a good kid."

"Are you feeling the connection?"

"Yeah, mostly. He misses his mom—and Millie, too. That makes me feel helpless."

"How much do you think he'll remember of Anne? He seems too young for much to have stuck."

"I'm trying not to let his memory fade. I've been reading up on it, and I know it's an uphill climb. But he'll have photos and videos. That'll help."

They went back to the cabin, Donovan studying it with fresh eyes. Inside, he took one look at Laura and knew she'd rather not go for a ride. He also knew she wouldn't renege, not because of *him* but because Ethan was expecting her to come along.

Suddenly the cabin became a metaphor for what his life had become in the past few years—dark and lonely. Was that what he wanted to bring Ethan into?

"I think we're ready to go," Donovan said.

Laura passed the baby to Keri. Ethan hopped up beside Laura and took her hand. His ease with her tweaked Donovan a little, since Ethan hadn't yet showed much spontaneous physical affection with him. Donovan was very much looking forward to time alone together, to finding the closeness that Ethan had felt with Anne and Millie—and apparently already with Laura.

"Guess what, Laura?" Ethan said. "When I'm five, I'm going to take the training wheels off my bike."

"You are? That's only a couple weeks away."

"I know. I'm very brave, you know. Mum always

said so." His face lost its glow in an instant. "She was sick a long time. I had to be brave." His voice cracked, fading to a whisper.

Donovan ached to hold his son. He met Laura's gaze, could see her dilemma. Ethan had already pressed himself against her, so Donovan gestured for her to go ahead. She knelt. He wrapped his arms around her neck and cried against her shoulder.

"I want my mum. I want her right now."

"I know you do, sweetheart," Laura soothed.

"I don't want her to be in heaven. She needs to be with me!" His heartbreaking sobs tore at Donovan.

Finally he stopped crying, although he kept his face buried against Laura. "I don't wanna go for a ride," came his muffled words.

"We don't have to," Donovan said, crouching behind, laying his hand on Ethan's back.

"I wanna go home."

"That's fine, bud."

"To Maine. I wanna go home to *Maine.*" He finally lifted his head and turned around.

His defiant look caught Donovan off guard. He set his hands at Ethan's waist. "That isn't possible, son."

"Why not?"

Keri handed Laura a tissue, then Ethan. He swiped at his cheeks and nose.

"It's a big trip going to Maine, and it takes planning," Donovan said, weighing his response. "And I think you want to go there because you want to see your mom again, and you know she's not there, Ethan. She can only be in your heart now. But the really good thing about that is that wherever you are, she'll be there, too."

He stared at Donovan for a long time, sniffling. "I hafta go to the bathroom," he said finally.

Donovan kissed his son's forehead, needing that for himself. "Okay."

"I can go by myself." He hurried off, shutting the door, something he didn't usually do.

Donovan dragged a hand down his face.

Laura squeezed his arm. "I know you don't think so now, but that was a good thing that just happened."

"In what possible way?"

"He's comfortable enough to test you. To test his limits with you. It's a *good* sign. He wanted to know if you would get angry, and you didn't."

"I agree," Keri said.

Jake shrugged. "No experience with this, Donny."

"Well, what about when I do get angry? Am I not allowed to correct him when he misbehaves?"

"It's *necessary* that you do," Laura said. "He needs the range of emotion—as long as he always knows you love him."

Donovan looked at the floor, scratching the back of his head. "I can't go just on instinct, can I?"

"To a degree."

"How'd you get to be such an expert?"

"I've watched lots of families relating to each other.

Lots. I've talked to child psychologists and pediatricians. Part of what I do is to counsel people on coping."

The bathroom door opened, and Ethan rushed out as if nothing had happened. "Can we get an ice cream on our drive?" he asked Donovan.

"That can be arranged."

Ethan charged out the front door and down the stairs.

"Mercurial," Jake said. "Look what we have to look forward to, sweetheart." He cupped Isabella's head and half smiled at his wife. Keri laughed.

At least you're not stepping into it five years after she was born. The uncharacteristically sarcastic thought stayed locked in Donovan's head. It wasn't their fault. It wasn't his fault, either. When it came to fault, Anne was—

"Come on!" Ethan yelled from outdoors.

"Oh, Mom offered to babysit Isabella tonight so that Keri and I can go out," Jake said. "We don't want to go too far, so we thought we'd head to the Stompin' Grounds. Want to come?"

"Sure."

"Laura?" Jake asked when Donovan didn't.

"Maybe." She waved and headed out the door.

"I was getting a vibe that you two were together," Jake said.

"Friends," Donovan said, which was both the truth and a lie. The lie part didn't sit well with him, but he was coming to realize that it was for selfish reasons. He wanted to be able to touch her, whether in public or private. "She's been a big help with Ethan, as you can tell. I'll see you tonight."

Outside, Ethan and Laura were crouched down, examining something at the bottom of the stairs.

"Come see," Ethan said. "It's a lizard. He's teeny tiny."

The lizard skittered off before Donovan got to see it. "Lots of creatures live around here, Ethan."

"Like what?"

"Fox and deer. Raccoons. Skunks."

"Skunks! Pee-euw." He skipped ahead as they went to the car, but before he climbed in, Donovan stopped him, put his hands on his shoulders and turned him to face the cabin.

"Does this look like home to you?" Donovan asked.

Ethan twisted around a little to look at his father, his brows furrowed.

Donovan phrased it differently. "Do you think you would be happy living here?"

The boy went still. He looked around again. "You mean, this is where we're going to live?"

Donovan stared back, stunned. He thought Ethan had understood that. Obviously not. "You know Uncle Jake and Aunt Keri and Isabella are moving into their new house. I told you we were going to move into their cabin."

"Oh. I remember now." He paused. "How do I get to Grandma's Aggie's from here?"

"We'll drive."

Ethan shifted his gaze to Laura, who stood beside

them, also looking around as if seeing the property for the first time.

"Can't we walk, Dad? Or I could ride my bike."

"It's a busy, curvy road, not safe for walking or riding."

"And there are lots of creatures."

"Yes, but they're nothing to be afraid of." Donovan crouched in front of his son. "Would you like to live here?"

Ethan hesitated, then finally shook his head.

"Me, either," Donovan said.

Ethan's eyes went wide. "Really?"

"Really."

"Can we live with Laura?"

Donovan didn't dare look at her. "We can't do that, but we can find ourselves someplace with lots of light and a big backyard where you can play."

"Where I can walk to Grandma's? Or ride my bike?"

"You won't be doing that alone for a long time, but yes, we would be much closer."

"Would you buy a house?" Laura asked, her voice tight.

Her face was about as expression free as he'd seen. "We'd rent, for now." He felt the tension in his shoulders ease. Making the right decisions usually resulted in that. "Why don't you and Laura hop in the car, bud? I'll go tell Uncle Jake we won't be moving here."

Ethan threw his arms around Donovan and hugged him hard. Donovan closed his eyes, gathering him close, his hair soft in the cradle of Donovan's palm. He only let go because Ethan squirmed.

Laura's smile was soft and knowing.

When Donovan returned to the car a few minutes later, Jake's understanding words echoing in his mind, Ethan greeted him with "We don't want to go for a drive, Dad. We really, really, really want ice cream."

"Ice cream it is." He started the car, then glanced at the solemn woman seated beside him.

"Are you okay?" she murmured.

He nodded. Or he would be, anyway, as soon as he figured out how to survive the emotional roller-coaster ride that was now his life. At least he'd made one good decision for them as a family unit. That was a step in the right direction.

In town they got their ice-cream cones and sat on a bench outside to watch the Saturday tourist crowd meandering along the wooden sidewalks. After a while they headed to Jake's to drop off the boxes.

"Since we're not going anywhere," Laura said, "how about coming to my house for a swim?"

"Brilliant!"

Donovan gave her a grateful look. "We'll drop you off, go get our suits, then pick up something for lunch later on."

"Sounds good."

He rounded the corner to her street and pulled into her driveway.

"What's that man doing, Dad?" Ethan asked, having

turned around to look at the house directly across from Laura's. "Can I go watch?"

That man was putting up a heavy wooden post. And attached to its crossbeam was a sign—For Rent.

Chapter Twelve

Laura had come *this* close to not showing up at the Stompin' Grounds. At home she'd paced, muttered and stewed. Finally she'd flipped a coin, which led to a second toss, then a third. In a best-four-out-of-seven losing conclusion, she ended up changing into her only Western shirt, black jeans and black leather cowboy boots with pointed toes and a pretty good heel.

As she drove into the parking lot, she didn't see Donovan's new SUV. Maybe he'd decided to skip coming. He'd had a busy day, after all.

She gripped her steering wheel and considered the speed with which everything had happened. They'd walked across the street and talked to the man installing the for-rent sign, Landon Kincaid, who turned out to have graduated from high school with Donovan. They walked through the house, a freshly painted two-bedroom with an upgraded kitchen and bathroom. The yard needed a lot of work, which Landon had intended to do before someone moved in, but Donovan offered, saying he needed a project now that Jake's house was done.

The deal was sealed with a handshake, the keys turned over right then. And starting tomorrow Donovan could stand at his kitchen sink, look outside and see her standing at hers.

Dispatching the image, Laura made her way to the door of the Stompin' Grounds. She hesitated, not wanting to go inside solo, then put her shoulders back and did just that.

She'd been to the bar once years ago and once recently, for a bachelorette party. It hadn't changed in however many years it'd been in business—the same dark-paneled walls, a jukebox churning out country tunes of love and devotion and heartbreak, and beer-sticky tabletops carved with a social minutiae of dates and initials.

She stood just inside the door, letting her eyes adjust to the dark room, counting up the customers. Thirty-two strangers. Then she spotted Dixie sitting at a dark corner table with two other women. Dixie waved her over.

"If I'd known this was your kind of place, I'd have invited you months ago," Dixie said, a twinkle in her eyes, as Laura pulled up a chair, relieved to find someone she knew. Dixie introduced her to the other two women, who decided to go choose some new songs from the jukebox.

"You came alone?" Dixie asked.

"Jake and Keri will be here any time now."

"And Donny?"

"He said so, but it's hard to know for sure. Something could've come up with Ethan." She decided to let Donovan tell Dixie the news about renting the house, although mostly Laura was holding back out of cowardice. Laura knew that Dixie would ask a lot of questions Laura wasn't ready to answer. He'll be within shouting distance? See each other's comings and goings? No privacy?

Not to mention the he's-just-across-the-street fantasizing she would be doing.

Dixie took a sip from her beer as Laura ordered one for herself. She drummed her fingers on the tabletop.

"You want to talk about it?" Laura asked finally.

"About what?"

Laura gave her a look that made Dixie laugh.

"It wasn't a date," they said at the same time, stopped, then grinned.

"You first," Laura offered, not in a hurry herself.

"We really were just having dinner at the hotel. Rick Santana owns Styles."

"The hair salon?"

"He's been a guest lecturer at my school twice this

month. Then he stayed to watch us work and critique it. He's courting me, all right, but for a job in his salon."

Laura leaned forward. "Maybe that's what he told you, Dix, but it's not all he wants. If you could've seen the way he looks at you..."

"I noticed. I was even flattered. But that's it. He's obviously a player. I don't need that."

"Are you going to take the job?"

"The money would be good eventually, since it's one of the most exclusive shops in Sacramento."

The waitress set a beer in front of Laura. She took a sip, wishing for a glass of merlot instead. "Did you factor in the cost of gas and time for the commute?"

"*You* do it."

"Not daily."

Dixie ran a finger around the lip of her mug. "If I took the job, I'd probably move down there."

Shock silenced Laura. Dixie's roots in Chance City ran deep. Her parents owned the hardware store. She had siblings who hadn't left, either, except for brief periods. "I can't imagine you leaving, Dixie."

She shrugged, but Laura could see how much it was costing Dixie to even be thinking about making such a move. Desperate times, desperate measures.

"Your turn," Dixie said in a tone indicating she was done talking about herself. "You can't in any way convince me that you and Donny weren't on a date. I've never seen your hair look like that. I haven't seen you look embarrassed before, either. You are so busted."

Laura had decided that if she ever felt the urge to open up, she would talk to Keri, who was new to town and the McCoy family. But Laura was feeling an affinity with Dixie, and had also come to trust her over the past few months.

"You can't really call it a date. We slept together. That's all. It'd been building for a long time."

"Since high school," Dixie said, nodding. "I remember your obsession."

Laura groaned, burying her face in her hands. "Did everyone know?"

"Pretty much."

"People have been laughing at me all this time?"

"I don't think so. Most seem to be in awe of you, frankly." She put a hand on Laura's arm. "People don't know you. I mean, you've lived here your whole life, and no one really knows much about you, except about your crowns and your job. Everybody loves your mom, but you've always been on a different, I don't know, level? In a different realm? I've wondered for years why you've stayed here."

Sometimes she wondered, too.

Dixie leaned close, lowering her voice. "Are you gonna do it again with Donny?"

"The first opportunity I get."

"You intend to keep the affair secret?"

"Yes."

"Okay. Then I will, too."

Dixie's friends returned, and the conversation

changed to gossip and speculation. Laura sipped her beer, surreptitiously checked out the front door every time it opened and thought about Donovan. Yes, she wanted to continue to sleep with him. But a new wrinkle was complicating that decision. She'd been almost in love with him for years—she'd acknowledged that to herself finally. But today she'd fallen deeper when he'd talked to Ethan about his mother, and then when he'd brought Ethan into the decision about moving into the cabin. Now she not only loved Donovan, she also respected and admired him. And wanted him. She'd never felt that for one man before, not all those things at one time.

Donovan was a born father, and that was the big complication. Without a doubt, he would want more children. All three of the McCoy brothers had been known as the men who wouldn't commit, but recently that label had been altered some. Jake had done a one-eighty and now was a devoted husband and father. Donovan had made a seamless transition to fatherhood himself. Laura had no doubt that Joe would follow in their footsteps. She'd watched him with his nieces and nephews for years, the easy way he had with kids and how well they related to him.

But as for her and Donovan having a future? It wasn't in the cards she'd been dealt. She just needed to get him out of her system now, while she had the chance, so that she could move on. She would find a way to fall out of love with him—not an easy thing but doable. People did it every day. She saw it in her practice all the time.

The front door opened, and in walked Jake, followed by Donovan and then Joe.

"Keri's not with them," Laura said, worried.

"It can't be anything serious or Jake wouldn't be here," Dixie said, having gone very still when Joe appeared.

Jake said something to his brothers, then crossed the room toward her and Dixie.

"Everything's fine," he said right away. "Isabella was fussy, and new mama couldn't bear to leave her. She put her foot on my butt, shoved me out the door and ordered me to have fun."

"Which means you'll have one beer and be gone," Laura said.

He grinned. "Probably not even that since I'll be driving. Anyway, I knew you'd be wondering." He walked off to join his brothers at the bar.

And while she couldn't see Donovan's eyes from so far away, she interpreted his body language just fine, making her wish she'd tossed the coin a few more times, enough times to grant her own wish to stay home and let him come to her instead.

Keeping her hands off him tonight would be a character-building experience.

Beers in hand, the brothers headed for a table. Donovan maneuvered himself into a chair where Laura was in his direct line of sight. She hadn't stood up yet, but he figured the view was going to be spectacular. He couldn't recall seeing her in jeans before, which seemed odd, jeans being the American uniform. Maybe it was a sign she was loosening up.

"Can we talk about Dad?" Joe said. "The other day, you two were wondering if he was happy. Why would you think he wasn't?"

Donovan had been giving the subject a lot of thought, too, since it'd first come up. "He never went anywhere but to work and home. Or an occasional trip to Sacramento or Tahoe or Reno, maybe. Can you remember taking any vacations?"

"With eight kids? Vacations cost too much." Joe sounded defensive. "He raised us and provided for us. I'm sure that's all he expected of himself. But we did lots as a family. We just stayed close to home."

"Maybe *you* did," Jake said. "You were the baby, so there were fewer kids to deal with as time went by, and more money. Mind you, I'm not criticizing. It was a great childhood." He looked at Donovan. "Do you think people have to leave home to be happy?"

"It seems like seeing the world a little would help you appreciate home even more. He wasn't even in the military." Donovan was still trying to figure out what Dixie meant when she'd said Joe was just like Jake and him, except he hadn't left home. "You haven't gone anywhere, Joe. Are you okay with that?"

"Doesn't matter, does it? I have a thriving business I can't leave."

"You also took over the man-of-the-family role when Dad died, and you were the only male offspring living here. You were stuck. But did you want to leave? Do you now?"

"I think about it." He took a good, long drink.

Donovan exchanged a look with Jake. Joe wasn't a complainer. In many ways he reminded Donovan of their father. He went off to his job every morning without griping about it, worked hard and had seemed okay with his life—until recently. Maybe the breakup with Dixie wasn't the only thing that had changed him.

"And if I decide to do something about it, I'll let you know, okay?" Joe said. "I may be the youngest, but I'm no kid." He stood. "I'm gonna say hi to some friends."

"Methinks he doth protest too much," Jake said when he'd gone.

"Yeah." Donovan watched Joe pull up a chair at a table with two women. Dixie turned away and focused on Laura, laughing as if she was having a great time.

"Despite what you said this afternoon, I know you're not just friends," Jake said, gesturing with his head toward Laura. "You can't stop looking at her."

"Hell, Jake. Even you said you'd been tempted through the years."

"I was joking. She's always only had eyes for you."

Why was it others seemed to know that but not him? Except for that time in high school, she hadn't come on to him again. And there'd been plenty of opportunities.

"You're stuck, aren't you?" Jake asked, humor in his voice.

"In what way?"

"You want to ask her to dance, but you can't—for whatever reason you think is valid. And you can't ask Dixie, because Joe would retaliate by asking one of the women he's sitting with. The potential for fireworks tonight is more than any Fourth of July celebration."

"And you sit there smirking, because you've got a wife and you're done playing the mating game."

"Damn straight. If I'd known marriage would bring such peace to my life, I would've done it years ago."

Peace. Was that what had been missing in his life? He recalled how reluctant he'd been to leave town this last time, how he'd stalled until the last moment—and that stall had resulted in his meeting his son, instead of being called back home by someone in his family. Plus, it hadn't even been a big deal to him that he was postponing an important article, the kind he usually craved researching and writing, his lifeblood. It should've been a big deal.

Peace. He wouldn't call his relationship with Laura peaceful. Arousing, frustrating, satisfying in some ways, yes. But not peaceful. And secret. He exposed secrets for a living. Was that why hiding the relationship wasn't sitting well with him?

And now he would be living across the street. They hadn't had a moment in private to talk about it, and he figured she must have plenty to say.

He studied her from across the room. She threw back her head and laughed at something Dixie said. He hadn't seen her laugh like that before. She was generally more subtle with him. He wanted to know the side of her that let go and laughed so boisterously.

"I dare you," Jake said, elbowing his brother.

"To do what?"

"Ask her to dance."

"She warned me she had two left feet. I verified it."

"So don't move much." Jake was laughing. "Never known you to be a coward, Donny."

Jake was right. Not only was Donovan being cowardly, he was also hesitant, something new for him. He decided to accept the dare. Several couples were on the small dance floor. They wouldn't be in a solo spotlight.

He stopped at the jukebox and punched in a song to follow the one currently playing. He zeroed in on her as he crossed the room. She glanced his way, looked back at Dixie, then did a quick double take when she realized he was heading directly to her. She ran her hands down her thighs.

He stopped next to her chair. "Evening, ladies."

"Hi, Donovan," Dixie said, her eyes twinkling.

She knew he and Laura had slept together, he thought, seeing pure sass in her expression.

"Do you know my friends Sheryl and Nancy?"

"I don't." He shook hands with each of them. "Can I buy you all a pitcher?"

"Well, sure," Dixie said. "That'd be nice."

He signaled the bartender, then turned to Laura. "May I have this dance?"

She fiddled with her napkin, shredding it. "You know I don't dance."

"It isn't a two-step, Laura. We'll take it slow."

He wasn't used to her not speaking her mind, and it was pretty evident that she wanted to have words with him. He put out his hand, counting on the fact that she would rather go with him than have to explain to the others why she wouldn't.

She stood, resistance in her stance.

Donovan did his best not to gloat.

Chapter Thirteen

Laura hadn't figured she'd ever have a second dance with Donovan. In some ways it felt even more important than sleeping with him, because it was public. Sure, lots of people who weren't lovers danced, but she could always recognize the difference. People who were intimate allowed the other person into their personal space comfortably. And it felt completely natural to be in his arms, even if she was furious at him. Even if she couldn't dance well.

"You're ticked," he said, sliding an arm around her waist, drawing her close but not too close.

"How could you do this? We agreed to keep our relationship to ourselves."

"Look around. No one cares what we're doing."

She did look around. "You're wrong. Several people are watching us."

"In the same way that they're watching everyone else who's dancing. Look, Laura, I've been thinking about this all day. What would it hurt if people knew we were seeing each other? I'm not talking about spending the night if Ethan's around, but in general."

Because it's going to end. The thought hurt, but it was the only truth she knew.

"I don't like lies," he said before she responded.

"We haven't lied to anyone."

"A fine point, and you know it. It's a secret. Secrets always involve lies. In my line of work, I uncover lies."

"This isn't about your job."

"True. It's about *me.* My integrity. And yours. Anne kept Ethan a secret from me. I will never forgive her for that. Never. And you can't convince me that a secret has less consequence than a lie. Either one is a deal breaker for me."

"I see your point." The point being, she'd been keeping her secret from him all along, when she'd always been honest with every other man she'd dated—semihonest. She didn't divulge the details, only that she didn't want to get married or have children. She hadn't told Donovan, and she didn't know why. Well, maybe she did. But now she'd sealed her fate with him by keeping the secret from him. She should come clean…

But she didn't want to give him up. Not yet.

"*But,*" she added, finally breaking her silence, feeling him tense. "It's still new. Let's see for ourselves where it goes before we involve anyone else."

"I can see we need a little more discussion about this before you agree with me." He sort of smiled and pulled her a little closer. "Enough talk about that. Let's enjoy our rare opportunity to dance. It's the only time I get to lead, you know."

She was more than willing to abandon the serious topics, but she wasn't sure dancing was going to solve anything. "That's because I don't know how to dance."

"Exactly. You're damn good at everything else. It's my turn to show off."

She had just begun to relax when the song came to an end. Grateful, she started to pull away. He tightened his hold as a new song began, the lyrics far too appropriate as Toby Keith sang about kissing—and getting lost on the dance floor. She didn't want to get lost. She wanted to keep her head about her.

"So. We're going to be neighbors," she said, trying to ignore the song.

He smiled, slow and sexy. "Life can change in the blink of an eye, can't it?"

"I guess you know that better than most people." She'd slept with him. She already knew what his body felt like, skin to skin. Yet dancing, fully dressed, had her just as revved up as being naked in bed with him.

"I guess I do." His fingertips pressed into her lower

back, something no one else would be able to see but that she could feel, heat expanding from that point.

Her head was spinning, just as the song said. "You've got a lot of work ahead, cleaning up that backyard."

"I'm always up for a challenge."

She had a feeling they weren't talking about the same thing, her feeling confirmed when he eased her close enough that their hips aligned. "Will you install play equipment?" she asked.

"It came already installed—thirty-three years ago." He flattened her other hand against his chest so that he now had both arms around her waist. "Works perfectly, as you know. Takes you soaring. Safe, too."

She couldn't look at him anymore, at the knowledge in his eyes and the anticipation of more. She shifted a little, touched her head to his cheek, looking over his shoulder. The action brought her breasts against his chest. He drew a long, slow breath.

"What will you do about furniture?" she asked, pointedly redirecting the conversation with what little remained of sane thought.

"There are these interesting places, counselor, called stores. If you haven't seen one before, I'll be happy to show you. They even let you test out mattresses. Decide whether soft works for you. Or maybe you like hard better."

She gave up trying to keep the conversation nonsexual. "I like both—for entirely different reasons."

"Really? You enjoy soft?"

"For what it implies. There's the breath-catching aftermath. And the anticipation of what could happen again. And don't forget the fascinating process of transformation."

"Ah. The adjustable mattress. I've heard of them."

"How about you? What do you prefer?"

"The kind you can sink into." He spun her around and around, matching the lyrics.

She felt dizzy but didn't stumble. It was a different kind of dizzy. One that had her leaning back, staring at his mouth. "Donovan…"

He bent low, brushed his lips against hers, an electrifying touch. She kissed him back, needing him…

Laura jerked back. What was she doing?

The song ended. She pulled herself free. "I knew this was a mistake," she said low and fierce. "Don't make a scene, okay? I'm going to leave now."

"I won't make a scene. But you don't need to leave."

Oh, yes, she did. And right now, before she made a fool of herself.

She said goodbye to Dixie, grabbed her purse and left. By the time she got in her car, she was shaking. He had a way of making her forget herself. She'd always been able to stay in control, except with him. And now everyone there had witnessed that. She'd kissed him. In public.

She fumbled with her key, trying to get it into the ignition, when her passenger door opened, and Donovan climbed in. "I need a ride," he said lightly. "I can walk to Mom's from your house."

She looked over her shoulder. "Your car is right there."

"I've been drinking."

Like her, he'd had time to drink half a glass. She turned back and stared out the windshield, swallowing hard. He was being thoughtful, not wanting her to drive when she was so upset.

"Do you want me to drive?" he asked quietly.

It was the quiet, understanding way he asked that had her nodding. Without speaking they got out, then traded places. She was angry, but more at herself for allowing herself to be in that public situation with him.

He started the engine. "I've been wanting to take your car for a test spin."

She latched onto the chance to change the subject. "You should've asked. I would've let you. It's just a car."

"No car is ever 'just a car,'" he said, backing out.

"You mean you wouldn't let me drive yours?"

"Maybe. After the new-car smell wears off."

"How long does that take?"

"About five years."

She laughed, still shaky but settling down. "I'll bet you don't keep a car that long." She tossed her head, the wind lifting her hair as they drove along the highway.

"If that turns out to be the case, I'll let you drive it once before I trade it in."

His palm rested on the gearshift. He could easily slide his hand over an inch or two and set it on her thigh. The fact that he could, even if he didn't, turned her on. And they weren't in public anymore.

"This is a great little car," he said. "Not stodgy at all."

"It's how I balance myself with my work."

"You balance it just fine without doing anything."

"So, you don't find me stodgy?"

"Depends on whether you're naked or dressed."

"Really? You find me stodgy when I'm naked?"

He shot her a look, then realized she was joking. "The librarian—or maybe in this case, the lady-lawyer—fantasy is popular for a reason."

"Hmm. Interesting."

He took the turn to her street. She pulled a remote from the glove box and opened the garage. He eased the car in and shut it off.

"Thank you," she said simply.

He dropped the keys in her hand. "Anytime." When she didn't say anything else, he started to open the car door. She hit the remote to close the garage door.

"Would you like to come in?" she asked.

The garage door touched ground. "Seems like you already answered that question for me."

"You know where the front door is."

He slipped a hand behind her head and pulled her toward him to kiss, something she'd been aching for him to do all day when they were together with Ethan and again then since he'd walked into the bar. Need sparked greater need, creating fire that crackled and flared between them.

The garage still held the day's heat, was stuffy and stifling.

"Let's go inside," he said.

"I thought you'd never ask."

Chapter Fourteen

By the time she opened her door and got out, Donovan was there, kissing her again, tasting her welcoming warmth, feeling the vibration of her moans transfer to him, rousing, tempting. They found their way into the house. She flattened her hands on his chest and pushed away slightly.

"I'll be back," she said, breathing hard. "I have to do something."

Birth control, he decided, shoving his hands through his hair. A diaphragm, maybe? They hadn't discussed it last night except that she'd said she'd taken care of it.

"Hurry," he said, impatient.

She disappeared down the hall into her bedroom.

Aroused and eager, he made his way to the living room. In almost no time he heard her door click open. She came down the hallway toward him, holding a few casebooks, her hair up, a pair of reading glasses on and wearing a white bra, panties and a skinny black tie.

Lady-lawyer fantasy. He knew enough of the legal lingo to say, "Looks like I've won my appeal. Habeas corpus, counselor." She did, indeed, "have the body."

She laughed as she continued moseying toward him, her hips swaying. He popped the snaps of his shirt, dragged it free of his jeans and hurled it toward the couch.

"Need help with your boots, newsman?"

He dropped onto the sofa and raised his foot. Leaning over him, she pulled one boot off, her breasts barely contained by her bra, her nipples hard and inviting behind the lace; then she turned around, settled his other boot between her thighs. He planted his other foot on her rear, while she yanked off the second boot. He wanted to tell her how exciting she was, how different, but he figured she'd take that as a comparison. No one wanted to be compared.

He stood. The rest of his clothes joined his shirt on the sofa, spilling like a Dali painting, looking as surreal as he felt. He'd been worried that they wouldn't repeat what they'd done last night, had figured she would find some way to stop the relationship in its tracks.

He was glad to be wrong.

"Shall we go sequester ourselves in my bedroom?" she asked, letting her hand glide down his torso, then wrap around him.

"Obviously, the evidence needs no oral argument," he said, drawing in a breath. "Although you can give that a shot, too."

She laughed, soft and sultry. "Let's go present our cases. Maybe we'll create a few precedents of our own."

She'd yanked the bedding off, as he had done at the hotel, except that his had been deliberate and neat. He was glad she'd been in such a hurry.

They fell onto the bed together, wrapped each other up in a tangle of arms and legs, then just stopped and held on, both breathing heavily and haltingly. After a minute he pulled back slightly and kissed her tenderly, remembering how upset she'd been earlier, wanting to make sure she knew he cared about her, that she wasn't just someone to have sex with. And vice versa.

"You are a constant surprise," he said against her lips as he got rid of her undergarments.

"Good." She deepened the kiss, indicating she didn't want to talk anymore.

But he always accepted challenges. "You're a lot more fun than you let on."

"I'm not laughing now, newsman."

He did laugh then, but at the same time cupped her breast, circling the nipple with his thumb, then sliding down her to taste the hard flesh. She arched, offering herself as he took his time exploring the landscape of her incredible body, drifting lower and lower, savoring her, enjoying every sound, every movement. He sent his hands on a journey, gliding and stroking, cherishing and arousing. Only when he was ready to give in to her increasingly demanding pleas did he let his mouth take over for his hands, enjoying her, appreciating all of the woman she was. Finally she gripped his hair and rose up, her pleasure and satisfaction audible, giving him a memory to cherish, too.

She came down slowly, breathing hard, her skin damp and hot, and then she went limp against the mattress, sprawled out, eyes closed.

He leaned on an elbow next to her. "What's the verdict?" he asked. As if he didn't know….

"Nolo contendere." She wasn't contesting it. She opened her eyes, ran a finger across his lips and smiled in that sexy way she had. "But I haven't made my closing argument yet."

He flopped onto his back. "I await your rendering."

She straddled him, her hair brushing his sensitive skin as she treated him to the reverence of her seeking hands, her tender lips, the swirl of her tongue over and around him. Her fingertips went on journeys of discovery, making promises of fulfillment, but delaying and delaying until he couldn't stand it a second longer. She finally let him find that elusive satisfaction, gifting him with incredible, amazing pleasure. Then he fell against the bed much as she had, limp, his needs quenched.

Later, when they were lying side by side recovering and he was contemplating round two, her phone rang. She let it ring. Her answering machine was turned up loud enough that they could hear the message being left.

"This is Jake McCoy. I'm sorry to bother you, Laura, but I'm looking for Donovan. If you see or hear from him, please tell him he's needed at home. It's not a medical emergency or anything, but Ethan needs some reassurance. Thanks."

Donovan and Laura looked at each other. "He probably had a nightmare," he said.

"Whatever the reason, you need to be with him," she said, rolling toward him and touching his shoulder.

He kissed her, softly, pulling back reluctantly. He wanted to ask if she felt better now, if she'd recovered from what had happened at the Stompin' Grounds, but it wasn't the way he wanted the night to end.

"I'll drive you," she said, getting out of bed when he did. "I can drop you off a block away."

He started to refuse, then didn't. It would save him ten minutes—and give him ten more minutes with her.

He dressed in the living room, where he'd left his clothes. Pulling his cell phone from his pocket, he saw that he'd missed two messages, one from Jake, one from his mother.

"Ready?" Laura asked from the door leading to the garage.

No. "Yes."

She handed him a brush.

They didn't kiss goodnight when she dropped him off. They just stared at each other for a few seconds. "I'll call you," he said, leaning back into the car.

"This has to stay private, Donovan. We had good reasons when this started. Nothing's changed."

He had no time to argue. She left, her taillights disappearing into the night as he climbed to his mother's porch. Inside the house, Ethan sat in Aggie's lap, his face tear streaked.

"Where *were* you?" he cried, resisting Donovan's efforts to take him from his grandmother.

"I explained that you went somewhere with your brothers," Aggie said, but she was silently questioning why he hadn't been with Jake and Joe.

He reminded himself that his son wasn't completely comfortable with him yet, and that Ethan was used to being with women, including a mother who'd been too sick to leave the house for as long as Ethan could probably remember. His grief was fresh and raw.

"I'm here now, son," he said quietly, rubbing Ethan's back. "C'mere, please."

At first Donovan thought Ethan would reject him, but he flung himself into Donovan's arms instead.

"Just don't go, okay? Don't leave me!"

Donovan carried him outside and sat in the rocking chair, the still-warm night quiet enough to hear the crickets. He rocked his son for the first time in his life, tucking him close, breathing the scent that was distinctly Ethan.

"I know this has been a big change for you," he said softly. "I know you miss your mom and Grammy, and the life you used to have. And I know you're a little worried about how different everything is. But the thing is, I can't promise to stay with you all the time. I need to go to work again soon. You'll go to school. I also need to go out sometimes with friends, just like you'll have sleepovers with Grandma Aggie or other people. You'll make friends at school."

He tightened his hold on Ethan. "But when we're apart, it will only be for a period of time." He wished he could assure his son that he would always come back, but it wasn't a promise he could make—just as Anne couldn't. "You'll always be with someone you want to be with, someone who loves you. Someone we both trust. Okay?"

Ethan drew a deep, shaky breath. "I was scared. I woke up and you weren't home."

"I'll tell you what. From now on, I'll tell you if I'll be going out, even if you're already going to be asleep before I leave. Is that a deal?"

Ethan was quiet for a long time before he finally nodded.

"All better now?" Donovan asked.

"I need ice cream."

"Oh, you *need* ice cream."

Ethan giggled. "Yes, I need it."

"All right. I'll join you."

Crisis averted, Donovan thought, relieved. "Run in and wash your face and hands. I'll fix two bowls. And one for Grandma, if she wants." She'd disappeared, so he wasn't sure if she'd gone to bed.

As Ethan skipped into the bathroom, Donovan dialed Laura.

"He's okay," he said when she answered, her hello soothing. "Abridged version is that he woke up and got scared because I wasn't here."

"Thank you for letting me know."

"We're going to have ice cream."

"The perfect cure-all."

He heard the smile in her voice. "Thanks again for tonight."

"We both know you were the one deserving of thanks. I appreciate your coming to my rescue, newsman. For noticing I needed rescue. Even though I didn't think so at the time. I'm a little used to controlling situations."

She would've been fine, but he was glad she saw it the way she did. "And my thanks to you for bringing one of my fantasies to life," he said, a clear image of her dressed like a lady lawyer glaring like neon in his mind.

"That actually was my pleasure, too. Good night, Donovan."

He snapped his phone shut, then tapped it against his thigh. Within the next couple of days, he and Ethan would move into a house and start their life as a family. And soon he would have to figure out what to do about work, a decision he'd put off for good reasons, but that he couldn't put off for much longer.

But all that could wait until he'd had a bowl of ice cream with his son.

Chapter Fifteen

"I can have a crew here and clear this yard in half a day," Joe said the next morning, standing next to Donovan on the back patio.

"What fun would that be?" Donovan peeled his T-shirt over his head as he watched Ethan drag a shovel through the foot-tall weeds, making motor sounds with his mouth.

"Fun? I don't get it, Donny. You're renting. Why put in the effort?"

"Because it's something I can work on with Ethan."

"Ah. Okay. That makes sense. So, what would you like me to do, aside from loaning you tools?"

"If you could help with the hauling, that would be

great. You've already put in extra time lately on Jake's place."

"Limited time. Keri wants to do her own thing. Anyway, what are brothers for?" He elbowed Donovan. "You'll let me choose the plants, right? And tell you where to plant them?"

His brother knew him well. "Yeah. Landon said he'd pay for them, within reason."

"Lucky him. He'll get my wholesale cost, so you can load up this place."

"Hey, Dad!" Ethan shouted from the far end of the yard, a good forty feet away. "Can we get a dog?"

"Nope."

"Why not?"

"Landlord's rules. No pets."

"Aw, man." He picked up the shovel again and started zigzagging around the yard.

"Is that true?" Joe asked.

"No idea. Didn't ask." He recalled the speech he'd given Laura the night before, and figured this lie might come back to haunt him sometime. Then he justified it by not knowing whether he was lying or telling the truth. He just didn't wanted to break Ethan's heart.

And he wasn't ready to commit to owning a dog.

Joe took a sip of his coffee, then said casually, "I'm gathering I had to drive your car home last night because you went off with Laura."

This was exactly the situation Donovan wanted to

avoid. Should he lie to his brother now, too? No. To hell with it.

"Yeah. I apologize for not asking you. I needed to catch her in a hurry."

"So Jake told me when he gave me your keys. I understand the attraction, Donny. In fact, I've seen it coming for years."

"But?"

"But watching you two on the dance floor? I know I'm not the king of relationships, but yours didn't look comfortable."

Donovan considered that, and decided Joe was wrong. In private it was comfortable much of the time, exciting much of the time and also frustrating much of the time. He could talk to her more easily than anyone else, even his brothers, with whom he shared the most.

"Appearances are deceiving," Donovan said, swiping a pair of gloves from the ground and grabbing a shovel.

"There's an original choice of words."

He laughed. "I'm out of practice."

"Uh-huh. About that. What's your plan?"

"Still not sure. I'd like to have it figured out by the time Ethan starts kindergarten, which gives me about three and a half weeks. It's hard to believe he's only been here for a couple of weeks." And it'd only been a couple of days since he'd first slept with Laura, yet it felt as if they'd been together for a long time.

"Anybody home?" someone called out.

"Speak of the devil," Donovan said at the sound of Laura's voice from inside the house.

"Not really," Joe said, looking at Donovan oddly.

"It's just a figure of speech, Joe."

"I know what it is, but you weren't talking about Laura." Joe grinned. "I guess Ethan starting school wasn't what was really on your mind, after all."

Laura came through the open sliding glass door, her mother behind her. Donovan almost went to Laura, almost embraced her. She looked temptingly beautiful in a cool blue summer dress and sandals, her hair up, which always brought more attention to her pretty hazel eyes and her elegance, in general.

"Good morning," she said. "I hope you don't mind us just dropping in. Mom wanted to see the place."

"Hi, sugar," Dolly said, her red hair shimmering in the sunlight.

"Welcome, sweet 'ums."

"I think I'm missing something," Laura said, looking from Donovan to her mother in question.

"Inside joke," Dolly said, patting Donovan's arm.

"Laura! Dolly!" Ethan raced over. "Come see my bedroom."

"I saw it yesterday, Ethan," Laura said. "I'm sure my mom would love to, though."

"Lead the way, young sir."

He giggled and took her hand in his grubby one, dragging her into the house. Joe excused himself to get more tools from his truck out front.

"When my mom isn't working for me, she's an interior designer, did you know that?" Laura asked.

He took a couple of steps toward her. "How are you this morning, counselor?"

It took her a few seconds to refocus. She smiled. "I'm good, thank you. Did you sleep well?"

"Surprisingly well." He dragged his fingers down her bare arm, enjoying how her skin rose in bumps. "Did you?"

"I had very pleasant dreams."

"I didn't." He bent close to her ear. "I had dreams that would shock you."

"Spinning new fantasies for me, newsman?"

He liked how she returned his heated look. "Don't you have a few of your own?"

"I might." She ran a pink-polished fingernail down his chest, tracing the line that disappeared into his jeans, then hooking the edge of fabric and pulling him near.

Donovan grabbed a handful of her hair and squeezed. Her touch was feather-light. He lowered his head. She rose toward him—

A loud clatter had them jumping apart.

"More tools," Joe said before striding out the gate again.

"He knows about us," Donovan told Laura, who had put a little distance between them. "He guessed, and I decided not to lie about it. But he'll also keep his mouth shut."

She nodded, which could mean just about anything.

"Dolly says I can decorate my room with fish," Ethan announced when he and Dolly returned.

"Fish?"

"As a theme," she said. "He said he likes to fish."

Donovan wasn't aware Ethan had ever been fishing, but a kid-size fishing pole would make a good birthday gift. "Okay."

"If you'd like help with the decorating, I'd be glad to, Donovan."

"I wasn't planning on getting much new, except mattresses. Until I know for sure what the future holds, I'm just accepting all donations."

"Do you have a style?"

"Early McCoy," Joe said, returning, pushing a rototiller. "It's too bad all that stuff from the Widow Braeburn's house already sold."

"Right," Donovan said. "Because the spindly-legged tables and prim little love seats would've looked great here in the man house."

"Man house?" Laura asked.

"'Cause we're men," Ethan said, then high-fived his dad.

"I can still help," Dolly said. "I do staging for sales all the time. I'm good at it. Just have everyone put their donations in the garage. I'll take it from there."

"Ethan and I get veto power, though, okay? We don't want frills or doilies or knickknacks, right, bud?"

"Right." He frowned. "What's doilies?"

"Something we don't want. Not manly."

Ethan puffed up. "Right."

"It's a cute little place," Dolly said. "Won't take much to fill it up. As for the backyard—good luck."

"It'll be great, you'll see." He looked around the space, envisioning it finished. "Yards like this are just begging to be filled up with kids."

Silence fell like a heavy quilt. Even the birdsong stopped.

"We have to go," Laura said briskly. "We have reservations for brunch."

Donovan saw her exchange a look with an obviously surprised Dolly. Laura was lying. Why?

"Drop by anytime, neighbor," he said as evenly as possible when what he wanted was to sit her down and make her tell him why she'd lied. "And, Dolly? I'll take you up on your offer, thanks. See you later, Laura."

"Bye. So long, Ethan. Have fun."

"I will!"

They left through the side gate. He would've picked apart everything that had happened except that all of a sudden his yard teemed with people—sisters, brothers-in-law, nephews, even a couple of nieces. He tried to stop them, but none of them paid any attention.

Which was the price one paid for being a McCoy—a pushy support system that ignored your requests when it decided you were wrong.

Well, maybe help cleaning out the yard wouldn't be so bad. He and Ethan could do the planting themselves, and perhaps install a small jungle gym or swing set. There would be enough projects for the two of them to do together.

And he was counting on Ethan inviting Laura over a lot. At least there was one McCoy male she couldn't seem to say no to.

"So, in order to turn a lie into the truth, we have to go eat a second brunch?" Dolly asked as she and Laura got into the Miata and headed to Dolly's house. "Because I couldn't possibly do that, no matter how much I love Honey's blueberry pancakes."

"I'm sorry I put you on the spot. I just wanted to get away."

"I know, sweetie." Dolly patted Laura's hand as she put the car in Reverse and backed out of her driveway. "You're in love with him."

"Yes."

"Wow. No hedging at all. This is serious."

"Semiserious." Laura turned the corner and headed for her mother's house, a few blocks away. "Because it just can't be, you know?"

"Do I?"

"Of course you do. You heard him yourself. He wants to fill the yard with kids."

"I heard him. I also saw the way he looked at you. You haven't told him, I gather."

Laura shook her head. She pulled into her mother's driveway. They went into Dolly's house, a charming little cottage that showcased her extraordinary talent with paint and fabric. Summer roses from her garden filled vases in every room, the fragrance filling the air until she opened the windows, releasing the heat.

"Iced tea?" Dolly asked.

"Sure." She followed her mother into the kitchen. The tea would be home brewed and peach flavored, the goblets cut crystal.

They took their glasses and sat inside a screened sunroom off the back door, the view of the rose garden peaceful.

"So," Dolly said. "Talk."

Laura swallowed. "I hardly know where to start."

"Maybe I will, then. I've got a few questions myself."

Relief spread through her. "Okay."

"Did you honestly think you could be with him and not fall in love? He's been your one-and-only for most of your life, even when you've been with someone else."

"Yes, I thought I could. I figured it would help get him out of my system. Maybe I was naive. Maybe I was rationalizing. When it came down to it, I couldn't pass up the opportunity."

"And now you're in deep. Too deep to recover?"

"Everyone recovers, Mom. Eventually. You got over Dad, right?"

Dolly looked away, took a sip of her iced tea. "Sure."

Laura went still. "You're lying."

"I'm not, sweetie. I was just remembering. I got over him, but it took years, and him getting married to someone else."

A sandbag seemed to have dropped onto Laura's lap. "You never told me."

"I was furious. Then devastated. I had to put him out of my head."

Laura could barely breathe. "Did he have more children? Do I have siblings?"

"I don't know. I can tell you where he's living, if you want to find out for yourself. He lets me know when he moves."

"Why?"

She shrugged. "After the first note, I stopped opening them. But I have them in a file, and you're welcome to have them, if you want."

"Why is this the first time I'm hearing about it, Mom?"

"You never asked."

Laura fixed her gaze on her mother.

"Oh, all right. I didn't want you to get hurt anymore. He walked out without looking back. If he had regrets later, he could've come here and made amends. I never moved, would never have denied him the chance to see you." Dolly squeezed Laura's hand. "I thought he was my soul mate. I loved him with all my heart. But love wasn't enough. It really never is, no matter how much people spout otherwise. And it's certainly not enough when it's one-sided."

"Why did he marry you?"

Her mother's smile was crooked. "I guess you're old enough to know now. Because of you, sweetie."

"You were pregnant?" Too many revelations at once had Laura's head spinning.

"Four months."

"Why didn't I ever know about this?"

"What purpose would it have served?"

Laura couldn't believe she hadn't heard it at some point through the years, especially during high school, when teenagers sometimes took great pleasure in revealing others' dirty laundry. "It's part of my history, Mom."

"Mothers do what we can to protect our young."

"You act like you're a mama bear and I'm your cub, needing to be kept safe from predators. I haven't been in need of protection for a long time."

"I thought about telling you when you graduated and became an adult, more as a cautionary tale, so that you wouldn't make the same mistakes I did. Then you got sick. You had a hard enough row to hoe then."

Laura decided she could waste time and energy being angry at her mother for keeping such a secret—or just get past it. She chose the gentler path. "Do you regret it? Having me? Making your way in the world solo?"

"Not one bit. Not one single bit. I could've married again. I had opportunities and even a few marriage proposals, frankly. But I think you learned how to build a wall around your emotions because I did, too. I'm sorry for that."

"You denied yourself the possibility of happiness."

"My life is far from over, you know. I'm only forty-nine—an age you'll find yourself before you know it." Dolly leaned toward Laura. "Does he love you?"

"He hasn't said so. More important, we want different things, Mom. He hasn't figured out his own life yet. I'm not sure he's going to be around much."

"He won't leave Ethan alone for long periods."

"I don't think he has a choice. He's in the top tier, and he thrives on it. He'll want to set an example for Ethan, too—that you should do what you love. I figure he'll take off more time than he used to, but that's it."

"Well, you know him better than I do."

They went quiet for a long while. Laura couldn't go home, not without being seen, and she needed some time alone. Needed to cocoon.

She'd known it was going to be hard, having him living across the street. She just hadn't realized it was going to be impossible.

Chapter Sixteen

"Where the hell are you? The Giants' ballpark?"

Even with all the noise surrounding him, Donovan recognized the *NewsView* executive editor's voice over his cell phone. "Close," Donovan said. "My mom's backyard. My son's birthday party. What's up?"

Rupert Cole liked to brag that he'd discovered Donovan, who'd decided years ago to let Rupert think that. It never hurt to be an editor's favorite.

"How do you like the sound of Special Projects Editor?"

Donovan walked away from the party, going out the side gate and onto the front porch, sensing that this phone call was going to be one of the most momentous of his life. "How do I like it for what?"

"For the job of a lifetime."

"Are you making me an offer?"

"Yeah. One you can't refuse."

Donovan sat on the stoop of his mother's house. He knew all the titles at *NewsView.* Special Projects Editor wasn't one of them. "You created a job for me?"

"You got it."

"Why?"

"Because we want to keep you."

"What makes you think you wouldn't?"

"Gimme a break, D. You have no interest in going overseas for months at a time anymore. Or maybe even days. Tell me I'm wrong."

He couldn't—but he hadn't known for sure until Rupert just said it, making it real.

"Right," his wise editor continued when Donovan said nothing. "So, here's the deal. Special Projects Editor. You get to run your own show, and you'll answer only to me. You'll work out of the bureau here in D.C. I think the salary will make you happy. Plus, you'll have benefits. Profit sharing. Stability. That's what you want most, right? For you and Ethan?"

Benefits. Stability. Not the edge-of-the-cliff life of before, but a grown-up job. Calling his own shots. A chance to own a home. A steady income. Excellent schools for his son. Donovan already had a wide circle of friends and contacts in D.C.

"When do you need an answer, Rupert?"

"Schools here start in three weeks."

Three weeks. And in Chance City, ten days. Ethan was already registered. They'd walked the campus, checking it out, had peered into the kindergarten classroom, analyzed the playground equipment for the level of fun and challenge.

"I appreciate this more than I can say," Donovan told his editor. "I need to tell you that I've got something else in the works."

"I heard." He chuckled. "It's a small world, our world. I don't have a problem with you pursuing that at the same time."

It was more than he could've hoped for—but was it an offer he couldn't refuse? "I'll get back to you. Thanks, Rupert. Not just for the job offer, but for what it represents, too. I appreciate the confidence."

"You've earned it, D. I'll e-mail you more details. Figure you're interested in how much we think you're worth. I know it won't be as exciting as being in the field, but being in charge should help. I'll be home the rest of the weekend, if you want to talk."

Donovan slid the phone into his pocket but continued to sit on the stair, aware of the party noise from the back side of the house, but not ready to face it yet.

"Donovan?"

Laura stood in front of him. He hadn't heard her approach.

"We're about ready for the piñata."

He straightened. "Yeah, okay. Thanks."

"Is everything okay?"

He ran his hands along his thighs, then stood. "Maybe. Any chance I can come by later and talk to you about it?"

"Of course."

"It'll have to be after Ethan goes to bed. I'll ask one of my nieces to babysit."

"That's fine."

He returned to the backyard with her, aware of her curiosity. Aware of her, period. As he always was. They'd had little time together the past couple of weeks. It had been more complicated than he'd thought, living across the street. He knew when she came and went. He saw her in the kitchen. Saw when her lights went out at night, wishing he could join her.

The days she worked in Sacramento now, she stayed until dark, something new. Ethan was already in bed when she drove in.

The house was too quiet when his son was sleeping. Donovan had gotten used to people coming in and out all the time at his mom's house. He'd never expected to miss that.

He and Laura had slept together only twice since he'd moved into the house, both times rushed, both times physically satisfying but vaguely unsatisfying, too. She'd seemed a little distant, and he'd started to feel uncomfortable with the…arrangement. He couldn't call it a relationship, since they still hadn't gone public with it. He didn't like the hiding.

But maybe it'd been the right thing to do, after all. It could make leaving easier, not just on them but also

Ethan, since he didn't have a clue about how Donovan and Laura felt about each other.

He stopped in his tracks. Did *he* even know how they felt about each other?

"You're scaring me," Laura said, her gaze intense.

"I apologize." People were looking at them—his brothers, his mom. Nana Mae. He hadn't yet followed through on his promise to take his grandmother to lunch. She wouldn't let him off the hook too much longer. "Everything's all right, Laura."

She walked away, sat between Dixie and Keri again, and Donovan made himself get back into the spirit of the celebration. Ethan had met three other five-year-olds recently, who were now waiting their turn to hit the piñata. He was settling in, making friends. How could Donovan take him away from that?

For the job of a lifetime? How could you not?

As Joe handled the piñata portion of the party, Donovan lingered in the background. He knew why he'd left Chance City all those years ago. He'd had good reason, a calling, and a need to fulfill it. He'd done that, could continue to, probably at even greater success and fame. And personal satisfaction, something he'd gloried in.

He could admit that now. He'd reveled in his success. Anne had been right—he'd been driven by his career, to the detraction of all else. He'd set a course and stayed on it, picking up speed year by year.

And what do you have to show for it?

Plenty. Success beyond his dreams. He'd been places most people never went, experienced firsthand what most never would. And he was only thirty-three years old. He still had a lifetime of such experiences ahead of him.

At what cost?

He studied his son, who was laughing uproariously as he tried to hit the piñata blindfolded. A mere month ago he'd been shy and cautious. He would've needed Donovan by his side, holding his hand.

Or Laura.

Donovan's gaze slid to her. Her eyes sparkled as she watched Ethan. She leaned closer to Dixie now and then to comment, but her gaze never strayed from his son.

She fit. She was surrounded by McCoys like a fine wine amid longneck bottles of beer. But she fit. He'd seen her go up to his mom today and give her a hug, something she wouldn't have done a month ago. Like Ethan, she'd settled in.

So have you.

Yes. So had he.

Donovan made his way to where his grandmother sat, enjoying the festivities. "I'm wondering what your calendar is like?" he asked, crouching beside her. "Do you have time for lunch this week?"

"As a matter of fact, I'm free tomorrow, after church."

"I'll pick you up at noon. We can take a drive up to Tahoe, have lunch, play the nickel slots a little."

Before her stroke a couple of years ago, she'd loved that kind of day.

"Let's just go to the Lode. It was sweet of you to offer, Donny, but I don't have the energy for anything more than that."

It was the first time she'd admitted it to him. She generally resisted any hint that she'd slowed down. How many years did she have left? She was eighty-nine. She had every right to take it easy.

"I'm fine," she said, patting his cheek. "Don't look so worried."

He'd observed the fragility of life so many times, in so many places. In the middle of a war there was no time to contemplate it. But here, where his life had begun and with his grandmother sitting beside him, aging minute by minute, he thought about it. She was becoming more fragile day by day, but only in body. In spirit she was as strong as ever, maybe stronger. Her perspective on his situation would be different, clearer.

"I love you," he said, kissing her cheek.

"Oh, my sweet boy!" She framed his face, her eyes glistening. "You always were the one to surprise me the most. And not always in a good way," she added with a laugh. "I love you, too."

His gut unclenched. He patted her shoulder and moved next to Jake, who happened to be standing behind Keri, and therefore close to Laura. He held Isabella, was swaying a little, bouncing a little.

Donovan studied his niece, her eyes drifting shut, then popping open at the sound of the stick hitting the piñata or people cheering.

"Could I take over?" he asked his brother. A couple of months ago, Jake had set Isabella in Donovan's hands, but he'd given her back almost instantly, unsure.

Jake didn't hesitate. He transferred his daughter to Donovan's arms. She stared at her uncle, serious and intent, then suddenly smiled, transforming her beautiful little face. His heart melted.

"There's nothing like it," Jake said.

"I missed this part of the dad experience." Another reason not to forgive Anne.

Laura twisted around to face him. "You look very natural," she said, a smile on her lips but not in her eyes.

Isabella slept finally as they finished up with the piñata, then throughout the opening of the gifts.

"Last one," Aggie said, carrying a large, flat, rectangular package. "The card says Ethan and Donovan."

"Come on, Dad! Help me open it."

Donovan passed the soundly sleeping Isabella back to Jake, then joined Ethan, who'd plucked the envelope from the package and handed it to Donovan.

"It's from Laura," Donovan said, reading the card.

"I already got a present from Laura." A pair of shields, encrusted in plastic gems, matching the swords from before.

"I guess she thinks you need two."

Ethan just grinned.

They peeled off the paper together, revealing a framed canvas painting of father and son. Oohs and aahs followed.

"Look, Dad! It's us!"

Donovan swallowed hard. Them, indeed, looking like a matched set, each of them wearing blue shirts, their heads touching, beaming with the same smile. He remembered that day in the park, had forgotten Laura had taken photographs. She'd had this one turned into a portrait, a tangible memory.

"Thank you," he managed to say to her. They might as well have been alone, because she was the only person he saw. "It's perfect."

"I'm glad you like it. Mom painted it."

The McCoy circle had expanded even more with the addition of Dolly, who'd spent most of the day talking with Aggie, as if they were old friends. Maybe they were. Donovan didn't know.

He sat back and looked around. This was his tribe. His village. His people.

His family.

"Have you had a good day?" he asked his son.

"The best." Ethan hugged him, long and hard, something he'd learned from his Grandma Aggie, Donovan figured.

"Me, too," Donovan said.

But was it enough? He was itching for more in his life, something the new job could provide. The backyard at his rental was finished, but the lawn too new and tender to host a family party yet, which was why they were at Aggie's. The fact that he'd even considered throwing a party still surprised him.

Aggie started singing "Happy Birthday," everyone joining in right away. Five candles were lit on the chocolate-cake-with-chocolate-frosting request from the birthday boy, who grinned from ear to ear.

If Donovan turned down the job, Ethan could grow up here, where he wouldn't have the global experiences of living in D.C., but where he was already loved and accepted. That trade-off for Ethan would be fine.

The question was, would it be fine for Donovan?

Chapter Seventeen

Laura climbed out of her pool and grabbed a towel, burying her face in it. She'd swum lap after lap after lap, had stopped counting how many. Her arms ached. Her hips and thighs swore at her.

Outside the French doors to her bedroom, she stripped off her suit, wrapped up in her towel and went inside. Nine-thirty, the clock said. An hour she'd been out there churning out laps. A full hour.

Compensating for the birthday cake and ice cream….

No. Countering a whirlwind of emotion.

Something was on the horizon for Donovan. Something crucial.

He'd called earlier, saying he'd be over around ten.

She still had time to shower, blow-dry her hair, put on a silk negligee she'd just bought. They usually didn't have time to set a romantic scene. She wanted to give him a memory—and herself, too, because she didn't know how many more opportunities there would be.

At precisely ten o'clock came a soft tap on the front door. Laura shook her hair back, more nervous than she could remember. And it *was* nerves, not anticipation that had her hands trembling and her breath shaky. It had to be nerves.

She opened the door. He didn't say anything, didn't have to. Desire flared in his eyes, in the hardness of his jaw, in his posture. He slipped inside, locked the door and pulled her into his arms, kissing her with a ferocity she returned in full measure. She wasn't interested in tender any more than he was.

He backed her against the foyer wall, attacked her mouth with his, hot, wet and deep, his throat vibrating with needy sounds. He squeezed her breasts, tugged at the straps of her negligee, dragging them down to savor her flesh, his tongue leading the way, nipping with his teeth, sucking her nipples into his mouth. He kept going, lower and lower, her gown pooling at her feet, his hands flattening her hips to the wall as he cherished her, stealing her breath, scattering all thoughts, leaving only sensation, rising, powerful sensation. She skyrocketed, soaring higher and higher until bursts of color shot through her with such force she had to brace herself.

Before she'd even come down all the way, he lifted

her, her legs wrapped around him, and carried her down the hall to her bedroom, dropping her on the bed. His shorts fell away. He didn't bother with his shirt, just plunged into her and drove hard, his face contorted as he moved rhythmically.

"Come with me," he murmured, slipping a hand between their bodies, dipping his fingers low, stroking her with incredible softness, considering his own need.

She slammed into a hard, fast climax that startled her with its intensity. He joined her, his body as hard as marble, his groans primal and flattering.

He said her name, low, almost painfully. She wrapped him in her arms and held him, wanting to soothe. He didn't move. Didn't roll off her, but lingered, his weight on his elbows but still heavy against her body, and exactly where he was meant to be.

"If I'd known you like negligees that much," she said when she couldn't stand the silence any longer, "I would've worn one sooner."

He lifted his head, kissed her gently, making no joke in return.

"What's wrong, Donovan?"

He finally moved away, pulling off his shirt, then settling down beside her. "Nothing's wrong. In fact, a case could be made for saying something's amazingly right."

"Are you going to tease me all night?"

He tucked a strand of her hair behind her ear. "That would be a first, wouldn't it? We've never had 'all night.'"

No, they never had. Never more than a few hours at a time. She'd come to resent that in ways that surprised her. "If you don't tell me right now what's going on, I'm leaving this bed."

He grabbed her hand, keeping her there. "I never expected we'd have this conversation naked," he said, smiling for the first time.

This conversation? Alarms blared in her head. Even before he started talking, she knew it would be about his work. Then he did talk, confirming it. And what an extraordinary job offer—life offer, really, because it would change his life forever. And Ethan's.

"When are you leaving?" she asked, wishing for the protection of clothes.

"I haven't accepted the job, Laura. I haven't even come close to it."

"How can you not? You know what your chances are of having another opportunity like this. Really, Donovan, how can you not take the job?"

"Because there are other things to take into consideration. Like Ethan."

She waited for him to add, "Like you," but he didn't.

She wanted to be done with the conversation. Wanted to give in to that bright ball of pain building inside her. She couldn't do that in front of him.

"What do you want from me?" she asked. "What's my role here?"

He moved back a couple of inches. "I'm thinking out loud so that you can help me see every angle."

She couldn't deal with it naked anymore, so she got out of bed and went into her closet, coming out wearing a robe. He'd pulled on his shorts and T-shirt and was sitting against the headboard, looking…distant.

Laura sat on the bed, facing him. "Ethan will grow where he's planted. You've already witnessed that. It only matters that you be together, and that his father is happy and fulfilled. That's all he needs."

He frowned. "I expected you to talk me out of it."

"I don't think you did. I think you came to me for honesty." She was glad now that she hadn't told him her secret, that she could continue to keep it. She could go back to her life as it was, which was just fine. Give her a few months—or years—and she would be fine, anyway.

"Actually, I've been dealing with something similar," she continued. "The partners are pushing me hard to come on board full-time. They've decided part-time no longer works for their purposes."

"What are you going to do?"

"I'm seriously considering it. It's not like the people of Chance City couldn't drive to Sacramento to consult with me." Except many would be priced out of it, probably, considering that her hourly rate in Sacramento was almost double what she charged here in town.

"But you told me you'd have to be working eighty-hour weeks," he said. "Add your commute, and you won't have a minute for yourself."

"I'd move to Sacramento." She figured she could buy a house or condo, and if Dixie decided to take her own job offer in Sacramento, too, they could share until she had the resources to go out on her own. It might be fun having a roommate, a true girlfriend. Laura had kept herself private for too long, far too long.

"Move to…? Are you serious? You said you'd have a full-time practice here, if you could make a living at it."

His memory was too good. "Well, I've rethought it. Like your offer, it's tempting."

He stared at her for a long time, a usually successful technique, she knew, for getting someone to say more. She didn't add anything. Couldn't add anything. Because any second now, she was going to break down and sob on his shoulder, pleading for him not to go, pleading for him to love her back.

She couldn't do that to him. They had no future. He wanted more babies, a real family life. She would even move to D.C. with him, if he asked, if she thought they could make a go of it, that he wouldn't eventually resent her for not giving him more babies. He'd made enough comments lately that she knew the inevitable.

"So," he said finally. "You'd be okay with me leaving?"

"I've had a great time with you. And you know I adore Ethan." That bright ball of pain was reaching epic proportions. If he didn't leave soon… "But, Donovan, you have an incredible talent. It shouldn't be wasted."

"And it wouldn't matter to you if I left?" he asked again.

I love you. "Do what you need to do."

"You didn't answer the question."

"Your decision has to be based on what's best for you and Ethan."

His gaze was steady. She looked right back.

He reached for her hands, held them in his, still staring at her. She thought she would spontaneously combust, so intense was the fire inside her. She wanted him with all her heart and soul, wanted him in sickness and health, for better or worse. Until death do them part.

She wanted to be a mother to Ethan, to watch him grow, to help raise him to be a man. Ethan was her only hope for that, because she would never give in to her emotions like this again.

"You're right," Donovan said finally, breaking a long silence. "You're right most of the time, you know?"

She shook her head, a lump in her throat preventing speech.

"I should go," he said.

She walked with him to the front door, her hand in his. He kissed her, thoroughly but without heat, the tenderness almost unbearable. Then he was gone.

One hand covering her mouth, one pressed to her stomach, she ran to her bedroom, fell facedown on the bed and gave in to everything she felt, all the pain, all the longing, all the love.

Maybe if she'd been honest with him from the beginning, it would've made a difference. Maybe. Regardless, she'd waited too long, had been too afraid that it would be the deal breaker for them. So she'd taken what she could from him, promising herself no regrets.

Which was the biggest lie she'd ever told herself. She was going to regret his loss for the rest of her life. Of that she had no doubt.

Donovan didn't sleep. He tried, several times, but he always wound up sitting in a chair on the back patio. If he'd been a list maker, he would've done the pros and cons, but there were too many factors to weigh, too many lists to compile and cross-check with others.

In the end, he would have to go with his gut.

By the time he picked up Nana Mae at noon and they were settled in their booth at the Lode, he was no closer to making a decision than when he'd gotten Rupert's call yesterday.

He didn't bring up the job offer while they ate, just kept the conversation light, getting her to reminisce about her life, asking questions he hadn't been interested in before, grateful she was still alive when he'd reached an age where he was genuinely curious about her history.

He noticed other things, as well. How elegantly she ate, using each utensil precisely, reminding him of the etiquette lessons she'd given all her grandchildren. He'd gone out into the world prepared to be tested over a meal by potential employers, heads of state, four-star generals or women on dates, knowing he could pass any test of manners with flying colors, not only because he knew which fork to use when, but how to converse, how to put people at ease.

She'd done that for him, for all of his siblings. He loved her, but even more, he respected and admired her.

When they were finished with their sandwiches and salads, Honey brought hot lemon tea and pound cake for Nana Mae, her traditional finish to any meal at the Lode.

"You drink too much of that stuff," she said to Donovan as Honey refilled his coffee mug. "Moderation in all things."

"Bores me."

Her eyes twinkled. "I know."

"Not likely to change, either."

"I know that, too. So, what's the real reason you invited me to lunch?"

He leaned toward her, remembering at the last minute not to put his elbows on the table. "I've been offered a job at *NewsView,* a full-time, permanent, regular-paycheck-and-benefits, big-challenge job."

"And the *but* is?"

"It's in D.C."

She nodded thoughtfully. "What are you going to do?"

"I don't know yet."

She took a careful sip of her tea, her way of gathering her thoughts. "Your father once had an offer like that."

Donovan sat back, surprised. "He did?"

"Not the same as yours, of course, but an offer that

would've suited him, a chance to leave town, be independent, see the world. He was twenty-one. He and Aggie had been dating about eight months."

"Mom would've been seventeen."

"That's right. They'd known each other for years, but when she started her senior year, he took notice of her in an entirely new way. She was so different from him, you know? Outgoing, bubbly, cheerful. She's the same now, just more mature, of course. I could see why he fell for her. He'd been too serious all his life. She brightened his world in ways I can't even describe.

"Then along came this job offer just as he was about to propose, the day of her high-school graduation. He came to me, wanting advice. I told him then what I'm going to tell you now, Donny. You need to do what makes you happy. If you're not happy, no one around you will be. It all may seem complicated, but it's really quite simple."

Donovan had figured that his grandmother would talk him into staying in Chance City. If he'd given it more thought, he would've realized she wouldn't do that. His mother might, but not Nana Mae, which was probably why he was talking to her and not his mom. "Dad didn't take the job."

"He did not."

"Did he regret it?"

"You grew up with him. What do you think?"

His father had remained a quiet man, dependable, patient and consistent. But he'd loved his wife openly, lovingly, their affection public, if subtle on his part. "He seemed content," Donovan said. "But if he had regrets, we never would've heard about it."

"Yes, you would, Donny. Not directly, but he would've been telling you one way or the other all your life. And if he were here today, he would tell you to check with your heart first before you make a decision, not your head. Not your practical side, but your selfish side. And once you've made a decision, don't look back. Don't regret. Have no remorse. Keep moving forward."

A hot lump settled in Donovan's throat. "Mom and Dad were incredible role models. I always knew I wouldn't settle for less than what they had."

Which was why he'd never asked Anne to marry him, even though he'd thought he'd loved her. If he'd loved her enough, he would've sacrificed for her, and he didn't. She must've known....

Nana Mae patted his hand. "You'll make the right decision. Whatever you decide will be right, because it'll be for the right reasons. Let your walls collapse for a while. See what's behind them."

Walls. The word triggered a memory of his conversation with Dolly. What had she said? That Laura had put up some pretty solid walls.

Why?

He hadn't asked why, hadn't gotten deep enough into her head to know why she'd built walls, why she'd needed them in the first place. Last night, he'd seen her pull back from him. She'd encouraged him to take the job, to go all the way across the country—for a job. She hadn't expressed any hope that he wouldn't go—not in words or even in her eyes.

Why? She'd said, too, that Ethan would bloom where he was planted—even though Donovan knew she loved Ethan, knew she loved being with him, and he with her.

And why was it so important to Donovan that she wanted him—and Ethan—to stay?

"You just made a decision," his grandmother said, watching him.

"I checked with my heart, like you said. It made it for me, loud and clear." He captured her hand across the table. "Thank you. Maybe I would've come to the same conclusion, made the same decision, but I would've probably suffered for days trying to make it. You made it simple. You couldn't have given better advice."

"When it comes down to it, Donny, most things in life are simple."

But not people. People were complicated and complex, with walls built around emotions and old hurts. You could chip away at them or shatter them all at once with a wrecking ball.

And there wasn't time to chip away at Laura's walls.

Chapter Eighteen

Laura left her hand cradled on the telephone receiver after ending the call, one that had taken her a week to work up the nerve to make. She didn't know how she felt yet except—

Her doorbell rang. Through the peephole she saw Donovan staring right back at her, waving, smiling.

He'd made a decision.

She drew a steadying breath, then opened the door. "Hi."

His smile went away. "What's wrong? You're pale."

She choked up a little, wanted to throw herself in his arms and let him hold her. She clenched her fists instead. "I just talked to my father. Come in."

He did, but stood just inside the front door, not trying to lead her into the living room, but cupping her elbows, steadying her.

"Did he finally track you down?" he asked.

"I called him. Turns out my mom has known all along where he lives—Orlando." She swallowed. "I have a brother and a sister. Twins. They just graduated from college. He—my father—wants to see me. He wants forgiveness."

"What are you going to do?"

"You know, given what I do for a living, I've seen how easy it is for people to become estranged and not know how to fix it, even when they desperately want to. I'm willing to give it a shot. It won't be easy, but I want to try. In some ways, I need to forgive my mom, too, for keeping his existence a secret from me. I'm in the mood to forgive." There were more important things in life, she'd decided, than holding grudges.

"I forgave Anne," Donovan said.

The short, simple sentence filled the entire room with significance. "I'm glad. How'd you come to it?"

"By realizing I hadn't done my share in the relationship. That I was at fault, too. She was wrong not to tell me I had a son, but it's done and can't be changed. I want a clean slate."

Laura's blood ran cold. She couldn't move. "So you've decided to take the job."

He cocked his head. "That's an interesting conclusion you've jumped to, counselor."

She would miss that, him calling her counselor in that playful way.

"Let's go for a walk," he said.

"Where?"

"Not far. Come on, Laura. Be spontaneous with me."

"Bully," she said, his dare a tempting one.

"Whatever works."

She grabbed her keys and left the house with him on what was probably the hottest day of the summer so far.

"One of the things I thought about during my sleepless night last night," he said as they walked, not holding hands, but occasionally bumping arms, "was your decision to move to Sacramento and take on an eighty-hour-a-week job. I wondered what had changed during the past few weeks, because I didn't get the impression that was something you wanted to do. So the only answer I could come up with was that you'd gone into self-protection mode. More important—into sacrifice mode. You wanted me to leave here with the knowledge that you, too, were moving on to something bigger. Your life would go on without me."

"You say in all humility." She didn't like that he could figure her out so well, so easily. *Yes, you do. You like it a lot.* Her heart was doing the talking now, instead of her head. No one else had ever read her so well.

He smiled gently. "I understand you. Is that so bad?"

"What do you think you know?"

"I'll tell you in a minute."

They rounded a corner and kept walking toward the park. She could usually summon up a great deal of patience, but not today. Not now. She wanted to get this over with. She especially didn't want to walk by the house. *Her* house, as she always thought of it. The place where life could be perfect, where a family could be made—and a wonderful life.

"Ever been inside this place?" Donovan asked, pointing to the house. Her house.

She shook her head.

He held up a key. "Let's take a look."

"How…?" She stopped the question cold, because she didn't really need to know how he'd gotten the key, but rather how he'd known that this was the house. Her house.

They went inside. She saw peeling paint, water-damaged hardwood floors, a filthy stone fireplace. She also saw beauty and warmth, peace and fun, which echoed through the house like their footsteps as they walked from room to room, checking out each of the five bedrooms, three bathrooms, unusable kitchen and gorgeous sunroom.

Donovan stayed uncharacteristically quiet, as if they were visiting a shrine. Maybe they were. Her own shrine to family and dreams that she'd given up on twelve years ago.

Finally he leaned against a pillar in the sun room. Still he hadn't touched her. She needed so much to be touched, to be held. The house, her house, was calling to her, as it always had, making promises she knew couldn't be fulfilled.

And somehow she knew Donovan was about to make things harder on her.

"I know you do need a partnership offered to you, Laura, and I'm here to do just that," he said, his voice sounding strange after the long silence. "There's a catch, however."

"Isn't there always?"

"How'd you get to be so cynical?" he asked, smiling slightly but not waiting for an answer. "The catch is, this partnership would require more than eighty hours a week. Also, the revenue can't be counted in cash, but it's immeasurable, refilling itself to overflowing all the time. Marry me, Laura. Live here with me. I love you."

He loved her? The room spun, not just with joy but worry. "But—"

He pressed his fingers to her lips. "No buts. Just love me and my son, and whatever other children we're blessed with."

How could the best day of her life also be the worst? "Children," she repeated.

"Yeah. I'm not talking a dozen or anything, but a couple more. I didn't realize how much I'd wanted kids until Ethan came along. This house could hold just the right number, don't you think?"

"You're not accepting the job offer?"

"I'm not. When I asked myself if I wanted the job

of a lifetime or the chance of a lifetime, it was a simple choice. I've been out in the world. I know the value of life, the importance of love, the necessity of a true partnership. I could have all that in D.C., too, if you were willing to move there. But this is where I want to raise my children—with you. I've learned that nothing is forever, that life constantly shifts and changes. I *can* go home again."

She walked away from him, staring at the overgrown backyard. He didn't give her time or space, but was beside her in an instant.

"Yes? No? Maybe? Give me time? Drop dead? Not if you were the last man on earth?" he said, covering anxiety with humor.

"I've been keeping something from you, Donovan. Something important. No, more than that. Something critical."

"I'm listening."

"I didn't tell you in the beginning, because I thought this would be temporary."

"This?"

"Us. Our affair." The word sounded harsh in her ears. Affair. It really was what they'd had, but it sounded tawdry now, especially knowing she loved him—and he loved her. She'd ignored that declaration, not letting him see how much his words had meant to her. It was what she'd wanted—and feared—would happen.

"Our affair," he repeated. "Is that how you see what we've had? No emotions involved, just sex?"

"I can't have children." There. She'd said it. Now they could deal with it.

He waited a few beats. "How do you know that?"

"Because twelve years ago, I had uterine cancer. I had a hysterectomy, then chemotherapy and radiation, all of which saved my life, but took away my ability to have children."

She felt him staring at her, but she didn't make eye contact, continuing to look out the window, seeing nothing. He turned away.

She trembled from keeping herself so still, so rigid. She wished he would just go, get it over with, let her get on with the healing she would need to do. Go to D.C., she wanted to scream. Get out of my life. Take your adorable son with you.

After what seemed like an hour, he faced her, took her shoulders and made her look at him. His eyes were wet. "Cancer."

She nodded.

"You could've died," he said, low and hoarse.

He pulled her against him so hard she bounced off him a little, held her so hard she could barely breathe. That she'd started crying didn't help.

"You could've died," he said again.

"I didn't," she said, comforting him, running her hands over his back, up into his hair, as he pressed his face into her shoulder. "I'm here."

He kissed her, emotion spilling from him. If she'd had any doubts that he loved her, they were gone now.

His fear, his relief, all poured out of him in that kiss that was tender and grateful and life-affirming.

"Why didn't you think you could tell me?" he asked, touching his forehead to hers.

"My reasons were purely selfish. I'd wanted you for so long. I finally had a chance. I didn't want to give you up until I had to. When you turned me down in the high-school parking lot, I was devastated. I wanted a memory this time."

He finally straightened. She brushed his cheeks with her hands, as he did hers, both of them smiling a little.

"You know why I turned you down, don't you?" he asked.

"You said I was too young."

"I also told you I was leaving. Believe me, I was more than tempted. But what kind of man gets involved with a woman when he knows he's going to leave?"

The silence that dropped between them was palpable.

"Yes," he said, without her asking the question. "Yes, I must have already decided I wouldn't be leaving Chance City when we first slept together. I didn't know it consciously, but I must have known, because that's not the way I operate. And you haven't answered my question, Laura."

She believed he loved her. Still, a big issue needed to be addressed. "You said you wanted to fill your yard with kids."

"You're too literal, counselor. What makes you think I wouldn't be open to adoption? Or if that's not right for you, we borrow the neighbors' kids or my nieces and nephews from time to time. But can you imagine the number of children I've seen who've been orphaned? How many kids I wished I could take home and keep safe? Are you willing to do that? Adopt?"

"Yes," she said instantly, the word scraping along her throat. "I never saw myself as a mother, never allowed it, but I've learned I have a lot to give a child, especially when I love his father."

"So that's a yes, you'll marry me?"

"That's about the biggest yes in the history of the world."

He kissed her, softly, sweetly, then framed her face and asked, "Aren't you curious about how I'm going to support us?"

"Yes, I am, in fact, although I have to tell you that you'd better come up with something good, because I'm quitting the firm in Sacramento. My income's dropping by a whole lot. We may not be able to afford this house."

The thought of not having this house now that she'd come to believe it was hers struck fear in her.

"Relax. We can afford this house," he said right away, reading her expression perfectly. "Remember last month when you were giving me ideas about work I might do that would allow me to stay here with Ethan? Well, it seems a publisher wouldn't mind paying me to write fiction, based on my experiences. I'm going to create a series starring an ace journalist who makes a name for himself by going where the story is, risking his life for it, no holds barred, and the enemies he makes."

"Will he ever fall in love and settle down?"

"What? Turn him into a boring, everyday—"

She shoved him away. He laughed and pulled her back. "Maybe. Maybe he needs some heartbreak first so that he realizes what he's got when he finally finds it."

"Much better," she said. "So, where's Ethan?"

"At Mom's." Donovan ran his hands down her, curved his palms over her rear and brought her close. "We have plenty of time to go back to your house for a while."

"Actually, I'd like to go tell him, if you don't mind." Excitement filled her to near bursting. "I'm going to be a mother. I'm kind of in a hurry to celebrate that. Actually, I'm in a big hurry. It's something I thought I'd never have the chance—" She swallowed.

His expression was one of total indulgence to her happiness. "We can go tell him right now."

"Do you think, since he calls Anne Mum, that maybe he'll be able to call me Mom?" she asked, worried. "I don't want to replace her, just add to what she's already given him. And I know we need to give him time to come to terms with it all first. Plus, it means another move for him—here, to this beautiful house—"

He laughed. "Slow down. Take a breath."

She inhaled shakily. "Okay. O-kay."

"All right. Anything else on that list of yours?"

"Probably lots, but for now? No."

He hooked an arm around her, and drew her back inside the house. "This place needs a lot of work."

"Of course it does. But then, anything that's worthwhile does. I love you, newsman."

"It's about time you said it."

"I've said it in my head so many times, I thought I already had."

They stopped in the middle of their future living room and kissed. "Don't ever stop," he said against her lips. "I'll never get tired of hearing it."

"I love you with all my heart." She would tell him that every day, for the rest of their lives. She would let herself be spontaneous. She would laugh and love and cherish.

They would have big family parties. She would be a full-fledged McCoy for the rest of her life.

"I'll learn how to cook," she said.

Donovan laughed then, and the house—her house—smiled, too.

* * * * *

Turn the page for a sneak peek at

Wealthy Australian, Secret Son,

the exhilarating new novel from international
bestselling author Margaret Way
available this month from all-new
Mills & Boon® Cherish™.

CHAPTER ONE

The present

IT WAS an idyllic day for a garden party. The sky was a deep blue; sparkling sunshine flooded the Valley; a cooling breeze lowered the spring into summer heat. A veritable explosion of flowering trees and foaming blossom had turned the rich rural area into one breathtakingly beautiful garden that leapt at the eye and caught at the throat. It was so perfect a world the inhabitants of Silver Valley felt privileged to live in it.

Only Charlotte Prescott, a widow at twenty-six, with a seven-year-old child, stood in front of the bank of mirrors in her dressing room, staring blindly at her own reflection. The end of an era had finally arrived, but there was no joy in it for her, for her father, or for Christopher, her clever, thoughtful child. They were the dispossessed, and nothing in the world could soothe the pain of loss.

For the past month, since the invitations had begun to arrive, Silver Valley had been eagerly anticipating the Open Day: a get-to-know-you garden party to be held in the grounds of the grandest colonial mansion in the valley, Riverbend. Such a lovely name, Riverbend! A private house, its grandeur reflected the wealth and community standing of the man who had built it in the 1880s, Charles

Randall Marsdon, a young man of means who had migrated from England to a country that didn't have a splendid *past*, like his homeland, but in his opinion had a glowing *future*. He'd meant to be part of that future. He'd meant to get to the top!

There might have been a certain amount of bravado in that young man's goal, but Charles Marsdon had turned out not only to be a visionary, but a hard-headed businessman who had moved to the highest echelons of colonial life with enviable speed.

Riverbend was a wonderfully romantic two-storey mansion, with a fine Georgian façade and soaring white columns, its classic architecture adapted to climatic needs with large-scale open-arched verandahs providing deep shading for the house. It had been in the Marsdon family—*her* family—for six generations, but sadly it would never pass to her adored son. For the simple reason that Riverbend was no longer theirs. The mansion, its surrounding vineyards and olive groves, badly neglected since the Tragedy, had been sold to a company called Vortex. Little was known about Vortex, except that it had met the stiff price her father had put on the estate. Not that he could have afforded to take a lofty attitude. Marsdon money had all but run out. But Vivian Marsdon was an immensely proud man who never for a moment underestimated his important position in the Valley. It was *everything* to him to keep face. In any event, the asking price, exorbitantly high, had been paid swiftly—and oddly enough without a single quibble.

Now, months later, the CEO of the company was finally coming to town. Naturally she and her father had been invited, although neither of them had met any Vortex representative. The sale had been handled to her father's satisfaction by their family solicitors, Dunnett & Banfield. Part of the deal was that her father was to have tenure of the Lodge—originally an old coach house—during his lifetime, after which it would be returned to the estate. The coach house had been converted and greatly enlarged by her grandfather into a beautiful and comfortable guest house that had enjoyed a good deal of use in the old days, when her grandparents had entertained on a grand scale, and it was at the Lodge they were living now. Just the three of them: father, daughter, grandson.

Her former in-laws—Martyn's parents and his sister Nicole—barely acknowledged them these days. The estrangement had become entrenched in the eighteen months since Martyn's death. Her husband, three years older than she, had been killed when he'd lost control of his high-powered sports car on a notorious black spot in the Valley and smashed into a tree. A young woman had been with him. Mercifully she'd been thrown clear of the car, suffering only minor injuries. It had later transpired she had been Martyn's mistress for close on six months. Of course Martyn hadn't been getting what he'd needed at home. If Charlotte had been a loving wife the tragedy would never have happened. The *second* major tragedy in her lifetime. It seemed very much as if Charlotte Prescott was a jinx.

Poor old you! Charlotte spoke silently to her image. *What a mess you've made of your life!*

She really didn't need anyone to tell her that. The irony was that her father had made just as much a mess of his own life—even before the Tragedy. The *first* tragedy. The only one that mattered to her parents. Her father had had little time for Martyn, yet he himself was a man without insight into his own limitations. Perhaps the defining one was unloading responsibility. Vivian Marsdon was constitutionally incapable of accepting the blame for anything. Anything that went wrong was always someone else's fault, or due to some circumstance beyond his control. The start of the Marsdon freefall from grace had begun when her highly respected grandfather, Sir Richard Marsdon, had died. His only son and heir had not been able to pick up the reins. It was as simple as that. The theory of three. One man made the money, the next enlarged on it, the third lost it. No better cushion than piles of money. Not every generation produced an heir with the Midas touch, let alone the necessary drive to manage and significantly enlarge the family fortune.

Her father, born to wealth and prestige, lacked Sir Richard's strong character as well as his formidable business brain. Marsdon money had begun to disappear early, like water down a drain. Failed pie-in-the-sky schemes had been approached with enthusiasm. Her father had turned a deaf ear to cautioning counsel from accountants and solicitors alike. He knew best. Sadly, his lack of judgement had put a discernible dent in the family fortunes. And that was even before the Tragedy that had blighted their family life.

With a sigh of regret, Charlotte picked up her lovely hat with its wide floppy brim, settling it on her head. She rarely wore her long hair loose these days, preferring to pull it back from her face and arrange it in various knots. In any case, the straw picture hat demanded she pull her hair back off her face. Her dress was Hermes silk, in chartreuse, strapless except for a wide silk band over one shoulder that flowed down the bodice and short skirt. The hat was a perfect colour match, adorned with organdie peonies in masterly deep pinks that complemented the unique shade of golden lime-green.

The outfit wasn't new, but she had only worn it once, at Melbourne Cup day when Martyn was alive. Martyn had taken great pride in how she looked. She'd always had to look her best. In those days she had been every inch a *fashionista*, such had been their extravagant and, it had to be said, *empty* lifestyle. Martyn had been a man much like her father—an inheritor of wealth who could do what he liked, when he liked, if he so chose. Martyn had made his choice. He had always expected to marry her, right from childhood, bringing about the union of two long-established rural families. And once he'd had her—he had always been mad about her—he had set about making their lifestyle a whirl of pleasure up until his untimely death.

From time to time she had consoled herself with the thought that perhaps Martyn, as he matured, would cease taking up endless defensive positions against his highly effective father, Gordon, come to recognise his family responsibilities and then pursue them with some skill and determination.

Sadly, all her hopes—and Gordon Prescott's—had been killed off one by one. And she'd had to face some hard facts herself. Hadn't she been left with a legacy of guilt? She had never loved Martyn. Bonded to him from earliest childhood, she had always regarded him with great affection. But *romantic* love? Never! The heart wasn't obedient to the expectations of others. She *knew* what romantic love was. She *knew* about passion—dangerous passion and its infinite temptations—but she hadn't steered away from it in the interests of safety. She had totally succumbed.

All these years later her heart still pumped his name.

Rohan.

She heard her son's voice clearly. He sounded anxious. "Mummy, are you ready? Grandpa wants to leave."

A moment later, Christopher, a strikingly handsome little boy, dressed in a bright blue shirt with mother-of-pearl buttons and grey cargo pants, tore into the room.

"Come on, come on," he urged, holding out his hand to

her. "He's stomping around the hall and going red in the face. That means his blood pressure is going up, doesn't it?"

"Nothing for you to worry about, sweetheart," Charlotte answered calmly. "Grandpa's health is excellent. Stomping is a way to get our attention. Anyway, we're not late," she pointed out.

It had been after Martyn's death, on her father's urging, that she and Christopher had moved into the Lodge. Her father was sad and lonely, finding it hard getting over the big reversals in his life. She knew at some point she *had* to make a life for herself and her son. But where? She couldn't escape the Valley. Christopher loved it here. It was his home. He loved his friends, his school, his beautiful environment and his bond with his grandfather. It made a move away from the Valley extremely difficult, and there were other crucial considerations for a single mother with a young child.

Martyn had left her little money. They had lived with his parents at their huge High Grove estate. They had wanted for nothing, all expenses paid, but Martyn's father—knowing his son's proclivities—had kept his son on a fairly tight leash. His widow, so all members of the Prescott family had come to believe, was undeserving.

"Grandpa runs to a timetable of his own," Christopher was saying, shaking his golden-blond head. She too was blonde, with green eyes. Martyn had been fair as well, with greyish-blue eyes. Christopher's eyes were as brilliant as blue-fire diamonds. "You look lovely in that dress, Mummy," he added, full of love and pride in his beautiful mother. "Please don't be sad today. I just wish I was seventeen instead of seven," he lamented. "I'm just a kid. But I'll grow up and become a great big success. You'll have *me* to look after you."

"My knight in shining armour!" She bent to give him a

big hug, then took his outstretched hand, shaking it back and forth as if beginning a march. "Onward, Christian soldiers!"

"What's that?" He looked up at her with interest.

"It's an English hymn," she explained. Her father wouldn't have included hymns in the curriculum. Her father wasn't big on hymns. Not since the Tragedy. "It means we have to go forth and do our best. *Endure*. It was a favourite hymn of Sir Winston Churchill. You know who he was?"

"Of course!" Christopher scoffed. "He was the great English World War II Prime Minister. The country gave him a *huge* amount of money for his services to the nation, then they took most of it back in tax. Grandpa told me."

Charlotte laughed. Very well read himself, her father had taken it upon himself to "educate" Christopher. Christopher had attended the best school in the Valley for a few years now, but her father took his grandson's education much further, taking pride and delight it setting streams of general, historical and geographical questions for which Christopher had to find the answers. Christopher was already computer literate but her father wasn't—something that infuriated him—and insisted he find the answers in the books in the well-stocked library. Christopher never cheated. He always came up trumps. Christopher was a very clever little boy.

Like his father.

The garden party was well underway by the time they finished their stroll along the curving driveway. Riverbend had never looked more beautiful, Charlotte thought, pierced by the same sense of loss she knew her father was experiencing—though one would never have known it from his confident Lord of the Manor bearing. Her father was a handsome man, but alas not a lot of people in the Valley liked him. The mansion, since they had moved, had undergone very necessary repairs. These days it was superbly maintained, and staffed by a housekeeper, her husband—a sort of major-domo—and several ground staff to bring the once-famous gardens back to their best. A good-looking young woman came out from Sydney from time to time, to check on what was being done. Charlotte had met her once, purely by accident…

© Margaret Way, PTY., LTD 2011

are proud to present our...

Book of the Month

Prince Voronov's Virgin
by Lynn Raye Harris

from Mills & Boon® Modern™

Paige Barnes is rescued from the dark streets of Moscow by Prince Alexei Voronov—her boss's deadliest rival. Now he has Paige unexpectedly in his sights, Alexei will play emotional Russian roulette to keep her close...

Available 17th December

Something to say about our Book of the Month? Tell us what you think!

millsandboon.co.uk/community
facebook.com/romancehq
twitter.com/millsandboonuk

BEAUTY AND THE BROODING BOSS *by Barbara Wallace*

Working for author Alex sounds like Kelsey's dream job until she meets her new, rude, unwelcoming boss. Yet beneath his gruff façade could Alex be her Prince Charming?

FRIENDS TO FOREVER *by Nikki Logan*

Marc and Beth were best friends—until a heated kiss exposed secrets and ruined everything. Ten years later, are they ready to forgive the sins of the past?

CROWN PRINCE, PREGNANT BRIDE! *by Raye Morgan*

Monte believed love had no place in his world, until courageous Pellea made him reconsider. Although she's promised to another, he's now determined to fight for her.

VALENTINE BRIDE *by Christine Rimmer*

Reserved Irina was the perfect housekeeper for playboy Caleb. Then she found out she was being deported. So Caleb came up with the ideal solution: marry him!

THE NANNY AND THE CEO *by Rebecca Winters*

CEO Nick can handle billion-dollar business deals with his eyes closed —but a baby? Driven Reese is the perfect nanny, yet could she be something more?

Cherish

0111/023a

On sale from 4th February 2011
Don't miss out!

Available at WHSmith, Tesco, ASDA, Eason
and all good bookshops
www.millsandboon.co.uk

THE FAMILY THEY CHOSE

by Nancy Robards Thompson

Struggling to have a baby is shaking Olivia's marriage to the core. Despite the heartache, Jamison's intent on bringing back his wife's happiness—one kiss at a time.

PRIVATE PARTNERS

by Gina Wilkins

No one knew about the secret wedding vows Anne had exchanged with Liam. But now her irresistible husband is back and ready to claim her all over again.

A COLD CREEK SECRET

by RaeAnne Thayne

Brant is hoping to put the past behind him and find some measure of solitude and peace at his ranch—but those hopes are dashed when spoiled heiress Mimi arrives!

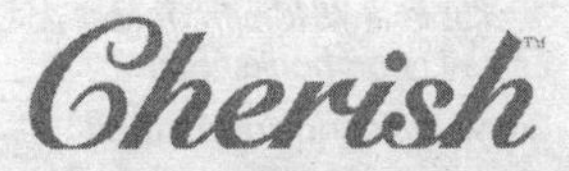

0111/023b

Live life to the full – give in to temptation

Four new sparkling and sassy romances every month!

Be the first to read this fabulous new series from 1st December 2010 at **millsandboon.co.uk**
In shops from 1st January 2011

Tell us what you think!
Facebook.com/romancehq
Twitter.com/millsandboonuk

Don't miss out!

Available at WHSmith, Tesco, ASDA, Eason and all good bookshops
www.millsandboon.co.uk

Walk on the Wild Side

by Natalie Anderson

Jack Greene has Kelsi throwing caution to the wind—it's hard to stay grounded with a man who turns your world upside down! Until they crash with a bump—of the baby kind...

Do Not Disturb

by Anna Cleary

A preacher's daughter, Miranda was led deliciously astray by wild Joe... Now the tables have turned—he's her CEO! But Joe's polished exterior doesn't disguise his devilish side...

Three Weddings and a Baby

by Fiona Harper

Jennie's groom vanished on their wedding night. When he returns, he has his *toddler* in tow! Jennie can't resist Alex's appeal and, for a successful businesswoman, one kid should be easy...right?

The Last Summer of Being Single

by Nina Harrington

Sebastien Castellano, prodigal city playboy, has mysteriously returned home to his sleepy French village. Now he's reminding single mum Ella how much fun the *single* part can be!

On sale from 4th February 2011
Don't miss out!

Available at WHSmith, Tesco, ASDA, Eason and all good bookshops

www.millsandboon.co.uk

0211/24/MB328

ULTIMATE ALPHA MALES:

Strong, sexy…and intent on seduction!

Mediterranean Tycoons

4th February 2011

Hot-Shot Heroes

4th March 2011

Powerful Protectors

1st April 2011

Passionate Playboys

6th May 2011

Collect all four!

www.millsandboon.co.uk

Discover Pure Reading Pleasure with

Visit the Mills & Boon website for all the latest in romance

- **Buy** all the latest releases, backlist and eBooks
- **Join** our community and chat to authors and other readers
- **Win** with our fantastic online competitions
- **Tell us** what you think by signing up to our reader panel
- **Find out** more about our authors and their books
- **Free** online reads from your favourite authors
- **Sign** up for our free monthly eNewsletter
- **Rate** and review books with our star system

www.millsandboon.co.uk

Follow us at twitter.com/millsandboonuk

Become a fan at facebook.com/romancehq

0111_S1ZED

2 FREE BOOKS
AND A SURPRISE GIFT

We would like to take this opportunity to thank you for reading this Mills & Boon® book by offering you the chance to take TWO more specially selected books from the Cherish™ series absolutely FREE! We're also making this offer to introduce you to the benefits of the Mills & Boon® Book Club™—

- **FREE home delivery**
- **FREE gifts and competitions**
- **FREE monthly Newsletter**
- **Exclusive Mills & Boon Book Club offers**
- **Books available before they're in the shops**

Accepting these FREE books and gift places you under no obligation to buy, you may cancel at any time, even after receiving your free books. Simply complete your details below and return the entire page to the address below. You don't even need a stamp!

YES Please send me 2 free Cherish books and a surprise gift. I understand that unless you hear from me, I will receive 5 superb new stories every month, including two 2-in-1 books priced at £5.30 each, and a single book priced at £3.30, postage and packing free. I am under no obligation to purchase any books and may cancel my subscription at any time. The free books and gift will be mine to keep in any case.

Ms/Mrs/Miss/Mr ____________ Initials ____________

____

Surname ______________________________

Address ______________________________

____

____________ Postcode ____________

E-mail ______________________________

Send this whole page to: Mills & Boon Book Club, Free Book Offer, FREEPOST NAT 10298, Richmond, TW9 1BR

Offer valid in UK only and is not available to current Mills & Boon Book Club subscribers to this series. Overseas and Eire please write for details.. We reserve the right to refuse an application and applicants must be aged 18 years or over. Only one application per household. Terms and prices subject to change without notice. Offer expires 31st March 2011. As a result of this application, you may receive offers from Harlequin Mills & Boon and other carefully selected companies. If you would prefer not to share in this opportunity please write to The Data Manager, PO Box 676, Richmond, TW9 1WU.

Mills & Boon® is a registered trademark owned by Harlequin Mills & Boon Limited.
Cherish™ is being used as a trademark.
The Mills & Boon® Book Club™ is being used as a trademark.